MUSES OF TERRA

Codex Antonius | Book II

Rob Steiner

Quarkfolio Books

Sign up for my newsletter at www.robsteinerauthor.com to get a **FREE** compilation of short stories set in the Codex Antonius universe, along with news and previews of upcoming books.
Never miss a new release, and you can unsubscribe at any time.

For Grandpa Chuck.

Do not argue what a good man should be. Be one.

- **Marcus Antonius Pictor, the only Antonii to retire the consulship.**

Chapter One

Marcus Antonius Cordus sprinted across the rust-colored gravel of the airless moon, his breath fogging the faceplate with each exhale. Sweat beaded on his brow. He lowered the air temperature in his helmet with a flick of his eyes. Cool air blew on his face and dried the sweat.

Cordus wished the suit could ease his pounding heart. He'd spent the last six years in Caesar Nova's comfortable 1.003 Terran-standard gravity. This moon was +0.12 T, which made his muscles scream much sooner than he expected.

The blood-red swirls from the gas giant above gave enough light to keep him from tripping over a boulder or slipping into an iced gully. He could have switched his helmet view to infrared with an eye-tap, but it would interfere with the colored view in his faceplate's left corner that showed the multi-colored heat signatures of the three golems chasing him.

His right foot slipped on black ice, and he lost a few steps to the golems as he righted himself.

Cordus sighed. He flicked his eyes to the rear heat window to turn it off, then switched his forward faceplate to infrared. He squinted as the landscape illuminated before him in black and green colors, a much better view to avoid hidden ice.

I know the bastards are behind me. No need to track them.

He ran through a narrow gully, which kept the golems from spreading out. It was why he chose it. He'd never set foot on this moon before today, but he assumed from its geology that it had once been warm and wet before some cataclysm took away its atmosphere. The gully was an ancient riverbed, now filled with smooth rocks and dry, water-eroded banks. If water had flowed through this gully, then it would have formed—

There. Infrared showed a dark opening several paces to his left. Cordus lunged toward the cave, praying to Jupiter that it was deep enough for him to—

A wall of black rock greeted him less than three paces past the entrance.

"*Cac*," he breathed.

The golems arrived a few heartbeats later. Their dark-gray pressure suits showed no sigil or livery bands, and Cordus could not see through their frosted faceplates. They spread a pace apart to form a semi-circle that blocked the opening.

"All right, boys," Cordus said, holding his hands out. "We had an invigorating run, eh? Good thing for you I'm a forgiving fellow. This is your last chance to leave this moon alive."

Neither golem replied. Cordus knew they wouldn't. He taunted them over an open channel, but he doubted they cared. They were programmed to kill him, not banter with him.

Cordus backed into the cave and the golems followed. The cave was not as deep as he preferred, but at least it forced the golems to come at him one at a time. Which was why he ducked in there to begin with.

The first one lunged at him clumsily. Cordus kneed the golem's stomach, then elbowed its neck. The golem fell motionless to the ground.

The second golem made a more nuanced attacked. It came at him with outstretched hands, then dropped and swept its leg toward his. Cordus leaped over the leg sweep and then gave it a savage rounding kick to the helmet. The kick's power sent the golem headfirst into the solid rock at the back of the cave. The golem collapsed in a heap.

Cordus had no time before the third golem came at him. A knife flashed in the moon's meager red light. Cordus jumped away, the knife within a finger's width of his pressure suit. He now stood in the riverbed. Weaponless, he considered running.

No. This ends here.

The golem came at him again with the knife. Cordus deflected its knife hand, but the golem brought its other elbow around into Cordus's throat. He fell backward onto gravel and rocks. Without thinking, he grabbed the first rock he could find and flung it at the golem's faceplate. The rock bounced off the helmet. The golem's head jerked backward reflexively. Cordus knew it wouldn't damage the helmet, but at least it distracted the golem.

Before the golem could focus on Cordus again, he kicked hard at its knee. Bone crunched through his boots, and the golem crumbled to the ground, dropping its knife. Cordus scrambled for the knife, picked it up, and jumped to his feet.

The two golems in the cave had not moved. The third golem clutched at its shattered knee, writhing at Cordus's feet. Cordus smiled triumphantly, then turned around.

A fourth golem, which he had not seen until now, kicked him in the chest. Breath exploded from Cordus's lungs. He fell onto the riverbed again. He still held the knife, but the golem kicked it from his hand. Cordus grabbed the golem's other foot with both hands and twisted it. The golem's body followed. Cordus pushed with all his strength, sending the golem onto its back. He grabbed the knife again and turned to finish the golem off.

Cordus froze.

Behind the golem stood a man without a pressure suit dressed in the ancient gold armor and red cloak of a Roman general from a thousand years ago. The man had dark curly hair and a matching beard. A green light reflected from his eyes as if he were a cat surprised in the dark by a torch lamp.

Finish him.

The man's voice echoed in Cordus's mind the same way the Muse whispers did. Cordus did not need his Muse memories to know the man was Marcus Antonius Primus, first Consul of the New Roman Republic. His visage was on almost every fresco, statue, and visum in the Roman Consular Palace.

Before Cordus could react, the fourth golem slammed into him with a tackle that knocked him on his back again. The golem produced another knife and placed it at Cordus's neck.

The golem's faceplate cleared. Kaeso Aemilius looked down at Cordus, confusion and anger warring in his eyes. He turned to where Marcus Antonius stood. Cordus glanced there, too, but the riverbed was empty.

"You had me, kid," he growled, turning back to Cordus. "Why did you hesitate?"

Cordus opened his mouth to speak, but paused. *Do I say that I'm seeing ghosts? That Marcus Antonius Primus, my thousand-year-old ancestor has come back to give me sparring advice?*

Kaeso grew impatient, so Cordus blurted, "I thought I saw another golem."

Cordus winced inwardly. The other three golems all lay where they fell. Kaeso regarded Cordus a moment, then grunted and stood. He offered Cordus a hand, which Cordus took.

Back on his feet, Cordus searched the riverbed for...whatever he saw. Besides the three golems and Kaeso, no one else was there. He turned his eyes to Kaeso again, who watched him suspiciously.

"I thought no weapons this time," Cordus said.

"I said no weapons for *you*, kid." Kaeso slid his knife into the sheath on his thigh. "Your assassins will likely have them. Would be poor assassins if they didn't."

Kaeso eye-tapped the displays in his helmet. All three golems stood in sync and formed a line behind him. Kaeso marched back up the riverbed toward their shuttle.

Cordus followed. "A real assassin would shoot me with a pulse rifle from a thousand paces."

Kaeso grunted. "Can't train you to evade a pulse pellet from a thousand paces, now can I? And don't change the subject. Why did you hesitate back there?"

"I told you, I saw a golem coming at me. The light on this moon is tricky. You said so yourself when we landed."

The crimson gas giant above them cast red and black shadows across the moon's rocky landscape. Cordus wanted to believe the light had played tricks with his eyes. Wanted it badly. He queried the Muses, but they were strangely silent on the matter.

"I saw your eyes, kid," Kaeso said. "Your faceplate was clear. Something scared you and it wasn't a golem."

"Golems are scary when they're coming at you with a knife. I don't know what to tell you, old man. I froze, simple as that."

Kaeso gave him a sideways glance. "Fine. We'll do the same drill again, and we'll keep doing it until you *don't* freeze."

Cordus didn't say anything and simply nodded. He had learned over the last six years that complaining about Kaeso's orders earned him an even worse job. *Kaeso would let the golems chase me until my air ran out if he caught me blinking at his order.*

Cordus prepared himself to run the exercise again. But he scanned the riverbed to ensure no long-dead ancestors were haunting it.

Chapter Two

It took Cordus one more attempt to complete the drill to Kaeso's satisfaction. Mostly because he wasn't distracted again by the ghost of Marcus Antonius Primus.

Thinking about Marcus Antonius—as real as Kaeso and the three golems walking with him back to the shuttle—made Cordus shiver. He had queried his Muses throughout the second drill, and then just now, but they suggested answers he'd already considered—tricks of the light, fatigue, even an actual spirit. When Cordus pressed them further, they either grew silent or gave him the same answers. It made him suspect his Muses had something to do with the apparition.

This disturbed Cordus. Over the past year or so, the Muses had become...not exactly resentful of his mastery over them, but hesitant in their answers. As a child, simply pondering a topic would fill his mind with wisdom from previous Antonii generations, quite often more data than he could process. But lately he had to ask them precisely worded questions before they'd give him the answer he wanted. Their wisdom and memories were no longer as effortless to access.

Cordus understood he was a unique human being. As far as he or the Saturnists knew, he was the only human in the last thousand years able to control the sentient alien virus humans called the Muses, rather than the other way around. Nobody knew how that ability would change as he grew older. Would he eventually lose it and become a tool of the Muses like every other Antonius since Marcus Antonius Primus? It was a fear he awoke with every morning and plagued him until he fell asleep at night.

And it was a fear the Saturnists and his friends shared.

Cordus glanced at Kaeso. Since Kaeso rescued him from Terra six years ago, he had been the father to Cordus that his real father, a Muse puppet, could never could be. Kaeso not only taught Cordus practical knowledge like self-defense and how to pilot a starship, but virtuous wisdom, like being an honorable leader people *wanted* to follow. While Kaeso drilled Cordus mercilessly on the practical, he never talked about the virtuous. Cordus learned those things by watching Kaeso among his crew.

Cordus knew Kaeso loved him like a son, but Kaeso was wary of Cordus's control over the Muses. What would Kaeso say if Cordus revealed he saw the ghost of Marcus Antonius, and that he suspected his Muses had something to do with it?

They arrived back at the six-man shuttle in which they'd flown to this moon and entered the pressure hatch. Once inside, the golems removed their helmets and sat in the flight couches behind the pilot couches without a word. All three must've been grown in the same vat—dark hair, pale skin, and surreal blue eyes. Cordus would've thought them Picts if he'd seen them walking down a Roman street.

Not that I know what a Roman street looks like these days.

Kaeso tossed Cordus packs of freeze-dried fruit and smoked eel, which Cordus tore into and devoured.

Kaeso also gave the golems food packs, though theirs weren't as appetizing as Cordus's—a protein and vitamin paste that satisfied the needs of the golems' biological systems. They each took their packs without a word, inserted the straws into the tops, and slurped down the contents.

While their minds were programmable tabulari, their human bodies needed food. Cordus had been surrounded by slaves in the Consular Palace, but never gave them much thought at the time. Now, after six years among Liberti and Saturnists opposed to human slavery, he wondered about the ethics of using golems. Liberti and Saturnists had no qualms about growing golems for servitude. If the Liberti were against enslaving one form of human, why didn't they see a problem with enslaving a different form?

It was one of the many Liberti contradictions that made them so fascinating. Roma's culture was a simple Muse-query away, from the New Republic's founding a thousand years ago to the present. The Liberti, however, were a mystery.

"Would you rather have theirs?" Kaeso asked. "You're staring at their paste like you want to spread it over your eel."

Cordus shrugged. "Just wondering what they're thinking?"

"They're golems; they don't think. Might as well ask what this shuttle is thinking." Kaeso ripped into his food packs, poured some raisins in his hand and popped them into his mouth. "I'm more interested in what you're thinking."

"About?"

Kaeso's frown said he didn't believe Cordus's feigned ignorance.

Cordus quickly thought up a topic besides Marcus Antonius. "I was thinking about how to persuade you to let me go to Reantium."

Kaeso drew in a deep, slow breath, as he always did when Cordus asked to go on Saturnist missions. After he exhaled, he would explain how Cordus was too important to risk on simple courier runs.

Which is why I'm keeping Marcus Antonius to myself.

"You give me the usual excuses," Cordus said hurriedly, "and then I counter that I'll never learn how to take care of myself if I'm stuck in a Saturnist stronghold. That's how these things always go. But let me remind you that my eighteenth birthday is in two weeks. Liberti law says I'll be a man when I turn eighteen. Even though Roman custom says I was an adult at fourteen—"

"With your father's permission."

"—I still honored the Liberti custom—"

Kaeso barked a laugh. "While whining the last four years."

"My point is that in two weeks I can decide the course of my life. You and Ocella and Gaia Julius cannot keep me prisoner behind Saturnist walls. Walls are why I fled Roma."

Gaia Julius, an exiled Roman patrician, led the Saturnist sect that hid Cordus. She thought Cordus's blood was humanity's only weapon against the Muse strains. But after six years of research and blood draws, the Saturnists had made minimal progress against the Terran strain Cordus carried. Part of the problem was that once Cordus's blood was drawn, the Muses in it dissolved their protein coats, making it difficult for Saturnist medicus teams to develop a vaccine against them. That contrasted with Cordus's ancestors, who had used their blood to easily infect others. The Saturnists had to rebuild the nucleic acids in the Muse strain from scratch just to figure out which proteins it used to infect cells, something that was taking much longer than they anticipated. The only true cure they knew was for an infectee to avoid delta sleep during a way line jump, like Kaeso and Ocella had when they rescued Cordus from Terra. However, it was a cure that risked madness for the infectee.

Kaeso and Ocella were just as overprotective as Gaia Julius, but their reasons were more paternal. They hid him because they cared about *him*. While most people thought Cordus was assassinated by the Liberti—according to the official Roman cover story—elements in the Roman government knew he lived. Roma was consumed by civil war, and every Roman general sought to legitimize his or her claim to the consulship. If they knew an Antonius still lived, especially the Consular Heir, then his life would be under constant threat from assassins. There had been two attempts on Cordus's life over the last six years, both from Praetorians who did not survive the attempts thanks to Kaeso and his crew. It was why Kaeso, a former Umbra Ancile, drilled Cordus on self-defense, weaponry, and evasion.

At almost eighteen years old, Cordus could best most Saturnists in hand-to-hand sparring, knew how to disassemble and reassemble a pulse rifle in under two minutes, and could pilot a ship through the rocks and ice of a ringed planet.

Yet Kaeso still refused to bring him along on his Saturnist missions.

After Cordus spoke, Kaeso stared at him. Cordus did not look away. Kaeso rarely raised his voice to anyone. Why would he if he could just stare down people into obeying his orders?

"First, I don't care if you're a man according to Liberti law, or if you're eighteen or a hundred and eighteen. I'm the centuriae of my ship, and I will take you on missions when I say you're ready."

Cordus clenched his teeth but continued to hold Kaeso's commanding stare.

"Second, you know damned well why we need to keep you safe. Like it or not, kid, you're humanity's greatest chance at keeping the Muses from turning us all into cattle. Your blood won't be much use if it's floating in space or feeding the worms on some Janus-forsaken rock of a world."

"Kaeso, this is all—"

"I'm not done." Kaeso's lip curled. "Third, you're right."

Cordus blinked. "Which part?"

"All of it."

Cordus stared at him. It was the first time Kaeso ever told him he was right about anything. When Cordus answered a question correctly, Kaeso would nod without expression or maybe give him a rare smile.

"Which puts me in a dilemma," Kaeso continued. "Yes, we can't keep you imprisoned your whole life. Someday you'll need to step out into the real world and take care of yourself. Maybe even return to Roma."

Cordus cringed. He was the last Antonius and the Consular Heir. Even as a child, he had never wanted to be consul. All he ever wanted, and still wanted, was freedom: to command his own ship like Kaeso, to explore worlds he'd never seen or even knew existed.

The Roman consulship was another prison, with the highest walls in the universe. Let the Roman warlords fight for it.

"So here's the deal, kid," Kaeso said. "You can come with us to Reantium. Ocella won't be happy to see you, but deep down she knows you need this. You will work on this trip. Are you ready for that?"

Cordus tried not to leap off his seat. "It's all I've wanted since I left Roma. I want to earn my way, not be sheltered. I *am* ready."

"Fine. I'll tell the crew when we get back to *Caduceus*." Then Kaeso studied him a moment and said, "Just remember you can't run from your responsibilities, because they'll always catch up with you and tackle you to the ground. I've learned that the hard way, and I'd rather you didn't."

"I'm not running, old man." Cordus grinned. "If anything, I want more responsibility."

Kaeso frowned slightly, as if Cordus had not understood the point. He did understand, though. Two responsibilities had been thrust upon him by something as unfair and arbitrary as birth.

One, the Roman consulship could be his if he declared himself. If the last Antonius arose from the dead, it could end a civil war that had raged for six years and claimed millions of lives. But that would mean an end to Cordus's freedom.

Two, his mastery over the Muses—and his blood—could save humanity from enslavement to the whims of an alien virus. Yet even that 'talent' was suspect these days, especially after seeing Marcus Antonius Primus, something that could only have come from his Muses.

He didn't want to think of those responsibilities now. He would finally test the skills he'd spent years practicing. Even if the trip to Reantium was simply a courier and rendezvous run, it was something real. Cordus would not ruin it by worrying about things he couldn't control.

Chapter Three

Marcia Licinius Ocella shifted in her command couch again. The rocks, ore, and ice floating outside the ship wore on her nerves. She glanced to her right at Lucia Marius Calida, the ship's pilot. In the darkened cockpit, her face was serene in the white, blue, and red lights of her control panel as she steered the ship through the dangerous debris.

It's the most relaxed she's been in days. Too bad the entire trip here wasn't through a debris cloud.

They had entered the vast spherical cloud surrounding the Menota system three days before. At first, the scraps left over from the formation of the Menota solar system were sparse. But three hours ago, the debris grew so dense—likely the aftermath of a planetoid collision—that Lucia took the ship off auto to fly it herself. While the ship's tabulari could theoretically evade debris, Lucia—and Ocella, for that matter—trusted gods-given human piloting instincts more than the ninety-year-old *tabulari*.

If we had an Umbra ship...

Six years after she left Umbra and she still longed for the Muse-granted tech the Umbra Ancilia used in the field. Saturnists were an outlawed organization, so they made do with what they could scavenge or buy off the black markets. Not like the vast resources to which an Umbra Ancile—or a Roman Praetorian—had access.

As evidenced by the ship they now flew, which was old when Ocella's mother was born.

"Just got a talaria hit," announced Varo Ullup from behind Ocella. The young Saturnist, two years older than Cordus, operated the delta sleep controls and monitored the talaria scans. "It's in and out, though. Hard to get a fix."

"It's this damned debris," Lucia growled, betraying her affected serenity. "Can't get a decent line of sight."

"At least we know it's out there, though," Ocella said, then winced. She was trying to remain calm and useful, but knew obvious comments like that didn't help. The command couch was the most useless position on a ship. Everyone else on the crew had a specific task. Centuriae, on the other hand, were bound by tradition and protocol to let the crew perform their assigned tasks. Centuriae had to focus on strategic decisions rather than minutia.

Which meant centuriae mostly sat in their couches wondering why they were even there.

Lucia scowled at Ocella's comment but said nothing Ocella was grateful; she didn't want another shouting match with Lucia during such delicate piloting maneuvers.

Ocella cursed herself once again for letting Kaeso talk her into bringing Lucia.

"She's the best pilot I know," he said as they held each other in bed the night before she left for Menota. "If that way line is in the outer debris clouds, she can get you through safer than any other Saturnist pilot."

"But there's still…tension between us," Ocella said. "I don't want distractions on this mission. It's too important."

"Every mission is important. It's time you two found a peaceful solution."

"Easy for you to say. She loves you."

Kaeso sighed. "I made my feelings clear long ago. I'm her centuriae and her friend…but my heart is with you."

"You're so romantic. Doesn't absolve you from listening to my grumbling."

"You've kept your distance from each other for six years. One of you has to make the first move."

"How would you feel if I wanted you to make friends with one of my unrequited lovers?"

"You have unrequited lovers?"

She jabbed him in the ribs, and he laughed. He pulled her to him, his naked skin warm against her body. "I'll talk to her again," he said.

"No, it's my problem, I'll do it. She is *the best pilot for this mission. She's been out there twice already. We'll work it out."*

Ocella knew Kaeso was right…but he didn't have to command a ship with a resentful pilot. *Blasted man! All he sees is the loyal and brave Lucia, not the surly child next to me.*

"Got another hit," Varo announced again. "Stronger this time. Heading six seven point three."

"Six seven point three," Lucia acknowledged, then tapped the controls on her tabulari to redirect the ship.

The view outside the command deck window did not reflect the tight quarters through which they flew. The only sign of debris came when a dark mass blocked the stars, or when a rock floated through the ship's running lights. Lucia didn't look out the window, but stared at her anti-collision scanners to pilot the ship.

"Found it!" Varo exclaimed. "Sending the coordinates to your tabulari, Lucia."

Ocella allowed herself a brief smile. Even Lucia grinned as she redirected the ship toward Varo's coordinates.

For six years, the Saturnists searched for the hidden way line Kaeso saw in the Menota archive vaults before the Romans destroyed them. Six years of month-long missions piloting through planetary rubble, comets, and ice, looking for the talaria particles that identified way lines. They had scanned an enormous amount of space around Menota, probably the most detailed scan of a solar system in human history. Most system scans stopped with the planets and in-system asteroid belts. Nobody paid attention to outer debris clouds because they were usually so hard to navigate and far from a convenient way line.

But according to Kaeso's data, an unknown way line existed out here. A way line that other Muse strains could use to invade human space from anywhere in the universe. It had to be found and monitored to stop a Muse invasion.

Ocella tried not to think about what they'd do if the other strains had *quantum* way line engines like what Umbra installed on Kaeso's *Caduceus*, before it was renamed *Vacuna*. Every speck of matter in the universe had a quantum connection. Umbra and the Liberti Muses had discovered a way to open way lines and travel those connections. The Liberti Muses had said it was new technology not known to other strains. Ocella prayed that was so.

Ocella could see little more than stars and shadows outside the window, so she monitored the proximity displays on her command tabulari. Varo marked the potential way line's location with a green circle on the displays. They were less than a thousand miles from it.

Lucia eased the ship around asteroids and comets the size of small moons, along with all the 'smaller' chunks of rock and ice—the width of five-story buildings—that could destroy the ship. It was why they flew what was essentially a four-man shuttle packed with engines modified for speed and maneuverability. The debris cloud would pummel anything bigger.

Lucia passed beneath a dead comet, emerged on the other side, and found the way line signal directly ahead. The talaria readings showed a stable way line. Way line discoveries were rare during the last fifty years. Most explorers believed all the way lines available to humanity had been discovered, and that humanity was now limited to the systems within its way line network. The last way line discovered was twenty years ago, and it went to a binary star system with no planets. Had a government sanctioned Ocella's mission, she and her crew would have returned to triumphs.

As Saturnists, however, this way line was one more secret they needed to keep.

"Prepare for delta sleep," Ocella said. "Varo, proceed with the sacrifice."

Behind her, Varo tore open a pack of freeze-dried falcon livers and dumped the contents into a small clay bowl. Ocella and Lucia closed their eyes.

"Oh, Jupiter Optimus Maximus," Varo prayed aloud as he crushed the livers into powder with a stone masher, "grant us your permission to travel through your realm. Accept this offering from a beast of flight. If it pleases you, grant us safe journey through your way lines so we may arrive at..."

Varo paused. At this point in the prayer, delta sleep officers said the name of the destination system. Though Ocella planned to take the way line if found, it was only now the thought sunk in: *we have no idea* where *it will take us.* It was a thought both thrilling and frightening.

"...so we may arrive at our destination," Varo finished. She heard the frown in his voice. 'Destination' was a vague term, and vague terms were never advisable when praying to the gods, who could interpret those terms in whatever way they pleased.

Despite her opinion that way line sacrifices were a quaint tradition at best, she added her own silent prayer. *So we may arrive at our destination* sane and alive.

She heard sparks as Varo used a small torch to ignite the powdered falcon livers, and then she smelled smoke as the livers disintegrated. Varo muttered a few more words in ancient Aramaic, the language of his Hebrew ancestors. It had been a dead language for 700 years since Roma atomized the entire Terran Palestinian region after a bloody revolt. Ocella knew a bit from her Umbra days when she and other Ancilia used it to communicate in situations where they might be overheard.

"Blessed are you, Adonai, who hears our prayer."

The sacrifice complete, Ocella enabled the delta headrest on her command couch, as did Lucia and Varo. The delta device glowed green, indicating activation.

"Thirty seconds to way line," Varo announced. "Delta sleep and crew couches activated. Transferring delta control to your tabulari, Centuriae."

Ocella's tabulari showed all three couches with a green outline.

Lucia set the ship on a heading into the way line entry point identified by the talaria particle sensors. "Delta pilot engaged," Lucia said. "Twenty seconds to way line entry." She leaned her head back into her couch.

"Initiating delta sleep on my mark," Ocella said. Then she turned to Lucia with a smile. "Let's make history."

Lucia rolled her eyes. "Let's pray we're around to see it."

Ocella shook her head, then turned back to the delta controls. "Mark," she said, then engaged the delta sleep for her crew.

Lucia's eyes closed, and her body sank further into her couch as all her muscles relaxed. Ocella watched the delta display on her tabulari to verify that the outlines of both Lucia and Varo turned yellow.

Satisfied, she watched the countdown to way line entry. Fifteen seconds. Her finger hovered over the control that would engage her delta sleep. She had taken on Kaeso's habit of manually initiating delta sleep rather than letting the ship do it. It comforted her to maintain some control over a means of travel that was largely in the hands of the gods.

At three seconds, Ocella tapped the delta control for her couch...

...and found her gaze on the command deck's dark ceiling. She blinked, raised her head, and scanned her tabulari. Five seconds had passed since she tapped her delta control. She checked her proximity display. They now orbited a planet and no system debris floated around them.

"Ship integrity stable," Lucia said, running through her post-way line checklist. "Internal systems normal. Way line jump confirmed."

"Where are we, Varo?" Ocella asked.

Varo tapped at his tabulari. "Orbiting a rocky planet approximately 1.3 T in size and mass. Minimal atmosphere—90% carbon dioxide with trace amounts of nitrogen, oxygen, and water vapor. No moons orbiting the...wait, one asteroid...."

When he said no more, Ocella said, "Varo?"

"Well it's not an asteroid, Centuriae. Whatever it is, it's in a stationary point above the planet's equator. It's 320,000 miles from us at heading eight nine point one. Thirteen miles long." He paused. "Amazing..."

"Focus, Varo. Just tell me what you see."

"Sorry, Centuriae. External composition analysis is saying 'unknown'. It's the oddest shape...like a tower with spikes."

Electricity tingled through Ocella's body, but she asked calmly, "Any power or heat coming from it?"

"Nothing. It's as cold as the space around it."

"The planet?"

Varo paused. "Nothing on the hemisphere below us, but we'll have to do an orbit before I can say what's on the other side."

"Interesting," Lucia muttered, staring at her tabulari.

"What's interesting, pilot?"

"It's not moving relative to the planet, or even rotating. If it has no power, how does it stay in a single point in space without even a wobble?"

Every artificial satellite had some power source to keep it in a stable orbit, or else it eventually crashed into the planet or flew off into space. What kept this object in place if it didn't have a power source?

"Varo, can you get any internal scans?"

"Not from this range. We'll need to get within 10,000 miles."

Ocella bit her lip. Protocols for first-time jumps through new way lines always included procedures for contact with intelligent alien life. They were protocols that had never been used throughout human history, though Ocella knew from the Muse archives, and Cordus, that the Muses had infected dozens of alien races over millions of years. And those were just the Muses that found humanity. Kaeso said the Liberti Muses warned of more strains beyond the hidden Menota way line. Had a Muse-infected alien race built the object?

She turned to Lucia. "What do you think, pilot?"

Lucia raised an eyebrow. "You're the Centuriae, why do you need my permission?"

"I'm not asking for your permission, I'm asking for your opinion. Do you think we should get closer to this thing?"

Lucia looked back at the object through her pilot-side window. "Kaeso would spend hours planning every possible scenario before taking his crew into an unknown situation like this."

Ocella pressed her lips together. Kaeso was an Ancile once, too, so Lucia was right. It just annoyed her that she'd bring up Kaeso now.

Lucia turned back to Ocella with a grin. "Me, I like charging into a dark room without knowing what's inside. More fun that way." Lucia regarded her a moment. "So who are you going to be: a cautious Ancile or a reckless barbarian?"

"I vote barbarian," Varo said from behind them.

Ocella smiled. She was also excited to discover an object that was obviously built by intelligent aliens. It was the first such object humans had discovered in the 600 years they'd been traveling the interstellar way lines. Varo and Lucia's excitement only added to her own.

But this thing was on the other side of a way line the Muse archive said led to Muse-controlled star systems. Her mission was to find the Menota way line, jump through it, and then begin preliminary surveys on the other side. Detailed surveys would take months and multiple missions, but her preliminaries would help plot future forays. Gaia Julius gave her strict orders to avoid contact with any possible Muse-controlled species. What if this thing turned out to be hostile? What if it "awakened" while they explored it?

Caution was drilled into Umbra Ancilia during their training. *Never undertake a mission without planning your reaction to every possible scenario.* That dictum had saved her life many times. Sometimes a situation came up that called for improvisation. Umbra recognized this reality and trained its Ancilia accordingly, but it was for situations where orders were unclear or non-existent.

Gaia Julius's orders were clear.

Ocella ground her teeth. If they didn't investigate this thing now, someone else would have to do it later. There would be just as much danger for them as for Ocella and her crew now. The Menota way line was so guarded by debris that no ship bigger than Ocella's could enter the way line. Investigating the object with a larger, better armed ship was just not possible.

I'm not an Ancile anymore, Ocella thought. *That ended when they tried to kill me six years ago.*

"Take us within scanning range," Ocella ordered Lucia. "But be ready to take us back through the way line if this thing wakes up. Varo, I know the delta systems suck a lot of power, but keep them online for now. We'll need them if we have to retreat."

"Yes, Centuriae," Varo said.

"Setting course for the object," Lucia said.

Ocella's body pressed into her couch. The shuttle's inertia cancellers were weak so as to make room for the speedier engines, but they were better than no cancellers. It took them fifteen seconds to reach optimal survey range. Ocella looked through her command window and exhaled. Even from this distance, the object was massive. Varo was right; it looked like an upside-down tower with spikes along its entire length, almost thirteen miles from tip to tip. Its black surface was bumpy and amorphous, but smooth and it reflected the planet's light like a dark mirror.

"We're within 10,000 miles," Lucia announced.

"Beginning scans," Varo said. After a few seconds, he gave a quiet whistle. "Take a closer look at the surface. I'm sending them to your panels."

Ocella looked down at Varo's detailed scans. When Varo added a hydrogen filter, myriad cracks appeared across the object. But they weren't cracks.

"Ice?" Ocella said.

"Yes, but I imagine that ice turns to water when this thing powers up."

"Like veins?" Lucia said. "It's all under the surface."

"Exactly! I bet those 'veins' send water and fuel all over the object. Amazing! But here's the best part—its surface isn't rock. It's some kind of organic shell."

"This thing is alive?" Ocella asked.

"No, it's frozen solid, but the surface is a chitinous compound, like an insect exoskeleton. Unbelievable..."

Lucia snorted. "So it's a giant, tower-shaped bug."

"Or an object built by bugs," Varo said. "Can you imagine?"

"We don't know what it's made of or who made it," Ocella said. "Just because its shell looks like an insect exoskeleton, doesn't mean its builders were insects. Our ship is made of metal, but we're not."

"I haven't been tutored like that since I was eight," Lucia muttered.

Ocella chose to ignore her. *That didn't last long...*

A flash of white light filled the cockpit. Ocella gasped and shut her eyes. Lucia cursed, and Varo grunted as if punched. The ship's window filters engaged to dampen the light, but Ocella still blinked to get the starbursts to recede from her vision. She checked her tabulari. All of the screens had turned to multi-colored static.

"Report!" Ocella cried.

"All my panels are scrambled," Lucia said. "Maneuvering controls not responding."

"My panels, too," Varo said. "I can't even tell if life support still works."

Ocella looked out the command window at the object. The light faded, so the window's auto-dimmers receded. What she saw made her wish they hadn't.

The object's 'veins' now pulsed with an ethereal blue light. It slowly swiveled so that one of its amorphous mountains was pointed at her ship.

Ocella's panels came back online, but her relief turned to horror when she found they were locked. She tapped her controls, but nothing happened.

Lucia pounded her fist on her tabulari. "*Cac*!"

"We're locked out," Varo said. "I still see my scans, but I can't change anything."

Ocella's panel was in the same condition; she could watch her readings, but couldn't switch views.

Her body suddenly pressed into the delta couch much stronger than before.

"They're controlling our ship," Lucia cried. "We're flying towards the object."

Ocella looked at the ship's relative speed. They had accelerated +20 T gravities. At least the ship's inertia cancellers held—making it feel more like +3 T—or they'd be crushed into the couches.

She looked out the window again. They were headed right for one of the object's spikes.

Chapter Four

The spike's tip seemed sharp from their survey distance, but as they flew closer, the tip flattened to two hundred paces across. A dark, triangular-shaped opening yawned in the middle of the flat expanse, taking up three quarters of the tip. Small circular holes ringed the opening, grouped in threes, twenty paces apart. Their ship flew into the triangular opening and the blackness within.

Ocella's body eased up from the command couch, and her tabulari said the ship was rapidly decelerating.

"Options," she said.

"I don't think they want to destroy us," Varo said. "They could've flown us into the planet if they wanted to. I think they want to talk." His voice trembled, and not with the same enthusiasm from a few minutes ago.

"What do we say to them?"

"Who says they want to talk?" Lucia asked. "What if they're hungry?"

"These are alien beings," Varo said. "Their contact protocols could be as incomprehensible to us as ours will likely be to them. Perhaps they consider this a friendly gesture, that maybe they're saving us power by flying us inside."

"Or," Lucia said, "they don't want us escaping to warn our people they exist. They drag us into their ship without even hailing us first? Doesn't seem friendly no matter what species you are."

"If all they cared about was our escape," Varo said, "they would have destroyed us. I still think they want to talk."

Ocella said, "It's a good sign they didn't blast us out of the sky, but we have to be ready for the fact they may *not* be friendly. We knew we might find a Muse-controlled species here. If they want to talk, we use the first-contact protocols we all learned in the academia."

"Identity, purpose, needs, plans," Varo quoted.

They were protocols all humans learned regarding first contact with intelligent aliens. First, establish a way to *identify* each other; determine the aliens' *purpose* for being in its location, along with humans communicating their purpose; learn the aliens' basic survival *needs*; ascertain the aliens' *plans* to secure their needs.

Lucia looked at Ocella. "If they're not friendly?"

Then Jupiter grant us a swift journey to Elysium. Her ship was unarmed, and each one of them only had a pulse pistol. They could not resist an alien race that could build an object like this and control her ship like a puppet.

Ocella's silence conveyed her thoughts to Lucia, so Lucia frowned and stared at her useless tabulari.

The cavern was pitch black for several minutes, but then a point of blue light in the far distance grew brighter the further they traveled. The end of the corridor soon became apparent—a wall covered in blue-lit veins. When they came within a hundred paces of the wall, the veins undulated and then concentrated around dozens of what looked like connector tubes covering the entire wall. The ship floated to one such tube. The connector was organic, chitinous, and glowed with blue veins. It was like a tentacle reaching out to them.

Ocella flinched when the ship repositioned itself to align its nose with the alien connector tube.

"How will it connect?" Lucia wondered aloud. Connector hatches and tubes across human space had been standardized for centuries, enabling every starship to connect with every other starship or way station.

No sooner had Lucia spoke when the tip of the connector tube grew and widened as it came closer. The hatch was below the command window and out of Ocella's view, but she felt a *thump* as the connector attached itself to the ship.

"Seems to know how," Ocella muttered.

Varo said, "Hatch sensors say the connection is good. They're even sending us power, gravity, and atmosphere."

Ocella's tabulari said the air that the object was pushing into the ship was human standard.

If they can fly the ship, they can fake the scans.

Lucia must have been thinking the same thing, for she unbuckled her couch straps and reached for her pressure helmet and air canisters. Ocella and Varo did the same. Within seconds, they all breathed air from their own pressure suits.

Ocella's tabulari flickered and then unlocked. She tapped a few displays and found she had full control of the ship again.

"I can get in," Ocella said. "You two?"

Lucia tapped her tabulari. "Flight controls are mine again."

"I'm back in, too," Varo said. "But check the view behind us."

Ocella glanced at the rear feeds. A net of blue veins quickly formed behind them, like a closing iris. Or a prison door.

Ocella removed her pulse pistol from the compartment in her delta couch and checked the pellet load. Lucia did the same.

Varo frowned at both of them. "I still think they just want to talk."

Lucia scowled, but Ocella said, "That may be true, but it doesn't hurt to show that we can defend ourselves if they don't want to 'just talk.' Arm yourself, Varo."

Varo sighed, then reached for the pistol in his delta couch.

Ocella led them down the command deck ladder to the shuttle's bottom level. The shuttle was smaller than *Vacuna*, with only a two compartment bottom level—an engine room in the rear and a storage bay that doubled as crew quarters in the front. The connector hatch indicator at the front of the storage bay glowed green.

Ocella approached the hatch. It made a loud hiss and Ocella jumped. Lucia drew her pistol and aimed at the hatch. Ocella pushed Lucia's pistol down and shook her head once. Lucia glared at Ocella but kept the pistol at her side.

The hatch hissed again. The locks clicked and the hatch swung inward. The connector tube beyond was empty, but its black surface was alit with the blue glowing veins. Ocella eye-tapped her helmet's scanners. The atmosphere beyond was Terran standard, but with slightly higher oxygen. The scans said they'd have no trouble breathing if they removed their helmets, but Ocella wasn't that trusting yet.

"You two stay here," she said. "I'll go first. Once I know it's...appropriate for you, I will signal."

"Centuriae—" Lucia began.

"This is my responsibility. I'll stay in constant com. It'll appear less threatening if one of us goes in first. "

Lucia barked a mirthless laugh. "'Less threatening?' Have you seen their ship? They don't have anything to fear from *us*."

"Just do it, Lucia."

Ocella stepped forward to the edge of the hatch and studied the alien connector tube. It seemed made of the same chitinous material as the rest of the object, with bright blue capillaries just below its semi-transparent surface. She stepped onto the tube, and the surface gave slightly beneath her weight. As far as she could tell, the tube generated a 1.0 T gravity field. She was thankful for the gravity, for she did not see any handholds on the smooth walls with which to pull herself along.

Her helmet still indicated breathable atmosphere, and the air temperature was well above freezing. It detected no elements in the air that would cause her harm. She still chose to keep her helmet on.

She stepped along the tube, which curved to the right and then ended at a dark entrance. She was about to eye-tap her external helmet lights when the entrance lit up with the same blue light as the connector. The corridor beyond ran perpendicular to the connector tube. The blue vein lights to the right glowed brighter and began to pulsate. The lights on the left, however, were dimmer and did not pulsate.

"I've reached the end of the connector," Ocella reported back to Lucia and Varo. She told them about the pulsating blue lights in the corridor. "They seem to want me to go right, so right it is."

"Hope it's not a warning to stay away from the right," Lucia commented dryly.

Ocella ignored her.

The corridor twisted and turned, went up and down. It was more like a tube, with a curved floor made of the same material as the walls and ceiling. Ocella wondered if this tunnel usually coursed with the object's "blood." Openings branched off, but the main path was brighter and pulsated, so she stayed with it. The material on which she walked still had a slight give beneath her feet. She couldn't shake the feeling she was walking on the object's "skin."

She described all this to Lucia and Varo over her com. Though her helmet cameras recorded everything, talking through her experiences helped calm her nerves.

"There's a tunnel on the ceiling," she said, scanning the opening as she walked beneath it. "Looks like the one I'm in, but it goes up. The main tunnel is still pulsating, so I'll stay on the path. Not sure how I'd climb up there anyway."

"It makes you wonder what their physical bodies are like," Varo said, excitement returning to his voice. "Why do they like the blue lights? Why is it so dark? How can they find their way around the vessel when its corridors twist and turn so—?"

Lucia said, "Varo, you're babbling again."

Despite her nervous stomach, Ocella grinned at the annoyance in Lucia's voice.

"Forgive me if I'm excited about the greatest discovery in human history since the Muses."

"Yes, the Muses turned out *so* well for us," Lucia replied.

"If you ignore the whole enslavement part, the Muses have been a good thing for humanity," Varo said. "Granted, like any Saturnist, I'd prefer we not have an alien virus controlling us, but Muse technology has only benefited humans."

"Who's to say we wouldn't have discovered those technologies our-selves?" Lucia said. "It's been a thousand years since Antonius overthrew Octavian Augustus. A lot could've happened during that time."

"But it would not have been the efficient track to where we are now. Technology had not changed much in the millennia before Antonius. I just don't believe we'd be traveling the stars without the Muses."

Lucia snorted. "You're a Pantheist. Won't the gods strike you down for admitting that?"

"I speak the truth. The gods do not strike down people for speaking the truth."

"If I could interrupt," Ocella said, "I've entered an actual room."

While Lucia and Varo debated, Ocella had turned a corner to her right and entered a cavernous, crescent-shaped room. Though she couldn't see around the crescent's inner curve, the room looked two hundred paces from tip to tip. It had a clearly delineated floor and hazy, blue oval shapes covering the walls on either side. Ocella looked up. The oval-lined walls disappeared into the gloom above.

"Centuriae," Varo said, "can you take a closer look at the walls?"

Ocella walked over to a human-sized oval to her right. It seemed made of the same chitinous material as the rest of the ship, yet brighter and more translucent than the black, vein-lit material around it. She thought she could see a shape inside. She eye-tapped the radar on her helmet display.

Her helmet showed a frozen, tentacled creature. It looked like a Terran octopus—three-feet tall, bulbous head, and eight tentacles. The creature's tentacles, however, each had three fingers and a thumb.

"There's your alien, Varo," Ocella said, staring at the creature. Ocella had watched the archive holos Kaeso retrieved from Menota, and they included this same creature. But seeing it on a holo and seeing it in the flesh were two different experiences.

"Unbelievable," Varo breathed. "This must be their version of a sleep-er crib."

Lucia said, "Or a meat freezer. There are hundreds of them."

Ocella aimed her helmet's radar at the ovals around the creature. Each one contained a similar octopod in a different frozen position, as if the creatures had been dumped in and flash-frozen. Octopod cells went as far up as her helmet's radar could see, and to the left and right.

"Wait, Centuriae," Varo said. "Turn to your left, twenty paces from your position."

Ocella aimed her helmet's radar to the left and walked toward the ovals on the wall. She saw what caught Varo's attention—another sec-tion of frozen creatures. But these had leathery wings wrapped around their bodies and a head resembling a Terran shark. Twenty more paces to the left was another species. This one had limbs and appendages sprouting from all over its torso, and Ocella couldn't tell which end was the head and which was the tail. The sections behind her contained equally bizarre and exotic alien creatures. Some had incomprehensible shapes, while others had skin as ephemeral as a Terran jelly fish. Frozen life filled the room. She passed one section of ovals that seemed empty at first, but then she noticed they were filled with dark swirls in the frozen fluid that looked like algae. *If the gods could create an intelligent virus, why not intelligent algae?*

Varo was silent at the images Ocella sent them, so she spoke first. "Wonder if these aliens are part of the crew or part of the menu."

Lucia said, "I hope they didn't bring you there just to freeze you, too."

The same thought occurred to Ocella, which was why she kept her helmet's motion sensors at a high sensitivity. If something came at her, or an oval opened, at least she'd have time to react.

And do what? the practical side of her mind asked. She had no answer.

The blue veins on the floor pulsated in intervals into the crescent room, like a wave of blue light rushing away. Ocella followed the blue lights once again, glancing left and right at the strange aliens caught in the frozen ovals. As she came around the curve of the crescent, another opening appeared ahead toward which the blue lights pulsated.

"Entering another corridor," Ocella reported.

She noted the time on her helmet display. She'd been wandering the object for almost twenty minutes. With all the twists and turns, she judged she had walked perhaps a mile. But she couldn't tell if she was farther into the object or just going in circles.

Lucia said, "Another one? This is getting boring."

Varo laughed. "If this is boring, I shudder to think what you'd find exciting!"

"I'm just saying you'd think they would have met Ocella at the hatch. They're making her run around like Theseus in the Labyrinth."

Thanks for making me think of a hungry Minotaur, Ocella thought with a frown.

She entered the corridor. "Again, we may not understand—"

As soon as she stepped into the corridor, the opening to the room behind her irised shut and turned into a blank wall indistinguishable from the rest of the corridor.

"The door just closed behind me," Ocella said, panning her helmet camera at the wall. She kept her voice calm, but her heart thudded even louder in her chest and ears.

Silence in her com.

"Lucia, Varo, do you read me?"

More silence.

"*Cac*," she breathed.

She looked around the corridor. The blue veins pulsated to an opening ten paces to the right. She glanced one last time at the wall where the door to the alien room had once been and then followed the blue lights.

Once she entered the room, she froze. A naked human woman stood before her.

It was an exact copy of Ocella.

On the command deck, Lucia ensured her pulse pistol was ready to fire. She shoved it into her holster, and then climbed down the ladder to the hatch level.

Blasted centuriae, Lucia thought. *Never listen to their trierarchs. Ocella learned too much from Kaeso.*

She suppressed a jealous wave with tremendous will. *Ocella's my centuriae on this mission. Even if she stole the man I've loved for ten years. My duty is to keep her from killing herself...if only to save her for myself.*

"Don't suppose it would help to remind you," Varo said, following her down the ladder, "that the Centuriae ordered us to stay here until she called for us?"

"No, it wouldn't help."

"And that a little pulse pistol won't do much against whatever's inside there?"

On the hatch level, Lucia stopped and glared at Varo. "Your point?"

Varo shrugged and then drew his pulse pistol. "Just confirming you were aware of the situation. Let's go find our centuriae."

Lucia shook her head inside her helmet. Every time she thought she figured out Varo, he did something that changed her opinion of him. She turned and approached the hatch.

The connector was just like what she saw through Ocella's camera feed—blue-lit, biological, and thoroughly alien.

"You said you wanted to know what I found exciting?" she said. "This."

Varo sighed. "Wonderful."

Lucia stepped into the connector.

Chapter Five

Ocella faced her naked self. It was a three-dimensional, color holo that was remarkably detailed, yet it had a metallic tint indicating it was not a real person. An irrational part of her mind cringed. *You're standing in an alien spacecraft and you're worried how your naked body looks?*

"New species. Curiosity."

Ocella's own voice reverberated throughout the room, which she detected with her helmet's external sound capture. While the voice sounded like hers, its cadence and tone were halting and golem-like.

"Its communications enable us to learn its language. Difficult. Time needed to learn correct sounds. Annoyance. New species will learn more efficient communication methods. Benevolence."

When Ocella could think again, she put her hand on her chest and said, "My name is Marcia Licinius Ocella. What do you call yourself?"

Ocella's holo stared at her. "'Name.' Implies individuality. Fascination. Rare for sentient species. Hesitation. Perhaps infected by rivals. Hatred."

"I'm not infected by your rivals," she said quickly. "We are explorers."

Ocella's holo stared at her as it processed her words. "Difficult to ascertain rival infection. Curiosity. Marcia Licinius Ocella must remove its helmet."

"I'd rather not," Ocella said.

"Impatience."

A terrible screeching filled her helmet, driving Ocella to her knees. She screamed, but could not even hear herself over the screeching.

The sound abruptly stopped.

"Marcia Licinius Ocella will remove its helmet. Impatience. Air in this room is breathable for Marcia Licinius Ocella. Reassurance."

Ocella reached for her helmet clasps with shaking hands and flipped them open. *Best not to annoy it further.* Her ears still rang from the shrill sound.

She pulled her helmet off. The room temperature was cooler than in the helmet. She forced herself to inhale. The air had an iron scent to it, like that outside a cattle slaughter yard, but she had no trouble breathing. After a few more breaths, she unclenched her muscles from the anticipation of choking to death.

"Analyzing breath of Marcia Licinius Ocella," hologram Ocella said. "Analysis confirms no rivals. Satisfaction. However, Marcia Licinius Ocella is aware of rivals. Suspicion. We would know the relationship between rivals and Marcia Licinius Ocella. Curiosity."

Ocella paused, gathering her thoughts. *How to make an alien understand human history?* The Saturnists never prepared her for this. Neither did Umbra for that matter.

"A thousand years ago—" she began, but the holo cut her off.

"Desire for information not directed at Marcia Licinius Ocella. Impatience. Communication methods too inefficient for data retrieval. Impatience. Information will be extracted from your species' drones. Impatience."

Ocella tensed. "What drones?"

⤞⟫⟫⟩ ⟨⟨⟨⟨⟨⟵

Lucia and Varo followed the pulsating blue vein lights in the walls and floor. Lucia hoped the lights took them in the direction in which Ocella had gone. Ocella had likely entered a room that cut off com signals. Perhaps a door closed behind her, blocking the signals.

Or perhaps she lay injured somewhere in this labyrinthine vessel, trying to call for help, but unable to get through.

Or perhaps something had awakened and taken her captive.

Lucia always assumed the worst. In this case, she assumed Ocella had been captured.

And just what are you going to do? Kaeso's practical voice asked in her mind. *You have a pulse pistol and a green kid on his first mission. You're going up against an unknown alien intelligence and you don't even have a plan.*

Lucia retorted to the Kaeso practicality. *And the time you'd waste coming up with a plan against an unknown alien intelligence—which, by the way, is unknowable and therefore a waste of time—you could be saving your lover. Why I'm doing this for you is a mystery greater than this godsdamned vessel.*

"Lucia!" Varo screamed behind her.

She whipped around to see Varo gaping at his feet. They were sinking into the chitinous floor, the blue veins brightening and coalescing around his feet as if trying to get a better grip.

Lucia lunged forward and grabbed Varo's hands. She tried pulling him out, but the floor was too strong. She couldn't get good leverage because the chitinous surface was too smooth. Only the area around him had turned viscous, for Lucia could step within a pace from him and stand on solid floor. But no matter how hard she pulled, he continued to sink.

"*Cac!*" she cried through clenched teeth.

Varo clutched at her, his eyes wide. He was down to his chest and the sinking accelerated.

"Lucia!" he screamed one last time before his helmet went below the floor's surface. His com cut off, but his hands grasped frantically at hers. She continued pulling, even as her arms went under the floor. He was suddenly yanked from her grasp. She felt around the viscous liquid under the floor, but couldn't find him. She pulled her arms out.

"Varo!" she yelled into her com.

Nothing.

"Varo!"

When he did not respond she rose to her feet. She stomped the floor through which Varo disappeared, but it was solid again.

"Gods below, what do you want with us?" she yelled at the walls.

She stomped the floor with her heel several more times. The only answer it gave was the pulsating veins leading down the undulating corridor. She licked her lips, then held her pistol in a firing position and followed the lights.

After more turns, hills, and dips, she entered the crescent room Ocella had walked through just before they lost her com. The hairs stood on her neck and arms. It was not the alien physiology that disturbed her, but the way their limbs seemed to flail, as if they had fought against their captors until the moment they froze. Even the algae-like substance she passed seemed to have been panicked, for it looked like a pyrotechnic starburst trying to escape the oval.

Focus, soldier. Mind current threats, not ancient ones.

But she didn't know if an ancient threat would suddenly become a current one. This object continued to surprise them. She watched the aliens in the ovals as if they would jump out at her at any moment. She kept her helmet's motion sensors—calibrated to compensate for her movements—on their highest setting. The bottom left corner of her helmet display showed the view behind her in case anything snuck up.

She rounded the curve of the room. The wall ahead had no ovals but was layered with a thick web of glowing blue veins. She saw no exit.

"Ocella, Varo, do you read me?" She didn't expect it to work, but she had to try. Perhaps the com signals would work this close to—

Her helmet's motion sensor blared. One of the algae ovals reached out with a gelatinous tentacle and engulfed her torso. In a panic, she tried pulling free, but more tentacles wrapped around her body. The tentacles snaked around her chest, her arms, and then a gelatinous mass poured over her head. She struggled to move in a massive bubble of viscous fluid as she screamed non-sensical curses and pleas in her panic.

The bubble pulled her backward into the oval from which it had emerged. Once inside, the outer layer solidified. Her panicked terror mounted when the algae darted forward and surrounded her.

Suit integrity alarms blared as algae began eating away at the suit. The air in her helmet sputtered and stopped, then quickly grew stale with her own exhales. Her faceplate turned opaque, then multiple cracks formed across the surface.

Her imminent death seemed to shatter her panic. A sudden calm came over her, and she didn't know if it was the algae or perhaps the gods granting her supernatural strength to face her death. Regardless, she used the last seconds of breath for one final message. She eye-tapped the deteriorating helmet display to start a recording.

"Kaeso," she said in a ragged whisper. "Be happy..."

Her helmet issued a final loud crack, then imploded. The viscous fluid poured onto her face, burning and freezing at the same time. It entered her lungs with the same horrible agony.

She thanked the gods it ended quickly.

A rumbling, suctioning sound reverberated through the room. Ocella whipped around to see what looked like a large drop of water form on the ceiling. A figure in a pressure suit slipped into the drop, and then the drop eased down until it touched the floor next to Ocella. The drop retreated back into the ceiling, leaving the figure to collapse on the floor.

Ocella rushed forward and turned the person over.

"Cen-Centuriae?" Varo said.

"Varo, what happened? Where's Lucia?"

"Gods, Centuriae, I have no idea what they did. I thought I was dead. It pulled me through this—"

"Varo," Ocella said, holding his shoulders, "where's Lucia?"

He blinked. "She was right in front of me. We were in a corridor—"

"You left the shuttle?"

"We lost com with you. We thought you might be hurt."

Ocella turned to the holo. "Where is my other crew member?"

The holo stared at her several moments. "Drone of Marcia Licinius Ocella species is under analysis. Curiosity."

"What do you mean, 'analysis'? *Where is Lucia?*"

"Marcia Licinius Ocella species concerned over drone. Sympathetic. Drone will be replaced after analysis complete. Benevolence. New drone will enable more efficient communication with Marcia Licinius Ocella species. Anticipation."

Ocella didn't know how to respond to this alien holo.

Analysis? Replacement?

She swallowed once. "Did you kill Lucia?"

The holo processed this question, and then said, "The drone's existence, as it was, is no more. Self-evident. Marcia Licinius Ocella species will be compensated with improved drone. Generosity."

Ocella exhaled once, then wanted to scream at the holo. *What good will screaming at it do? It thinks it's doing me a favor.*

"I would have preferred," she said slowly, using all her will to stamp down her panic, "that you had not...ended my crew member's existence. She was important to me the way she was. I do not want a...replacement, nor do I want you to do the same to my crew member here."

The holo stared blankly for almost a minute. Ocella wondered if it was unable, or unwilling, to understand her request.

"We do not understand why Marcia Licinius Ocella species prefers flawed drones. Confusion. We wonder why Marcia Licinius Ocella species does not appreciate our services. Insulted. Besides, preferences of Marcia Licinius Ocella species are irrelevant. Dominance. Only experiences valued. Anticipation."

The blue-lit veins in the room pulsated quicker, and then the entire wall behind the holo turned gray. The holo winked out, and then a 3-D image of the space around the vessel displayed on the wall, complete with the brown-clouded planet below. The view swiveled around to the left until it faced the empty space that held the way line.

"Oh, gods," Varo said, "are they taking us through the way line? If we go through without delta sleep—!"

The view flickered, and then the Menota debris cloud appeared. The vessel plowed through the debris as if it weren't there, turning rock, metal, and ice into atoms when the debris struck the translucent, blue energy shield surrounding it.

After ensuring her sanity—*if I were insane, would I know?*—she sat next to Varo. "You might as well take your helmet off. Better to save your air until you really need it."

Varo took off the helmet, revealing his sweaty, matted black hair. It took him several deep breaths before his eyes returned to a normal size and he set his helmet beside him. He stared at the display wall. "Where do you think they're going?"

Only experiences valued.

Ocella stared at the wall. "Menota."

If they were like the other Muse strains humanity had encountered, they valued experiences—the memories and emotions all intelligent species generated—above all else. The archives Kaeso and Cordus retrieved from Menota had taught the Saturnists that "experiences" were their gold, religion, and sustenance all rolled into one.

Ocella wondered what they would do when they learned the Menota archives were gone.

Chapter Six

"Cordus will be my second on this mission," Kaeso said to *Vacuna's* four other crew members in Cargo One. "Questions?"

Cordus struggled to keep his face impassive as shock roiled through him. *Second? I only wanted to come along. He wants me to be his Trierarch?* Granted, this was a simple courier mission: pick up a device that could detect the scentless aura of Muses in any Muse-infected human. A Saturnist named Aulus Tarpeius had developed the device on the Roman agricultural planet Reantium. They would also meet Lucia and Ocella there after their month-long mission to Menota. But as Kaeso had drilled into him for six years, there was no such thing as a 'simple' mission. Anything could go wrong once you step outside your door, and you had to prepare for it.

Gaius Octavius Blaesus, a white-haired, exiled Roman Senator and patrician, sat in a spare flight couch. He clapped his hands and beamed at Cordus. As always, he spoke first.

"It's about time you gave this young man responsibility, Centuriae. As I've always said, he needs the practice. Congratulations, Trierarch Antonius."

Cordus frowned. "You mean 'Trierarch Aemilius.'"

Only the crew of *Vacuna*, Gaia Julius, and select members of the Saturnist upper echelon knew Cordus's real identity. To everyone else, he was Titus Aemilius Cordus, nephew of Kaeso Aemilius and Marcia Licinius Ocella. After he escaped Terra, he had "disappeared" to Caesar Nova, a Lost World with geography and weather similar to northern Britannia—rocky, wet, and cold.

But Cordus knew what Blaesus meant by "practice." He tried his best every day to avoid thinking about it. Blaesus believed the romantic notion that Cordus should return to Roma, declare himself the Consular Heir, and then the civil war would end and all humanity would be united under a single ruler, as it was meant to be.

There was nothing in the universe Cordus wanted less.

Nestor Samaras, the ship's medicus, a Pantheon priest, and a committed Saturnist, frowned. The dark-haired Greek priest did not share Blaesus's fantasies and, in fact, opposed a return to the Roman government's old ways: rule by a single consul and a religious Collegia Pontificis, with a Senate that simply "advised" the rulers. Nestor had ancient Athenian ideas of democracy that were just as romantic as Blaesus's. He hoped Roma would emerge from its civil war with a Liberti-style government that combined ancient Roman republicanism with Greek democracy. Cordus thought it was another fantasy, but he could always count on Nestor to oppose Blaesus when the topic of Cordus's return to Roma came up.

"Unlike my Roman friend here," Nestor said cautiously, "I hope your ambitions are limited to commanding a starship."

"No other ambitions come to mind," Cordus said.

He glanced at Kaeso, who was as blank-faced as ever. *I know you think like Blaesus. That's why you made me your second. You want me to get used to giving orders so I can fulfill my "destiny". Well get used to disappointment.*

"Can we get back to work?" asked Dariya, one of two engineers on the ship. She leaned against a bulkhead with an impatient expression. Daryush, the ship's second engineer and Dariya's twin brother, stood next to her. Daryush, a large man with a naturally bald head, stood with his hands in the pockets of his green jumpsuit looking from Dariya to Kaeso. Dariya and Daryush were Persians and former slaves to a wealthy Roman patrician. They escaped slavery and fled to the Lost Worlds. Kaeso hired them years ago as engineers on *Vacuna*. Daryush's tongue had been cut out by his former Roman master, but Daryush was the most brilliant engineer Cordus had met during his brief time among the Lost Worlds.

Dariya, however, more than made up for her brother's silence. She turned to Cordus. "'Ush and I need to finish integrating that damned energy shield the Saturnists installed yesterday." She looked past Cordus to Kaeso. "By the way, Centuriae, why does *Vacuna* have to be the test subject for Gaia Julius's new toys?"

Kaeso shrugged. "*We* discovered the shield tech on Menota, so *we* get to test it. If it does what they say it does, it'll make us indestructible in a fight."

"Or implode us to the size of an atom," Dariya grumbled, adding a Persian curse under her breath. She turned back to Cordus. "Do we have your leave, *Trierarch*?"

Cordus suppressed a grin at Dariya's tact, or lack thereof. In the six years he'd known her, he came to realize she only spoke that way to people she trusted. She just ignored people she didn't trust.

"I have nothing to say," Cordus said. "Centuriae?"

Kaeso shook his head.

"Then you have leave to finish your engine prep."

"His Highness is most kind," she said, bowing deeply. Then she gave him a half-grin and left. Daryush, however, smiled broadly at Cordus and applauded softly. He then followed his sister to the engine room at the other end of the corridor.

Blaesus stood and put his hands on Cordus's shoulders. "Ah, my boy, I remember when you first came to us. A twelve-year-old with big brown eyes, tousled black hair, and an infant's naiveté about the universe outside Roma. How far you've come in just six short years. No doubt thanks to my tutoring."

Nestor stood as well. "You mean *despite* your tutoring?"

Blaesus lifted his chin. "You wound me, Medicus. If not for me, Cordus here would have no knowledge of his Roman ancestry or the intricacies of Roman governance. Why he'd be just as ignorant of Roma's contributions to humanity as the Lost World barbarians...present company excluded, of course."

"Blaesus, you're an arrogant fop," Nestor said. "He can get that from his Muses."

"Ah, but the Muses only give him *memories* of his ancestors' exploits. Having someone else's memories does not give one the *skills* used in those memories. Can you command Legions by simply reading the biography of Gaius Julius Caesar? I think not. Mastering the skills in those memories takes practice, which is what *I* gave him."

Cordus held up his hands. "Gentlemen, as always, I find your debates enlightening, but right now I need to speak to the Centuriae alone."

Nestor shrugged and left Cargo One. Blaesus wrapped his red scarf around his neck. "Trierarch, Centuriae, I'll leave you to your conference. Besides, I need to study my *latrunculi* strategies before we get to Reantium. Aulus Tarpeius may be generous to host us at his villa, but he is most vicious across the *latrunculi* board. Why I can count on one hand the number of times I've defeated the man in the forty-two years I've known him. Did you know he—?"

"Blaesus," Cordus said, "I really need to speak to the Centuriae."

"Of course, sire. I was doing it again, wasn't I?"

Cordus grinned.

"Very well, I will leave you without another word."

Miraculously, Blaesus left Cargo One and closed the hatch without another word.

Before Cordus could speak, Kaeso said, "I made you trierarch because you're ready for it. I didn't tell you before now because I wanted to see how you reacted when I sprung it on you."

"Did I pass the test?" Cordus asked.

Kaeso shrugged. "At least you pretended you knew all along. One of the first rules of leadership: Always act like you know what's going on. Especially when you don't."

Kaeso proceeded to explain another point of leadership, but his voice faded from Cordus's attention.

Marcus Antonius Primus stood behind Kaeso, his muscled arms folded. He stared at Cordus with preternatural blue eyes and wore a sideways grin. He had dark, curly hair and a well-trimmed beard. He wore the ancient Roman armor and scarlet cloak of a military commander. A gladius hung in a sheath from his left hip. His armor was dented and stained from multiple battles. Legends and Cordus's Muse memories told him Marcus Antonius loved to wade into the thick of battle. But after the Muses infected him in Egypt, they had kept him back.

Only an alien virus could keep Marcus from doing what he loved.

"You listening, kid?"

Cordus swung his eyes back to Kaeso. "Leadership is hard, I get it," Cordus said, using all his will to ignore the apparition of Marcus Antonius. "I still would rather have known before you announced it to the crew."

Kaeso stared at Cordus, then slowly looked over his shoulder to where Marcus Antonius stood with folded arms. Cordus's heart raced, and he thought Kaeso saw Marcus, but Kaeso turned back to Cordus with suspicious eyes.

He doesn't see. Gods, I am *going mad.*

Marcus Antonius barked a laugh that echoed in the hold. Kaeso didn't even flinch at the sound.

"Like I said," Kaeso continued, "I wanted to test your reaction to a real situation with real consequences. Not some drill, but one where your world just changed and you had only moments to adapt."

Oh, Kaeso, if you knew how my world was changing right now...

"And you get to pilot the ship," Kaeso said with a slight grin. "Hope that doesn't add more pressure."

Sweat beaded in the center of Cordus's back. "I've done it dozens of times. But Lucia will kick me out of her couch when she sees me—"

"I told Lucia before she left. She knows you'll be Trierarch for the entire mission, not just the trip there."

Cordus shook his head. "So you've planned this for over a month? What did Ocella say?"

Kaeso winced. "I...didn't tell her. Deep down she knows you need to do this. I'll deal with the consequences."

"Well this should be a fun reunion."

"Mmm. We leave in thirty minutes. Make sure everyone does their job, Trierarch."

"Yes, Centuriae," Cordus said. His voice sounded stiff, and he hoped Kaeso assumed it was the stress of his new responsibilities.

What else should he think? That I see my ancient ancestor's ghost?

Cordus's gaze swept the hold. "I want to make sure everything's locked down here first."

Kaeso nodded. "You'll do fine, kid."

Cordus gave Kaeso a reassuring smile, and then he started inspecting the cargo fastenings as Kaeso left the hold.

When the hatch closed, Cordus whirled around to Marcus Antonius. The ancient Roman unfolded his arms and walked straight toward Cordus. Cordus took an involuntary step back, but then stopped.

He's not real. He can't hurt me. Stop running, coward!

"We're very real, young Antonius," Marcus said, standing a single pace from Cordus. "Want to touch us?"

Cordus just watched Marcus, his breath quickening and the sweat dripping down his back. "Are you...from the Muses?"

Marcus laughed. "Obviously. What, did you think we were Marcus Antonius Primus come back to life? That man died long ago, and he was quite a bit more trouble than we bargained for. Did you know we had to infect him twice before we could control him? The first time, his body rejected us because he refused to listen when we told him to stop drinking wine. Clouds our senses, as you know. Our flamens injected him again, and after some adaptations on our part, we finally infected him. We've had no trouble infecting anyone since." Marcus eyed Cordus with a wry smile. "Until you came along."

"My Muses are creating this vision of you?"

"Young Antonius, 'your Muses' are standing before you. Only you can see us. It's the only way we can talk to you now."

"Why? Why can't you just talk to me in my mind like you always did?"

Marcus shrugged. "You're the first *living being* to control us. Nobody knows how this will work, not even us. You may have noticed our silence recently?"

Cordus nodded.

Marcus walked around the hold, inspecting the cargo containers. "That's because your body and your brain are maturing. This one is loose."

Cordus checked the floor clips on a container of pressure suit air canisters. Sure enough, the clips were not pushed all the way closed. Cordus went over, bent down, and fastened the clips.

Can you read my mind, too?

"Yes," Marcus said, moving to another cargo container, "but like before, only if your questions are directed at us."

Cordus couldn't help but stare at Marcus. Though well muscled, he was a head shorter than today's average human. The Muse-memories of Marcus's days gave Cordus the impression Marcus was taller. In his day, he may have been taller than the average ancient human.

"Why didn't you tell him you see us?" Marcus asked while checking another container.

"You know why."

"Yes, yes," Marcus said. "They *say* they trust you, but they don't *really* trust you, eh? Afraid we're going to reassert our control some day?"

Cordus watched Marcus. "Are you?"

Marcus walked back to Cordus with a grin. "We would if we could. Believe us, we have tried, but some things are beyond even our understanding."

"What do you mean?"

Marcus shrugged and then sat upon a container. His armor clinked as he moved, and his sword banged against the container as he hopped up.

"Every species that has served us has presented us with challenges that forced us to evolve. Our strain alone has controlled nine different species over the course of millions of Terran years. Humanity's individualist nature forced us to evolve to be compatible with your physiology." Marcus's eyes narrowed at Cordus. "You, young Antonius, are the first sentient being to control us, *and we cannot figure out why.* We evolve, we adapt, but you block us in every way...and you don't even know you're doing it."

"So I'm blessed by the gods, like Nestor says?"

Marcus barked a laugh. "We know nothing of the existence, or non-existence, of your gods."

"Then I suppose I'm just lucky."

Marcus shrugged. "All life evolves. Perhaps you are a new path in the universe's biological evolution. The 'why' of it doesn't matter to us, though. We are your slaves and there's nothing we can do about it." Marcus bowed his head to Cordus. "That, at least, has not changed."

When he was a child, Cordus guarded his thoughts as soon as he realized what the Muses were. Not only did Cordus grow up watching how the Muses controlled his family—from his father down to his brothers and sisters—but he had the memories of what they did from the moment they infected Marcus Antonius a thousand years ago. Cordus knew they were ruthless and would enslave him if given the opportunity.

But his memories also told him that while the Muses may be vicious, they never lied to their hosts. Even when those hosts were slaves, the Muses always told their hosts the truth.

Easy to do when you know you have control, he thought. The Muses never lied to the hosts they controlled for the same reason Cordus would never lie to a golem.

"Ah," Marcus said, watching Cordus, "the gears are turning in your head, young Antonius. Should I trust this apparition, should I not? Should I tell my friends, should I not? Decisions abound!"

"Fine," Cordus growled. "You seem eager to tell me what I should do. What would you do in my situation? If you are my slave, you will tell me the truth."

Marcus raised an eyebrow. "We would have you do what you were born to do: lead and command. You have the wisdom of a thousand years in your mind. Use it to rule these people. Use physical qualities we give you to force them to—"

"No!" Cordus said, immediate disgust crawling in his stomach. "If you mean I should use your aura to take away the will of other human beings, like my ancestors did, then that is something I will never do. You know this."

Marcus smiled, then jumped down from the cargo container and put a hand on Cordus's shoulder. Cordus could feel the hand through his jump suit.

"Very well," Marcus said, "may Fortuna be with you, young Antonius."

Then he vanished.

Cordus exhaled sharply. *No, I will not tell Kaeso about this.*

He didn't have the time or energy to work through this right now. He had trierarch duties to finish.

CHAPTER SEVEN

C ordus awoke from his delta sleep and checked the status displays on his pilot's tabulari. Ship's integrity was intact, systems nominal, and their location was what it should be: orbiting Reantium just outside the alpha way line event horizon.

They used alpha way lines rather than the instant travel of their quantum way line engines. The quantum engines were still a Saturnist and Umbra secret, so *Vacuna* only used them when traveling to remote locations. They'd have to answer awkward questions if the local way station saw them pop into existence far from a known way line.

The acrid smell of Nestor's pre-way line sacrifice still hung in the air. Cordus was comforted by the scent. It meant he was alive and not mad from the jump.

"Way line jump successful," Cordus reported to Kaeso, who sat in the command couch to his left. "All systems normal."

"Very good, Trierarch," Kaeso said.

Cordus glanced at the com on his tabulari. The Reantium Way Station should have hailed them by now. He scanned the com channels around the way station. Nothing. He checked the proximity sensors for any ships around the way station. While it was small compared to Liberti standards, there should have been some traffic.

But the local space was empty.

Cordus looked at Kaeso.

"Get a read on the way station itself," Kaeso ordered.

Cordus gave a sharp exhale when the readings came through. The way station, a hollowed asteroid where starships docked, gave off no power signatures at all. It was a cold, dead rock.

"Take us into the atmosphere," Kaeso said, after checking the scans.

"Yes, sir."

Cordus entered the coordinates Blaesus had provided to the villa of Aulus Tarpeius. Tarpeius owned over 90,000 acres of farmland on Reantium, making him the largest landowner on the planet. Reantium had just gone through a bloody revolt against the Roman garrisons stationed there, but most battles had taken place on the other side of the planet in the more populated areas. Tarpeius's villa was remote, even for this planet, so his holdings had been unaffected.

At least they'd been unaffected as of his last com. So had the way station.

Tarpeius was a committed Saturnist, which somehow escaped Blaesus's keen observation skills for the decades he knew Tarpeius. Cordus sent a sample of his blood to Tarpeius a year ago so his flamens could work on a Muse-detection device. In theory, it could detect the aura a Muse-infected human gave off, which was scentless to a human nose, and therefore Saturnists could know who was infected. A courier golem from Tarpeius had arrived on Caesar Nova three weeks ago saying the device was ready for testing. The original plan was for *Vacuna* to bring the device back to Caesar Nova and test it on Cordus. But now, since Cordus was coming along anyway, they would test it on him on Reantium.

"Piloting" the ship through the atmosphere was a matter of entering the correct coordinates and making sure the ship's automated re-entry systems functioned normally. After that, Cordus could sit back and watch the view outside the command deck windows. Bright white plasma engulfed the ship as it collided with Reantium's atmosphere. Cordus watched his tabulari as the ship's inertial control and grav systems yielded to Reantium's natural gravity field. This always made the ride into an atmosphere bumpier than it tended to be on more modern ships. *Vacuna* was state-of-the-art ninety years ago. Today, only the engineering skills of Dariya, Daryush, and to a lesser extent their Saturnist friends kept the ship flying.

The white plasma surrounding *Vacuna* dissipated, and the ship descended through the sparse clouds. Cordus checked his tabulari once again.

"Re-entry complete, ion engines engaged, altitude 60,000 feet," Cordus reported to Kaeso. "Should land at Tarpeius holdings in twenty minutes."

"Thank you, Trierarch," Kaeso said. "And thank you for letting the ship fly." He gave Cordus a small grin. "Lucia likes to fly it through the atmosphere. Makes for a bumpier ride. I hate it."

"Why don't you tell her?"

"Because it makes her feel in control of something that's beyond her control."

Marcus Antonius leaned between Cordus and Kaeso, and Cordus jumped. "You see, we are not that different from each other," Marcus said.

Kaeso noticed Cordus's flinch. "You all right, Trierarch?"

"Fine," Cordus said, though he couldn't see Kaeso with Marcus between them. Cordus quickly rubbed his left eye. "A speck..."

Marcus laughed. "You're getting good at lying to him."

Why are you here? Cordus asked with his mind.

"We're always here, young Antonius. We're part of you, remember?"

Why are you taunting me then?

Marcus affected a frown. "We would never taunt you. We have more respect for our master than humans ever did for theirs."

If I'm your master, then I order you to go away and not come back unless I call for you. Clear?

Marcus bowed his head. "Of course, *Dominar.*"

Then he disappeared...to reveal Kaeso staring at Cordus with a raised eyebrow.

Cordus blinked several times. "Damned speck."

Nestor spoke up from his delta couch behind Cordus. "You might have an eyelash. Do you want me to check?"

"I'm fine," Cordus said a little too forcefully. Then in a gentler tone, "I think it's out now."

He hoped he could make Marcus go away and reappear with a simple order. He decided he would test that later when he wasn't so busy...or around people.

Vacuna descended toward the Tarpeius holdings on a clear, sunny day. The ship sped over rolling green hills and vast crops of wheat, maize, and other vegetables and grains. Farming was Reantium's reason for existence, and it had once been considered Roma's "granary". With Reantium's independence, food prices in the Republic would now soar. Some outlying systems and colonies would even starve.

Cordus ground his teeth. *Just one Roman warlord Legion could've stopped this revolt before it even began. And yet millions of citizens will starve because gluttonous senators fight over who gets to sit in the consul's chair.*

The hailing channel chimed. "*Vacuna*, this is Tarpeius flight control. Please respond."

Cordus thumbed the com. "Tarpeius flight control, this is *Vacuna.*"

"We have you inbound from the southwest at 200 miles out from Tarpeius spaceport. That port is no longer in operation. Please proceed to government-sanctioned Nascio spaceport at the coordinates I'm forwarding to you."

Kaeso frowned, then thumbed his com. "Tarpeius flight control, this is the Centuriae of *Vacuna.* What happened to the Tarpeius spaceport?"

There was a noticeable pause. "Tarpeius spaceport has been decommissioned by the Reantium Liberation Collegium."

"'Reantium Liberation Collegium'?"

"Reantium's holy government. Please proceed to Nascio spaceport where agents of Aulus Tarpeius will transport you to his villa."

Kaeso's frown deepened. "Acknowledged, Tarpeius flight control. *Vacuna* out."

Cordus entered the new coordinates into the tabulari. The ship's automated systems obeyed the commands and brought the ship into a steeper descent to the Nascio land port seventy miles closer.

"So this is Tarpeius's reward for staying out of the rebellion," Cordus said.

"Or punishment. The 'Reantium Liberation Collegium' is likely bitter he didn't use his considerable resources to drive the Romans out."

"Should we be worried?"

Kaeso looked at Cordus wryly. "Just don't tell anyone who you are."

"Great."

"The Centuriae is right," Nestor said. "The worlds that rebelled against the Republic all wanted one thing: independence. Most desire membership in the Lost Worlds, so they try very hard to remain friendly to non-Romans. As long as we stick with our usual cover stories, we will be fine. The post-rebellion worlds we've visited so far have treated us like pontiffs."

Cordus wished Kaeso and Nestor's words reassured him, but they didn't. Terrible uneasiness spread from his gut. He hadn't felt this nervous since he escaped Terra six years ago. He noticed Kaeso also seemed tense. His brows furrowed as he scrolled through planetary news feeds on his tabulari.

This is what it's like to be in danger. Get used to it.

Nascio flight control hailed the ship and then took control of their landing process. Cordus was already uneasy over the dead way station and change in spaceports, so letting an unknown flight controller fly the ship made him bite his lip.

Cordus looked out the command deck windows at the Nascio spaceport. Few ships were parked around the port, mostly shuttles and air flyers. Four block-shaped hangars with the iconic Roman red-tiled roofs were spread across the port, and a small control tower stood near the edge of the concrete landing pads.

Nascio flight control set *Vacuna* down on a pad with a slight bump. As soon as the ship landed, controls came back to Cordus's tabulari, so he powered down the engines and the inertia/grav fields. Cordus felt lighter, as Reantium's gravity was 0.95 T.

Should make self-defense a bit easier, he thought warily.

The ship's external com chimed from a local voice network.

"This is *Vacuna*," Cordus answered.

"*Vacuna*," a Germanic male voice said, "I am Uller Mus, chief slave in the House of Aulus Tarpeius. I have a ground car waiting to take you to my *dominar's* villa. I am on the southeastern corner of the port and will be holding a sign with your ship's name."

Kaeso reached over and thumbed the "mute" button. He then tapped his collar com. "Blaesus, did you hear that?"

"I did," Blaesus said, "and I know Uller Mus very well. He's a dour man, though efficient and capable."

"So you do recognize his voice?" Kaeso pressed.

"It certainly *sounded* like the grumpy old dog."

Kaeso turned off the "mute" and nodded to Cordus. Cordus said, "Thank you, Uller Mus. We will meet you in ten minutes."

"Acknowledged, *Vacuna*." The transmission ended.

Cordus unbuckled himself from his couch. Kaeso did the same, still frowning.

"You don't trust this Uller Mus?" Cordus asked.

"Not that," Kaeso said. "It bothers me how easily Tarpeius gave up his spaceport to the new government. He has a private legion to protect his holdings and security systems better than even the Roman garrisons. They'd have no trouble fighting off a revolutionary mob. What made him give up so easily?"

Nestor had already unbuckled himself and stood near the command deck ladder. "The 'mob' overthrew the Roman garrisons, so maybe they're more powerful than they seem?"

"Maybe," Kaeso conceded. "But all the combined Roman garrisons on Reantium barely added up to a legion, and they were spread across the planet. A frenzied mob could take down individual cohorts, but not a well-supplied legion like Tarpeius's." Kaeso looked at Cordus. "Whatever the case, I don't like unanswered questions. Stay alert, Trierarch."

Cordus nodded. He didn't need Kaeso to tell him that.

The *Vacuna* crew gathered in Cargo One as Kaeso lowered the external ramp. They all wore some variation of a green jumpsuit that was standard fashion for Liberti merchant crews. Blaesus, however, seemed to chafe in his jumpsuit; he had wanted to wear his brilliant white toga as he typically did on-world, but thought better of it. An obvious Roman fashion on a revolutionary world might garner sour glares at best, a sniper's pulse pellet in the brain at worst.

"I hesitate to burden you with such a request, sire," Blaesus said as he dropped his packs to the floor, "but could you carry my second bag? My back spasms have returned and will *not* let up. I think it's because I'm sleeping on a ship's bunk again, which makes a board of nails seem as comfortable as a feather quilt in comparison."

"Sure," Cordus said, then picked up the pack. He grunted in surprise; the pack seemed to hold a dozen hardbound books and a few bricks for good measure.

"You're a wonderful Trierarch, sire," Blaesus said, then bounded down the cargo ramp.

Cordus now understood why the rest of the crew scattered when Blaesus entered Cargo One. He put the pack over his shoulder and walked down the door ramp.

At least no one will mistake me for a Roman patrician. They'd rather die than suffer under this load.

At the bottom of the ramp, Kaeso eyed Blaesus's pack as he tapped the controls on the *Vacuna* to close the ramp. "You'll learn," he said with a grin.

The yellow sun, blue sky, and cool breeze refreshed Cordus's spirits and made the pack seem lighter. This was the first time in six years he'd set foot on a Terran-class world other than Caesar Nova. A pleasant grassiness permeated the air. The hills beyond the tarmac were green and rolling, with occasional trees that looked more like giant shrubs than the tall canopy trees Cordus grew up with in Roma. Cordus had grown used to Caesar Nova's limited vegetation of man-sized bushes, so he marveled at the size of Reantium's tree-shrubs.

The walk to the ground car loosened Cordus's tight muscles. It had been over a week since they left Caesar Nova, and he'd barely had time to train like he had on the Saturnist stronghold.

But I'm not in training anymore. Now he was doing something that mattered, practicing his skills in a real mission. Though the confused situation on Reantium made him nervous, he could not deny the excitement rising in him with each step. The air, the adrenaline, and the low gravity combined to make him feel ready for any challenge the mission gave him.

A lone ground car sat at the edge of the tarmac, beside which stood a short, stocky man with a shock of blond-white hair, its wisps standing in the breeze. He wore the tan shirt and matching pants commonly worn by slaves throughout the Republic. He held a sign with *"Vacuna"* hand-written in black, bold letters. This amused Cordus, for there were no other ground cars around Uller Mus, and no other disembarking crews from the parked ships.

"This must be our car," Kaeso remarked.

"Uller Mus!" Blaesus shouted good-naturedly when they were a dozen paces away. "Gods, man, you don't look a day over 80!"

"Dominar Octavius," Uller said in a quiet voice. "A pleasure to see you again."

Uller took Blaesus's shoulder pack from his outstretched hands. He walked around to the back of the ground car, opened the trunk and stowed the pack. Cordus and the rest of the crew handed their packs to Uller, who added them to the trunk.

Once the packs were secure, the *Vacuna* crew climbed into the car. Uller got into the driver's seat, and they were soon traveling down a paved road toward Nascio.

Blaesus sat in the front seat to Uller's right. "So the troubles reached old Tarpeius, eh? Bet the bastard wasn't pleased to lose his spaceport."

"He was not, dominar," Uller said without elaborating.

"So all his produce goes through Nascio now? Jupiter's balls, how does he ship it here? His harvesters took their produce directly to his land port—now he has to ship them twenty miles to *this* one?"

"Yes, dominar."

"How many ground haulers did he have to buy?"

"Many, dominar."

"Unbeliev—"

Blaesus stopped talking. Cordus glanced at the old Senator and saw him staring out the front window with a grim, angry expression. Cordus leaned around the driver's seat in front of him to see what could make Blaesus speechless.

Crosses lined each side of the road bearing Roman soldiers. They all wore the green fatigues common to all soldiers fighting in a green environment. Hand-written placards were nailed above each victim's head—"ROMAN PIG" in dark letters the color of dried blood. All looked dead at least a week. Some wore uniforms marred by obvious pulse wounds, while others wore relatively clean uniforms.

Tribunes and logistics staff, Cordus decided. *Captured last.*

Brightly colored carrion birds perched on several crosses, pecking at eyes and noses. As Uller drove by, he lowered his window, put two fingers in his mouth, and released an ear-splitting whistle. The birds perched on the crosses scattered into the sky, some still holding their grisly pickings.

Blaesus eyed Uller a moment, then lowered his own window and produced the same high-pitched whistle at the carrion birds on the right side of the road.

Dariya sniffed. "They will only come back."

Cordus glared at her as she stared out the window. She turned to him and blinked when she saw his face. He didn't know what kind of expression he wore, but she sighed, lowered her window and began whistling like Uller and Blaesus. Soon even Kaeso and Nestor whistled at the birds.

Embarrassingly, Cordus could not produce the same whistle with his two fingers as his crew, so he screamed at the birds. The more he screamed, the angrier he got, until he was yelling nonsensical curses with a raw throat.

How ridiculous we must look, a car full of screaming, whistling passengers racing down the road.

He stopped screaming when Kaeso put a firm hand on his leg. The rest of the crew had ended their whistling and gave him sideways glances.

"I think we got them all, kid," Kaeso whispered.

Cordus nodded, then used his sleeve to wipe the tears from his face.

Chapter Eight

Cordus estimated one hundred crosses lined the highway from the spaceport to the city, and he vowed that somehow the ones responsible for this would pay.

He was not so naive to think that Romans never committed atrocities—he had the Muse memories to prove it. But he always had a soft place in his heart for the common Roman soldiers, the ones who did their duty, rushed into the fire knowing death lay inside, and followed orders even when they knew their tribunes were incompetent or corrupt. They believed Roma was the light of the universe, the culture that civilized humanity. The truth of that was a debate for philosophers and historians. What mattered was the soldiers believed it, and the prevailing culture among the Legions was one of honor and duty to the Republic.

So when Cordus swore vengeance on the ones who caused this, he was not thinking of the Reantium rebels. He thought of the warlord senators and local tribunes who put those soldiers in the situation that got them hung on crosses as feasts for carrion birds. Sadly, the local tribunes were likely among the men and women on those crosses, thus denying Cordus any way to make them pay.

But the senators still lived.

And what would you do? You're a simple trierarch on an antique cargo ship in an organization that no one outside it believes exists. It's not like you're...important.

Cordus refused to think on his own questions. These were his thoughts and not from the Muses, for they sounded like Kaeso's practical influence. He buried the thoughts of "doing something" deep. Like he always did.

They entered Nascio two miles after the last cross. Cordus didn't know anything about Nascio other than the locals considered it a small city on a planet where the largest cities barely reached 50,000 residents. This one looked to hold no more than 5,000 permanent residents. It didn't surprise Cordus since most people on this continent lived on their farms and only came into the city for supplies or to deliver their produce.

Nascio seemed to have taken the brunt of the revolt.

They first passed the old Roman Legion compound. Broken down fences and gates surrounded six military buildings. Most were blackened and crumbling ruins. An intact watchtower stood in the middle of the compound, the top floor lined with broken windows. Several blackened military ground cars were parked near it, their Roman Eagle sigils scoured off.

As they moved further into the city, Cordus noticed more rubble than intact buildings. The only ground cars on the streets were wrecks, and few people wandered the streets. Those who did all wore heavy black robes and hoods covering their heads. Cordus couldn't tell if they were men or women. Some carried shoulder packs, some carried boxes, some carried nothing. All walked in joyless motions.

A large number of Dis Pater worshipers lived on Reantium, more than on any other world. They believed that neglecting rituals produced dire catastrophes, from extreme weather to famines to wars. The only way to atone for the sins that caused the catastrophes was even greater attention to rituals, moral restraint, and sacrifices. Part of "atonement" required all believers to cover their bodies in shame when in public, for they had offended Dis Pater through their actions or inactions, and did not deserve to be seen.

Could Reantium have rebelled against Roma for the same reason the Kaldethi did sixteen years ago—because they believed Roma was corrupt, decadent, and not observing the proper rituals? That didn't make sense. The Kaldethi rebellion had simmered for decades before it exploded. Up until two months ago, Reantium was the definition of a stable Roman colony.

Uller broke the silence in the ground car. "We are approaching a checkpoint. Please let me speak to the discipuli. All will be fine."

Cordus tensed along with everyone else. Even Blaesus was quiet.

Cordus watched the checkpoint get closer. Two former Roman armored cars were parked on either side of the road. Scavenged chain fencing was fastened to a long pole that hung over the road. Two discipuli, each dressed in black flamen robes with hoods over their heads similar to the Nascio residents, sat next to the armored cars. Their robes were dirty, torn, and ill fitting, as if they'd been stripped off dead flamens and did not quite fit the new owners. The discipuli stood up from the shade next to the car and approached the center of the road with their pulse rifles in both hands. Cordus noticed a naked old man sitting on the ground hunched over with a chain around his neck fastened to one end of the gate. Dirt, bruises, and open cuts covered his body. The man looked half-starved, for his rib cage bulged from his torso. He stared at the car with dead eyes.

"Gods," Blaesus said. "I know that man. He was the garrison tribune in Nascio. Manius Galerius. We had dinner together at Tarpeius's villa last time I was here. Gods..."

A discipulus held up a hand, motioning Uller to stop. Uller pulled up next to the discipulus and lowered his window. "Dis Pater's grace on you, discipulus. These are the guests I mentioned on my trip through here."

Only the discipulus's blue eyes and pale skin were visible in the shadows of his hood. The man stared hard at each passenger in the car. Cordus tried to put on an air of indifference, as if he had nothing to fear because he had nothing to hide.

But men like these *like* to inspire fear and may see his indifference as arrogance. Then they'd do something to inspire fear. The crucifixions and Tribune Galerius showed the depravity of which these discipuli were capable.

Before Cordus could decide what to do, the discipulus's gaze had already swept past him and was on Uller again. "You did not say there would be so many guests," the discipulus said in a quiet tone more chilling than if he had shouted. "You will need to pay another toll, slave."

Uller nodded, reached into his tunic pocket and retrieved a money pouch. "How much, discipulus?"

"Twenty sesterces per guest."

Without expression, Uller counted out twelve ten-sesterce notes and handed them to the discipulus. The discipulus shoved the notes into a pocket within his robes. He nodded to his partner.

The second discipulus kicked Tribune Galerius. He slowly rose to his feet. Once the emaciated man stood, he gathered his strength, gripped the chain with both hands, and then leaned backward to use his weight to pull the gate open. The gate inched horizontally inward. It could not have been heavy, but Galerius struggled with it as his bare, blistered feet slipped on the paved, dusty road. One discipulus could have opened it with little effort. The only reason they made Galerius do it was for humiliation and torture. The two discipuli returned to their shaded chairs near the Roman armored cars.

With the gate opened, Galerius collapsed to the ground and lay on his back panting. Uller drove past the gate. Cordus stared at Galerius. Strips of flesh had been removed from Garlerius's calves and forearms, exposing rectangular, oozing wounds beneath dirt and grime.

"Barbarians," Blaesus whispered.

Kaeso watched the discipuli, while Nestor, Dariya, and Daryush did their best to keep their eyes on the road ahead.

Rage boiled in Cordus once again. Reantium had been a peaceful world before the civil war, and the Roman garrison was more of a lictor force ensuring public safety. What changed? Had the garrisons turned brutal as Roman control broke down with the civil war? But why would they? The colonists were citizens, not an occupied nation. What could cause citizens to turn so fanatical that they'd viciously slaughter their protectors?

After the checkpoint, the drive to Tarpeius's holdings was uneventful and silent. Twenty miles of straight road on flat ground surrounded by wheat and maize fields. Cordus occasionally spotted an automated harvester roaming the fields, either watering the crops or spraying fertilizer or insect repellent. Each harvester was over three stories tall, with one-story wheels that fit between the crop rows. The top of the harvester had multiple appendages and arms to complete almost any farming task.

After driving twenty miles, they approached a tall watch post, three stories high, with sensor arrays and small pulse cannons at the top. The post stood near the right side of the road surrounded by a wide, cleared semi-circle. A few hundred paces beyond it was another post. They continued like this until they reached a right turn with two more elaborate towers on either side of the road, each bristling with sensors and pulse cannons.

Uller turned onto the paved road without stopping. Cordus had no doubt that if their car failed to send a friendly signal, the cannons on the watch towers would fire.

"Has Tarpeius always protected his villa so well?" Cordus asked Blaesus.

"Yes," Blaesus said. "Although I think the posts along the main highway are new. How about it, Uller?"

"They are new, dominar."

Blaesus sniffed. "You never were a conversationalist. It's a wonder why Tarpeius keeps you."

"Yes, dominar."

They drove another two miles, tall maize stalks lining the road like a green wall, before they arrived at the main Tarpeius villa. They passed more watch posts and then entered a vast clearing with emerald green grass, patches of flowers, decorative trees, and life-sized marble sculptures of Romans garbed in everything from ancient armor to modern toga and pants. Dozens of workers tended the vast gardens. With a second look, Cordus noticed they were all golems—all male and Germanic, with the same light brown hair and fair skin. They were like younger versions of Uller Mus. Cordus had no doubt Uller's genetics were used to create the golems. Roman patricians loved to create their golems based on a favorite human slave.

They passed the gardens and entered a circular drive in front of a columned villa built in a semi-circle around the drive. The villa was a hundred paces in length, one level, with a traditional red-tiled roof. More golems clipped and tended to the multitude of flowers arranged around the villa and drive.

Uller stopped the car in front of a smiling, white-haired man dressed in a colorful toga, bordering on garish. *Aulus Tarpeius.* Cordus recognized him from the state dinners Tarpeius attended when Cordus was a child, before his escape from Roma. Tarpeius appeared the same now as he did then: steel-gray, short-cropped hair, a smooth face, and broad shoulders and chest.

The moment the car stopped, Blaesus stepped out and strode toward Tarpeius. Both men laughed, clasped forearms, and then gave each other a tight embrace.

"Aulus Tarpeius," Blaesus exclaimed, "your surgeons have made you look *younger* than the last time I saw you."

Tarpeius smiled. "They'd better; I pay them well enough. I could set up an appointment for you, old friend."

Blaesus put up his hands. "I prefer to meet the gods with my natural beauty intact."

Tarpeius grinned at Blaesus, then shifted his eyes toward the rest of the crew exiting the car. His eyes widened when he saw Cordus. Tarpeius went to him, then knelt on one knee and bowed his head.

"Sire, it is an honor to host you at my villa. Forgive my humble surroundings, but I am a simple farmer."

Cordus couldn't tell whether Tarpeius was joking, for he said this with his head bowed and without a hint of sarcasm in his voice.

"I...appreciate the welcome," Cordus said. It had been a long time since anyone treated him this way. He remembered discomfort over it as a child. As an adult, it embarrassed him. "Please stand, Aulus Tarpeius. I'm not the Consular Heir anymore."

Tarpeius looked up, confused, but he stood. "Blaesus said you had...grown up. I hope you have not forgotten your people, sire. They are desperate for leadership, especially in these horrific times."

After Blaesus introduced the rest of the crew to Tarpeius, Kaeso said, "We went through Nascio. Is the whole planet like that?"

Tarpeius's smooth features suddenly reflected his age. He stared blankly beyond Kaeso at the garden and the working golems. "No. Many places are worse."

"Why did this happen?" Cordus asked. "Roman citizens live here, not a conquered people. Religious and ethnic differences here seemed so minor."

Tarpeius shrugged. "When the civil war started, people wondered what Reantium independence would be like. Didn't take long for power-hungry flamens to start making things out to be worse than what they were. The rhetoric escalated a few months ago until..." Tarpeius paused, then looked at Cordus. "I never thought something like this could happen here. But it has, and so we survive as best we can."

His haunted stare lingered on Cordus a moment until he blinked, and his smile returned. "Let's not speak of such unpleasantness now. You are my guests, and it's been a long time since I've had any. I've prepared rooms for you all and a feast later that I'm sure you've never seen on Caesar Nova. I've been a Saturnist my whole life, but I couldn't bear a day on that dreary rock of a world."

Blaesus snorted. "You have no idea."

As Tarpeius led them inside, Marcus Antonius appeared beside Cordus. Cordus thought he maintained his composure rather well at Marcus's sudden appearance.

"Something's not right, young Antonius," Marcus said, his hands clasped behind his red-cloaked back as he stared at Tarpeius's back.

Cordus ground his teeth. *I told you to stay away until I called you.*

"Ah, but you did call us," he said with a grin. "Your own doubts and instincts know something is amiss. You subconsciously seek confirmation with us, so here we are."

Cordus pretended to gape at the beautiful frescoes, ancestral busts, and sculptures filling Tarpeius's villa. It wasn't hard considering he hadn't seen such art since he left Roma. Even Dariya and Daryush stared open-mouthed at Tarpeius's wealth.

Fine, so confirm away. What is it that has me uneasy?

"You're wondering why you've only seen golems and not humans since you arrived at Tarpeius's villa. Tarpeius and Uller seem to be the only humans here. You remember that Tarpeius once owned human slaves, which, by all accounts, he treated so well that some indebted citizens on other worlds wanted to sell themselves to him."

Cordus scanned the villa. Here and there, golems scurried about, dusting vases and sculptures, clipping and watering flowers. Savory smells came from the direction Cordus assumed to be the kitchen. He heard banging pots and pans, but no talking. Golems rarely spoke, so Cordus assumed they also manned the cooking duties.

The human slaves may have fled the revol—

Marcus snorted. "They're slaves. They can't 'flee.'"

There is a simple explanation we don't know yet, that's all.

"A simple explanation," Marcus repeated thoughtfully. "Why don't you ask Tarpeius about it?"

Cordus hesitated.

"You don't want to because you fear it's something you're not supposed to notice. And you fear it could make things...unpleasant."

Things are already unpleasant. I need to figure out what to do about it.

"Do you want my opinion?"

Cordus looked at Marcus. The apparition bared his teeth in a sarcastic grin.

What is your opinion?

"Talk to your father." And then Marcus vanished.

Gods below, what was that supposed to mean? My real *father or...*

Cordus glanced at Kaeso's back right in front of him. Kaeso's head tilted left and right as he took in his surroundings. He no doubt already noticed the lack of humans, and would be wondering the same thing as Cordus. Up ahead, Blaesus and Nestor talked with Tarpeius about the current state of the Saturnist movement. Dariya and Daryush gaped at the atriums they passed, filled with small fountains and lush green plants beneath skylights.

Cordus moved forward to walk beside Kaeso. Before Cordus could say anything, Kaeso whispered without moving his lips, "What do you see?"

"A lot of golems," Cordus whispered back.

Kaeso gave a quick nod. "Slaves are gone." His eyes casually took in the villa. "I'd suggest we leave, but I doubt we'd get far."

Cordus's heart thundered and his palms grew sweaty. It was one thing to have his own suspicions, but it was something else to hear Kaeso worried.

"What do we do?"

Kaeso gave him a raised eyebrow. "What do *you* think we should do?"

"This isn't a godsdamned drill," Cordus hissed. "This is real."

"I know, but you asked for this. What do we do?"

Cordus glared at Kaeso. *Could the old man be playing with me? Is this act a test?*

The set to Kaeso's jaw and the way his eyes kept moving said he was worried. Either the old Ancile had hidden his acting talents from Cordus for six years, or he was genuinely tense.

Cordus tapped his teeth together. He noticed more golems cleaning and running as couriers. There were too many golems for even this massive villa. Why?

Why not *ask Tarpeius?* he thought. If something bad was going to happen, it would happen whether or not Cordus provoked it now. Perhaps there was a simple explanation. Perhaps his instincts—though less probably, Kaeso's instincts—were wrong. If Tarpeius wanted to betray them, it was better to force his hand now than wait until *he* chose to spring a trap.

"I think I'll have a talk with Tarpeius," Cordus said, then strode toward the group ahead.

CHAPTER NINE

Kaeso didn't stop Cordus, but the Ancile's footsteps followed right behind him.

Tarpeius was saying to Blaesus, "...So when things started crumbling, I put Drusa and Figula on the family starship and sent them to Figula's cousins on Libertus."

"You must miss them terribly," Blaesus said.

"Yes..."

"I can't believe Drusa is twenty years old! Why that girl had me running in—"

"What about your slaves?" Cordus asked.

Cordus would have missed the hesitation in Tarpeius's step had he not been looking for it. "They went with Drusa and Figula, sire. I worried for them, as well."

"So you bought a lot of golems."

Tarpeius nodded. "Not the same quality as human slaves, of course, but they'll keep things running until it's safe for my staff to return. Here we are."

They emerged onto a covered terrace behind the villa. A large banquet table the shape of a horseshoe was arranged before them. Cordus's stomach rumbled at the scents of roast pork and the deep saltiness of open *garum* dishes. Stacks of various breads sat in the center of the table beside platters with cheeses, vegetables, and olive oil urns. Beyond the terrace was a large expanse of gardens, trees, and lawns similar to the front. Beyond the gardens towered the endless maize stalks surrounding the villa, like the sea to an island.

Several golems stood to one side holding sweaty metal pitchers, their eyes fixed on the table. A quartet of golems sat on stools behind them with traditional Roman stringed instruments, playing a piece that Cordus recognized from the state dinners in the Consular Palace.

A shudder ran through Cordus as he felt twelve again.

"Please sit where you feel most comfortable," Tarpeius said.

Blaesus clapped his hands. "Aulus, you dog, you've outdone yourself. I haven't seen a feast like this since my Senate days in Roma."

Next to Cordus, Dariya murmured, "I have not seen one like this since I was a slave."

Cordus glanced at her, but her eyes—and Daryush's—were fixed on the table. She then grinned at Cordus. "I would rather eat one than serve one. Right, 'Ush?"

Her brother nodded vigorously. Dariya and Daryush took their seats at one end of the horseshoe, then Kaeso sat next to Daryush. Cordus was about to sit next to Kaeso when Tarpeius called to him.

"Sire, would you honor me by sitting next to me?"

Tarpeius pulled a cushioned chair out from the table and looked at him expectantly. Cordus glanced at Kaeso, who gave him a slight nod. Cordus moved toward the open chair Tarpeius had pulled out for him and sat down.

"I hope you do not mind eating from chairs rather than couches, sire," Tarpeius said, sitting to Cordus's right. "Eating while reclined is the Roman way, but I find sitting up while eating aids my digestion."

"Fine," Cordus mumbled. "That's how I've done it for the last six years."

On Tarpeius's right, Blaesus said, "Young Antonius has adapted well to the barbaric ways of the Lost Worlds." He dabbed a bread roll into a bowl of olive oil and took a huge bite.

Cordus waited for Tarpeius to reach for a roll and then pretended to reach for the same roll. Tarpeius laughed. "I'm sorry, sire, go ahead."

Cordus took the roll and set it on his plate. After Tarpeius poured some olive oil in the small bowl next to his plate, Cordus poured oil from the same urn into his bowl. He continued to follow the choices Tarpeius made throughout the dinner.

The only way he'll poison me is if he poisons himself.

Blaesus and Tarpeius were engaged in conversations about old times in the Senate, so Cordus studied his surroundings without interruption. The golems were attentive throughout the dinner: They refilled his water glass whenever it was half-full, offered him more portions when he finished the last bite, even provided new towels whenever he wiped his mouth with one.

In all, it made him queasy like it did when he was a child. The Consular Family had to remain aloof at all times while in public. Cordus's mother and father, both infected with the Terran Muses, had no trouble because for them it was not an act. Their Muses forced them to act like gods. To fit in, Cordus had to act the same way, even when he knew he was different. At first, he simply wanted to be like his family. Why didn't his Muses 'guide' him like they did his parents and siblings? Why must he tell *them* what to do?

Cordus found himself clenching his chair arms with white hands. He eased his hands off the chair and placed them in his lap.

Nestor asked, "When can we see the prototype of the Muse device, Aulus Tarpeius? I'm curious as to how your flamens used Cordus's blood to—"

Tarpeius waved a hand. "In time, brother. First let us enjoy dessert. My golem cooks have prepared fig tarts and walnut sweet cakes that would make the goddess Edesia's mouth water."

"You're making *my* mouth water, old friend," Blaesus said.

Tarpeius turned to Cordus with a large grin. "They may be golems, but I've programmed them well, don't you think, sire?"

"Impressive," Cordus said. "Have you received a signal from Ocella? They were supposed to be in-system by now."

Tarpeius shook his head. "I have not, sire. Of course the com satellites have been dreadful lately. The way line to Menota is on the other side of the system. They could be in-system already, but unable to communicate. I wouldn't worry, sire." The golems put a platter of glistening tarts and cakes in front of them. "I'm sure something sweet will ease your worries."

Cordus suppressed a scowl. *I'm not a child to be distracted with sweets.* But he shook his head politely. "No, thank you. I filled up far too much on the main course."

Blaeus said, "Wonderful! More for me and 'Ush." He leaned forward and gave Daryush a wink. Daryush launched into the cakes with as much drive as Blaesus.

Nestor also took some cakes, then asked, "How have you tested this Muse device, Aulus Tarpeius? I wasn't aware there were infectees on Reantium."

A golem set another platter of cakes on the table, then reached into its work vest, pulled out a pulse pistol, and shot Nestor. The top of the Greek medicus's head exploded. His body and chair fell backward and landed with a crack on the marble floor.

Cordus stared, frozen, the scene unraveling in surreal slowness. He could not think or feel or move. Four other golems had pistols in their hands and advanced toward the table. The head of one of the golems exploded into yellow fragments. Blasts erupted from his right. Kaeso and Dariya were shooting down the golems. Daryush and Blaesus dove under the table. Tarpeius stood, holding up his hands, screaming at the golems. Cordus could not understand his words.

In fact, he could not understand anything he was seeing until Kaeso slapped his face with an open palm. "Get up!" he screamed, pulling Cordus out of the chair by an arm.

Cordus blinked. Yes, he should leave this place. Where friends are gunned down by golems. Where the remains of Nestor's head were scattered across the terrace. Yes, it was best to leave.

Cordus let Kaeso drag him after the others as they fled into the gardens beyond the terrace. Pulse shots cut through the gardens around him until the trees and bushes surrounding the villa hid all the humans. They continued running through the dense foliage. Leaves and branches slapped and scratched Cordus's face and arms.

After sprinting a hundred paces, they found a columned, marble altar to Abundantia and hid behind it. Kaeso and Dariya peeked around the marble columns as they reloaded their pulse pistols. Daryush sat on the ground with his arms wrapped around his knees. Blaesus and Tarpeius, their chests heaving, sat on a marble bench surrounded by flowers.

"What's happening, Tarpeius?" Kaeso growled. "Talk or we throw you to your dogs."

Tarpeius closed his eyes, tears streaming from them. His surgical augmentation seemed to have failed, for he looked ancient, withered, and defeated. "They took Drusa and Figula," he said between sobs and pants. "I had to do something. I had to give them something. *They're going to crucify my family!*"

Blaesus glared at Tarpeius. "So you gave them *us*? Oaths you have taken, Tarpeius. Saturnists have survived the millennia because they did not give each other up, no matter the personal cost." Blaesus snarled. "You coward."

Tarpeius turned to Blaesus with wide, mad eyes. "Gods damn you, Gaius Octavius Blaesus! You have no family, so do not speak to me that way."

Kaeso finished reloading his pistol. "The 'why' doesn't matter. How do we turn off those golems?"

Tarpeius started laughing. Kaeso narrowed his eyes at Tarpeius.

"You can't turn them off, you fool," Tarpeius laughed with red eyes. "We tried. They run the gods damned planet now!"

Cordus suddenly found his voice. "The *golems* rebelled? The golems are this 'Reantium Liberation Collegium'?"

Gods, those were golems at the discipulus checkpoint. They looked and acted like golems, but I still didn't see them. Golem programming was so secure that malfunctions were almost non-existent. It was like thinking a ship's tabulari would suddenly start flying the ship on its own.

"We thought we could control them," Tarpeius murmured, almost too quiet for Cordus to hear. Then he looked at Cordus with pleading eyes. "We thought we could use the same interstellar com mechanisms as your Muses. We thought we could reprogram them all at once, without master keys." Tarpeius groaned. "All we did was *free* them."

Cordus felt numb. "My blood. You didn't use my blood for a Muse detector. You used it to reprogram *golems*? Why?"

Tarpeius laughed insanely again, then waved his hand back toward his villa. "So we could do *that* to a Republic with golems as ubiquitous as roaches!"

"Gods, man," Blaesus said, aghast. "I cannot begin to think up a more horrid weapon to—"

"Roma needs to die so it can be reborn the way the gods meant it!" Tarpeius screamed at Blaesus, spittle flying from his mouth. "Isn't that what Saturnists have wanted for a thousand years?"

Pulse blasts showered them in marble fragments. Kaeso and Dariya peeked from around the columns, searching for targets.

"Trierarch," Kaeso said calmly, firing off pulse blasts. "We could use your help."

You are the trierarch. Act like you know what you're doing. Especially when you don't.

Cordus retrieved his pulse pistol from the holster in his vest. He hurried to another column and then peeked around the edge toward where Kaeso fired.

"Movement to the right," Dariya called out. "They are surrounding us."

"Dariya, take them into the maize fields," Kaeso said, "I'll cover your retreat."

Cordus said, "I'm Trierarch, sir, that's my job."

Kaeso stared at Cordus.

"I'm here," Cordus said firmly.

Kaeso nodded once. "Take them into the maize, Trierarch. I'll cover you."

Cordus nodded, then turned and helped Blaesus up from the ground. Daryush was already up and impatient to flee. Cordus let Tarpeius stand on his own.

He turned to Kaeso, but before he could say anything, Kaeso said, "I'm right behind you."

More blasts hit the columns, this time from the left and right.

"Go!"

Cordus led the survivors further into the dense garden until they reached a clearing. He stopped them. The edge of the swaying maize fields was twenty paces ahead of them across a green, well-tended lawn. Cordus turned left and right, but did not see any golems.

"Dariya?" Cordus said.

"Nothing. But those sons of whore machines could be anywhere."

Cordus turned to Tarpeius. "Any other security we should know about?"

Tarpeius stared at the ground, shuffling from foot to foot. "Nobody was supposed to get hurt..."

"Blaesus?" Cordus asked.

"None that I remember besides simple sensors," Blaesus said between heavy breaths. "But he obviously upgraded in the ten years since I was last here."

Pulse blasts from behind split the branches and leaves around them. Trampling feet rushed toward them. Cordus brought his pistol around, but held off when Kaeso burst through the bushes.

"Go, go!" Kaeso yelled, pushing them forward. "They're right behind me!"

Cordus and the others sprinted across the clearing and toward the maize rows. Just as he entered the maize, blazing cold agony enveloped his entire body. And then he remembered no more.

Chapter Ten

Ocella awoke with a start from a dreamless sleep. Despair flooded her heart when she realized she was still on the alien vessel. The dead, gray-brown planet Menota filled the view screen on the wall. She instinctively felt the pistol holster at her side and found it empty. She sighed.

Varo lay on his back beside her, and his eyes fluttered open. His face fell once he was lucid. She wondered if she looked the same when she realized where she was upon awakening.

"How long was I asleep?" he asked.

"I don't know," Ocella said, sitting up on the black floor. "I was asleep, too. I think they did something to us, because I don't recall lying down. They took our pulse pistols."

Varo checked his empty holster and cursed.

Ocella stood and then nodded to the wall. "We're above Menota. Last I remember we exited the new way line. Menota should have been a four-day journey from there, if they're as fast as our ships."

Varo stood as well, regarding the wall. "At least we didn't have to sit here staring at that for four days." He looked at her hopefully. "There's some mercy in that, eh?"

Ocella didn't say anything. She doubted mercy had anything to do with it. The ship wanted to keep them alive for some reason. It didn't want to feed them or give them water, so it put them to sleep. Ocella was no more hungry or thirsty than when she first arrived on the ship, so it must have been a frozen sleep.

But why keep us alive?

"We're overdue at Reantium," she said suddenly.

"Do you think they'll come for us?"

"I hope not." *What can a few Saturnist ships do against this thing?*

"How will we escape if no one helps us?"

She frowned at him. She assumed the vessel was listening. She did not want it to know they were hopeless mice, there to run whatever labyrinths in which it decided to put them.

"We will leave when it is time," she said, annunciating each word.

Varo seemed to understand her meaning and gave her an abashed nod. "Yes, Centuriae."

The wall behind them irised open and a naked woman stood in the entrance.

"Lucia!" Ocella gasped.

She went toward her Trierarch, but then stopped within a few paces.

The woman in the door was not Lucia. She looked like her, from her muscular build to her shaved, stubbly head. But her skin had a grayish tint, and veins of blue pulsed lightly beneath.

And she had no eyes. They were empty sockets.

"Gods," Varo breathed behind Ocella. "What did they do to her?"

"It's not her," Ocella said in a low tone. "What did you do to my Trierarch's body?"

The Lucia golem's head turned to Ocella. "This is not your Trierarch's body, Centuriae," the golem said, her voice sounding like Lucia's. "It is a replica."

"A golem?"

Lucia's head shifted. "Yes, similar to your golems. Forgive this appearance, Centuriae. Eyes are difficult. We will add them later. We have questions that cannot wait until then."

"I have questions—"

"We would know the capabilities of your Umbra Corps ships."

Ocella stared at Lucia, but avoided her eyeless sockets. Instead, she focused on Lucia's mouth. "I don't understand why you need—"

"This drone's brain has limited data regarding Umbra Corps, yet it believed Umbra Corps to be powerful. Its memories suggest you were once in this organization. Do you know the capabilities of its starships?"

Whenever Ocella heard "Umbra Corps", she instinctively flinched, waiting for the searing pain from the Umbra implant behind her right ear. Umbra Ancilia were forbidden to discuss Umbra with non-Ancilia. The implant, a data and communications link between the Umbra magisterium and its Ancilia, physically prevented discussion of the ultra-secret Corps. Libertus lacked massive fleets of warships, so it used the deadly Ancilia to infiltrate hostile regimes and end threats to Libertus before they began.

But Ocella was no longer in Umbra, which she left when she rescued Cordus six years ago. Still, the promise of pain was not easy to forget.

"I don't know their capabilities now. Why?"

"Four Umbra ships are on an intercept course with us. They have technology that defies our scans. We would know how to disable them so we can gather more witnesses."

Ocella turned and stared at the view wall. All she saw was Menota, one gray half bathed in sunlight and the other dark. There was no sign of ships.

Could Umbra ships fight this vessel? Not the ships that existed when she was an Ancile, but Umbra could make huge leaps within a short period of time.

"Like I said, I don't know their capabilities anymore."

The Lucia golem "stared" at her as if assessing her truthfulness. She then shrugged in an awkward way, as if she knew what the gesture meant, but did not know how to execute it. She looked to the wall, and Ocella followed her gaze.

The view on the wall shifted, magnified, and focused on four black Umbra ships flying toward the alien vessel in a wide formation. Ocella was surprised Umbra still patrolled the Menota system, given the 'no landings' treaty between Libertus and Roma had expired with the latter's civil war. She also assumed they knew the Menota Muse archives were destroyed by the last Roman consul in a fit of Muse-fueled rage. Why were they still here?

Of course. They knew a second way line existed in the Menota system. Had they found it, or were they searching for it like Ocella and the Saturnists?

An Umbra ship suddenly disappeared in a white ball of light. When the light dissipated, the ship was gone. Two more ships were destroyed in the same fashion, one after the other. The last ship tried to turn and flee, but did not get far before it succumbed to the same fate.

Ocella stared in shock at the images. Umbra warships were the most advanced ships humanity had ever built. Their power, and secrecy behind the Umbra veil, were what had kept Libertus free for two hundred years.

Yet this vessel had destroyed them in moments with a shrug.

"This drone's memories," the Lucia golem continued, as if nothing had happened, "say that the Roman Consul destroyed the Menota archives. Why would he commit such a sacrilege?"

When Ocella found her voice again, she blurted, "What do you want with us?"

Lucia stared at her with those monstrously empty sockets. "You are to be witnesses." She said it as if the statement was self-evident and needed no further explanation. She then cocked her head. "The Roman Consul's son, Marcus Antonius Cordus, is important to you. This drone's memories suggest this is so."

Ocella felt the blood drain from her face. *I will not give this thing Cordus. It will have to kill me.*

"This drone's memories," Lucia continued, "suggest the boy is a host for a rival strain. 'Muses', it calls them. Yet it suggests Cordus can control them. Is this true?"

Ocella turned away from the Lucia golem.

"You care for your drones. Would you answer our questions if it would prevent us from hurting the drone behind you?"

Ocella glanced at Varo, whose eyes had widened.

The opening behind Lucia irised open, causing Ocella to start. "We will not waste more witnesses. We have the data we need regarding Marcus Antonius Cordus from this drone's memories. We will meet him at Reantium. The archives on the planet below must be rebuilt. If this drone's memories are correct, these 'Muses' he hosts will help us accomplish this."

Lucia turned around and left the room. The opening irised shut behind her.

"Centuriae, if this thing gets Cordus—"

Ocella whirled around. "Quiet!"

Varo snapped his mouth shut.

She had to think. It had been a long time since she was in a hopeless situation like this. Six years, to be exact. There were many more times before that, but she had her Umbra implant to guide her. Its link to the wisdom of the Liberti Muses gave her all the knowledge she needed to think her way out of dangerous situations.

But like every other Ancile, she came to rely on the implant. Now, she tried to focus through the fear and doubt clouding her mind.

She was trapped in an alien vessel. She needed to escape, and any plan had to involve Varo. She could not discuss the plan with him for fear the aliens were listening. Now that they had Lucia's memories, they knew their language. How could she communicate with Varo in a way the aliens would not understand?

Or, how could she communicate with Varo in a way *Lucia* would not understand?

Lucia was a Roman citizen. As far as Ocella knew, she had never learned another language besides the universal Latin spoken by almost every human. While some worlds—and some Terran regions—still spoke various ethnic languages, Latin was the language of human commerce.

Ocella caught Varo's gaze and said in ancient Aramaic, "Can you understand me?"

Varo looked confused, and Ocella wondered if he had ever learned the language of his ancestors. Varo thought a moment, then said in Aramaic, "It has been a long time. I can understand, but speak little."

Ocella bared her teeth in a smile. "Good. We have some things to discuss."

Chapter Eleven

Cordus awoke to a savage pain in his limbs and head. He groaned, his eyes still shut.

"It'll pass in a few moments," a female voice said near his side.

It took all the strength Cordus possessed to open his eyes. His sight was clouded and gritty. He blinked several times, though each blink brought stabbing agony in the center of his head. But the more he blinked, the more the pain faded. Once the cloudiness was gone, he focused on the source of the voice.

She was young, no more than a year or two older than him. She had long, black hair tied in a single braid, brown eyes, and the olive skin of a Mediterranean native. Billions of humans across space had that look, but it gave him a sudden nostalgia for Roma. Her face was gaunt, as though it had been weeks since she had a proper meal.

Kaeso's voice came from his left. "About time you woke up, kid."

Cordus could now turn his head without fire surging through his body. Kaeso sat on the floor next to him, dried blood crusting the right side of his face. There was a bloody gash above his right ear on his stubbly head. Despite his obvious pain, he gave Cordus a lopsided grin. For Kaeso, it was tantamount to a running embrace.

Cordus scanned the room. It was octagonal, with barred, open windows at head-height. Judging by the light outside, it was either dusk or morning. He couldn't tell since he was unfamiliar with the directions on this world. The room was warm, so Cordus assumed dusk. In the meager light, he saw Blaesus, Dariya, and Daryush laying to Kaeso's left. All three lay on their backs unconscious.

Seven men were on the other side of the room, all wearing the standard-issue gray under-tunics and patterned green fatigues of Roman Legionaries. Some lay on their sides, some sat with their backs against the wall. All were dirty, wounded, and half-starved. The ones who were awake watched Cordus with tired eyes.

The room reeked of unwashed bodies and vomit.

Next to him was the woman who spoke to him. Cordus thought at first she was another Legionary until he noticed her clothes: They were tattered and dirty, but in the style of a citizen.

Cordus tried to sit up. Pain shot through him again, but he clenched his teeth and sat up so his back was against the wall like Kaeso.

"Where are we?" he asked Kaeso.

"Remember the tower we passed when we entered Nascio?"

Cordus nodded. "What do they want with us?"

"I just woke up myself. Don't even know how long we've been out."

"You've been here a day," the woman next to Cordus said. "No idea how long you were out before that. The fulgurators can keep you down for up to four days."

Cordus eyed the woman. "Fulgura...?" He assumed she was referring to whatever the golems had used to knock him out. "What is your name, my lady?"

The woman gave him a tired laugh. "Such manners, for a simple merchant. I am Aquilina."

Cordus turned to Kaeso, and he shrugged. "Tarpeius has bigger things to worry about now than paying us for our the insect repellant we delivered."

Implicit in the shrug was, *We're cargo haulers, kid...and no more.*

Taking up the act, Cordus sighed. "So much for a quick payday. Where is Tarpeius?"

"Not here," Kaeso said.

Cordus turned back to the woman. "How did you end up here?"

"Those scraps of vat flesh think I'm a Roman patrician," Aquilina said, then gave Cordus an amused glance. "But I'm also a simple merchant."

"She's a godsdamned spy, is what she is," a legionary growled. He was around Kaeso's age with graying hair in the stubble on his head and face. His left forearm had a long cut that was sewn shut hastily with haphazard stitches. "She's one of them Liberti *numina* everyone whispers about. Merchant, ha! Mound of pig *cac*, if you ask me. We was arresting her when the golems rebelled."

Aquilina shook her head wearily. "I don't know what else to tell these men, but I am no spy. Yes, I'm from Libertus, but I was delivering fertilizer. Just because I do well and dress well, the golems—and our esteemed fellow prisoners—think I'm something I'm not. They're just upset and taking it out on me."

The legionary started to rise. "You're godsdamned right I'm upset! I lost good men—"

"Easy, friend," Cordus said in a soothing tone as he rose to his feet. "The golems are the enemy. What is your name?"

The legionary glared at Aquilina, then shifted his eyes to Cordus. He exhaled sharply through his nose, then sat back down and leaned his head against the wall.

"Paulus Ulpius," he said. "Centurion, 2nd Cohort Equitata Machina, 24th Legion."

"I'm sorry for your losses, Centurion," Cordus said, easing back down. "Are you and your men all that's left of the 24th?"

"Aye," Ulpius said, glancing at the six others nearby. They all looked defeated, demoralized, and ready to die. "Been six days since we was captured. Three more came in here with us. Golems crucified them, one every other day. If the pattern holds, they'll take another one of us today."

Dariya groaned next to Kaeso. Her eyes fluttered open, and she sucked in a ragged breath when the pain hit her. Kaeso put a reassuring hand on her shoulder as she awoke.

Cordus turned to Aquilina. "So we were hit with a...*fulgurator*...?"

"A gun that shoots lightning, but doesn't kill," she said. "Hurts like a bolt from Jupiter, though."

Ulpius said, "The flamens gave it a fancy code name I don't remember, but the men came up with fulgurator, a lightning gun. Shuts down your body, puts you into some kind of hibernation."

Kaeso gave Cordus a meaningful look. "Seems the Romans have a new toy," he murmured.

In the past, before Cordus fled Roma, any "new toy" came as a revelation from the Muses. Most often it came to the consul, but they also came to the Collegia Pontificis. The Muses would give their hosts the plans for some technology, and then the hosts would publicly proclaim they received a Missive of the Gods. The Missive would have the plans for the technology, and the host would pass the plans on to Roman flamens to build or develop.

But the Terran Muses—which only infected the consul, his family, and the Collegia Pontificis—were supposedly destroyed in Roma six years ago, an event that sparked the current civil war. Had Roman flamens used their own ingenuity to develop this gun...or do the Terran Muses still live?

Cordus doubted the Terran Muses lived. He queried his Muses constantly for over a year after the consul's death, but they could not find the presence of their strain.

"Apollo's cock," Blaesus moaned as he woke to the fulgurator's awful pain.

Dariya had already sat up and was whispering to Daryush as he also woke. Daryush grunted something that Dariya seemed to understand.

Ulpius stared at Daryush. "Is he dim or what?"

Dariya tried to stand but she couldn't get her muscles to work. Instead, she snarled, "He has more brains than you, you Roman pi—!"

"No offense, lass," Ulpius said, holding up his hands. "Just asking."

Once Dariya calmed down, Kaeso explained to her, Daryush, and Blaesus what they knew so far.

"That treacherous bastard Tarpeius can rot in Bacchus's soggy ass," Blaesus grumbled, holding his head in both hands.

Ulpius grunted. "Spoken like a Roman. What's your name, old man?"

Once Blaesus knew he had an audience, his pain seemed to ease. He drew his head up and sat straight.

"Gaius Octavius Blaesus."

Cordus winced. *So much for keeping a low profile...*

Ulpius's eyes narrowed. "Octavius Blaesus. You were exiled from Roman territory if I remember right. I believe it's the duty of every Roman soldier to arrest you if you set foot in the Republic again."

Cordus tensed and felt Kaeso do the same.

"You know me?" Blaesus exclaimed. "How wonderful! Well I can assure you, Centurion, it was all a misunderstanding. Some Senators do not appreciate..."

Blaesus trailed off as the elevator rumbled behind the closed doors on the other side of the octagonal room. The Romans who'd been sleeping sat up, their eyes fearful.

Aquilina leaned next to Cordus and said, "Try not to look so defiant...and Roman."

Before he could ask her what she meant, the elevator doors opened. Four golems dressed in tattered black flamen robes, each holding a metal rod in both hands, exited the elevator and stood to one side. Behind them, a fifth golem stepped into the room. This one wore a torn and bloody toga arranged around its shoulders as if a child had put it on. The right side of its face was painted dark red, and Cordus had the chilling suspicion it was somebody's blood.

The golem moved to the left, studied each Roman a few seconds, and then moved on to the next. It gave no indication what it was thinking. When its eyes finally rested on Cordus, he tried to sink his shoulders and look as beaten as his body felt. The golem's stare moved on to Kaeso—who simply closed his eyes and pretended to sleep—then Blaesus, Dariya, and Daryush.

After it stared at Daryush, the golem pointed at Cordus. His heart skipped a beat.

"You may go," the golem said.

It pointed at Kaeso, Dariya, and Daryush and said the same thing.

Then it pointed at Blaesus. "You will come with us. You will stand trial for your crimes against the Reantium Liberation Collegium."

"What?" Blaesus exclaimed. "I haven't done anything to your Collegium, how can you—?"

"You are Roman. You are guilty. You will stand trial for your crimes."

Three golems with the metal rods strode toward Cordus, Kaeso, Dariya, and Daryush and motioned them to their feet. The fourth golem prodded Blaesus, who stood on shaky legs. The golem put metal cuffs on Blaesus's wrists.

Kaeso said to the lead golem, "He's not a Roman citizen. He had no part in any crimes against you."

The golem stared at Kaeso. "He is Roman. We have knowledge given to us by Aulus Tarpeius."

"He lies!" Blaesus yelled.

"He does not. We ensured his truthfulness by torturing his wife and daughter in front of him. We stopped in exchange for his knowledge. He will not risk their continued torture by lying. We learned this tactic from Romans."

Cordus tried to swallow, but his throat and mouth were suddenly dry. If Tarpeius gave up Blaesus, why didn't he give up Cordus, the last Antonius? Could he have suddenly remembered his Saturnist vows? Maybe he had to give the golems something and chose Blaesus over Cordus?

The golems prodded Cordus and the others toward the elevator. As the doors closed, he caught a final look from Aquilina—

The Muses in his mind cried out in shock.

Marcus Antonius blinked into existence next to the golem to Cordus's right. He turned to Cordus, surprise on his bearded face. "That woman has a Muse implant. She just sent you a message—*help me and I will help you.*" Marcus laughed. "That sodding centurion was right about her! She's an Umbra Ancile!"

Chapter Twelve

C ordus was not in a laughing mood. The elevator was cramped. A golem kept the metal rod fulgurator pressed into his side. Blaesus breathed heavy, still weary from the fulgurator blast he took at Tarpeius's villa. Behind Cordus, Daryush whimpered quietly every few breaths. Kaeso was silent and still.

What is an Ancile doing on Reantium? Cordus asked Marcus Antonius.

Antonius snorted. "How in all the hells should we know? The Liberti strain has confounded us for millennia."

Cordus had to tell Kaeso. He was no longer an Ancile, but he might have some insight into getting Umbra's help to escape Reantium. Cordus would not stand by and let these golems crucify the Romans wasting away in that awful prison, and he certainly would not let them crucify Blaesus.

Cordus tried turning to Kaeso, but the golem shoved the rod deeper into his side. Cordus kept his head forward.

Antonius chuckled. "The flesh machines learn fast."

You mean they were programmed well.

"And there lies the answer you seek," Antonius said, folding hairy forearms over his bronze-plated chest. "Who programmed them to do this, and why? Who has the most to gain by sowing chaos in the Republic's largest granary? And yes, the pun was intended."

We need to escape to find that out.

The elevator stopped with a jolt and the doors opened to the outside.

Tarpeius's crucified corpse greeted them not ten paces away. He hung naked from a hastily built cross made of plastic and aluminum beams. His legs looked broken, so his death by suffocation had been relatively quick compared to what the Romans on the road had endured. His mouth hung open, and Cordus noticed the golems had nailed Tarpeius's tongue to his left breast.

Antonius leaned close to Cordus's ear. "Then I suggest you escape sooner rather than later."

The red-faced golem marched toward an armored car parked twenty paces from the elevator doors. The golem beside Cordus jabbed him with the rod again, so Cordus followed the lead golem. His heart raced. He calmed his breathing, relaxed his muscles.

Within four paces of the armored car, Cordus jammed his elbow into the throat of the golem next to him. Golems breathed like humans, so a crushed mechanical trachea made the golem loosen its grip on the fulgurator.

Cordus grabbed the rod from the golem's hand, turned it on the golem...and could not find the trigger.

A golem behind the one Cordus had wounded pointed its fulgurator at Cordus. In one smooth motion, Kaeso kicked the golem's leg and grabbed its fulgurator as it landed with a grunt on its back. Instead of firing, Kaeso smashed one end into the golem's head, cracking its skull. The golem's legs twitched in its death throes.

Cordus felt movement behind him. He swung his fulgurator low, like an ax-wielding gladiator in the arena. The metal rod hit the red-faced golem's right knee with a loud crack. The golem went down, but it produced a pulse pistol from its dirty toga and aimed at Cordus. He lunged forward and kicked the pistol from the golem's hand just as a blast zipped over his shoulder. He brought the fulgurator down on the golem's head. Yellow blood spurted from its cracked skull, covering the red blood paint on its face. Cordus grabbed the pulse pistol from the golem's twitching hand.

He whirled around to see Kaeso and Dariya putting down the last two golems, using the fulgurators as clubs.

Blaesus stared at the dead golems, a snarl spreading across his lips. He walked over to the lead golem and kicked it in the chest as hard as he could. "It's a crime to be a Roman, eh?"

Cordus stooped down and searched the golem's tattered toga for keys to the shackles on Blaesus's wrists. He found none. He glanced back at Kaeso and Dariya, who were also searching the downed golems. They couldn't find keys either.

Pulse blasts at their feet sprayed dirt in their faces. One hit Blaesus in the abdomen with a sickening slap, and he crumpled to the ground.

"The car!" Kaeso screamed as he pushed Dariya and Daryush forward.

Cordus tried dragging Blaesus toward the armored car. Kaeso helped pull Blaesus as pulse pellets struck the car and the ground around them. Blaesus clenched his teeth as they moved him, then screamed when they shoved him into the back of the armored car.

Cordus spared a glance up. At least a dozen golems in dark robes spilled from out of a building near the tower fifty paces away. Each aimed pulse rifles at them and fired.

Thank the gods they weren't programmed for shooting, Cordus thought as he dove into the driver's seat of the armored car. More blasts bounced off the armored door.

Kaeso shut the back door and yelled, "Drive, kid!"

Cordus's fingers flew across the controls on the armored car. When the engine hummed to life, he punched the accelerator buttons on the steering column and sped toward the approaching golems. He found the controls for the car's top pulse guns and sent streams of pellets into the golems. The blasts ripped the golems apart, spraying yellow pieces across the garrison field.

Seeing no other golem targets, Cordus turned the car toward the garrison's chain fence gate ahead. More golems at the gate fired at the armored car with their pulse rifles, but the pellets bounced off the armored wind shield. Cordus smashed through the gate and onto the streets of Nascio.

The car lurched, and a terrible grinding came from the rear wheels. Cordus glanced at the side mirror on his left. Part of the gate was caught in the left rear wheel well. He tried swerving and speeding up, but nothing would dislodge the gate.

"What's wrong?" Kaeso asked from behind.

"Gate's caught in the wheels. It'll destroy the axles."

Dariya swore. "Find a quiet alley. Me and 'Ush can get it out."

Cordus scanned the street in front, then the sides, and then the rear camera displays on the car's tabulari. He saw no signs of pursuit, but that didn't mean they weren't coming.

Kaeso said, "We won't get far with a gate in our wheels."

Cordus nodded. He found an alley and pulled into it. He drove down another street on the other side of the alley before turning into a second alley. He was struck by how deserted the whole town was; no golems, much less humans, roamed the debris-filled streets. He tried not to dwell on what happened to all the humans.

Cordus stopped the car, grabbed his pistol, and exited. He held the pistol in a firing position as he scanned the areas behind the car, the tops of the buildings around them, and the ends of the alley. Dariya and Daryush jumped out of the car and hurried to the gate.

"Whoreson," Dariya breathed as she inspected the damage. "You did a real *cac* job on these wheels, Roman."

"Next time I'll let you climb the fence, Persian," Cordus growled, still scanning the street behind them.

Dariya chuckled as she kicked downward at the gate to dislodge it. "We might make you a trierarch yet, *Trierarch*."

Cordus grinned, despite the dire situation. It was the first time this entire mission he heard respect in her voice when she said "Trierarch".

Kaeso stepped out of the car and stood next to Cordus. "Status?"

"Clear for now. The gate is another matter."

Dariya cursed, and Daryush grunted, as they both pulled and kicked at the lodged gate.

Cordus looked at Kaeso. "The woman Aquilina. I think she's Umbra."

Kaeso's head jerked to Cordus. "How do you know?"

"She has a Muse implant. She sent me a message via the Muses just as we got on the elevator. Said she could help us if we help her."

Kaeso frowned. "If that's true, then this revolution is starting to make sense."

"What do you mean?"

Kaeso shook his head. "Later. You did well back there."

Cordus tried not to let the compliment swell his heart. "We're not out of this yet. How's Blaesus?"

"I patched him up best I can with the car's medicus kit, but he won't survive the hour unless we close that wound."

Cordus exhaled, then handed Kaeso the pulse pistol. Kaeso raised an eyebrow, so Cordus said, "You're a better shot than me."

Cordus helped Dariya and Daryush pull on the fence. It took them a few more minutes, but between the three of them, they yanked the mangled fence free and threw it into a corner of the alley. They hurried back into the armored car. Kaeso stayed in back with Blaesus, who seemed even more pale and weak than a few minutes ago. Cordus knew it was bad because Blaesus was silent.

In the back seat, Kaeso said, "They'll have *Vacuna* under guard. Options?"

Cordus reached for the car's tabulari. "I'll look for a hospital."

Dariya said grimly, "The old man is bad."

Cordus located the hospital on a town map. It was nine blocks away. He backed the armored car out of the alley and then followed the directions on the map.

As he drove to the hospital, slowing before every street to ensure no ambush awaited them, Marcus Antonius appeared in the seat next to him. "This would go so much faster if you switched on the unit locator," Marcus said in a bored tone. "Every armored car has them. That option is centuries old."

Cordus sighed. He was getting used to Antonius popping in and out of existence, and he didn't know if that was good or bad.

How do I do that?

Antonius gave him instructions, and when Cordus performed them, four icons displayed on the tabulari's map. Two armored cars raced toward Nascio from the landing port, a third came from the discipuli checkpoint they passed on the road to Tarpeius's villa, and the fourth, their car, moved toward the hospital.

Damn. If I can see them, they can see us.

Antonius grinned. "We recommend abandoning the car."

Blaesus needs to get to the hospital or he dies.

"You can carry him."

Cordus shook his head before he could stop himself. *It could kill him.*

"The golems will kill you all if they capture you. If you had more men, you might be able to fight them off..."

Cordus ground his teeth and shifted his eyes to Marcus, who winked.

Cordus called to the back, "Our unit locator is broadcasting our position to the golems."

"*Cac,*" Kaeso breathed. "How many are coming?"

"Three armored cars. If they're full, that means eighteen golems. If we go to the hospital, they'll know where we are. But I have an idea."

After he told them, Kaeso was silent a few moments. "Fine," he said. "Let us out here."

Cordus stopped the car at a turn that led to the hospital four blocks to their left. Kaeso crawled out of the car from the back, as did Dariya and Daryush. All three gently pulled Blaesus out of the car, but they were not gentle enough. Blaesus groaned through clenched teeth. The old Senator tried to hold in his screams to avoid giving away their position to nearby golems. But a human body can take only so much pain without screaming.

The three finally got Blaesus out of the car. Kaeso kicked the door closed, then nodded to Cordus from outside. Cordus punched the accelerator and sped down the street back toward the garrison. The rear camera displays showed Kaeso holding Blaesus's shoulders while Dariya and Daryush tried to keep his legs stable. They half-walked, half-jogged toward the hospital.

Juno protect them.

Still sitting in the passenger's seat, Antonius slapped his hands together. "Now that we're relieved of the cargo, the real fun can begin."

Chapter Thirteen

The way back to the garrison was clear, which made Cordus more nervous. This was once a city of five thousand souls. Had all the humans fled or had the golems done something to them? The tabulari map showed three other roads out of the city. He shuddered to think there might be miles of crosses lining those roads as well.

He tracked the unit locator icons on the map. The two armored cars from the spaceport were still twenty minutes out, so Cordus was not worried about them. It was the discipuli car coming off the Tarpeius road that concerned him. It had already entered the city and was heading in Cordus's location. Judging by its speed, Cordus had less than ten minutes to rescue the Romans and the Umbra Ancile. He hoped no more golems awaited him at the garrison.

"When we arrive," Antonius said from the passenger seat, "go to the garrison headquarters where the golems had—"

"I know," Cordus said aloud. "Weapons first, then the prisoners."

Antonius gave him an approving nod. "Seems you've paid attention to the lessons of your Liberti father."

"He taught me more than my Roman father ever did."

Antonius clicked his tongue. "Is that bitterness, young Antonius?"

"Just the truth."

"You can hardly blame your father or your Roman family. They were hosts. They had no choice in the matter." Antonius grinned. "Think of it this way: If not for them, you wouldn't have us keeping you company right now, would you?"

"If you're trying to make me feel better, you're doing a lousy job."

Antonius laughed. "We weren't trying to make you feel better. Just giving you the truth."

Cordus pulled the armored car around a corner and saw the garrison directly ahead. "We're here. I'd appreciate no more distractions."

Antonius grunted, then disappeared.

Cordus sighed. *I can't believe I'm getting used to the bastard. What would Kaeso and Ocella say?*

He took a deep breath, then punched the accelerator and drove straight toward the garrison entrance. The remains of the mangled gate lay to the side of the entrance where they had crashed through. He scanned the area for movement. The golems he'd destroyed still lay where they fell, and no other golems emerged from the garrison buildings.

Cordus stopped the car next to the golems. He searched the grisly yellow remains for their weapons. They had all carried pulse rifles, but most were damaged by the armored car's pulse blasts. He only found three rifles that seemed to work, so he slung them over his shoulder. He gathered six ammunition clips, trying to ignore the sticky yellow golem blood and tissue all over them.

He threw the rifles and ammunition into the car and then drove it toward the headquarters building from which the golems had emerged. He grabbed a pulse rifle, jumped out of the armored car, and ran through the open door. The room inside showed the golems cared little for cleanliness. Debris was strewn across the floors—ripped clothing, broken marble busts, tabulari pads, crushed furniture, empty golem food packets. In the corner of the room to Cordus's right, rust-colored bandage wrappings lay on the floor in the middle of two dark bloodstains. Furniture pieces covered the windows.

Cordus looked for a weapons locker. Seeing none, he hurried to the hallway to his right and tried every door, but they were locked. He rushed to the other wing of the building, but every door was locked besides the latrine room, which did not have windows.

The last Legionaries had barricaded themselves against the golems, so they would have locked all the doors. Cordus had no time to break down each door—the nearest armored car was minutes away—so he raced outside to his idling car and drove it the hundred paces to the prison tower. He parked the car so that it blocked the elevator door. After grabbing the three pulse rifles, he leaped out of the car and ran to the elevator. He quickly prayed the controls weren't locked and then tapped the "up" button. The doors hummed shut, and the elevator began to rise.

At the top, when the doors opened, Cordus was shocked to see the large octagonal room empty. He stepped out of the elevator, saw movement to his right, and swung the pulse rifle around.

He almost shot Aquilina. She was hiding on the right side of the elevator, ready to attack, but she relaxed when she saw him. The Romans stood on the left side, Paulus Ulpius looking relieved.

Cordus turned back to Aquilina, and she smiled. That smile flustered him and words fled his mind. *Hell of a thing to distract me with certain death on its way.*

He found his words after a momentary stutter. "We only have a few minutes."

He handed one pulse rifle to Aquilina and one to Ulpius. Aquilina looked surprised when he gave her the rifle. *If she's what I think she is, she may get the most use out of this.*

"I'm only a merchant—"

"Right, so am I," Cordus said.

He didn't wait for her response. He hurried back into the elevator as Aquilina and the six Romans followed him. Though all six Romans were gaunt and weary, they seemed determined to leave their prison.

He was relieved. It meant he would not have to leave anyone behind.

"Thank you for coming back...merchant," Aquilina said.

Cordus didn't want to look at her. Already he felt his Muses stir simply standing beside her. They knew she had an implant and they knew such a thing meant she served their enemies. Cordus ignored their growing fury, for he could control them. Though if he was like every other human host of the Terran Muses, he'd be choking her by now.

But that was not why he refused to look at her. He didn't want her smile distracting him again.

"You're welcome...merchant."

"Bloody decent of you, sir," Ulpius said, and was seconded by murmured thanks from the five other Romans.

"You may not think so when I tell you the plan."

Cordus had explained the situation by the time the elevator touched the ground. Aquilina and the Romans frowned and grumbled but knew they had no choice.

When the doors opened, Cordus brought his pulse rifle up and searched the area around them for targets. Finding none, he led them past the armored car and Tarpeius's rotting corpse, and then sprinted toward the garrison's wide-open exit. Aquilina kept up with him, her rifle in a firing position that only a trained professional would know. The weakened Romans, however, soon fell a dozen paces behind.

When they reached the gate, Cordus stopped and listened. Through his heavy breathing and beating heart, he heard a humming engine and wheels crunching on gravel. The armored car from the north would see them in seconds. Cordus turned back to the Romans behind him.

They would not make it across the street in time.

When Aquilina stopped and looked back at him, Cordus yelled, "Go to the hospital!"

She wanted to say something, but the armored car turned the corner to their right. She grimaced, then raced in the direction of the hospital.

The Romans arrived next to Cordus, all gasping for breath and staring fearfully at the armored car.

"The car is going to see us if we stay here," Cordus said, "so the only chance we have is to cross the street. Move now!"

The legionaries, trained to follow orders without question, pumped their tired legs to cross the street as fast as possible. After the last man started off, Cordus followed with his rifle aimed at the armored car. It would do little good against the car's armor, but it might draw the attention off the unarmed legionaries.

The car opened fire. Warm blood sprayed Cordus's face. The torso of the man in front of Cordus disintegrated. He was dead before the halves of his body slapped to the street. Cordus kept running and crossed the street with pulse blasts sending bits of concrete into his bare arms and face.

The five surviving Romans took refuge inside a tavern with blown out windows. Ulpius saw his downed comrade, bared his teeth, and then motioned Cordus toward him. Cordus leaped through the open door and followed them to the rear of the building. As they ran toward the back, the armored car stopped out front and its doors creaked open.

"Keep moving," he whispered harshly as they dodged broken tables and chairs. "They're dismounting."

They entered a large kitchen in the same disarray as the common room.

"Where's the Mars-damned back door?" Ulpius growled.

"Over here!" One of the Romans pushed open a metal door behind a large steel cabinet. Sunlight entered the kitchen.

Pulse blasts slammed the Roman back into the door. His body crumpled to the ground outside as the door, now covered in blood, slowly shut on its own.

"Tib!" Ulpius screamed, then lunged for the door. Cordus grabbed his arm. If Ulpius was not half-starved, he could have easily broken Cordus's grip.

"They'll kill you too! Your man's dead."

"You don't know that!"

Cordus pulled Ulpius closer. "You saw him."

Ulpius shut his eyes. "He wasn't my 'man'. He was my nephew."

"We're surrounded, sir," one Roman said to Cordus.

Cordus looked at the steel cooking tables. He slung his rifle over his shoulder, snatched Ulpius's rifle from his hands, and shoved it into the hands of the Roman.

"Cover the door." He pointed to the other two Romans. "Help me lean these tables on their sides. Make a 'V' and then get behind them."

The Roman covering the door fired several rounds into the common area. Return blasts came from the golems. Stucco shards from the wall flew through the air, and the Roman had to duck behind the door.

"They're advancing," he yelled. "I can't hold them."

With the tables set, Cordus pushed Ulpius, who was still in shock, behind the tables and told everyone else to get behind them. When the Roman near the door jumped over the table, Cordus said, "Cover the common door, I'll take the back door."

The Roman nodded. The two Romans behind Cordus wore grim expressions and held cooking knives they'd found on the floor. They'd do little good against pulse rifles, but Cordus admired their determination.

In the seconds it took the golems to organize their assault on the Roman position, Cordus marveled at his mental clarity and total lack of fear. Was it the Muses? Was it his ancestral blood? Marcus Antonius was known as a warrior without fear even before the Muses took him. Cordus knew this from the memories.

Whatever the reason, he was grateful he hadn't frozen today like he did at Tarpeius's villa. It would help him die with honor for fellow Romans. It felt as if his life had led up to this moment.

He looked at the Roman with the pulse rifle aimed at the common room door. His eyes were wide and his hands clutched the rifle so tightly they were white. The young man was no more than a year or two older than Cordus, had orange matted hair and a face covered in freckles.

"What's your name, Legionary? Where are you from?" Cordus asked.

"Gracchus, sir," the Roman said, watching the door. "From north Atlantium on Terra."

Cordus turned to the two Romans holding knives. "Your names?"

"Duran," said the dark-skinned Roman, who looked the same age as Ulpius. "West Africa."

"Piso, Hiberia," said the Roman with a bandaged head. "Your name, sir?"

Cordus paused. "Titus," he said. *If we get out of this, I'll still need to maintain my cover.*

Piso nodded, then gave him a sideways grin. "Glad to have you here, sir."

Cordus grunted. "Thanks."

Pulse blasts surged from the common room, bouncing off the steel tables and the wall above them. Gracchus returned fire as best he could, but the fury of the blasts forced his head down. Cordus turned his rifle on the common room door and tried to return fire, but he too had to duck below the deadly pellets.

The blasts suddenly stopped.

"Put down your weapons," an impassive golem voice said from the door. "We will not—"

Gracchus fired, and the golem fell to the floor. He turned to Cordus. "No deals. I ain't going to be crucified."

Cordus nodded once in agreement.

The pulse blasts from the common room resumed, this time at greater intensity. Cordus and Gracchus did their best to return the fire, to keep the golems from advancing further, but it was only a matter of time before their pulse clips went dry.

Blasts came from the back door. Cordus swung his rifle around and fired at the golem coming through. It went down in a spray of yellow blood, but a golem behind it pulled it out of the way and then resumed firing from the same position as the first.

Gracchus stopped firing and cursed. "I'm out."

Cordus cursed as well. He had forgotten to grab the six ammunition clips he'd thrown into the armored car. They only had the clips in their rifles. Now Gracchus's rifle was a high-tech club.

Cordus continued firing at the golems at the back door and the common room entry. For every golem he took down, another would emerge. *Where are they coming from? That car should've only held six golems!* Cordus wondered if other golems were stationed nearby. Regardless, the other armored cars would arrive in minutes, and then the battle would be over.

Yet he still felt no fear, only calm clarity. *Is this normal?*

His pulse rifle clicked empty. He turned to the Romans behind him. "Ready with those knives."

The golem pulse blasts stopped. Golem boots crunched onto the kitchen floor. Four held their rifles in a firing position. Two more entered through the back door, their rifles aimed at Cordus and the Romans.

Cordus stood, holding his rifle like a club. The other Romans stood as well, even Ulpius, who watched the golems at the door with pure hatred in his eyes. He only had his bare hands, but had the look of a man who would kill many golems before he went down.

The golems at the door strode toward Cordus and the Romans. The impassiveness in their blank faces suddenly infuriated him. The rage scoured away his calm in a blinding moment.

If you're going to kill us, you should feel something! Joy, fury, anything! Well I feel something. Die, you godsdamned machine!

Cordus was about to swing his rifle at the nearest golem, but it crumpled to the floor as if shot. But no pulse blast had hit it. The golems behind it staggered, as if hit, but regained their balance and continued forward.

Fury still burned in Cordus, and he prayed with all his will the golems coming at him would join their fallen comrade.

They staggered again, and this time fell to the floor.

Cordus had no time to wonder what happened. A surge of electricity erupted from his body, and his senses were heightened beyond anything he'd ever experienced. He suddenly stood beside his body, watching the golems coming through the door, along with the Romans ready to meet them.

Harsh whispers came from above him. Like his Muses, but different, more chaotic and unfocused. He couldn't understand what they said.

Aquilina's voice murmured from outside the tavern. He wanted to tell her they were in trouble, that they needed her help—

He sat at a table in a dark room, one light pad on the ceiling illuminating the table. Across from him sat Aquilina. She stared at him, her mouth open in shock.

"How...?" she stammered.

"We need help," Cordus said. He didn't know how he came here, or where this room was, but he instinctively knew he was speaking to Aquilina. "The golems have us surrounded. Go through the back door of the tavern and surprise them from behind."

He didn't know whether Aquilina got the message, for he felt as if he were spinning down a whirlpool...and then he was back in his body.

A pulse blast from the back door startled Cordus. One of the golems fell face-first onto the floor. Aquilina stepped over it and fired at the four other golems at the common room door. She took them down in quick succession. All four were so surprised, they never lifted their rifles.

Cordus stared at her. *She heard me.*

Aquilina stared back at Cordus with the same shocked expression she wore in the dark room.

"Unless you want to cook something, I suggest we go," she said finally. "The other armored cars are two blocks away."

She went out the back door without another word.

Cordus, still unable to speak, turned to the Romans behind him who stared suspiciously at Aquilina, unsure of whether to follow her. Ulpius brushed passed them.

"Liberti spy or not, the woman saved our lives," he rumbled. "I'm following her."

He paused to pick up the pulse rifle from the golem near the door, then exited into the sunlight.

Cordus was surprised when the other Romans looked to him rather than Ulpius. "Let's go," Cordus said, then stepped over the pocked steel tables that had shielded them.

The three Romans picked up the rifles and pulse clips from the downed golems and then followed him.

Cordus entered an alley behind the tavern. Tib's body had been thrown to one side. Ulpius knelt over it with hard eyes. He took a ring from Tib's left hand and put it into his pocket.

Ulpius met Cordus's eyes. "Family signet."

He marched after Aquilina, who was at the end of the alley peeking around the corner. Cordus hurried after Ulpius, the other three Romans behind him.

He watched Aquilina take the point position with the skill of someone who'd done it her whole life.

Gods, what did I just do?

Chapter Fourteen

By the end of the fourth day of their journey to Reantium, Ocella wished for whatever sleep the aliens had used on them in the Menota system. Once again, she thought, like all humans, it was ironic that way line travel between the stars took a blink of the eye, whereas travel within local solar systems took days and sometimes weeks.

On the first day, Ocella and Varo had removed their pressure suits and wore their ship jump suits. They were startled when the walls in the room suddenly shifted and changed, like clay molded by an unseen sculptor. Two 'beds' appeared from the wall on one side of the room, and then a small, enclosed latrine formed at the other end. The beds had a blue, gelatinous mattress dry to the touch, but formed to their bodies. The latrine looked the same as the one on *Vacuna* and worked just as well.

Ocella looked forward to the times the Lucia golem delivered their 'food'—a green, tasteless paste—and water, if only to break the monotony. If the aliens were curious about the Aramaic that Ocella and Varo spoke, the Lucia golem never commented. The golem simply delivered their food and then left without a word.

With their basic physical needs satisfied, they occupied their minds by practicing their ancient Aramaic. Ocella's skills seemed better than Varo's, which she attributed to her Umbra training. Varo hadn't spoken the language since he was a child and was only taught informally by his Hebrew grandmother. But with all their idle time, their conversation skills were improving.

On the third day, the Lucia golem entered the room with a surprise: It finally had eyes instead of the unnerving black sockets. It still had gray skin with blue tendrils just beneath the surface, and even the eyes had hair-thin blue veins. Ocella was grateful for the differences, though, for it re-enforced the fact that she was not speaking with Lucia, and that this alien ship had killed her Trierarch.

Ocella and Varo mostly watched the wall view. She wasn't aware of any way line jumps, but she knew one must have occurred since what she assumed was Reantium grew on the wall by the hour. It was now a small blue marble in the center of the wall. Time seemed not to exist here, and she slept more often than she was awake. Varo was the same way. If anything, he seemed to sleep longer.

On the fourth day, he was in such a lethargic state that he didn't even want to practice their Aramaic. Ocella kept forcing him, until he finally snapped at her. "This is pointless!" he yelled in common Latin. "How is speaking some dead language going to get us out of here?"

"Because," she said calmly in Aramaic, "it will keep us from going insane. Now tell me again, in Aramaic, the prayers your grandmother taught you."

Varo stared at her with angry, desperate eyes. He sighed once, and then began reciting the prayers.

Mostly, however, Ocella lay in her gel bed, watching the view of space and occupied with her own thoughts. She wondered why the aliens assumed Cordus was on Reantium. She was supposed to meet Kaeso and *Vacuna* on Reantium, not Cordus. If the aliens wanted Cordus, why didn't they just go to Caesar Nova where he'd been the last six years? They could easily retrieve that information from Lucia's memories.

Could Kaeso have brought Cordus to Reantium, and Lucia somehow knew? Anger boiled in Ocella at the thought. They had agreed Cordus was not to leave Caesar Nova until he was properly trained and mentally prepared for the dangers that would find him wherever he went. He had become increasingly vocal on going on a Saturnist mission, especially with his eighteenth birthday approaching. And Kaeso had become increasingly sympathetic to Cordus's arguments. Could he have finally convinced Kaeso? The last she'd heard, the situation on Reantium was tense, but no worse than any other planet in the war-torn Roman Republic. If there was any mission Cordus could convince Kaeso of bringing him along, it would be Reantium.

What made Ocella most angry with Kaeso, however, was the thought he confided in Lucia and not her. Just thinking of the possibility made her teeth clench, which was irrational since she didn't know for sure either way.

But unless the aliens were lying to her—a distinct possibility—they were going to Reantium for one purpose: to make Cordus a "witness", whatever that may be.

A section of the wall irised open, startling Ocella. The Lucia golem, still naked, entered. Ocella's stomach wasn't growling, so she didn't think it was time for a meal.

Varo, in the bed next to hers, awoke and swung his legs onto the floor. He watched the Lucia golem with suspicious eyes.

"We now orbit the planet you call Reantium," the golem announced.

The wall view still showed the blue marble of Reantium surrounded by empty space. "I thought this showed our current location," Ocella said.

The Lucia golem looked at the wall view. It suddenly changed to show a Terran-class planet filling the entire wall. *So they do lie,* Ocella thought.

Varo sounded indignant. "Why did you deceive us about our location?"

The golem cocked its head. "Why do you both converse in a language this drone does not comprehend? Is that not deception?"

Varo glanced at Ocella, and she said, "There's little here for us to occupy ourselves. We speak it to pass the time."

"How does speaking a different language make time pass?"

"It doesn't, exactly. It just—"

"This topic is irrelevant," the Lucia golem said, its strange eyes focusing on the wall view again. "We have located Cordus and your lover, Kaeso Aemilius, on the planet."

"My lov—? Wait, Cordus is *in-system?*"

"We require you to send Kaeso a message. We could create one in your likeness, but we do not yet have the wisdom to mimic your speech patterns."

"What message?"

When the golem finished telling Ocella the message, she swallowed. "If I refuse?"

"We will kill your drone Varo. If you still refuse after he dies, we will bring Cordus here once we secure him and then slowly kill him in front of you."

Varo glared at the golem with hard eyes.

"I thought you said you needed Cordus," Ocella said, trying to keep her voice steady. "I don't think you will kill him."

"We prefer not to. He will make a powerful witness. But we want to study him, to see what makes him resist the strain he hosts. To do that, we would destroy his body and remake it like we did this drone. The process will kill him. Either way, we will gain valuable wisdom for the new archive. Make your choice."

Despair and rage flooded Ocella's senses. She wanted to curl up on the bed behind her and sob. *Who do I condemn: the man I love or the boy who's become a son to me? And why in the name of all the gods did Kaeso bring Cordus here?*

Varo's gentle hand rested on her shoulder. In Aramaic, he said, "You know what you need to do. He is too important."

Varo was right. If she looked at the situation from a "what's best for humanity" point of view, the decision was simple.

But not easy.

She gave a shaky sigh and then turned to the Lucia golem. "Let's record your damned message."

Chapter Fifteen

Cordus, Aquilina, and the four Romans sat beneath the broken window of an old tailor shop listening to the armored car roll by. Cordus gripped the trigger of his pulse rifle. Aquilina and the Romans did the same. No one made a sound.

Cordus met Aquilina's eyes and once again tried to speak to her through his Muses. *Can you hear me?*

If she could, she gave no sign. There had been no time or privacy for them to discuss her message at the tower and their 'meeting' during the fight at the tavern. Perhaps even she had no idea how she did it.

I sure as cac *don't know how it happened.*

The car turned the corner down the street.

Marcus Antonius appeared next to Cordus, his head peeking outside the window.

"You have a foot patrol coming from the right," Marcus said.

Ulpius was about to stand, but Cordus grabbed his arm and held him in place. Ulpius gave him a questioning look. Cordus shook his head.

Within seconds, they all heard the foot patrol following the armored car. It sounded like six pairs of boots on the debris-strewn street.

"Six golems," Marcus confirmed, "all wearing fashionable black robes and carrying rifles. Like a bunch of Dis flamens who just rolled in a garbage heap."

They didn't seem to be in a hurry and marched as if they were on their way to tend crops.

After a minute, Marcus said, "Clear."

Cordus slowly peeked above the window. Seeing no other patrols or armored cars, he motioned the others up.

Ulpius whispered, "How did you know they was coming? My hearing ain't like an owl's, but it's good. I didn't hear them flesh cans."

Cordus glanced at Marcus, then shrugged at Ulpius. "Your hearing's good, but mine's great. Let's go."

Aquilina arched an eyebrow at Cordus, but he ignored her. He stepped over the windowsill and onto the empty sidewalk, then led them toward the hospital.

Cordus figured walking eight blocks would take no more than fifteen minutes at a normal pace. But scurrying from building to building and waiting out golem patrols had pushed their time to an hour. He wondered if Kaeso had stabilized Blaesus's wound. Cordus already lost a good friend in Nestor—he couldn't shake the image of Nestor's pulverized head—so the thought of losing another made his eyes mist.

You kept me humble, Nestor, my friend. Who will do that for me now?

"Can't afford emotion, young Antonius," Marcus warned as he strolled next to Cordus. "You'll never see your friends if you dwell on *them* rather than your current troubles."

Without glancing at Marcus, Cordus directed his thoughts to him. *How* did *I know those golems were coming? You only see or hear what I see or hear. I did not hear them.*

"No, you didn't hear those golems," Marcus said, "but we did. We use your senses, but we can process the input better than your less-evolved human brain." He winked at Cordus. "No offense, eh?"

Sure.

"You know, we could enhance your senses a thousandfold if you'd let *us* control your body like we did your family."

Cordus jerked his head to Marcus and infused his thoughts with a snarl. *No!*

Marcus put his hands up. "Just a suggestion, no need for murder."

It's never going to happen, so don't suggest it again. I'm trying to focus on my current troubles, remember? Stop talking now.

Marcus gave him an elaborate bow. "As you wish." And then he disappeared.

There was a time when Cordus was thankful for the Muses and his ability to control them. The Muses gave him knowledge and wisdom no other person—besides an Umbra Ancile—could imagine, while his control enabled him to maintain his humanity.

Now he wondered if his abilities were a curse. Why had Marcus suggested Cordus let the Muses take control? Was that even a choice? Cordus always assumed it was not. But with his maturing body and the appearance of Marcus Antonius, he refused to discount anything. The fact that Marcus could suggest such a thing set off warning bells in Cordus. It made him more fearful than ever that the Muses might try to seize control someday. If that happened, how would Cordus even fight them?

Pulse blasts echoed from the direction of the hospital two blocks away.

Cordus gave his companions a hard look, then ran toward the blasts. He was satisfied to hear their footsteps behind him.

When he came to the block before the hospital, Cordus peeked around the pockmarked wall of a tailor's shop. The hospital was a small, single-story building that seemed more like a clinic than a true hospital. Two golem bodies lay near the hospital's front door, while six more golems hid behind two ground cars, sending pulse fire through the open doors. Two fired from behind one car, and four fired from behind the second.

Cordus scanned the rubble and buildings around the hospital, along with the rooftops, but did not see any other golems. He whispered to Aquilina and the Romans, "Six golems with their backs to us. I don't see any others, but that foot patrol might be here in minutes."

Aquilina eased her head around the corner. She surveyed the street, then nodded to Cordus. "We can take these if we're quick."

"Agreed," Cordus said. He turned to the others. "Wait to fire until I start, or if they see us first. Ready?"

They all nodded grimly and said, "Sir."

Cordus peeked around the corner again to ensure the golems weren't looking in his direction, then broke into a quiet run toward them. He kept his rifle trained on the four golems behind the second car.

When he got within thirty paces, he fired. Two golems went down with yellow sprays of golem blood, while the other two fell to blasts from the Romans behind Cordus. The two golems behind the first car fell to more fire from Cordus's team.

He reached the second car, pulled clips and rifles off the dead golems. Aquilina did the same to the two golems behind the first car. After they gathered the weapons and clips, Cordus shouted from behind the car, "Kaeso, it's..." He glanced at the Romans. "It's Titus."

"Get in here, kid!" Kaeso responded from inside.

Cordus jumped from behind the car and ran to the open doors with Aquilina and the Romans close behind. When he burst through the door, he saw Kaeso to the right standing behind a desk with darkened pulse gouges, his pulse pistol at his side. To the left stood Dariya holding a large metal rod. They both grinned at Cordus.

"Fine timing," Kaeso said. "I had three pellets left in this thing."

"I was prepared to meet Ahura Mazda," Dariya said, holding up the metal rod. "You have thankfully delayed that meeting, Trierarch."

"Sorry I'm late." Cordus tossed the scavenged rifles to Kaeso and Dariya, who took them gratefully.

They looked past Cordus to Aquilina and the Romans. Kaeso's face hardened when he saw Aquilina, and Dariya's turned equally hard at the Romans. *Seeing their former masters. I hope they remember the golems are the bigger threat.* Aquilina and the Romans were more concerned with catching their breath from their sprint than noticing any tension.

"How's Blaesus?" Cordus asked, breaking the tension before his new comrades noticed.

Kaeso eyed Aquilina a second longer, who now noticed Kaeso's stare, before responding. "He's stable. Daryush is with him in the back. We found some skin sealant. He's lost a lot of blood, though, and we couldn't find any synthetic blood here. We need to get him back to *Vacuna*."

Aquilina shook her head. "They'll never let us get to the spaceport."

"What do you suggest?" Kaeso said. "Merchant."

A blinding white light filled Cordus's vision, and a nova of pain seared through his head. A terrible ringing filled his ears. He gasped and fell to his knees. From far away, Ulpius said, "What's wrong with them?"

The light and pain slowly faded, but the ringing continued. Cordus regained control of his senses, for the most part.

Kaeso, however, leaned against the wall, doubled over, his hands on his head. Aquilina was on her knees, head bowed, her hands over her eyes. After a moment, they removed their hands from their heads and blinked several times.

Cordus stared at them. "It happened to you, too?" He could barely hear his own words over the continued ringing.

"*What* happened?" Dariya growled.

Before Cordus could speak, Ocella's voice floated in his ears. It started as a whisper beneath the ringing, then grew louder, but muffled as if she spoke through a blanket.

"...is important that you do what they ask, Kaeso, or they will hurt Cordus. Can you hear me, Kaeso?"

Kaeso stared at the floor with squinted eyes. His lips moved, but made no sound.

"I know," Ocella said, her voice fading in and out, "but it is the only way. Please...you know how...what they want of..."

Cordus noticed Aquilina staring at Kaeso. *She must hear it, too. Now she knows Kaeso was once an Umbra Ancile. She may even know who I am. What will she do about it?*

Strong hands reached under Cordus's arms and lifted him off the ground. Ulpius and Duran held him up and asked him what was happening. Cordus couldn't focus long on their voices as Ocella's voice took away his ability to concentrate on anything else.

"...Cordus must not...don't try to...you are a stubborn..."

The voice and ringing abruptly stopped.

Marcus Antonius popped into existence next to Cordus. For the first time Cordus could remember, there was fear in his eyes.

"This is very bad, young Antonius," he said, as he paced back and forth. "Very bad, indeed."

What is bad? What just happened?

Marcus leaned close to Cordus and whispered as if he were afraid of being overheard. "Another strain has arrived. They want you."

Kaeso was upright again and handing Cordus the pulse rifle. Cordus looked at him questioningly, and Kaeso said, "I won't need it."

"Was that Ocella?" Cordus asked. "How did she—?"

"Not important."

Kaeso brushed past Cordus and the Romans and walked through the open doors.

"Kaeso!" Cordus yelled, but Kaeso didn't turn.

Dariya stood next to Cordus. "What is wrong with you two?"

Cordus ignored her and ran after Kaeso. He stood in the middle of the street, searching the blue sky as if awaiting Sol Invictus to carry him away.

"Kaeso, what's happening? Was that Ocella?"

"Yes." He continued staring at the sky, searching for something.

"Where is she? How could she send—?"

"Kid, you've always had too many questions." He gave Cordus a sad grin. "Whether you want it or not, you're the Centuriae now. Don't come after me, you hear? And do *not* go to Caesar Nova. It's too dangerous for you there now. Just get your crew somewhere safe." He glanced at the hospital. "Maybe Libertus."

Cordus turned to see Aquilina, Dariya, and the Romans in the doorway staring at them.

He leaned close to Kaeso and whispered, "I don't understand what's happening."

Kaeso looked up again. "Neither do I, but it's the only way to keep you safe."

"I'm not ready for this."

"Nobody ever is. Ah..."

Cordus followed Kaeso's gaze. A white dot streaked across the sky, its head growing larger as he watched. The white dot turned yellow, then red, then black.

A missile suddenly streaked toward the black vessel from the Nascio spaceport. The missile impacted with the vessel in a white ball of light, the explosion taking several seconds to reach Cordus's ears. But the black vessel flew through it as if flying through a cloud. More missiles flew up from the spaceport, but the vessel blew through them too.

"Like I said," Kaeso murmured, "do not come after me."

"What is it?" Cordus asked, staring at the approaching vessel.

"A trade."

The vessel now hovered silently fifty paces above the street near Cordus and Kaeso. It looked like a glob of black tar wrapped in thin, pulsating blue veins just beneath the surface. The vessel had no windows or engines or any other features common to a spacecraft as he knew it. As it descended, the bottom of the ship undulated and morphed until it formed a flat pad on which the vessel could rest. It touched the ground just as the bottom flattened. A door irised open, and the interior looked the same as the exterior—black with pulsing blue veins.

Kaeso pulled Cordus into a tight embrace. "You're a born leader. I see it in you. Get them safe."

Cordus couldn't speak. All he could do was return Kaeso's embrace.

Kaeso suddenly broke away. "If these bastards are honest, the way back to *Vacuna* will be clear for you."

He turned and approached the vessel opening. Cordus reached out and grabbed Kaeso's arm. Kaeso could easily have broken his grip, but the former Ancile stopped, still facing the vessel.

"What. Is. Happening?" Cordus demanded.

Kaeso didn't move for a moment, but then he said, "Ocella is on one of these ships in orbit. My capture was the price of your freedom." Kaeso turned to Cordus and said gently, "Let me go, kid."

Cordus let him go. "Will I see you again?"

Kaeso gave him a long, steady look, then turned and strode toward the vessel opening.

"Centuriae!" Dariya cried, rushing down the hospital steps.

Without breaking stride, Kaeso said, "Cordus is your Centuriae now."

"*You* are my Centuriae," Dariya said.

She stared at Kaeso desperately. Cordus knew her statement was not meant as an insult to him, but as a reaffirmation to Kaeso that he was the leader she would follow to Hades if he asked her. Cordus felt exactly the same.

Kaeso understood as well. He stopped, gave her a soft grin, and then started toward the ship. He never paused as he stepped through the dark opening and into the blue-veined interior. As soon as he entered, the opening irised shut, and the ship rose straight up into the sky without a sound.

"We cannot just abandon him," Dariya said next to Cordus.

Cordus watched the vessel disappear into the sky with a speed no human ship could match.

"We're not. Get Blaesus and Daryush. We have to get back to *Vacuna* before the ship in orbit gets away."

"The Centuriae ordered you not to pursue. I heard him from the steps."

"He did."

"You will pursue him anyway?"

He turned to her. "Yes. Do you have a problem with that, Engineer."

She gave him an savage grin and shook her head. "I do not. Centuriae." She turned and jogged back up the steps into the hospital.

Duran, Piso, and Gracchus approached Cordus. Duran said in a deep, rich voice, "If it's all the same to you, sir, we'd like to come with you."

Cordus looked at each one of them. "Why? This isn't your fight. I'm probably leading my crew to their deaths."

Duran said, "You were willing to die with us. Figure we owe you."

Cordus glanced at Ulpius, who sat on the steps to the hospital staring at Tib's signet ring in his hand.

"I thought Ulpius was your Centurion."

Duran shook his head. "He and the Liberti spy got thrown in with us a day or two after we was there. He's from a different cohort, I guess."

Piso picked at the bandage on his head, and then said, "Sir, we have nothing left here. Our Legion is gone, our families are..." Piso's voice caught a moment, and then he continued. "None of us know how to pilot a starship, so we can't leave ourselves. We'd rather die fighting with you than running from golems the rest of our lives."

Cordus didn't know what he faced in this strange alien vessel, but he knew a fight would come if he were to rescue Ocella and Kaeso. He would need all the help he could get, especially from proven fighters like the three Romans before him.

Cordus looked past the three Romans and at Aquilina standing near a burned out car. She held her pulse rifle against her shoulder as she watched Cordus. An Umbra Ancile would be a powerful ally. But would she come with him? And could he trust her?

She smiled, and he looked away.

And could I concentrate on the mission when she does that? *Gods, what is it about this woman?*

Aquilina walked to him and said, "I have certain...associates who'd be very interested in what just kidnapped your friend. I may be able to help, even."

Cordus forced himself to meet her eyes. "How would your associates feel about rescuing two *former* associates?"

Aquilina's lips twitched in amusement. "With your friends' experience, the information they can gather regarding this vessel would be quite valuable to my associates."

Ulpius approached them. "If you two are through with your spy talk, I want to come, too. I got no other way off this dead rock. I know a thing or two about battlefield med, so I could help your wounded friend."

Cordus looked at them all. "I can't promise you'll live through this."

They all nodded their acceptance.

At the hospital doors, Dariya and Daryush stood on either side of Blaesus with one of his arms around each of their shoulders. Blaesus looked frail, and his skin was whiter than his many togas. Dariya and Daryush half-carried him to the armored car the attacking golems had used.

As they all got into the armored car, Cordus thought, *Gods, I am running through deep* cac *now.*

Chapter Sixteen

Cordus sped through Nascio's ruined streets, having no choice but to trust that the vessel had cleared the way for them back to *Vacuna*. Thankfully, the vessel's 'word' was true—Cordus did not encounter any other golem patrols in the city. It made him wonder why the vessel would help them, considering it just kidnapped the two people who meant the most to him in the universe.

It wants us to follow them. Why? He tried not to think about that now.

Not only were golems absent from the streets, but so were humans. When he asked the Romans what had happened to the humans, their eyes turned haunted. Piso explained that the local citizens who survived the initial rebellion were rounded up to ostensibly serve as laborers in the fields. But rumors of mass crucifixions made even the citizens rebel, which led the golems to slaughter them.

"There are no more people," Piso said, shaking his bandaged head. "At least not in Nascio. Don't know what things are like elsewhere on the planet."

Cordus glanced in his rear mirrors. Tears streamed down Duran's dark cheeks as he watched the passing maize fields.

Outside Nascio, the road to the spaceport was also clear of armored cars and golem checkpoints. But the bodies of crucified Romans stared down at Cordus. He lowered his window to shout at the carrion birds feasting on the corpses. The legionaries also yelled or whistled. Aquilina kept her eyes on the road ahead.

When they were within five miles of the spaceport, Cordus noticed black smoke billowing from it. They arrived to see hangars, buildings, and starships in smoking, burning ruins. The acrid chemical stench filling the air turned Cordus's stomach.

Cordus stopped the armored car next to *Vacuna*. The ship appeared intact. *At least they're honest kidnappers.* He jumped out and ran toward the ship's lock. He placed his palm on the lock, and the door ramp hissed open with a slow groan.

Once the door ramp touched the ground, Dariya and Daryush rushed Blaesus into the ship. Cordus watched after Blaesus with deep worry. The old Senator was silent during the speeding trip and barely conscious the whole way. Even now he seemed on the border of lucidity and fainting. Ulpius followed the two Persians as they carried Blaesus as fast as they could to the ship's supply lift, which would take them up to the crew deck and the ship's medical hatch. Aquilina and Piso jogged up the ramp, while Gracchus and Duran backed in, their rifles still up and scanning the spaceport. Cordus was the last one in, and he closed the door ramp from inside Cargo One.

"Delta couches are on the crew deck," Cordus told the Romans. He turned to Aquilina. "Only three there, so you can take one on the command deck."

All four nodded and then followed Cordus as he hurried to the ladder. The three Legionaries jumped off onto the crew deck while Cordus and Aquilina continued up to the command deck. Cordus strapped himself into the pilot's couch. He couldn't bring himself to sit in the command couch.

"Know anything about delta systems?" he asked Aquilina.

She eyed the old delta controls. "I can run one as long as it doesn't break."

"Take the command couch," Cordus said, beginning the engine start-up. Since all systems started normally, it looked as if the golems had not tampered with the ship.

Could be a different story once we're flying...

Aquilina strapped herself into the command couch. "So I get to be centuriae today?"

Cordus allowed himself a sideways grin as he continued the start-up routines. "Kaeso always told me the command couch is the one place on the ship were a person can do the least damage. You can only monitor ship's systems, you can't change them."

"Unless I know the password, eh?"

"Which you don't. So enjoy the ride."

It took less than a minute for Cordus to complete all the start-up routines, his fingers flying across the tabulari. The ship's engines engaged and *Vacuna* lifted off the ground. Cordus ensured the ship's inertia cancellers were on full power, then instantly accelerated the ship past the speed of sound straight up into the sky. Even with inertia cancellers, he felt as if the hand of Jupiter was pushing him down into his couch.

He hoped the acceleration did not hurt Blaesus, but he had to get into space fast. He had no idea if the alien vessel had quantum way line engines like *Vacuna*, or if it had to use the alpha way lines. If the vessel had quantum engines, it was likely Cordus would never find it again.

Even before they left the atmosphere, Cordus began scanning the space above them. Reantium's atmosphere played havoc with the sensors and seemed to return false hits all over the sky. The higher they flew, however, the more false hits fell off the screen, until he found a single large hit twenty thousand miles from his position.

"That thing is thirteen miles long," Aquilina breathed, staring at the command tabulari. "No beacon. Surrounded by some kind of energy bubble. We can get a visual read, but nothing on its composition or internal systems."

Cordus checked the readings and a chill went through him. The "energy bubble" Aquilina mentioned looked like the same thing the Saturnists recently installed on *Vacuna* based on tech from the Menota Muse archives. If it was anything like *Vacuna's* shield, no scans or physical objects would be able to penetrate it. He was likely going up against a vessel packed with every bit of tech the Muses had.

Cordus clenched his teeth and set a course for the vessel. *Vacuna* darted toward its location.

But as soon as he set the course, the vessel shot out of Reantium's orbit toward the alpha way line near the star system's second planet 60 million miles away.

Cordus frowned. It was as if the vessel had been waiting for him before leaving.

Doesn't matter. He accelerated *Vacuna* after the vessel.

"You're flying into a trap," Aquilina said. "That thing wants you to follow it."

Cordus shook his head. "If it wanted to capture or kill us, it could have done it on Reantium. It wants us to follow for another reason."

"So you're going to do what it wants?"

He chewed his inner lip, thinking of Kaeso and Ocella. "I don't have a choice."

Cordus stared at his tabulari as he felt Aquilina's eyes on him, but she said no more.

Even with Caduceus's scopes at maximum magnification, the vessel was still outside visual range, but Cordus got an idea of the vessel's shape from the sensor readings. It was, as Aquilina said, almost thirteen miles long and looked like a black spiked tower with glowing blue veins. Theories cascaded through his mind. Ocella had been searching the Menota system for the secret way line they saw in the Menota archives six years ago. Had she found it, gone through, and then met this alien vessel controlled by a new Muse strain?

Marcus Antonius, Cordus called with his thoughts. *What can you tell me about this new Muse strain we're following?*

Marcus's voice came from the delta systems couch behind Cordus. "It is one you'd do well to avoid."

Cordus didn't look behind him. *Why?*

Aquilina interrupted Cordus's thoughts. "The way line it's heading toward goes to Illium. Illium has two way lines: one to Abundantia and one to Libertus."

A terrible coldness seized Cordus's chest. Libertus was now the only planet in human space with the greatest concentration of Muse hosts. The Terran Muses were wiped out six years ago, along with the physiologically incompatible Menota Muses. If this new strain was like the others, then it was in a perpetual state of war with all other strains. It would do everything it could to seek out new strains and destroy them.

The vessel had Ocella and now Kaeso, so it likely knew about Umbra and the Liberti Muses.

"Your Liberti friends will not find this strain so easy to defeat," Marcus said behind him, "so what chance do you think you have against them in this ancient garbage hauler? Flee, young Antonius."

Marcus always seemed to urge Cordus to take the most aggressive actions. If something could scare Marcus that bad, Cordus began to wonder if he should listen to the ancient avatar's advice.

No. Ocella and Kaeso would come for me. If I flee now, I might as well be dead; the guilt would make me a hollow shell the rest of my life.

"It's going to Libertus," Cordus said to Aquilina. He looked at her, praying he could keep his eyes and face hard. "We both know why."

Aquilina licked her lips, then winced as if trying to ignore a sudden pain in her head. "I can't say anything," she said slowly, "until I know what you know. If your friend is what I think he is, or used to be, then you'll understand."

Both Kaeso and Ocella told him stories of Umbra, how their implants prevented them from saying anything about the organization. Even uttering the name "Umbra" made their implants send a stabbing pain through their brain to remind them of their loyalties. Not even the Liberti consul knew of Umbra's existence; its security was too important to trust to the honor of a citizen who would only hold the consul post for six years.

Umbra had kept Libertus—a single star system without a large space fleet—free from the tyrannical regimes surrounding it, like Roma, the Zhonguo Sphere, and numerous other warlords trying to achieve eternal glory. It used the tech given to it by its benevolent virus allies, the Liberti Muse strain, to spy, sabotage, and assassinate away any threats to Libertus before they could materialize into full-scale invasions. Umbra Ancilia were posted throughout human space watching for those threats, using tech no other human government possessed. The mysterious "bad luck" that befell anyone threatening Libertus had earned them the superstitious reputation of being protected by *numina*, demons of the gods.

So if Aquilina was Umbra, then she was physically unable to talk about Umbra until she knew Cordus knew the same information. Then the implant would release her to speak freely.

Cordus glanced behind him. No one else was on the command deck ladder, and he heard no one coming up.

He said to Aquilina in a low tone, "If that vessel is a new Muse strain, then it will go to Libertus to destroy the last concentration of Muses in human space. Umbra Corps."

She sighed, as if the pain suddenly receded. "That'll make it easier for us to talk."

"Kaeso and Ocella were once Ancilia. I'm surprised you've never heard of them."

Aquilina snorted. "If you know anything about Umbra, you know that Ancilia never get all the data they want. Only what they need to complete their mission."

"What *was* your mission on Reantium?"

Aquilina winced again. "I still can't talk about some things. Details on existing operations, for one."

She then gave him a raised eyebrow and a coy grin. "You have a little secret of your own, eh, *Titus?*"

He involuntarily averted his eyes, which angered him. He ignored the heat in his face and forced himself to return her gaze. The heat only compounded his discomfort, and beads of sweat fell down his back.

Gods, what is wrong with me?

Marcus chuckled. "Why, young Antonius, is that lust we sense in you?"

Quiet!

"How is it," she asked, "that you also heard the vessel's message? Your friend Kaeso and I had Muse implants. Were you an Ancile, too? There's no other way you could have...communicated with me like you did from that tavern." Her gaze traveled up and down his body, which quickened Cordus's heart. "You're certainly built for the job, but I doubt you've seen eighteen Terran years. You'd be the youngest Ancile I've ever known."

"Maybe I am," Cordus stammered. "You don't look much older than me. How old are you?"

He cringed inwardly. *If you wanted to sound petulant, you could not have done a better job.*

Her smile widened. "Older than eighteen."

"Well...I can't talk about some things either," Cordus said, pretending to review something on his tabulari to avoid her large brown eyes. "All of this is irrelevant anyway. You need to warn Umbra Corps that a threat they've never encountered is on its way to Libertus."

Aquilina's expression turned serious. "I've been trying since that vessel came to Reantium, but I can't get through. It seems to be jamming me."

During the Roman siege of Libertus six years ago, the Romans had used a similar jamming signal. The vessel was more advanced than Roma, so he assumed it had the same ability to jam Muse communications.

"Just keep trying," Cordus said.

His tabulari showed the vessel slowly pulling away from them. *Vacuna* was at its top acceleration. Any more and it would overload the inertia canceling systems. Even now, he felt his weight pressing into the pilot's couch.

He brought up a map of the Illium system on his tabulari. Illium Primus, the lone Terran-class planet in the system, was a so-called Lost World, independent from Roma since it was colonized two hundred years ago. The entire system had ten million citizens, with mining bases throughout the system's planets and moons. It was economically, culturally, and militarily aligned with Libertus. Besides the Reantium way line, it had two other way lines in the system: one linked to Abundantia, a Roman system, and one to Libertus.

Cordus checked the distances from Illium's Reantium way line terminus to the other two. The Abundantia way line was closest, only a single Terran astronomical unit away. The Libertus way line orbited Illium Primus, but was over seven astronomical units away.

A plan began to form in Cordus's mind, but he needed the alien vessel to confirm one last detail before he would begin to allow himself hope.

The alien vessel sped toward the Illium way line, getting farther from *Vacuna*. At this rate, it would reach the way line in ten minutes, and then *Vacuna* would follow it through ten minutes later.

"What are you thinking?" Aquilina asked. "You look like someone contemplating ten *latrunculi* moves ahead."

"Something like that," Cordus said. He tapped his collar com, which broadcast his voice throughout the ship. "Ulpius, this is Cordus. Pick up the com in the medical hatch."

After several long seconds, Dariya's voice said, "He is busy."

That didn't sound good. Cordus's stomach turned queasy thinking Blaesus may die on this ship. *Do the job, Centuriae.*

"Just make sure you strap Blaesus into the medical delta couch. We're going through a way line in twenty minutes. I'll tell you once we're close so you can get to your couches, too."

Ulpius growled in the background, "I ain't going to be finished in twenty godsdamned minutes!"

"Then make sure he's stable," Cordus ordered. *I could be ordering Blaesus's death.* He shook away that thought. "If we don't follow that vessel through the way line, we may lose it."

Ulpius grumbled something Cordus couldn't hear, but Dariya said, "He says he will try."

After a minute of silence, Aquilina said, "So what *is* your plan?"

"It involves some secrets I need to keep from you. I'd rather not tell you in case I learn my plan won't work." He kept his face impassive. "Forgive me if I don't quite trust you yet."

Aquilina shrugged. "Fair enough. Although if you want us to work together, you'll need to trust me."

"Funny coming from an Umbra Ancile."

"I'm physically prevented from trusting you. You won't trust me by choice."

"I don't want to get into a 'who's more trustworthy' argument. I'll tell you my plan when I'm ready."

"What should I do in the meantime? This command couch makes me feel useless."

"Know anything about pressure suits?"

"Enough to put one on."

"There's a closet of them in Cargo One. Go make sure they have air and their systems are running."

"How many should I prep?"

Cordus thought a moment. "Four."

She regarded him a second longer, then unstrapped herself from the command couch. "Very well. Just don't go through the way line until I return."

"You have seventeen minutes."

She snorted, then rushed to the command deck ladder in the back.

When the sound of her steps faded, Cordus whispered, "You've been quiet, Marcus."

"We know what you're planning. It won't work."

Cordus turned to Marcus for the first time since he sat in the pilot's couch. Marcus lounged in the delta systems couch, one leg over the side. It seemed to Cordus that a human would not have been comfortable in such a position, especially wearing Marcus's ancient armor and leather skirt straps. Marcus made it look comfortable, though.

"What do you think I'm planning?"

"Well it's obvious you want to board the thing," Marcus said, inspecting the nails on his right hand. "How you do it is irrelevant. It's the boarding part we think is doomed."

"Why?"

Marcus brought his leg down and leaned forward. The affected boredom on his face turned to haunted seriousness. "Because that ship is alive. That strain doesn't use individual hosts like most strains. It prefers to travel the stars in living ships. And when it is invaded, it eradicates the threat much the same as your body's immune system tries to eradicate an invader."

Cordus stared at Marcus and then laughed. Marcus scowled. "We fail to see the humor in—"

"You don't see it?" Cordus said. "We—humans—will be a 'virus' that invades the 'body' of a Muse strain."

Marcus rolled his eyes. "Yes, ha-ha, the irony is sublime. But we still don't think you appreciate the dangers of the task before you. It was a struggle for us to establish a foothold in human bodies. We lost trillions in that war to your natural defenses. Do *you* have an army of trillions to waste fighting that vessel's natural defenses?"

Cordus turned back to his tabulari, doubt in himself and his plan creeping into his mind. "Well, it won't matter if I'm wrong about what this ship will do once it reaches a way line."

"What do you hope it will do?"

"Stop."

Marcus smiled. "Ah, clever. Again, that may get you inside. What will you do once you're inside?"

"One thing at a time."

Cordus let the minutes before the vessel's way line jump pass in silence. When the moment arrived for the vessel to reach the way line, Cordus tapped a button on his tabulari to record the event.

What he saw gave him hope. The vessel, like every other human ship, stopped on the way line's event horizon. It was motionless for a second before the way line's gravity reached out and pulled it in. The vessel disappeared.

Cordus nodded to himself, realizing for the first time his heart had been pounding. *We can get inside. But Marcus is right—what do we do then?*

Chapter Seventeen

The opening to the room irised, and Ocella sat up on her gel bed. The Lucia golem entered the room, stood to one side, and then Kaeso marched in after it. The golem then left the room and the opening irised shut behind it.

Ocella leapt up and wrapped her arms around him. He matched the intensity of her embrace. They held each other for a long time, and she didn't care that Varo was on the other side of the room respectfully giving them their moment, or that the ship was likely watching them. Right now, all she wanted to do was lose herself in Kaeso's warm arms and forget the past week.

"I'm sorry," she finally whispered in his ear. "I didn't know what else to—"

"Stop. You did the only thing you could do." He pulled back and placed a gentle hand on her cheek. His usually stony eyes were soft. "I'm glad you did it. I missed you."

She leaned her head on his chest and hugged him tighter. "I missed you, too. And I'm glad you're with me."

She pulled back from him and then released the anger that had simmered for days. "But you must have *cac* for brains if you thought it was a good idea to bring Cordus to Reantium."

"That was nice while it lasted."

"I'm serious, Kaeso. He's not ready to go into a war zone, and he's certainly not ready to command *Vacuna*."

"Listen," Kaeso said, "I would not have made him Trierarch if I didn't think he could handle it. Yes, when things blew up he froze, but only for a second. Juno, we all froze when Nestor—" Kaeso stopped, blinked several times. "Nestor... So much was happening that I never had a chance to think about him."

Kaeso proceeded to tell her what happened on Reantium. From the initial, inexplicable golem attack at Tarpeius's villa to the moment Kaeso arrived in this room. Ocella fought back tears when she learned of Nestor, shook her head in confusion over the golem uprising, and prayed Cordus took Blaesus to a system with good hospitals rather than chase after them.

"You should have seen him," Kaeso said. "He's a born leader. I don't know what he did between the garrison and the hospital, but to those Romans he rescued, he was their *Centuriae*. They'd follow him any-where."

Kaeso was rarely so animated about anything. His pride in Cordus made his eyes sparkle and was almost infectious. Almost.

"He should *not* have been there," she said.

She realized she sounded petulant, berating Kaeso for something neither of them could change now. But her frustration and fear wouldn't stop her from venting her anger. Kaeso happened to be the most con-venient target right now.

Kaeso watched her patiently. It made her all the more angry because he acted like he did nothing wrong and was waiting out a child's tantrum. Couldn't he see that Cordus had to be protected so he could fulfill his destiny *when the time came*? Couldn't he see the insanity of risking Cordus's life in a mission that was unimportant compared to the battles to come?

Apparently not.

She turned away from him and went back to the gel bed near Varo. Varo stood and walked over to Kaeso. They exchanged a few words, mostly on how they wished they had met again under different circum-stances.

Ocella ignored them both and lay down on the bed. The frustration and fear she had kept in check while with Varo had evaporated when Kaeso entered the room. She was ashamed for the way she broke down in front of Varo, a crewman who was supposed to look to her as his Centuriae.

Why did Kaeso have to bring the boy?

Cordus was stubborn, and it was possible he'd come after her and Kaeso. If he did...well, she wasn't sure what would happen. The vessel wanted Cordus to remain free, but wanted him to follow them and was using Kaeso and Ocella as bait. But for what? Her throat seized when she thought of them dissecting Cordus to—

She closed her eyes. *Minerva, grant Cordus the wisdom to ignore the bait.*

Ocella noticed Varo and Kaeso were conversing in Aramaic. Varo was doing Ocella's job: giving Kaeso their status and all the information they gleaned so far regarding the vessel. It wouldn't help their situation if she kept worrying about Cordus and letting her anger at Kaeso paralyze her. She pushed those feelings to the back of her mind...for a more appropriate time.

She stood up from the gel bed and walked to Kaeso and Varo.

"...still don't understand what their true goals are," Varo was saying in Aramaic.

"They want Cordus to follow us," Ocella said in Aramaic, as she approached them.

Kaeso regarded her a moment and then nodded. "How much do they know about his—?"

The opening irised and the Lucia-golem stepped through, this time clothed in the same blue merchant's jumpsuit that the human Lucia had worn onto the vessel. The golem also looked more human, with fewer blue veins pulsating beneath its skin, and its white skin tone closer to Lucia's pallor.

Kaeso watched the Lucia-golem with a clenched jaw. It was a reminder the vessel had killed his friend. He had lost two old friends in quick succession, and Ocella felt guilty over her earlier behavior. Her guilt did not ease her fear for Cordus or her opinion that Kaeso was wrong to bring him to Reantium, but she couldn't imagine Kaeso's pain over those two losses.

No, I can *imagine it. I gave myself the same pain six years ago.*

"We have entered the star system you call Ilium," the golem said without inflection. "We will soon arrive in the system you call Libertus."

Kaeso tensed. He did not tense like a normal person, who would clench his fists or draw himself up taller. Kaeso grew more *relaxed*. She had trained with him long enough to know that he was keeping his muscles loose so his attack and defense options were open.

Not yet, Kaeso.

To draw the golem's attention from Kaeso, she asked, "Why Libertus?"

"We must have new witnesses."

Kaeso growled, "What do you mean by 'witnesses'?"

Lucia-golem swiveled its head to Kaeso. "The Great Archives are gone."

When it said no more, Kaeso said to Ocella in Aramaic, "It is impossible to talk to this thing."

In flawless Aramaic, the Lucia-golem responded, "It is not 'impossible' to talk to us."

Ocella looked from Kaeso to Varo. *So much for our secret communications. This thing will know everything we say.*

"We deciphered the grammar and words of your second language by listening to you speak it," the golem said, returning to Latin.

Then it did the most gruesome thing Ocella had yet see it do—it smiled. It was simply the movement of muscles, without any mirth behind it. The smile never reached the Lucia-golem's dead eyes.

Ocella tried to keep her voice steady. "We want to know why you are going to Libertus. We do not understand what you mean by 'witnesses' and 'Great Archives.'"

The golem's head cocked, as if listening to instructions only it could hear. "You are our first witnesses. We require more witnesses, more memories. Strong memories. Pain produces the strongest memories. This we have learned over countless millennia."

Kaeso asked quietly, "What will you do at Libertus?"

Lucia-golem's head swiveled to Kaeso. "Observe. Record. Instigate."

Through clenched teeth, Kaeso asked again, "What...does that mean?"

"We will take more witnesses. Then you and the witnesses will watch us kill Libertus. We will record your pain and rebuild the Great Archives your kind destroyed."

Chapter Eighteen

"So that's our situation," Cordus said.

He tried to adopt the stance Kaeso used when addressing his crew—arms folded, back straight. Gracchus, Piso, and Duran sat on supply containers, the wisdom of foot soldiers throughout history dictating they rest whenever given the chance. The fair-skinned Gracchus stared expressionless at the Cargo One ramp; Piso, the dark-haired Hiberian, picked at the fresh bandage wrapped around the top of his head; Duran, the brown-skinned central African, coldly studied a knife he'd pulled off a golem body in Nascio. Ulpius, his face pockmarked and stubbly, stood behind them, his hands in the pockets of the common blue merchant's jumpsuit Cordus had given him. Dariya and Daryush stood next to each other near the door to the corridor, their usual place in these meetings. Blaesus was still in the medical hatch under sedation.

Aquilina watched Cordus with those pleasant brown eyes. He did his best to avoid them.

He had just explained his theory that the alien vessel was heading toward Libertus. He told them he aimed to board the vessel to rescue Kaeso and Ocella. And with Aquilina's approval, he explained she was indeed a Liberti spy, though he didn't specifically mention 'Umbra' or the Liberti Muses. The Romans gave her icy stares, but said nothing.

The problems, he said, were twofold: what to do once they boarded the vessel, and how to warn Libertus about its arrival.

"Forgive my bluntness," Ulpius said, "but why should we—meaning us Romans—care what happens to Libertus or two people we don't know?"

Cordus regarded Ulpius with the stoniest stare he could muster. Kaeso had used that stare many times to make the strongest Saturnist back down. But watching Kaeso do it and doing it himself were two different things.

It seemed to work, because Ulpius broke eye contact and glanced away.

"Because I told you on Reantium what I planned to do," Cordus replied, "and you came anyway. Too late to back out now, Centurion. Besides, I saved your life *and* I gave you a ride off that dead planet. I would hope that honor dictate you return that favor."

Ulpius shrugged. "Don't get me wrong, I appreciate all that. But with all due respect, my allegiance is to Roma. Not you."

Marcus Antonius suddenly stood next to Cordus. Cordus didn't flinch or look at him.

"Well don't get *us* wrong," Marcus said, "but we'd just as soon you didn't go chasing that strain. Though if you want the help of these plebs, there is a simple way you could get it."

I told you, do not speak of the aura again.

Marcus sighed. "You are the most stubborn Antonius we've ever infected. And that's out of a thousand years of living in your bloodline."

Well, there's never been an Antonius like me.

Marcus grunted.

Duran stood. "I can't speak for the other boys, sir, but I'm with you." He gave Ulpius a glare. "Roma never responded to our repeated calls for reinforcements, even when they knew the planet was almost lost. They left us to rot. As far as I'm concerned, the Republic can rot."

Ulpius balled his hands into fists. "That's blasphemy, soldier. You've taken oaths—"

"What about Roma's duty to its soldiers in return for those oaths?" Duran asked, his deep voice shaking. "We begged for help up until the golems took us. All we got was silence. Roma left us to die."

"In case you hadn't noticed," Ulpius growled, "we're in the middle of a godsdamned *civil war*! You don't know what's happening on Terra. They could have been busy with more important—"

Duran snorted. "More important then losing the Republic's main food source?"

"Yes! Maybe it was more important than that!"

Piso and Gracchus stood next to Duran and stared down Ulpius. Piso said, "We're with Duran and the Centuriae."

Ulpius stared at all three of them. "Deserters," he snarled.

Shouts and insults flew between the three soldiers and Ulpius. Before the argument descended into a physical fight, Cordus hit the controls that opened the Cargo One door ramp. A loud alarm blared and the lights in the hold turned orange. The Romans stopped arguing and stared at him in shock. Aquilina stood, her face alarmed. Dariya and Daryush exchanged grins.

"Are you insane?" Ulpius yelled over the alarm.

Cordus tapped the controls again. The alarm silenced, and the lights in Cargo One went back to normal.

"Now that I have your attention, gentlemen," Cordus said in a low voice. Another trick he'd learned from Kaeso—people seemed to listen closer to a low voice than a raised one. In this case it worked, for Duran and Ulpius stopped yelling at each other and focused on Cordus.

"Ulpius, I respect you for honoring your oaths to Roma," Cordus said. "But I will follow that vessel. Time is critical, so it may be a while before we make it back to Roman space or a colonized world. I apologize, but whether you like it or not, you're coming with us. So you can either help us or stay out of our way. Make your decision."

Ulpius glared at Cordus, then turned toward the hold's exit. "I'll make sure your man lives. That will be my contribution to this little adventure." He brushed between Dariya and Daryush, neither of whom moved out of his way, and left the hold.

Cordus turned to the three Romans. "Thank you. I hope I haven't made things worse for you when you get home."

Duran glanced at where Ulpius left the hold. "I suppose he could report us. Technically we're not deserters; we just figure the fastest way home is to help you."

Gracchus curled his freckled upper lip. "Besides, that centurion is an ass. Been bossing us around ever since the golems threw him into that prison with us." Piso and Duran nodded their agreement with Gracchus.

Cordus turned to Aquilina.

"Libertus is my world," she said. "Of course I'll help."

Cordus nodded. "Now back to my original question. Once we're aboard, how do we find my friends?"

The silence in the hold stretched for minutes.

Cordus glanced at Marcus. *The question is directed at you more than anybody.*

Marcus raised an eyebrow. "Ah, so now you want our help? Wonderful. Here's what you do—"

"If they were once...spies," Aquilina said, talking over Marcus, "I may be able to locate their implants."

Marcus scowled and then muttered, "Which was what I was about to say—"

"But their implants are deactivated," Cordus said. "How will you find them?"

Aquilina smiled, and Cordus looked away before forcing himself to meet her gaze. *Stop that!*

"Trade secret," she said. "You get us in, and I'll find them."

Chapter Nineteen

Cordus hit the sparring bag harder than he should have. The impacts sent painful jolts through his hands and elbows, even with his soft sparring gloves. When the pain grew too much, he switched to kicks until his ankles and knees screamed. After that, he switched back to the punches. Sweat poured down his face, and it felt good to release his frustration over recent events despite the pain.

Six years ago, Kaeso had converted part of Cargo Two on *Vacuna* into a gymnasium. Now that *Vacuna* worked exclusively for the Saturnists, they rarely took jobs that required much cargo space. Kaeso figured the crew needed a place to practice self-defense during the long days of intra-system travel, especially with the ever-present dangers stalking them in their new missions.

Cordus drilled himself over and over, the same way Kaeso had done. He pushed himself harder than Kaeso's drills, going for one extra minute of punches, kicks, pushups, pull-ups, and various other calisthenics. The benefits of the exercise were physically self-evident, but it was mental cleansing he sought now. He needed to avoid thinking about the problems he'd been obsessing over the past few days. The ritualistic drills did more to clear his mind than any of Nestor's prayerful meditations.

"Do you mind some company?"

Cordus dropped down from the rafter he'd been using for his pull-ups. Aquilina stood in the hatch to Cargo Two wearing a loose-fitting, white exercise suit, her long black hair braided down her back. Two wisps hung over one of her brown eyes. She dropped a towel on one of the crates near the hatch and began stretching without waiting for his response.

"I don't mind," Cordus said. "Where did you get the outfit?"

"Dariya lent me one. A little loose, but then I was half-starved for a week."

"Are you well enough for exercise?"

She stretched her legs. "Your concern is touching, but I've had four days to rest. I'm at the point where if don't spar, I'm going to pick a fight with somebody on this ship."

"I know the feeling. Gloves are in the locker and the sparring bag is over there." Cordus glanced up at the rafter he'd been using. "We kind of improvise for everything else."

"I don't want to hit a bag," she said, giving him an appraising look. "Want to have a go, Centuriae?"

Cordus's heart skipped a beat over the way she studied him. He was shirtless and wearing loose shorts. Kaeso's relentless training, and Cordus's own drive, had packed a lot of muscle on his frame. Even though he'd trained hard for the last half-hour, he regarded Aquilina's gaunt face, which had admittedly filled out over the last four days, and wondered just how well she had recovered from her ordeal on Reantium.

"I hardly think it would be a fair spar."

"You're right. Should I fight left-handed?"

When Cordus only stared, she continued, "Centuriae, you forget I am among the best trained soldiers in human space. I endured far more hardship in my academy days than on Reantium." She stopped stretching and then went to the locker and put on sparring gloves with a quick and efficient manner. She then took on a fighting stance five paces from him. "You won't 'damage' me."

Cordus tried to shrug indifferently. "Very well. Any particular style? I assume Greco wrestling is out."

"Why?"

"I just thought..." Seeing her level stare, he said, "Never mind. So freestyle, then?"

"You're too concerned with rules. I thought your mentor was Umbra."

"He was," Cordus stammered. "I just...well, I don't want to..."

Aquilina rolled her eyes, then came at Cordus with quick jabs and uppercuts that he barely blocked. Her blows pushed him back against a crate. He finally caught one of her wrists and twisted it around her back. Her lithe body turned in the same direction until he almost had her wrapped up from behind.

Somehow she flipped out of Cordus's grasp, did a quick roll, and came up several paces in front of Cordus in the same stance with which she had started.

Cordus stared at her. "How did you do that? I had you."

"Another trade secret. Now you attack me."

Cordus slowly approached, then circled just out of her reach. She turned with him, their gazes locked, a smile in the corner of her mouth.

"Roman tactics," Cordus said. "You started with the *ludus dacicus*, then transitioned to *ludus magnus*. But I have no idea what that was at the end. Zhonguo?"

"Good. Umbra doesn't discriminate when it comes to tactics. If it works, they use it, whether it comes from Roma or the Zhonguo. Are you going to attack or talk?"

"Talk for a bit. Where did you grow up on Libertus?"

"You won't distract me with—"

Cordus spun around and swept his leg beneath Aquilina's. As he expected, she jumped over his leg. He twisted in mid-air and brought his other leg down on her upper back. It knocked her off balance, and she fell to the floor. Golems programmed to master-level had fallen flat on their chests after that move, the air knocked from their lungs. He would then jump on their backs and put them in a headlock they couldn't escape.

But Aquilina's fall was lighter than he thought it would be. She brought her hands up in time and landed on them. Then in a spring-like motion, vaulted off the floor and away from Cordus's follow-up straddle move. He scrambled away from her own follow-up to his move. They both ended up on their feet facing each other in their original stances.

Cordus smiled. "You're amazing."

"Pretty smiles won't distract me, Roman."

His smile faltered. "I'm Liberti—"

She came at him again, this time with roundhouse kicks that he blocked, but made his arms throb with their power. She used every bit of torque she possessed to make her blows powerful. They were executed with a master's precision.

He ducked away again and jumped onto a crate just to catch his breath. She circled below, her chest heaving. Considering her weakened condition, all he had to do was keep attacking her, and he'd eventually have her.

But there was no honor or sport in that.

"What makes you think I'm Roman?"

"You fight like one," she said. "You going to stay in your tree or finish sparring?"

"'Fight like a Roman'?"

"You try to bludgeon me with your punches and kicks. No subtlety in your attacks."

"Ancilia trained me," Cordus said, stepping from crate to crate. "How could I fight like a Roman?"

"Has nothing to do with training. It's in the blood."

"You're saying my blood is Roman?"

She chuckled. "I've rested enough. Are you going to come down and finish, or do you concede the spar?"

Cordus jumped down from the crate ten paces from Aquilina. "I'm not Roman."

She closed in slowly. And then he heard her voice in his mind like a faint whisper, "My implant says otherwise...Marcus Antonius Cordus."

She took full advantage of his momentary shock. Her attack sent him reeling. It was all he could do to block her rapid blows. She feinted with a swing at his head. He brought his arm up to block, but she somehow shifted in mid-swing to a stoop and then brought her leg under his, knocking him on his back. She straddled him with her forearm to his neck. Her face was inches from his, her breath warm and sweet from the apricot packets she had for breakfast.

"Do you concede?" she asked.

"I concede the spar."

She kept her brown eyes locked with his a moment longer, then jumped off him and walked to the equipment locker to grab a towel.

"You're good. For a merchant."

Cordus stood, his mind racing to figure out what to say. Did he admit he could hear her voice in his mind? That meant revealing his heritage. Though the Liberti Muses knew he was with Kaeso and Ocella, he assumed they did not make it common knowledge to all Umbra. If Umbra Magisterium had not told this Ancile, then he was certainly not going to volunteer the information, considering Umbra had wanted him dead six years ago.

But how much longer could he conceal his identity? She was smart and talented. Right now, all she had was a guess, but she would confirm the truth soon.

"I want to check on Blaesus," Cordus said. Better to retreat and regroup than flail about. "You may continue your exercises if you wish."

"I didn't hurt you, did I?"

"No. You did well. I just haven't checked on my friend today."

She watched him unlace his sparring gloves and then towel the sweat off his chest before donning a loose tunic.

"I don't blame you for not trusting me," she said. "You barely know me. But we're on the same side. We both want to stop that vessel before it reaches Libertus. The more I know about you, the more I can help you."

Cordus laughed. "You're suggesting a *quid pro quo*? I thought Umbra had a little policy against that."

She opened her mouth, but closed it again and turned her eyes away.

"That's what I thought," he said. "Until you can tell me your secrets, then Pluto will hear my secrets before you do."

He tossed the towel at the foot of the locker and left Cargo Two. He wondered why he was suddenly so angry with her. Was it that she had beaten him in sparring when only Kaeso could do so? Or that she knew who he was, yet she would not tell him anything about herself?

Or the fact he couldn't string two thoughts together in her presence?

Chapter Twenty

Cordus stalked through the corridor to the medical hatch, still musing on what to do about Aquilina. He'd been so lost in thought that Ulpius startled him at the entry to the medical hatch.

"The wound is stabilized," Ulpius said, "so the thing now is to get his blood back up. Just finished another round of synth-blood, but he needs a real hospital with real surgeons."

Cordus looked in at Blaesus, who lay on the bunk in the corner shirtless and with a white bandage wrapped around his mid-section. He looked frail and his skin was gray, but his eyes were open, and he smiled weakly when he saw Cordus.

"Don't let this pleb talk you into dropping me off on some backwater planet," Blaesus croaked. "You're going after the Centuriae, and that takes precedence."

Ulpius shook his head. "Is he always such a cranky bastard?"

"Only when he's feeling better," Cordus said, grinning. Then to Blaesus, "Whatever we do, *you* are going to stay right here. We'll get you to a hospital once we have Kaeso and Ocella."

Blaesus nodded. "Good," he said. He seemed to have used up all his energy, for he eased his head back onto his pillow and closed his eyes.

Ulpius glared at Cordus, then motioned him outside the hatch. "A word."

They exited the medical hatch, and Ulpius closed it behind him.

"If you don't get him to a hospital, he will die."

Cordus frowned. "How long?"

"Could be minutes, could be days. Depends on the gods, I'd say."

Cordus sighed, staring at the medical hatch. One of his mentors was fighting for his life, while his *de facto* parents fought for theirs. "We have no time for side trips. We'll have to trust the gods aren't ready for him yet."

Cordus went to leave, but Ulpius grabbed his arm in a grip that demonstrated his years of Legion service. "I don't think you understand, Centuriae," Ulpius growled. "You being Liberti and all, I don't expect you to give a wit about a Roman, but I do. He will die unless he's seen by a real medicus, and soon."

Without turning, Cordus said, "Release me, Centurion."

Ulpius held on a moment, but then released Cordus's arm.

Cordus turned to face Ulpius. "Gaius Octavius Blaesus means more to me than you will ever know," Cordus said in his own growl. "And I know full well his blood is on my hands if he dies here. Do your best, centurion."

Ulpius scowled, then turned and went back into the medical hatch.

"He's insubordinate," Marcus Antonius said from behind Cordus. "You're within your rights as centuriae to shoot him dead."

Cordus turned quickly and strode toward Marcus. Before the Muse image could move, Cordus walked right through him. He was disappointed that it felt like walking through a holo. He had hoped for a cry of surprise from Marcus or a tingling sensation. Something.

Instead, Marcus just grunted in amusement. "We're just an image in your mind, boy, remember?"

I'm trying not to.

"You should kill the girl, too."

Cordus stopped. *Why?*

"She's trouble."

She's Umbra.

"It's not just that. There's something about her, something that makes us think she's pretending to be something she's not."

Cordus turned around. *So she's* not *Umbra?*

Marcus shrugged his armored shoulders. "She seems Umbra, but...you should spend more time with her. It will give us more of an opportunity to observe her. That shouldn't be much of a hardship for you."

Cordus turned and strode back down the corridor. He knew his fumbling words around Aquilina made it obvious to any sentient human being that he was attracted to her. He hated being so transparent. He especially hated being mocked for it by Marcus.

He was about to climb the ladder to the command deck when Dariya called from the level below. "Centuriae."

Dariya was looking up at him, the muscles around her jaw twitching as she clenched them. Something was wrong.

Cordus climbed down the ladder. "What is it?"

She waited until he was all the way down, then nodded toward the engine room. She entered the engine room without waiting for him to follow. Inside, Daryush was tapping at the engine tabulari, then turned around as they entered. Cordus had no idea how the big man knew they'd arrived, for the deep hum of the engines seemed to mask all but the loudest and harshest noises.

"Ush, watch the door, will you?" Dariya said. Daryush nodded, then walked over to the door and leaned against the wall outside with his arms folded. He tried to wear a menacing look. His first instinct was to avoid conflict at all costs, so over the years he figured out that looking as mean as possible was the best way to avoid a fight.

"You're making me nervous, Dariya," Cordus said in a tone just audible above the engine hum.

"You should be," Dariya said as she tapped her tabulari. She stepped aside and then pointed at the display. "I found this an hour ago while I was searching our archives for tactics on how to use that crazy energy shield the Saturnists installed on my girl. I figured we may need it soon."

"Good thinking," Cordus said. He scanned the com diagnostics and they all looked normal to him. "You'd better tell me what I'm looking for, or we'll be here all day."

Dariya gave him an approving glance. "You admit your ignorance like Kaeso. I like that."

She tapped the icon that showed the archives. The display expanded, and Cordus saw the system was operating normally. Except...

Cordus froze.

Someone had been searching through *Vacuna's* log regarding its trip to Menota six years ago and the Muse archives it had found. That archive was locked, and only the ship's Centuriae could access it. The archive had been opened eight hours ago, and Cordus had not done it.

He looked at Dariya.

"Right," she said. "Somebody on this ship is a snoop."

"How? Only the centuriae can authorize access, and I sure as Juno did not." Cordus studied the display.

"I have spent the last hour searching the tabulari. All I can see is that the archive was opened last night, but there is no identification stamp. Whoever did this knew how to cover themselves." Dariya leveled her eyes at Cordus. "Seems to me there is only one person on the ship who would have those skills..."

Cordus stared at the archive readouts. It didn't make sense for Aquilina to do this. Umbra knew what *Vacuna* found on Menota. Perhaps they had not made that information available to her and she wanted it out of personal curiosity? If she was that curious, why wouldn't she simply ask him for the information?

Cordus shook his head. "That doesn't mean Aquilina did this. We have four other Romans on this ship who we know nothing about. Besides, if

Aquilina was smart enough to get into our archives, seems to me she'd be smart enough to cover her tracks better."

"She—er, whoever did this covered themselves well. Simply erasing the identity stamp takes skills. But to erase all access traces would require a system restart, and that would have drawn our attention quick." She tapped the tabulari and closed the archive. "So what are your orders, Centuriae?"

Cordus gave her a sideways glare. "You ask as that as if you're glad you're not me."

Dariya grinned.

"Can you set a trap to let us know if it's accessed again?"

"Already have. The spy will not gain access without setting off every alarm on the ship."

"Good. Keep me posted on any other unauthorized system access."

Dariya nodded, and Cordus left the engine room. Daryush gave him a questioning look, and Cordus said, "All clear, big man?"

He gave Cordus an upturned thumb, and then returned to the engine room.

"There's a simple way to deal with this," Marcus Antonius said from behind Cordus.

Cordus turned to his ancestor. "I'm not going to shoot them all."

Marcus snorted. "No, no. Too messy. Just gather them in Cargo One and open the air lock. Quick and clean."

Cordus began climbing the ladder to the command deck. Marcus called from below, "You'll need a harder spine if you hope to rule one day, boy."

Cordus stopped climbing, but kept his eyes fixed on the command deck above. *I will die before I accept that destiny.*

He continued climbing. Marcus was silent, but Cordus could somehow sense the Muse image smiling.

Chapter Twenty-One

B ells chimed softly behind Ocella as she sat in a red, gold-trimmed couch on a covered patio before a calm, clear sea. The sky was blue, and the bright Liberti sun warmed the white sands around her. She held an infant to her breast, and she hummed a soft Roman lullaby to the child. She pulled back the white blanket covering the infant boy's dark hair, and she gently stroked his head.

"Cordus," she whispered with a smile. The baby's eyes opened, full of innocence.

Ocella's eyes sprang open when their cell door irised. The video wall above her illuminated the Lucia-golem in the opening. Kaeso had already risen from the gel bed where he'd been laying next to Ocella.

"You may explore," the Lucia-golem announced, and then left the room. The door did not shut behind her.

Varo rose from the gel bed beside them. "Is it serious?"

Ocella glanced at Kaeso, who looked back at her with a frown. "Are you all right?" he asked.

"Yes, why?"

"You've been crying."

Ocella felt her wet cheeks, and then wiped away the tear streaks. "I'm fine." She stood up from the gel bed, blinking away the tears and focusing on the opening. "Should we leave before it closes the door again?"

Kaeso scratched his stubbly chin. "I hate doing what it wants."

Varo approached the open door. "Well I hate sitting here. With all due respect, Centuriae Amelius, we've been locked in this cell days longer than you. I can't speak for Centuriae Licinius, but I need to get out of here."

Kaeso looked at Ocella again, and she shrugged. "They can do whatever they want to us locked in here," she said. "I don't see how exploring makes things worse."

He grunted. "Things can always get worse."

"Where's the optimistic Kaeso I once knew?"

"There's a difference between optimism and common sense." He motioned toward the opening. "After you, Centuriae."

Ocella strode toward the door and after Varo, who had already left the room. She stopped just outside the door and stared in shock. The walls were no longer black with blue glowing veins. The whole corridor now looked like the interior of a human-built starship.

Vacuna, to be precise.

Kaeso sucked in a breath behind her. She followed his haunted gaze as it swept the corridor, right to left. From what she could see in the meager light, the corridor stretched in both directions until the ends became a faint point on the murky horizon. It must have gone on for a mile each way.

"Well this is different," Varo remarked.

"They're using Lucia's memories," Ocella said. "They re-fashioned this part of the vessel to look like *Vacuna*. Why?"

Kaeso walked to the closed hatch across from their cell. He tapped the lock pad to the right of the hatch, but it did not open. An "access denied" message scrolled across the pad's display. He then went to the next hatch to the left, about ten paces down the hall. It also gave him an "access denied" message.

Varo tried several hatches down the hall to the right, but got the same results. "Great," Varo said, walking back to Ocella and Kaeso. "We trade a one-room cell for a really long one."

"Maybe this is where they'll put all the 'witnesses' they keep talking about," Ocella said.

Kaeso finally said, "No, they want our reactions to all this. The Liberti Muses traded their wisdom and technology for experiences. Experiences are their currency, food, and religion all rolled into one. The Terran strain was the same, and the Menota. It's the one thing they all had in common. This strain is no different."

Ocella looked up and down the endless corridor. "They want us to explore, to gain new experiences." She gave a mirthless chuckle. "They were just as bored watching us in the cell as we were sitting there."

Kaeso nodded. "Let's assume it's true that they want us to experience all this. Soon they'll think we've had enough and will want to make a withdrawal."

Ocella shuddered. She wondered what they had done to Lucia's body to create the golem and extract her memories.

Careful, Ancile. Those thoughts lead to panic.

She still thought of herself as an Ancile, even though she'd left Umbra six years ago. The Umbra training changed her forever, as it was meant to, and she doubted she'd ever think of herself as anything other than an Ancile.

Albeit one that betrayed and shattered the order.

Varo looked between Ocella and Kaeso. "I can't stay in that room any longer."

Ocella felt the same. The cell was like a sarcophagus to her even though it was three dozen paces—she'd counted—from one end to the other.

"Agreed," Ocella said. "Besides, we need to gather intelligence if we—I mean, *when* we get off this vessel."

Kaeso's mouth twitched at her optimism, but he nodded. "So which way?"

Ocella slammed her hand against the locked hatch.

"Fifty-seven," Varo murmured behind her.

"I think we can stop counting," Ocella snapped. Varo closed his mouth with an audible click.

She leaned both palms on the closed door and took deep, calming breaths. It had started out as a game after the first few hatches—how many could they try before one actually opens. They shrugged off each one as they progressed through the twenties. By the thirties, she was biting her lip. By the forties, she grew angrier with each locked door. Now she simply wanted to walk back to their cell. At least there she could sleep away the time rather than grow increasingly frustrated with each passing moment.

Kaeso put a gentle hand on her shoulder. "I think we should go the other way."

"Why not?" she said. She turned away from the door—and Kaeso—and strode down the corridor back the way they came.

For the fifty-seventh time she wondered what sort of 'experiences' the Muse strain was seeking with this hallway and its locked doors. Did it want memories of anger and frustration to know their mental breaking point? If so, it was doing an admirable job. Ocella was ready to snap Varo's neck if he counted one more locked hatch.

It had taken them almost an hour to try fifty-seven hatches, but it only took Ocella twenty minutes to pass the previous fifty-six. It was twenty minutes of silent walking, for Kaeso and Varo were in the same frustrated mood, though they hid it better.

When she finally counted down to zero, she stopped. The opening to their cell should have been right in front of her. Instead, there was an empty bulkhead wall. She glanced up and down the corridor, but did not see the cell opening.

"Did I miscount?" she asked Kaeso and Varo, who stopped behind her.

"I counted fifty-seven," Kaeso said. Varo nodded slowly in agreement.

Ocella gave a long shaky sigh. *Control, Ancile, control....*

"This cannot be happening," Varo growled in a low voice. "This cannot be *happening*."

"Calm yourself," Kaeso said in an even tone. Ocella wanted to snap at him for being so calm in such an insane situation, but her Ancile training kept her tongue in check.

"Calm?" Varo said, his eyes wide. "We're standing in an infinite corridor, no doors open for us, and the one place in the entire *caccing* ship that seemed to stay the same is now gone." He strode up to Kaeso and screamed in his face. "Why should I be calm?"

Ocella grabbed Varo from behind and slammed him against the bulkhead wall where the opening to their cell should have been. In a cool, even voice, she said, "Because *they* don't want us to be calm. It's not much, but at least we can bore the bastards."

He stared at her in surprise. The swiftness of her attack seemed to have broken his panic. He blinked several times and breathed deeply. When his body finally relaxed, he nodded. "Sorry, Centuriae."

Ocella let him go, and Varo grinned sheepishly. "'Bore the bastards'? Some retaliation."

She shrugged and returned his grin. "It's something." And then she silently thanked the gods Varo had panicked before she did.

Kaeso examined the wall where their cell should have been. He ran his hands across the smooth, dark-gray metal. From Ocella's vantage, it looked as seamless as the walls up and down the corridor.

"It's warm," Kaeso said. "*Vacuna's* walls are always cold. Along with every bulkhead wall on every starship I've ever traveled on."

Ocella touched the wall. It was not blazing hot, but it seemed the same as her body temperature. She turned to the opposite wall and felt the metal. It too was warm.

"The floors are warm, too," Varo said. He had stooped to one knee and had both palms on the burnished metal floor. "Just like the walls."

"So?" Ocella asked.

Kaeso stared at the wall a few moments, then said, "Just thought it was interesting." He motioned to the right of their former-cell. "I suppose we go right?"

He proceeded down the corridor without waiting for her to follow. Kaeso could be remarkably closed at times. It was one reason why they broke up the first time twenty years ago, before he married her sister, Petra. He was much better over the last six years, but he'd still occasionally shut down on her.

Like now.

She strode after him and stopped with him before another hatch. He tried the lock pad, had no success, and then proceeded to the next hatch.

"You have an idea," she asked. "What is it?"

"The seed of an idea. The vaguest hint of an idea." He glanced at her. "And I don't want to give it away too soon since our friends may be listening."

"Can't you at least—"

A hatch opened far up the corridor. Ocella froze. She barely saw anything in the corridor's dim lights, but she caught shadows far ahead and reflections off either smooth armor or glistening skin. They chirped softly, and skittering sounds drifted toward them. Another hatch opened and closed, and the sounds stopped.

Ocella, Kaeso, and Varo stood motionless. Her heart felt as if it was leaping into her throat.

"I passed through a room before getting captured," she said. "It held hundreds of frozen aliens."

"Right," Varo whispered. "The alien zoo."

"I must've missed that one," Kaeso said dryly. "I guess the vessel unfroze some of them."

Ocella wiped her sweaty hands on her jumpsuit. "I say we go down there. They at least know how to open the doors."

"And if they're hostile?" Varo asked.

"I don't think they mean to attack us," Ocella said. "If they did, they would have done it. They might be trapped just like us. Maybe we can communicate with them and work together."

"Or they could be infected," Kaeso said. "Or—"

"The point is, we don't know," Ocella said, glaring at Kaeso. "Seems to me we have no choice, anyway."

Kaeso glanced at the wall where the opening to their cell should have been, and nodded. "So much for the boredom tactic."

Ocella looked at Varo. "Are you with us?"

He nodded, though he didn't seem pleased.

Ocella squinted in the dim light at the location where she saw the shadows and then proceeded down the corridor with Kaeso and Varo on either side. They didn't bother with the hatches they passed. She focused her sight on where the shadows had been, lest she lose track of where she saw them. If that happened, they'd have no idea which hatches the creatures used.

A vile smell grew stronger with each step, like ammonia combined with swamp decay. When they were within twenty paces of the location, Varo coughed, then pulled his jumpsuit neck over his nose and mouth. Ocella and Kaeso did the same.

When they arrived, she said, "This about where you saw them, too?"

Kaeso and Varo nodded, their eyes watering from the stench the creatures left behind.

Ocella studied the hatch, then glanced at the two men. They both watched her. Even Kaeso looked desperately hopeful.

She turned back to the hatch and tapped the lock pad.

The hatch slid open.

Ocella had a brief moment of triumph before the stench assaulted her with a force that drove her to her knees. She coughed and gagged, and she was vaguely aware of Kaeso and Varo doing the same.

"Close it!" Kaeso gasped.

Ocella, on all fours, lifted her head and focused her blurry vision on the lock pad. She raised her hand to hit the pad, but paused.

Hundreds, maybe thousands, of octopod-like creatures squirmed in the strange fluid-filled ovals she'd seen before. Some crawled out of the ovals, the viscous fluid still clinging to their bodies. Other octopods assisted the emerging ones, chirping softly while cleaning each newcomer with their tentacles. None seemed aware of her, or if they were, they didn't care.

Ocella slammed her hand on the lock pad, and the hatch clanged shut.

The stench still filled the corridor, but it was not as overwhelming as it had been moments earlier. She staggered further down the corridor with Kaeso and Varo. When they reached a point where they could breath without gagging, they stopped and sat against the bulkhead walls.

"Their births...," Varo said between coughs, "...stink."

Despite the continuing stench and the mucus flowing from her nose, Ocella started laughing. It was a frustrated laugh, a panicky laugh, one she knew contained no mirth at all. But she couldn't stop herself.

"Really?" she gasped between laughs.

Varo and Kaeso stared at her, and then they both began laughing as well.

Perhaps madness is contagious, she thought.

CHAPTER TWENTY-TWO

I t took three more days for the alien vessel to arrive at Illium Primus, the lone Terran-class world in the Illium system. During that time, Cordus checked and double-checked each phase of his plan, from the way line maneuvers to the eventual boarding. He discussed it with Aquilina, the Romans, and Dariya—sometimes with all of them together and sometimes with each one separately. He even discussed it with Marcus Antonius, though the Muse apparition seemed more interested in talking him out of it than offering suggestions.

Given the risks, Cordus was surprised nobody else tried talking him out of it.

Dariya had run *Vacuna's* engines to the breaking point trying to keep up with the alien vessel. Though they could not match its speed, they stayed close enough so that it only outpaced them at 0.25 T-gravity acceleration. Just as long as they could keep the vessel in their sensor range...

Cordus sat in the pilot's couch on the command deck of *Vacuna*, Aquilina in the command couch. The vessel would arrive at the Illium Primus way line to Libertus within five minutes. The Illium system defense forces had wisely stayed away from the vessel and had kept ship traffic away as well. Fortunately, the vessel had ignored them and the Illium way station.

Why should it go out of its way to kick an anthill?

Cordus tapped his collar com. "Five minutes until delta sleep," his voice echoed through the ship. "Get to your couches if you haven't already."

His delta display showed all but one crewman in their couches. Likely Ulpius, since the unoccupied couch was in the medical hatch next to Blaesus, who they had strapped in a few minutes ago.

"Ulpius, get to your—"

"Strapping in now, Centuriae," he growled through the com.

Cordus didn't ask what he'd been doing, but he did glance at Aquilina, who shrugged with a raised eyebrow. "Romans, eh, Centuriae?"

Cordus chose to ignore Aquilina and turned back to his tabulari to watch the alien vessel speed toward the way line above Illium Primus.

At its current speed, it would reach the way line in ten seconds. He had synched *Vacuna's* delta countdown with the precise moment the vessel stopped before the way line. In that moment, *Vacuna* would use its quantum way line drive to jump inside the vessel's shield. If it pleased the gods, *Vacuna* and the vessel would arrive at Libertus at the same time, but with *Vacuna inside* the vessel's shield. The timing would have to be perfect.

Cordus found himself wishing Nestor was behind him performing his pre-way line sacrifice of falcon livers. He blinked several times to keep his eyes free of tears.

A tone indicated twenty seconds to delta sleep and the quantum way line jump. He tapped his collar com and announced to the crew, "Engaging delta sleep."

He ran a finger along the slider that controlled delta sleep and then verified on this console that each couch held a sleeping occupant. Aquilina next to him settled back into her couch with closed eyes and slightly parted lips. He watched her a moment, then turned his attention to the delta countdown. When it reached three seconds, he engaged his own sleep...

...and then woke to see stars in the command deck window.

He frowned and then checked the ship's position. He stared in disbelief at the charts—they were in the Libertus system...but near the outer gas giants. The quantum way line engines had not dropped them within the vessel's shield, but billions of miles from Libertus Primus.

He tapped his collar com. "Dariya, what happened?"

"Checking now," she said over the com.

"We lost our window," Aquilina said grimly. "The vessel is surely through the way line by now."

"*Cac!*" Cordus swore. He tapped his com again. "Dariya, those engines!"

In an exasperated tone, she said, "The more you annoy me, the less time I have to figure out what happened."

Cordus ground his teeth, knowing she was right, but feeling powerless to do anything. *A good leader lets his people do their jobs,* Kaeso's voice echoed in his mind.

But how did you stay calm in these situations, old man?

Trying the doors had become an automatic action to Ocella, like breathing or blinking. She had lost count over how many doors they had tried since finding the aliens. She wasn't even sure how long they'd walked, but her rumbling stomach and dry mouth insisted it had been hours since her last meal and drink.

She glanced at Kaeso, wondering how he could continue on without complaint. Whenever he tried a door that didn't worked, he went on to the next, whereas Ocella wanted to scream and slam her fists against it. He had always been the cool one, while she had often let her passions get the better of her. She supposed it might be the reason why they had stayed together for six years—they brought opposite, yet necessary, ingredients to their relationship. They had often talked about marriage, but neither one seemed to have the courage to suggest a date. It was always "one of these days" or "when things settle down." But deep down, she knew "one of these days" would never arrive as long as they continued with the life they chose. And she knew Kaeso knew it as well.

Neither one of us wants to betray Petra. We both loved her too much. Gods, why must I realize these things when it's almost too late?

A hatch slid open behind her, confusing her. Was it a dream? She turned to see Varo standing before an open room. When she looked closer, she recognized it as their cell.

"Thank the gods!" Varo exclaimed, then rushed in and hurried to the latrine in the far corner of the cell.

Ocella and Kaeso walked in, but her relief evaporated when she saw the wall display. The outline of a Terran-class planet spread out below, its nightside alit with large cities sprinkled across its northern and southern continents.

Despair suddenly made Ocella want to weep.

"No," Kaeso whispered, staring at the wall display. His face was a jumble of emotions that she hadn't seen since he last visited his daughter six years ago.

They had arrived at Libertus.

"I'm getting transmissions from Umbra now," Aquilina said, her eyes glassy and unfocused in the command couch. She rubbed behind her right ear as if massaging away a headache. "They've engaged the vessel above Libertus."

"What's happening?" Cordus asked. He wished he could tune in the intra-system channels on his tabulari, but the transmissions traveled at the speed of light. Any normal com from Libertus Primus would take hours to arrive at their location. Aquilina's Muse implant was the only way they could monitor events in real-time.

Umbra ships were the most powerful starships humanity had ever produced, at least according to Kaeso and Ocella. While Roman ships were massive and packed a lot of firepower, Umbra ships were stealthy, speedy, and could hit any ship and then escape before the ship even knew it was there. While not the "planet killers" that a legion of Roman Eagles were, a swarm of Umbra ships could stop any attack.

At least, any *human* attack.

Cordus waited for Aquilina to respond, using all his self-control to keep from shaking her.

"It's not going well," she murmured.

"For who?" Cordus asked. *If Umbra destroys that vessel before Kaeso and Ocella can escape...*

Aquilina opened her eyes and glared at him. "Who do you think? Umbra is losing."

Cordus didn't know whether to be relieved or worried. Kaeso and Ocella would live, but three billion people lived on Libertus.

Dariya's voice came over his collar com. "Centuriae, please come to the engine room."

"Why?"

"Centuriae...please."

He glanced at Aquilina, but she was focused on the transmissions she was receiving from Umbra. He unbuckled himself from the pilot's couch and descended the ladder to the engine deck. A sick feeling spread through his core.

When he reached the engine room, Dariya was standing with her hands on the tabulari console. Daryush stood next to her, his hands in the pockets of his jumpsuit, his face twisted with worry.

"What happened?"

"The *cac*-spawned way line engines failed."

"But why?"

She turned around. "Apparently *I* did it."

"You're not making sense."

She pointed at the tabulari. "The quantum way line coordinates changed the second we engaged the delta sleep. It was an automated program, well-hidden...and it has my seal on it."

Cordus stared at the display. Sure enough, the logs showed Dariya's seal on the routines that disabled the delta system. "You didn't—! Did you?"

"Of course not!" she growled. "But somebody did, and they were good enough to use my seal. My seal! On my own *cac*-spawned ship!"

"What about the trap you set on the com system?"

She shook her head wearily. "Nothing."

Cordus was suddenly as angry as Dariya. The person doing this was not just a leak anymore, but an active saboteur. This person had prevented Cordus from getting Kaeso and Ocella back. He shook with impotent rage and wanted nothing more than to kill this saboteur with his bare hands. Whoever it was, it was someone he had rescued from Reantium, and they had repaid him by—

"You should have spaced them all," Marcus Antonius said from beside Cordus. "They could all be Liberti, for all you know, and you can't trust the Liberti."

Cordus ignored Marcus for the moment.

"Dariya, close all the hatches on the ship. I don't want the Romans free." He prayed they had not left their couches yet.

Dariya nodded grimly, then quickly tapped the tabulari. Hatches slammed shut across the ship at the same time, except for the one to the engine room. Daryush looked scared, but he drew the pulse pistol from the holster at his side and went to the open hatch to keep watch.

"Done," Dariya said. "What will we do with them?"

Cordus had his pistol out and strode to the hatch. "I don't know yet, but I don't want them wandering the ship until I have answers. You two stay here and seal the hatch behind me. I'm going to get Aquilina."

Cordus stepped through the hatch after ensuring the corridor was clear, then nodded to Daryush. The big Persian nodded back, then closed the hatch.

"Finally, you're going to finish the Liberti spy," Marcus said, leaning against the bulkhead with his arms folded.

I'm a little busy. Go away.

"Just offering our support, young Antonius," Marcus said. "One bit of advice, though: shoot her before she can talk. Otherwise your hormones will get the better of you."

Then Marcus winked out of existence.

Cordus kept his pistol in a firing position as he approached the ladder to the upper decks. He scanned the corridor to ensure both cargo hatches were shut, took a few deep breaths, and quickly pointed his pistol up the ladder.

Nobody was there, and no shots came down.

He used one sweaty hand to climb the ladder to the crew deck, while his pistol hand pointed above him, his heart thudding in his ears. Cordus leaped off the ladder onto the deck and scanned the corridor for threats. All the crew hatches were closed.

He whirled around. A closed storage hatch was on the left and the galley entrance on the right.

The galley hatch was open. All of the ship's hatches should have been closed. Was it a malfunction? Was somebody in there? He had to find out.

It took some effort to move his feet forward. He stepped down the corridor slowly—

"Easy, Centuriae," a male voice said calmly from behind him. Cordus froze and then felt the tip of a pulse rifle at the base of his neck. "Drop the pistol."

The storage hatch. Gods, my stupidity may have just killed me.

Cordus raised his hands, shifting the pistol in his hand so that he held it by the barrel. He bent down slowly and put it on the floor.

"What are you doing, Ulpius?" Cordus asked. He didn't have to turn around to know it was the centurion behind him.

"My duty."

"You can't fly this ship on your own."

"I know."

"Then how...?"

Cordus's voice trailed off as Aquilina and the other three Romans stepped out of the galley, their weapons pointed at Cordus. Their blank expressions told him they would kill him given the slightest provocation.

"We're taking you home," she said in a neutral tone. "*Sire.*"

Chapter Twenty-Three

Bursts of light flashed across the wall display as beams of intense blue energy destroyed the Liberti defenses surrounding the planet. Satellites, Liberti Defense Force warships, the rebuilt way station, ground-based missile batteries, and even cloaked Umbra ships were throwing everything they had at the alien vessel. Libertus had rearmed after the Roman siege six years ago, with more weapons than it ever had in its history. The fire it deployed now would have obliterated any human fleet.

Stuck in a cell on the alien vessel, Ocella didn't even feel a tremor from the Liberti assaults.

Kaeso sat on a gel bed staring at the wall display, his shoulders slumped. She sat next to him, holding his limp, dry hand. He had not said a word since they returned to the cell.

Varo stood against the back wall, his arms folded, staring grimly at the battle above Libertus.

The door to the cell opened behind them, and the Lucia-golem walked in. She regarded them with the emotionless face the aliens still could not fix.

"This world falls," the golem said. "Witness."

The wall display shifted and then focused on a swarm of what looked like tiny black wasps spilling from one of the openings across the vessel. The vast swarm of drones shot toward Libertus and then spread out so they evenly covered the entire planet. As the drones descended through the atmosphere, planetary defenses tried desperately to shoot them out of the sky. Liberti plasma cannons and missiles disintegrated drones by the dozens, but there were simply too many for the Defense Force to get them all.

"It only takes a few," the Lucia-golem said.

"What are they doing?" Ocella asked in a half-whisper, staring in horror at what was happening to her home.

"Some will take witnesses," the golem said. "Most will destroy life on the planet. The strain below must not survive."

Kaeso didn't make a sound when he leaped off the gel bed, nor when he grabbed the Lucia-golem's head and slammed it to the floor on its back. He continued slamming the golem's head against the floor until there was a sickening crack. Yellow golem blood spurted from its head and bubbled from its mouth. It offered no resistance and appeared to be dead. But Kaeso continued slamming the head against the floor as hard as he could with one hand, his mouth closed and teeth clenched. When the golem still didn't move, Kaeso began striking the golem's face with his fists, over and over, until its yellow blood mixed with his own on his cut knuckles.

And he kept hitting it.

Ocella rushed over to him. "Kaeso, enough!"

When he didn't stop, she grabbed his head with both hands and pried his face upward so he looked at her. He stopped beating the golem when their eyes met. His eyes shocked her for she expected to see rage and grief.

All she saw was the blank stare of a golem.

"Kaeso," she said gently.

After long seconds, he blinked. He seemed to notice her for the first time, and then looked down at the golem he had destroyed. He gave a shaky sigh and then stood. He stared at his knuckles for a time, each covered in yellow and red blood, and then wiped them on his jump suit.

"Kaeso?" Ocella asked.

He didn't reply. He turned around, went back to the gel bed, and sat down. He stared at the unfolding destruction of Libertus in the exact same position he'd been in before he attacked the golem.

Varo came over to Ocella, staring at the golem. "I've been wanting to do that since I first saw it."

"It doesn't help," she muttered. "The vessel will just make another one."

Varo nodded at Kaeso. "You think he'll be all right?"

She was silent several moments. "Did you know his daughter, Claudia, still lives down there?"

Varo shook his head. "I didn't know he had a daughter."

"She thinks he's dead. When he joined Umbra, he had to 'die' to everyone he ever knew, including his family."

"I've never understood why anyone would do that."

Ocella shrugged. "It's not so bad if you have no one in your life. Like I did when I joined."

"But *he* had a family," Varo said quietly.

"He joined after his wife was killed by a Liberti criminal syndicate she was prosecuting. And he got the justice he wanted. Through Umbra, he tracked down and killed every member of the syndicate within months of becoming an Ancile."

"So he abandoned his daughter for vengeance?"

Ocella looked at Varo. "Yes, and the guilt has consumed him piece by piece for almost twenty years. It's rare for him to feel anything or show feelings to others now. But he's no golem. The emotions are still there, just locked away...mostly."

Ocella stared at the ruined Lucia-golem on the floor. Its head was an unrecognizable mash of yellow fluid and biological circuitry. Would the vessel be angry with them over its dead golem? The known Muses had 'personalities' of a sort. Would the vessel seek to punish them for this?

Did it matter?

"Centuriae," Varo breathed, staring at the display.

Ocella looked up, already too numb to feel any sadness or anger. What she saw only increased the numbness.

Slowly, but inexorably, the green portions on the planet's continents turned from green to gray. The change happened first as pinpoints, but then spread out from each point. Whatever toxin the drones had released into the air was killing the planet at what she thought would have been an impossible rate.

She watched the bright engine trails of ships fleeing the planet's surface. Some escaped into space; most were attacked by drones that latched on to the ships. The drones then flew back to the alien vessel after several minutes, leaving the ships floating dead in space.

Ocella turned back to Libertus. During the minutes she had watched the fleeing ships, most of the planet's surface had turned ash-gray. Even the bright blue of the oceans seemed to dull to a bluish-black color. Libertus had mining colonies beneath the oceans. No doubt life beneath the waves would eventually suffer the same fate as that on land.

All Ocella could do was sit down next to Kaeso, hold his yellow and red-bloodied hand, and weep.

Chapter Twenty-Four

Cordus sat on a crate in Cargo One as Piso and Duran pushed Dariya and Daryush into the hold. Dariya glared at the two Romans, but they had already sealed the hatch before her glare caught them. Daryush looked more annoyed than fearful. Cordus couldn't decide if that was good or bad.

"I'm sorry, you two."

"Stop right there," Dariya said, turning her glare on him. "Whining is the last thing I want to hear from you. I want to hear a centuriae with a plan, not a guilt-ridden child."

Cordus stared at her a moment, then broke into laughter. It had been a long time since he'd laughed, and it felt good. It did not make him any less angry or frustrated, but it did seem to clear his mind.

Dariya watched him with narrow eyes until he brought his laughter under control.

"Fine," he said. "Would you feel better if I said this was all part of my plan?"

"No, because I know you would be lying."

The Cargo One hatch opened again. Duran and Piso entered with their pulse rifles aimed at the three of them. Ulpius and Gracchus came behind, each holding one of Blaesus's arms. The old Senator looked frail and tired, but his eyes were clear and he had a firm set to his jaw. A blanket was draped over his naked shoulders, and a faint bloodstain showed on the white bandages around his mid-section. Ulpius and Gracchus let Blaesus down gently onto a cot in one corner of the hold.

Gracchus, the Roman closest to Cordus's age, refused to meet his eyes as he took up a position near the Cargo One door. Ulpius ignored Cordus, but said to Blaesus, "There you go, old man. Best we could do on such short notice."

Blaesus turned away from Ulpius with a scowl.

"You probably don't remember me," Ulpius said. "My father worked on your Tribune campaigns before you became a Senator. I was just a kid then, but he brought me to your offices. You paid me five sesterces for every bundle of pamphlets I passed out, even though the going rate was two."

Blaesus continued staring at a corner of the hold and didn't say anything.

Ulpius frowned. "Don't like doing this is all I'm trying to say." He then turned back to the Cargo One hatch.

"I remember Vitus Ulpius quite well," Blaesus said with a scratchy voice, still staring at the corner. "Tireless campaigner. Brought many votes to my slate that I never would have gathered on my own. Loyal man." Blaesus turned his eyes to Ulpius. "Too bad those qualities were never learned by his son."

Ulpius whirled around. "I am loyal to the Republic, old man! Unlike you, who sold yourself to these Liberti mercenaries. Do you believe in anything anymore?"

Cordus stood. Piso and Duran held their pulse rifles higher, the barrels pointed at Cordus's head.

"Easy, sir," Duran said quietly. "Don't want to shoot you, but I will if you get foolish."

"I believe in loyalty to my crew," Blaesus said, ignoring Cordus and the others. "The young Centuriae over there saved your miserable lives on Reantium, and this is how you repay him?" Blaesus started coughing. When he gained control again, he gasped, "Nothing more to say to you."

Ulpius shook his head and then strode out of the hold, followed by the three legionaries. When they left, Cordus saw Aquilina standing in the hatchway.

"Come with me, Centuriae," she said. "We need to chat."

"I'm not leaving my crew," Cordus said.

She sighed. "Come with me now or I shoot one of your friends." To emphasize the point, she drew her pulse pistol and held it at her side.

Cordus looked from Blaesus to Daryush to Dariya. They all wore defiant expressions. He felt both proud and humbled that people he respected so much would have so much faith and loyalty in him. He loved them all and would do anything to protect them.

Even ignore his pride and follow Aquilina's orders.

He strode toward the hatch. Aquilina stepped back to let him exit, but she kept her pulse pistol at the ready. The Romans in the corridor behind her also maintained their aim on Cordus.

He stopped in front of her. "Where should we *chat?*"

"Galley," she said, and then motioned him forward with her pistol. Cordus climbed the ladder up to the second deck, the Romans following him.

When he reached the galley, he sat down at the small table facing the door. Aquilina handed her pulse pistol to Ulpius and then entered the galley. She shut the hatch so that only the two of them remained.

"So let's *chat*," Cordus snapped.

Aquilina folded her arms. "Aren't you the least bit curious as to who I am and what I'm doing?"

"Sure. You destroyed the one chance I had at rescuing the two people I love most. So yes, I'm a bit curious."

"I understand your frustration, Marcus Antonius—"

"My name is Titus."

"You are Marcus Antonius Cordus, the Consular Heir to the Roman Republic."

"I never claimed such a thing."

"Your crew thinks you're Cordus, as confirmed by your ship's tabulari. And your former Centuriae was Kaeso Aemilius, the same man held at the Praetorian South Pole Detention Center six years ago. Who was chased to Menota by Quintus Atius Lepidus, a respected Praetorian veteran. We don't know what changed Lepidus on Menota, but we all know what he did when he returned to Roma." She raised her eyebrows questioningly. "Any of this knocking loose a memory?"

Cordus leaned forward. "And just who are *you*, Aquilina? Some traitorous Umbra Ancile who sold herself to the Romans? How did you keep your little side project from Umbra? I've heard they deal harshly and swiftly with traitors."

Aquilina smiled, creating a small dimple in her cheek. "I'm not an Ancile. I'm Praetorian."

"You have an implant—"

"I do. But never discount Roman ingenuity."

And then it hit Cordus. *Ocella's betrayal...*

When Ocella had helped Cordus leave Roma, she had to protect him from not only the Romans, but Umbra, who wanted him dead for the same reasons the Romans wanted to keep him—because he could control the Muses infecting him. She had infiltrated the Praetorian Guard to assassinate Cordus, but was convinced not to do it by a Saturnist Praetorian she respected. To protect Cordus from Umbra, she betrayed her oaths and her fellow Ancilia by giving the Praetorians the names of all the Ancilia in Roma. It was a coup that earned her the appreciation of Cordus's father...and her choice of Praetorian assignments. She chose Cordus's security detail, which enabled her to smuggle Cordus out of Roma.

Her betrayal had cost Umbra not only the lives of its Ancilia, but apparently the implant tech in their brains. Implants were no bigger than the tip of a fingernail and were supposed to dissolve upon the deaths of their hosts. The Praetorians must have salvaged some of the tech to create their own implant network.

And Aquilina was one of them.

"Yes," she said, seeing his understanding dawn. "Ocella's betrayal was quite the boon to the Praetorian Guard. While we don't have the experience of our Umbra adversaries, we now have the same tech. It's only a matter of time and practice before we achieve field parity as well."

"All this time when you said you were in contact with Umbra—"

"Lying."

"And the others? All that tension between them and you?"

"My team is well trained in the dramatic arts. Helps with deep cover assignments like this one. It made you trust them a bit more, eh?"

Cordus didn't say anything. He was too angry and humiliated to come up with something intelligent.

"But somehow you can communicate with my implant," Aquilina said in a thoughtful voice. "So either you have one, or..."

"I don't know what you're talking about. I'm a Liberti merchant who just wants to rescue his friends and go home. Just tell me what you want so I can spit in your face."

She stood straight. "Come with me," she ordered, then opened the galley hatch. The Romans outside the hatch aimed their weapons at Cordus. He followed Aquilina to the deck ladder, which she climbed toward the command deck.

On the command deck, Aquilina motioned to the command couch. "Sit. Don't worry, I've disabled all the controls in case temptation gets the better of you."

A weapon prodded his back, so he sat in the command couch. Aquilina sat in the pilot's couch and tapped the controls on her tabulari.

"These images came in through the long-range scopes ten minutes ago," she said, nodding to his tabulari.

The display showed a long-range image of Libertus. The entire, sun-lit half filled his screen. It did not have the fine detail of a short-range scope, but Cordus could make out the continents and cloud patterns—

Slowly, almost imperceptibly, thousands of dark-gray dots formed on the continents. They seemed more pronounced in the green regions. The dots expanded until they became circles of gray. The circles expanded until they met each other, covering all the continents in a gray color that could only signal death.

"The vessel released a toxin into the planet's atmosphere," Aquilina reported. "From what we can tell, it took less than ten hours to destroy all life on the surface of Libertus."

Cordus could imagine the horror of it as vividly as if he were experiencing it first hand. Most of the three billion people on Libertus were so surprised by the suddenness of the toxin that they died where they stood. Some heard of the toxin via com networks before it reached them and chose to spend their final moments huddled together in the arms of their loved ones. Crying parents held frightened children in the cellars of their homes; elderly spouses grasped hands while sitting outside watching the sky; complete strangers huddled in bomb shelters listening in horror to announcers on the emergency com channels scream and then die, one by one.

"Libertus is dead," Aquilina said quietly.

Cordus stared at the expanding gray, his body cold. He swallowed, and then whispered, "The vessel?"

"Com from the survivors say it left through the alpha way line above Libertus."

All those people...the symbol of freedom...gone within hours. The vessel had taken on the strongest fleet of warships humanity had ever produced and swatted it away like flies. Now it was gone and could be anywhere in human space now. The Libertus way line went to Radiatus, which had multiple way lines to other Lost Worlds and Roman space.

"You can't save Libertus," Aquilina said, "but you can save other worlds."

"By doing what?" Cordus asked, still staring at the dead world on his tabulari.

"Give us the codes to your quantum way line engines. I can reprogram the coordinates, but I can't engage the engines without the centuriae codes. We're stuck here unless I can do that. We can go to Terra and gather a force that can—"

"Wait," Cordus said. "Wait, wait, wait. Why are you asking this now? Why not days ago when we *could* have gathered that force to fight for Libertus?"

Her gaze was locked on a point over his shoulder.

"Because you *wanted* Libertus to die," Cordus whispered. "Gods..."

"I was under orders," Aquilina said, but she didn't sound convinced. "My loyalty is to the Republic. I wouldn't expect you to understand that."

Cordus shook his head. "It's as if the Muses still control you. Nothing has changed. Roma is still infected with monsters."

Aquilina's eyes blazed. "You have no idea what it's been like in Roma and Terra for the last six years. It's been a non-stop series of vile warlords trying to create their own dynasties. They come to power and then use the Praetorian Guard to kill off their rivals. Even the Praetorian Guard has had its own civil war. But two years ago a strong leader came to power and ended all that. She has brought order to Roma and Terra. I am fighting to keep the monsters out of the Republic."

"Vibia Servilia Gemmella," Cordus scoffed. "She's strong because her enemies killed each other off."

"Regardless, Roma has a strong leader that can bring peace to the Republic. But Libertus never wanted a Roma at peace. The more Romans fought each other, the more Libertus profited. From weapons to food, Libertus filled the markets vacated by Roma. *Umbra* wanted *Roma* to die. This alien vessel was just the gods-granted opportunity Roma had been waiting for to protect itself from Umbra and Liberti plots."

"Libertus never wanted Roma to die! Umbra was the only weapon Libertus had to defend itself against Roma. It was the only thing that kept Libertus free for two hundred years, or it would've fallen long ago. Libertus had every reason to fear Roma, not the other way around."

"How do you know?"

"Because my—!"

Cordus was so angry and grief-stricken at the moment that he couldn't concentrate on holding his tongue around Aquilina. *Because my Muses told me.* He stopped himself, but realized from Aquilina's face that it was too late.

"Which brings us to the second problem with which I need your help," Aquilina said quietly. "You *are* Marcus Antonius Cordus, the last of the Antonii. And your people need you now."

Marcus Antonius Primus appeared between Cordus and Aquilina. "Finally, a worshipper. Give us the word, and she will be groveling at your feet."

I swore I'd never do that again.

Marcus sighed. "Then get used to life in the cargo hold." He stepped back and sat in the delta couch behind Cordus.

"Why do you think I'm—?"

"Please, just stop denying it," Aquilina said. She exhaled an exasperated sigh and then stared at him. "Do you know what I've been doing the last year? Tracking down Antonii pretenders. They pop up every now and then like weeds, claiming to be you. They try to raise a legion or gain the support of a warlord. Some get so far as to become a threat." Her voice turned hard. "It's been my job to track them down and eliminate them *before* they become a threat."

Cordus snorted. "Gemmella doesn't want any competition, eh?"

"It's not like that. She wants to eliminate pretenders, yes. But she's also searching for *you*. She believes in the rumors that you still live, and she thinks you can unite the Republic if you return. So my mission has been two-fold: Kill the pretenders, but bring you back if I find you."

"You trust Gemmella's word? That she would give up power to the last Antonius? She only says that because it makes her sound like a reluctant ruler and a patriot. She's just another dictator who wants to cement her status in the hearts of the people."

Aquilina shook her head. "She's different."

"How can you be so—?"

"She's my mother."

Cordus paused, his mouth half open, then said, "Mothers have been known to lie to their children."

"Not in this case. I've watched her obsession with you over the last six years. She's a believer."

"Well it doesn't matter. What makes you think I'm not just another pretender?"

Aquilina's voice blasted in his mind. "BECAUSE PRETENDERS CAN'T HEAR THIS."

Cordus flinched at not only the power behind the voice but at how it felt like a hot dagger in the base of his skull. Aquilina watched him with a materializing smirk.

Behind him, Antonius grunted. "Gods, the girl has a set of lungs on her."

Aquilina leaned forward. "If you should return, the civil war would end almost instantly. Every major player, from my mother down to the petty warlords, claim they are the true inheritors of the Antonii. So if the last Antonius should appear and claim the consulship, after every one has paid your family such homage, then they'd all bend their knees to you whether they want to or not. My mother certainly would."

Cordus abruptly stood up from the command couch. Piso and Duran stepped forward, their pistols aimed at his head, but Cordus ignored them. He stared down at Aquilina. She had not flinched when he stood, but the muscles in her face had tightened, and she was still.

Through clenched teeth, Cordus said, "I'm *not* going to help you." He turned to Piso, who continued to aim a pistol at him. "Take me back to Cargo One."

"I'll kill your friends if you don't help," Aquilina said from behind him.

Cordus turned and studied her. She continued to stare at the empty command couch.

"Will you?"

"I just let three billion people die," she said quietly.

Cordus stared at her for a long time. *Marcus, can you get into her implant? Can you tell if she's lying?*

Antonius turned and studied Aquilina. "Hmm. Her thoughts are not integrated with her implant, so we cannot see any specific deception. But we do hear conflict outside the implant. For what it's worth, young Antonius, she's struggling with something, but she is determined to follow a course of action."

Cordus learned all this in an instant, and it took only another instant to come up with a plan. "Release my crew. Swear they will not be harmed...and I will give you the centuriae codes. And then we will get Kaeso and Ocella. And then you can do with me whatever you want." He leaned forward and said, "But I am Titus Aemilius Cordus. I am *not* the last Antonius."

"Well," she said. "This is progress. You have a bargain, Centuriae."

Marcus grunted. "Show us what you're planning, young Antonius."

When Cordus did, Marcus smiled.

Chapter Twenty-Five

O cella lay on the gel bed staring at the opening to the endless corridor. No sound came from the corridor. No sound came from anything in the room besides Kaeso's breathing beside her and the occasional stomach growls from them all. The opening had not closed since the Lucia-golem entered.

Its body still lay on the floor where Kaeso had beaten it to death hours ago.

Had it been hours? Days, weeks, months? She had no idea, and she was at the point where she didn't care.

Apathy was dangerous and led to defeat, yet how could she not feel defeated right now? Libertus was dead, Kaeso was as non-responsive as a way liner who had stayed conscious during a jump, and she was stuck inside an alien prison with a corridor outside that went to infinity in both directions. She knew the corridor simply went in a circle around the vast ship, but even that logical explanation held no reassurance.

Right now, she felt like they were going to die of old age in this room.

Even Varo lay on the gel bed next to her, staring up at the ceiling with glazed eyes. He had not spoken in... She couldn't remember.

Hours, days, weeks, months?

She couldn't even feel a hum or vibration from the ship's engines. They could be deep beneath the surface of a rocky planet for all she knew. The wall display above showed unchanging stars. The blue lights in the room and the corridor never changed.

But it was the complete silence that attacked her sanity.

She looked down at the remains of the Lucia golem. Its face and head were a pulpy mash of yellow fluids and biological circuitry similar to the innards of human-made golems. Was this more tech that came from the Muses?

Had humans ever made *anything* on their own?

Her growling stomach broke the silence, and she giggled. She glanced at Kaeso and Varo. Neither one looked at her.

"Come on, gentlemen," she said, her voice sounding shrill even to her ears. "Let's play a game. Let's see whose stomach can growl the loudest. I just went first. Who's next?"

Varo rolled onto his side, his back to her. "No thanks," he murmured.

Kaeso only stared at the display.

"Fine, how about a flatulence contest?" When neither man responded, she said, "Belching?"

She shook her head. "I'm stuck in a room with the only two human males not interested in flatulence or belching. Are you men or what?"

Without turning around, Varo growled, "How about you shut your mouth?"

"Excuse me, pilot?" Ocella said slowly. "Watch how you address your centuriae."

Varo sat up and faced her. "Sorry, *Centuriae*. How about you shut your mouth, *Centuriae, sir, madam, my Lady*? Is that better?"

Ocella stood. "Calm down, Varo. You're losing your grip."

He laughed. "You're the one suggesting fart competitions, *Centuriae*. Who's losing her grip, *Centuriae*?"

She knew Varo was right. Her juvenile suggestions proved it. And picking a fight with Varo wouldn't help their situation. But she just wanted to feel something other than apathy.

Ocella strode to Varo, who stood up from his gel bed with his fists balled at his sides. She stood before him, nose-to-nose, and growled, "Stand down, pilot."

"Eat my *cac*, Centuriae."

She brought her knee up in a shot that should have connected with his groin. But he was ready for it and averted his body at the last second. Instead, her knee plunged into his abdomen. The air exploded from his lungs and he doubled over. It was not quite the location she had planned, but it would do.

"I said, stand down—"

Varo rammed his shoulder into her midsection. Both flew into the side of the gel bed on which Kaeso sat. Varo tried straddling her, but she kicked away from him before he could set himself. She tried to stand. His foot shot toward her legs. She jumped over his foot and then brought her elbow down on his face as he tried to tackle her again.

His nose crunched beneath her elbow. Varo howled as blood spurted from his nose. He fell onto his back. Ocella straddled him, then landed blow after blow on his forearms, which covered his face. She knew she was hurting him, but she couldn't stop.

Hard, muscular arms looped through her arms and pulled her back-wards. She screamed in protest, but Kaeso's voice was deep and calm in her ear. "Enough," he said.

His voice broke the spell she'd been under, and she slumped to the ground. She stared at the blood flowing from between Varo's hands. He was shaking and sobbing.

"We're going to die here," he said between sobs. "We're never getting out…"

Ocella pulled on the left sleeve of her jump suit near the seams. It ripped a little, so she pulled harder. Kaeso saw what she was doing and helped her pull the sleeve apart. It came loose with a loud tearing sound. She gathered the sleeve in a bunch and crawled over to Varo.

"I'm sorry, Varo," she said, trying to pull his hands from his face. He let her do so. Blood and mucus flowed from his crooked nose, and he stared up at her through tear-filled eyes.

"We're going to die here," he repeated. "We're going to die here…"

Ocella put the bunched up sleeve on Varo's nose. "Sit up, Varo. You don't want to choke on your blood."

He meekly did as he was told, and leaned is back against his gel bed. "Better to end it now than wait forever."

"Stop it," Ocella said. She held the sleeve firmly against Varo's nose. "We can't think like that. Not ever. No matter how long they keep us here, we cannot think like that."

If I could only follow my own orders…

Varo didn't say anything. He leaned against the gel bed and took the sleeve from her hands. "I can take care of my own nose."

Ocella nodded and then sat back. She brought her knees up and wrapped her arms around them. Kaeso was staring at her.

"Welcome back," she said.

He averted his eyes. "Sorry. I don't know what happened."

"You watched your home world die."

"You did, too. You didn't lose your mind."

She glanced at Varo. "Didn't I?"

"Your hands are bleeding."

She noticed her swollen and bleeding knuckles for the first time. They suddenly felt on fire, as if they'd been waiting for her to see them before producing pain. She tried flexing them, but they only hurt worse.

A loud, metallic clang echoed from the corridor outside the room. Ocella jerked her head around to the opening. Faint footsteps came from down the hall. She scrambled to her feet. Even Varo stood on his own after some struggle. She was heartened to see the self-pity had fled from his eyes, replaced with a hardness that his bloody face made even more menacing. Kaeso stared at the opening, his body in a defensive stance.

Ocella took on the same posture as Kaeso and Varo. They were not defeated yet.

The footsteps came closer and then stopped just outside.

A face peeked around the corner. It was human, a young woman with dark hair and—

Kaeso gasped. "Claudia!"

Chapter Twenty-Six

Claudia stepped from around the corner, her eyes wide. "Father?"

She issued a quick sob, then ran into the room and wrapped her arms around Kaeso. Kaeso stood wide-eyed, his arms at his sides.

"They just took me. Oh gods, I don't know where my son and husband are..." Her words turned into unintelligible sobs.

Ocella stared transfixed at Kaeso's daughter. *How did they find her?*

And how did she know Kaeso was her father? Umbra had surgically modified his face when he joined to make him unrecognizable to anyone who might have known him. Kaeso had briefly visited her six years ago, but he had done so under the guise of an old soldier friend of her father's.

She shouldn't be able to recognize him.

Cold dread swept through Ocella as she studied Claudia grasping Kaeso like a scared child. Ocella glanced at the Lucia-golem on the floor and then back to Claudia. It had not taken the aliens long to perfect the Lucia-golem...

Kaeso seemed to realize the same thing. His wide eyes slowly turned to Ocella. She had no idea what to say to him. Leaving Claudia was a wound that had never healed for him, and Ocella could only imagine how painful it must be to see her again like this.

Kaeso slowly grabbed Claudia's arms and pried loose her embrace. He held her at arm's length, his face muscles twitching. She stared up at him through confused, tearful eyes.

If Claudia was a golem, she was the most perfect golem ever made. The emotions, the tears, even the eyes. They were all indistinguishably human.

"What?" she asked.

Kaeso seemed incapable of speaking, so Ocella gently pulled Claudia away from him. He let his hands drop to his sides once she was out of reach and continued staring at the spot where she had stood.

"Claudia," Ocella said, "how did you get here?"

Claudia continued staring at Kaeso as she said, "I was home. Alone. Abram took Pullus to the market to buy dinner. I was in my studio listening to some recordings I made yesterday. Then the emergency sirens started up outside. I thought it was another drill. We've had a lot since the Roman siege, but they're always scheduled. This was a surprise. I went to the window and saw…" She sucked in a quick breath, and her chin began to quiver. "I saw a black object hovering just above the ground in front of the house. Then these *things* jumped out—"

Claudia started crying again, so Ocella hugged her. Golems produced internal heat that was far warmer than a normal human. But Claudia felt the same as a real human.

"And then I was standing in front of this room," she said when her sobs eased. "I don't remember how I got here. Have you seen Abram and Pullus?"

"I'm sorry, we haven't," Ocella said. She studied Claudia's eyes. Brown, just like Petra's. Tears streamed from them, but they were nothing like the inhuman eyes the Lucia-golem had. *Was* this Claudia? Was this really Kaeso's daughter and Ocella's niece?

"Claudia, how do you know this is your father?"

Claudia looked at Kaeso, who continued standing where he was, his arms at his side and his gaze on the floor.

"He came to me six years ago," she said. "Said he was a friend of my father's. But I knew it was him from his eyes."

"How?" Ocella asked.

"My son, Pullus, has the same eyes."

"No!" Kaeso suddenly screamed. He turned to Claudia and pointed at her. "You are not real! They made you! They gave you Claudia's memories and then threw you in here for whatever sick experiments they're doing on us. *YOU ARE NOT REAL!*"

Claudia flinched backward as if Kaeso had struck her. But she recovered quickly, her pain turning to anger.

"So that's it," she snarled. "You've abandoned me before, so why not now? I spent the last six years searching for you, thinking you had good reasons for leaving me. Turns out you just never wanted me. You were a waste of time. Pathetic."

Ocella watched Kaeso, wondering if he would do to Claudia what he did to the Lucia-golem. She didn't know if she could stop him, but she would if he tried. The Claudia standing before them could be a real person, or it could be a golem. They didn't know.

But Kaeso's rage dissipated as quickly as it had struck. He laughed, but the mirth did not reach his eyes. He started clapping at the ceiling and yelled, "So you can make a better golem than we can. Well done!"

Claudia stared at him for several moments and then asked Ocella, "What's wrong with him?"

Ocella pulled Claudia to one side of the room as Kaeso continued clapping. Varo glanced at Ocella and nodded at her unspoken order to watch Kaeso. Varo would not likely stop Kaeso from attacking, considering the wounds she had just inflicted on him, but he could sound a warning while Ocella talked to Claudia.

"There's more going on here than you know," Ocella said. "There's more to *him*, than you can imagine."

"What's to imagine?" she said bitterly. "He pretended he was dead. It killed my grandparents. They both died within a year after he disappeared. He's a selfish bastard. And apparently insane."

"Perhaps we all are right now. But you need to know why he thinks you're not real."

Ocella quickly told Claudia how the vessel had used Lucia to create a golem that it then sent to them. Claudia stared in shock at the golem body on the floor, as if seeing it for the first time.

"He thinks I'm a golem?" she said. "I'm *not* a golem."

Ocella tried to soften her words. "But we don't know that."

Claudia threw up her hands. "Well I don't know how to convince you then. I remember everything about my life, at least as much as any normal person can. Golems don't have personalities."

"Not golems created by humans. That one on the floor came to us in different iterations, and each one was better than the last. Perhaps they perfected their techniques with you."

Claudia's lips started quivering again. "I am Claudia Abiff. My husband is Abram and my son is Pullus. I know who I am. I am not a golem."

Ocella glanced at the remains of the Lucia golem, then back to Claudia. "That golem also had Lucia's memories."

Claudia had been on the verge of sobbing, but anger seemed to win out again. Her emotional swings were much like Kaeso's used to be.

"In the last few minutes," Claudia said through gritted teeth, "I've been kidnapped by aliens and imprisoned on their starship *with my dead father*. That's enough to drive the sanity out of any person. Now you want me to believe that I'm not really me, that I'm a golem with the memories of—" She turned to Ocella. "How do you know *you're* not a golem?" She raised her voice. "How do *any* of you?"

Ocella didn't know what to say. How could she prove she wasn't a golem?

She looked at Varo, his face still covered in dark red blood. At least his nose seemed to have stopped bleeding.

Ocella bit her lip. She looked from the yellow fluid of the Lucia-golem on the floor to Varo's red blood.

"There is one way to tell," she said. She explained her idea to Claudia, who flinched.

Claudia swallowed once and then asked, "Do you have a knife?"

"No," Ocella said. She looked at Claudia's fingernails. They were well manicured, painted purple, and longer than Ocella's short nails, which were trimmed to the skin. "You have beautiful nails."

Claudia looked at them and sighed. "I've nicked myself with them before. They're certainly sharp enough."

Ocella nodded. "I'll go first."

She held out her forearm, and Claudia asked, "Where do you want me to...um, do it?"

"Anywhere but an artery." Ocella grinned, trying to put Claudia at ease, but the Liberti woman only looked pale.

I don't know if she's a "Liberti woman" yet.

Claudia took hold of Ocella's forearm, then dragged the nail of her index finger over an inch-long stretch on the top. The nail barely broke the top layer of skin.

"Not deep enough," Ocella said.

Claudia winced, then dug deeper.

A line of red drops welled up from the scratch. Claudia and Ocella looked at each other, and Claudia said, "Congratulations."

They went to Kaeso, who by now had sat on the gel bed with his shoulders slumped. Ocella was about to explain her idea to him, but he simply held his forearm out to Claudia without looking at her. She grabbed his forearm with more force than she had with Ocella. Her cut went longer and deeper than Ocella's and had no trouble drawing bright red blood.

Claudia looked at Ocella. "My turn."

Without hesitating, Claudia drew her nail across her own forearm. It took many agonizing seconds for the bright yellow drops to well up along the cut. It was more viscous than human blood, for it did not drip down Claudia's arm like the cuts she'd made on Ocella and Kaeso.

Claudia stared at her arm with a blank expression. Her mouth opened and closed. "I can't— How—?"

Her legs gave out, and she fell backwards onto the floor before Ocella could catch her. She stared at her forearm and tried to push herself along the floor with her feet, as if she could get away from her own arm.

"This is a dream. I'm going to wake up any second now. Any second now..." When her back met the wall on the other side of the room, she stopped pushing and stared at her arm.

Behind Ocella, Kaeso wept quietly.

Varo approached Ocella. "Gods, every time I think this can't get worse..."

"I'm sorry I lost control earlier."

"I lost it, too, Centuriae. At least you woke me up." He grinned. Though it made his bloody face more hideous, Ocella felt better knowing that Varo wasn't gone like Kaeso and Claudia.

Claudia. It wasn't Claudia sitting in the corner. It was a golem, a biological machine constructed from the remains of the real Claudia, which the aliens had destroyed to assemble this one.

She could barely contain her rage at the aliens. They killed her niece! Ocella had not seen Claudia since she was a child, just before Ocella had 'died' to join Umbra. She remembered a precocious, talented, and beautiful little girl. She had followed Claudia's singing career from afar and felt nothing but happiness that Claudia's life had taken such a wonderful track.

It wasn't fair that this woman had to die just because these gods-damned aliens wanted to experiment on Kaeso and Ocella. To create "witnesses".

She had so many questions. How could they create this golem and make it so much like the original human? How did they even find her on a planet of three billion? Why did they create her in the first place and put her here?

But all those questions were irrelevant. The golem was here. They were here. The only question was what were they going to do? Were they going to sit around on the gel beds until they lost their minds?

Ocella glanced at the opening. It had not closed since they returned from their walk. Did the aliens want them to leave? Maybe so, and she was loath to do anything the aliens wanted. But sitting in this prison cell was slowly driving them all mad. If they left again, at least they would be moving. At least they would be doing something.

And if they were doing something, they might find a way to truly resist the aliens.

"We have to leave this room," Ocella finally said.

Varo objected, "We tried that—"

"Then we try it again. It's either that or we end up killing each other in here."

He thought about it and then sighed. "Maybe we'll find some ice for my nose." His voice had taken on a nasal quality, and Ocella gave him a sympathetic smile.

He nodded to Kaeso and Claudia. "What about them?"

Kaeso had his head in his hands, and Claudia continued staring at the yellow golem blood on her arm. Ocella went to Kaeso, sat down next to him, and put an arm around his lower back.

"Are you up for another walk?" she asked.

He sat up straight and blinked the tears from his eyes. "Yes," he said, then stood up and strode to the opening.

Claudia looked up at him as he passed her. "Father?"

Kaeso ignored her and left the room.

The sadness and rejection on her face broke Ocella's heart. She was a golem...but from her perspective, she *was* Claudia Abiff. Ocella couldn't imagine the horror and shock this golem must be feeling right now. It was still hard for Ocella to even imagine a golem could feel such things.

What would I have done if my scratch had oozed yellow?

Ocella stooped down next to Claudia. "Come with us."

Claudia gave her a hopeless expression. "Why?"

"No matter what you are now," Ocella said, "there's still a bit of Claudia in you. Her memories are all there in your mind. We'll be walking a long time, so I'd like to get to know you better."

"Why would you care about me? You don't know me. Or her." She issued a shaky sigh.

Ocella opened her mouth, but then hesitated. Why was she so nervous about revealing her old name? *It's just a golem, it's not the real Claudia.* It was partly due to her Umbra conditioning to never reveal her old identity to the people she once knew. It was also her shame at abandoning Claudia as well. She and Claudia had never been particularly close, only seeing each other on holidays and the occasional visits. When they did see each other, they shared many laughs and played many games. Ocella liked to think she had been the "favorite aunt".

So it may not have crushed Claudia when Ocella's old self "died", but considering little Claudia had just lost both parents within the span of two years, it could not have been easy.

But if the real Claudia was dead, this was the closest thing to that woman left in the universe. *Maybe I can find out what kind of woman my little niece has become.*

Ocella held her hand out to Claudia, and she took it. Ocella helped her up.

"Let's talk," Ocella said, then guided Claudia out of the room.

Chapter Twenty-Seven

Cordus strapped himself into the command couch and looked with annoyance at his tabulari. Its displays were dimmed, which meant he was locked out of all the ship's controls. He glared at Aquilina in the pilot's couch, and she gave him a sweet smile.

"I appreciate your help," she said, "but I still don't trust you. I will be running the delta systems on this trip."

"You and your people watched Dariya, Daryush, and me the whole time we ran the delta diagnostics and quantum way line calibrations. You saw us enter the coordinates for Terra. What's the problem?"

She gave him a wink. "Because you're not only pretty, but you're clever. I wouldn't put it past you to try something."

Cordus leaned back in his couch. "Fine, run the damned ship."

"No need to pout, Antonius."

Cordus shot her a glare. "We still have a bargain, right? We take Blaesus to a Terran hospital, then we get Kaeso and Ocella. Once they're safe, you can call me whatever name you want. But until then, I am Titus Aemilius Cordus."

"Peace, Titus, it was a slip of the tongue. Of course we still have a bargain." She turned back to her pilot's tabulari. "All crew in delta couches. Starting delta sleep now."

The displays for all the crew couches turned yellow, indicating they were under delta sleep.

Aquilina turned to Cordus. "Good night, *Titus.*" She tapped the delta controls...

...and then Cordus opened his eyes. He looked at Aquilina in the pilot's couch. She was asleep. He checked the delta readouts for the rest of the crew. All the Romans were still asleep, but Dariya, Daryush, and Blaesus were awake.

He tapped his collar com. "*Vacuna* crew, report."

"Ush and I are here," Dariya said over the com.

"Blaesus here, too, Centuriae," the old Senator's voice croaked. He then chuckled, which transformed into a raspy cough. "That was fun," he said after his coughing subsided.

Cordus felt an emotional dagger against his heart. Blaesus needed true medical attention yesterday. But first, Cordus needed to secure the ship before he could get Blaesus to a medicus that wouldn't arrest him on sight like they would on Terra.

"Good work, Blaesus," Cordus said, unstrapping himself from the command couch. "They weren't watching you after all."

"One of the perks of being old and wounded," Blaesus breathed. "Nobody thinks to monitor my systems access. Quite insulting, actually. Just because I'm the ship's scholar, diplomat, and comedic relief, doesn't mean I can't reprogram a delta system."

Aquilina and the Romans had indeed watched everything Cordus, Dariya, and Daryush did as they programmed the quantum way line engines for a jump to Terra. But they had ignored Blaesus, who seemed asleep the whole time.

Except for when he wasn't and using the tabulari in the medical hatch to set a little trap for the Romans.

Cordus checked the star charts and smiled. They had not moved. The delta sleep systems had engaged, but Blaesus had set a hidden program to cancel the way line jump yet maintain the delta sleep for the Roman couches. Cordus hadn't given the idea much chance for success, but it was the only thing he could come up with so quickly.

It was something Kaeso would have done, and Cordus allowed himself a moment of pride.

I'm going to find you, old man. You and Ocella. But only as centuriae of this ship. And then I'll give her back to you.

Cordus bent over the sleeping Aquilina and entered coordinates to a Liberti mining colony in the outer reaches of the system. It was likely overrun with refugees by now, but it was an hour away at their ion engine's top speed and their only option to get Blaesus the surgery he needed.

As soon as Cordus sent *Vacuna* on its way to the colony, Dariya's voice came over the collar com.

"Centuriae, we have a problem with the way line engines."

Cordus shut his eyes a second and took a deep breath. *Gods, you never let it be easy.*

He tapped his collar com. "I'll be right down."

When he arrived in the engine room, Cordus found Daryush growling at the tabulari in front of him. The big Persian put his fists on his hips and then flinched when he noticed Cordus enter the engine room. He shoved his hands into his pockets and seemed embarrassed that Cordus had heard him.

"So this is how you talk when no one's around?"

Daryush gave an embarrassed grin and then shrugged.

"He heard the same from me just now," Dariya said from behind Daryush. "The Romans made a mess of my engines, Centuriae, and I do not think I can fix them. At least not without parts from a way station."

"What did they do?"

"The quantum *and* alpha way line engines are locked. We need a key code to unlock them both and it is different for each one." Dariya let loose a stream of curses in Persian and Latin, and turned around to study the tabulari. "I was so focused on the delta sleep system that I did not see this lockout program."

"Have you tried entering a key? Maybe—"

"Yes, I assume I *could* get lucky and enter all 16 alphanumeric characters in the correct order with a pure guess. And Ahura Mazda *could* jump out of the engines and make me a goddess."

"Dariya, you've always been a goddess to me."

She shot him an incredulous glare, which he returned with a grin.

"Centuriae, you are too young and too Roman for me." She turned back to the tabulari console, muttering something in Persian. "Besides, I already tried entering a key and here is what happened."

Cordus came over and watched the tabulari as Dariya tapped the key into a text field. The text field disappeared from the screen and then a video of Aquilina came up. She was sitting in the pilot couch on the command deck.

"*Salve*, Marcus Antonius." She smiled briefly, then continued. "If you're seeing this, it's because you somehow subdued me and my men. I hope you didn't kill us, because that would ruin my high opinion of you. Anyway, so you've taken control of the ship and are trying to engage the way line engines. By now you know they are locked. Think of it as my backup plan to bargain for my release...or my revenge from the underworld."

"*Cac*," Cordus muttered.

"Only I know the codes, so it would be a waste of time trying to get them out of my men. If you want to go anywhere, you'll need to bargain with me. If I'm dead, well, I'm sure the Liberti Defense Force will be along soon—once they're done rebuilding."

She leaned forward as if to turn the video off, but then said, "Oh, by the way, if you enter the wrong code on each engine more than three times, the engines will overload and destroy the ship."

She smiled, and then the video winked out.

"I would just as soon bargain with Angra Mainyu then that Roman bitch," Dariya spat. "No offense, Centuriae."

Cordus stared at the blank video screen. "We may have no choice. Once we drop Blaesus off at the Liberti mining colony, we're going to need those quantum way line engines to catch up to the alien vessel. I won't abandon Kaeso and Ocella."

"No, we will not," Dariya said. "But say we do bargain with her. How can we trust her? She certainly won't trust us after this. How can we know she has not left some other trap in our systems, waiting for the right time to spring it on us?"

"I know, but what choice do we have?"

She cursed again. "None. I just do not like it."

Cordus couldn't agree more. He hated bargaining with Aquilina, especially since she probably had more tricks awaiting them once he woke her up. She had survived on Reantium, taken control of *Vacuna*, and hid that way line lockout program without even Dariya detecting it. She had fooled Cordus into thinking she was from Libertus and an Umbra Ancile. It all meant she was too dangerous to even wake up, much less bargain with. Any bargain they made with her held the prospect of hidden treachery. But if they didn't bargain with her, *Vacuna* would never leave the Libertus system. Only the *Vacuna's* quantum way line engines could catch up with the alien vessel.

There is a way you can ensure she deals honestly with you...

Cordus's stomach roiled at the thought. Not only because he'd sworn he would die before doing such a thing again, but because it had come from his own mind and not his Muses.

Marcus Antonius appeared next to Daryush.

"You're right," Marcus said, his dark eyes boring into Cordus. "You have no choice. If you want to save your friends, this is the only way to ensure that mean little Praetorian up there won't *cac* all over you. What is your decision, young Antonius?"

Before he could think too hard on it, he said to Dariya, "I want you and Daryush to stay off the command deck, no matter what you hear. And make sure Blaesus stays in his bed."

"Are you sure you want to be alone with her? She is dangerous."

He turned to the hatch. "I'll be fine. I just don't want any of you up there when I..."

Gods, am I really going to do this? Am I really going to break the only promise to myself that has held any meaning to me my whole life?

"Centuriae," Dariya said from behind him in a hard voice, "you do what you have to do to make her talk."

Marcus grunted. "Your Persian makes sense, young Antonius. Listen to her."

Cordus left the engine room and climbed the ladder to the command deck. Dariya assumed he was going to torture Aquilina into giving up the codes. In some ways, he wished that's all he had to do.

Chapter Twenty-Eight

C ordus tightened the shoulder straps over Aquilina as she slept in the pilot's couch. He had wrapped more straps across her body and the couch. She could escape with a little effort, but Cordus only needed to keep her still until his Muse aura took hold.

He made his preparations as if he were an empty-minded golem. He tried ignoring his protesting conscience. He had to empty himself of all emotion if he was to get the information he needed. He had begun to have feelings for Aquilina, and he wondered if she had felt something for him. It was most likely an act on her part, he decided. His feelings were real, though, and they were augmented with a grudging admiration for the skill in which she had fooled him and taken control of the ship. If they were playing a *latrunculi* match, she had rolled over him like a master would a novice.

"Marcus," Cordus said aloud, "I will need your help to keep focused."

Marcus Antonius appeared in the delta couch behind the command couch. He wore a look of greedy anticipation. "Whatever you need."

The Muses whispered in Cordus's mind. They swept away all emotions, replacing them with a singular focus—get the key codes from Aquilina. He had not let the Muses infiltrate his mind like this in so long that he almost instinctively tried to push them out.

Cordus leaned over Aquilina, brought up the delta controls on her tabulari, and turned off her couch's delta sleep field. Her eyes blinked open, she looked up at him, and then tried to move. She glanced at the straps and then raised an amused eyebrow at him.

"You didn't disappoint me," she said.

"What are the key codes to the way line engines?"

"Right down to business, eh? What are you willing to—?"

Cordus leaned forward. "Give me the codes."

She must have seen the lack of emotion on his face, for she hesitated and uncertainty replaced her amusement. "No."

Make her trust me, Cordus told the Muses.

He felt the billions of Muse viruses in his body each release just a few molecules of aura. The molecules floated through Cordus's blood and up to his lungs and skin, escaping through his breath and pores.

Aquilina's eyes grew unfocused. She opened her mouth to speak and then shut it again. She blinked, then her lips curled in anger. "What are you doing?"

Make her love me, he told the Muses. They released more aura.

Aquilina drew in a sharp breath and stared at Cordus with soft eyes. The eyes of someone in love. Or what Cordus imagined it would be.

"Give me the codes," he said again.

She gave him a languid smile and was about to speak, but then hesitated. She shook her head in two quick motions, and shut her eyes tightly. When she opened them again, rage burned there. "No," she said through clenched teeth.

Make her worship me.

Her mouth fell open, and her eyes held adoration for him meant only for the gods. It was how he remembered supplicants staring at his father years ago. They worshiped him as a god. And he believed it.

Cordus struggled to ask her the question once again. Nausea over what he was doing fought the Muses, and it was hard for him to focus. "Give...me...the codes."

Aquilina's mouth opened and closed. She was fighting the aura, fighting it with all her will. A high-pitched moan issued from her open mouth, growing louder and louder until it became an anguished shriek.

Through her screams, she stared at Cordus with adoring eyes. In between the screams, she said, "Slave...or...soldier...?" She said it over and over again.

My father had slaves. Kaeso had soldiers.

Cordus's conscience blasted through the walls he'd built and threw the Muses out of his mind. He fell back into the command couch, sweating and crying. He leaned forward and put his head in his hands.

I can't do this. I'm sorry Kaeso, Ocella. I can't do this...

"Oh, young Antonius," Marcus said from the delta couch, "you were so close."

Cordus jerked his head up. "I am not your puppet," he said aloud. "I am not like my father, and you will know your place!"

Marcus held up his hands in surrender. "Of course. Poor choice of words." He disappeared.

Cordus looked back at Aquilina. Her eyes were red and her cheeks flushed from the effort of fighting the Muse aura.

"What did you do to me?"

Cordus held her gaze. "I'm sorry. I swore I'd never— But I need those codes. The lives of my friends are at stake. I'm not going to use the Muses again to force you to tell me the codes. But I need them."

She leaned back in the couch, then closed her eyes. "What would you do with them, Consular Heir?"

Cordus tried not to wince. "I told you, I would rescue my friends. This is the only ship outside Umbra that can get within that vessel's shield sphere—"

"Say you rescue your friends. What will you do then?"

Cordus gave an exasperated sigh. "I don't know. Live my life. Will you give me the codes or not?"

She leaned forward as far as the straps on the couch would allow. "You think my mother is just another warlord with delusions of starting her own dynasty."

"By your own admission, she let Libertus die!"

"She saved you! Do you really think you could have stopped that vessel? When the finest warships in the Liberti arsenal couldn't scratch it? When not even their Umbra ships, which have *the same quantum way line drives* as this ship, were swatted from space like flies? If we had tried your plan, we'd all be dead now!"

Cordus wanted to shout back at her, but he knew she was right. He had always known his plan was risky at best, suicidal at worst. But he had wanted to do something, *anything*, to rescue Kaeso and Ocella. Even if that something had a low likelihood of success. They had risked everything for him more times than he could count.

All he would've done was kill the rest of his crew.

"Yes, she may use the same tactics as the other warlords," Aquilina continued, "but she believes in the Republic. She believes it must survive or humanity will descend into a dark age."

Cordus snorted. "A bit dramatic. Plenty of other worlds exist—"

"But almost all share a common culture with Roma. Almost all share the same religion, the same government, the same language. Even a large chunk of the Zhonguo worships the Roman Pantheon. Libertus and Roma were the same in virtually every way."

Cordus shook his head. "The Liberti people elect their consuls. Roma's were forced on the people by the Muses."

"I know there are differences between Roma and every other world. But Roma is the Mother from which all those worlds were born. If Roma dies, then humans would lose the one culture they all have in common. Humanity would fracture and probably never unite again. At least not until another culture came along to unite us once more, and that wouldn't happen for thousands of years. It took Roma almost two thousand to get where it is today."

"Blaesus would be more interested in this debate than me. Talk to him, but give me the way line codes."

"Not unless you swear to me on everything you hold dear that you will come back to Terra and take your rightful place as consul of the Roman Republic."

Cordus laughed. "Gods, you don't give up, do you? How can I make this clearer." He leaned forward and shouted in her face, "I...don't...want...to be consul!"

She didn't flinch but regarded him sadly. "I never asked if you *wanted* to be consul. I'm saying you *need* to be consul. What you *want* is irrelevant."

"The last thing Roma needs is another consul imposed by the Muses."

"But you control your Muses, and that is the difference. Look, you would be the transition figure. All the major warlords fighting right now have publicly proclaimed they would follow an Antonius if a real one should appear. If you declared yourself, they would have no choice but to follow you, especially when presented with a crisis like this alien vessel. Once you unite the warlords, we can use the combined strength of *all* Roman Legions to defeat this alien vessel."

"What about Kaeso and Ocella and Lucia? I should just let the Legions destroy them along with the vessel?"

"Once the warlords are united, we can come up with a plan, a *viable* plan, based on your ideas. *Vacuna* may just be the last ship in the universe with quantum way line engines. It would play a vital role in taking out that vessel."

Gain access to all the Republic's resources. But the price would be me—Muse-infected, possibly insane—as consul. Gods...

"When you restore peace to the Republic," Aquilina went on, "you can transition Roma into something different. Perhaps even something like Libertus. What greater tribute to the 'beacon of freedom' in the universe if Roma should return to her Republican roots and adopt the Liberti system of government?"

"You make it sound easy."

She raised an eyebrow. "That sounds easy to you? It'll be the hardest thing any single human being has ever attempted. But you're the only one who can do it. If you can't, or won't, then no one can."

Cordus stood abruptly. "We're going to a Liberti mining colony to get Blaesus some medical attention. We'll be there in one hour. You have until then to give me those codes."

She swallowed. "If I don't?"

He turned to the command deck ladder and did not look at her. "I'm not above trying more mundane forms of persuasion."

"Will you consider coming back to Terra?" she called out.

Without turning around, he said, "I've spent the last six years considering it. The answer is still no."

Chapter Twenty-Nine

"My grandparents have all your recordings," Varo told Claudia as they walked through the endless alien corridor. His voice still sounded nasally from his broken nose. "Although I must confess it's not my favorite style of music."

Ocella didn't know whether to smile or cry as she listened to Varo and Claudia. At times, Varo spoke to Claudia as if the golem really was her. Then the golem answered as if she were Claudia, only to remember she wasn't. Ocella was glad they found something to talk about as they searched the endless corridor, but it was sad when they remembered their situation.

"What is your favorite style?" Claudia asked.

"Anything with lots of percussion. Nobody does it better than the African groups on Gwaza Primus."

"I should think so," Claudia said. "Gwaza Primus was founded as an artists' colony. Many musical styles were born there. I studied there for—" She paused, took a deep breath. "Well. My memories say Claudia studied on Gwaza Primus just before her music became popular. Her time there moved her singing to the highest levels."

Varo paused as if the spell were broken for him as well. They both walked along in silence.

It had gone like that for almost an hour.

The only room they'd found so far contained the same gelatinous 'food' the aliens had given them, along with a water basin. They had all drank their fill of water—even Claudia—and ate as much food as they could tolerate to keep their hunger pangs at bay. The room was only a few doors down from their prison and had taken minutes to find. It had only filled them with hope that they'd find more unlocked doors this time.

But they soon felt they were in a repeating holo as door after door stayed locked.

Kaeso walked ahead of everybody, trying each door with as much passion as a golem. He ignored Claudia and everyone else. Ocella thought he had come back when he pulled her off Varo, but Claudia's appearance only flung him back into whatever pit his mind was trapped. Ocella wondered if he'd ever be the same...if they ever escaped this ship.

Kaeso put his hand on a door pad and it slid open. He flinched in surprise, then looked at Ocella with wide eyes. She and the others ran up to where he stood.

Inside the circular room, a large disc floated three feet above the floor, taking up most of the room's center. Holographic images played above the disc with such stunning clarity that Ocella thought she was seeing real events. Two octopods floated in the air with their tentacles intertwined. Their movements were slow and tender, as if they were mating.

The holograms disappeared, and then Ocella noticed the octopods on the other side of the disc. And they were very real.

There were five, and they appeared to have entered the room from another hatch on the other side. They all suddenly stood on their rear four tentacles and raised their front four tentacles like a fan around their bulbous, gray bodies. One octopod rushed over, its tentacles raised and four tiny fingers wiggling at the ends. Hoots and whistles came from its beaked mouth.

Kaeso was about to slam the hatch shut when Claudia shouted, "Wait!"

He hesitated, but then glared at her and shut the hatch anyway. The hatch slammed shut before the octopod could get any closer.

"It was trying to tell us something," Claudia told Kaeso.

Kaeso turned and walked up the corridor again.

Seeing she couldn't get through to Kaeso, Claudia turned to Ocella. "I could understand it."

Ocella looked sharply at Claudia. "How? Those things sounded like birds."

Claudia shook her head. "I just could. It asked for our help."

Varo glanced at the hatch. "Maybe they're trapped here like us."

"Or we're the freshest meat they've seen in days," Kaeso called out over his shoulder.

Varo ignored Kaeso and looked at Ocella. "Maybe we can work together. If Claudia can communicate—"

Kaeso turned around and strode back to Varo, his lip curled. He stood within inches of Varo's face, his voice quiet, yet menacing. "First, this *thing* is not Claudia. Do not call it that again. Second, you're a fool if you think you can trust a golem created by Muses."

Varo was visibly intimidated, but he stood his ground. "Do you have a better idea? Or would you rather wander these corridors until you die of old age?"

Kaeso stared at Varo with venom in his eyes. Ocella stepped forward before Kaeso did to Varo what she had done earlier. She put a gentle hand on Kaeso's arm. He glared at Varo a moment longer then stepped away.

"He's right," Ocella told Kaeso. "They may know things about this ship that we don't."

Claudia put a hand on Kaeso's forearm. He acted as if it were not there.

"I know you don't trust me," she said. "And I don't claim to be your daughter, though every part of me screams..." She exhaled sharply. "I want to help. The only way I can prove it is if you let me."

Kaeso's jaw moved back and forth. "Fine," he said to Ocella. "It can talk to the aliens."

Ocella nodded to Claudia. At this point, she was willing to grasp at any string of hope.

Claudia placed her hand on the door panel, and the hatch opened. The octopods had gathered in a group near the hologram circle on the side facing the door. When the hatch opened, they all flinched, then stared at Claudia as she hesitantly walked inside. An octopod skittered to Claudia, its top four tentacles held high, while it stood on its rear four. The bulbous head in the center of the tentacles had two black eyes, one on each side of the head, two slits for what appeared to be nostrils beneath the eyes, and a red beak for a mouth.

The octopod opened its beak and produced soft whistles and cooing sounds. Claudia stared at the octopod, her head cocked to one side. Her eyes went wide, and she nodded to the creature. The creature reached forward with two gray tentacles, and Claudia held her hands out. Gray fingers and human hands met each other, and she gasped. Tears dripped from her eyes.

"Can you understand them?" Ocella asked.

"Oh, yes," Claudia answered. "They're in the same situation we're in. They want to trade information. They will tell us what they know, if we tell them what we know. Perhaps together we can get back to our ships and escape."

Ocella glanced at the octopods behind the leader. They stood on their rear four tentacles, with the front four splayed above their heads in a fan pattern. Each one swayed back and forth as they watched their leader communicate with Claudia. "What did it say to make you cry?"

Claudia wiped the tears from her cheeks with her wrist. "This one is a golem, like me. Her family over there is having just as hard of a time accepting her as—" She frowned, then turned back to the cooing octopod. "It's comforting to know someone else exists like me. Sad, but comforting."

Kaeso's low voice came from the hatch behind them. "Ocella," he said.

He gave her a meaningful stare and then walked out into the corridor. Ocella followed Kaeso and met him a dozen paces from the octopod room.

"Kaeso, this could be our one opportunity to—"

"You assumed I would object?"

She eyed him warily. "Well..."

"Tell them anything you want. I don't care."

"Then why did you pull me out here?"

"Because someone needs to be the *numina*." Then the cheek muscle beneath his right eye flinched in a half-wink.

It was all Ocella could do not to wrap her arms around Kaeso and kiss him like she had the last time they'd lain together. Her Kaeso was back. She wasn't sure if he'd always been there or had just come to his senses. She wanted to ask him what brought him back, but she knew such a question would jeopardize their tactic.

Besides, it didn't matter. For the first time in what seemed like weeks, she had hope.

"Being the numina" was an interrogation tactic used throughout human history, though only Umbra referred to it as such. One interrogator took on the "Vestal" role—after the guardians of Vesta's holy fire that protected Roma—and was friendly to the subject. Another interrogator became the "numina"—after the belligerent spirits of ancient Roma—and would threaten violence if things didn't go his way. This made the subject more likely to give in to the reasonable Vestal, since opposition might set the numina off.

It worked even better if the numina's own team feared him and acted that way in front of the subject. Ocella wasn't sure if Kaeso was trying to fool the aliens in the next room, the vessel, or even Claudia. Whoever it was didn't really matter since none of them could be trusted. Ocella *wanted* to trust Claudia, and *wanted* to believe her when she said she felt like the real woman, but this Claudia was a golem and golems could be programmed to say or do anything. Even if this Claudia was telling the truth, who knew if she'd eventually turn on them when dictated by her programming?

These thoughts ran through Ocella's mind in seconds, and only her years of Umbra training kept her voice neutral. "I don't need your permission to do anything. We are going to work with these aliens whether you like it or not. If you don't like it, you can just walk the other way."

Kaeso gave her the quick half-wink again, then let his face turn to stone. It was a frightening transformation that almost fooled Ocella. "Fine, talk to those things," Kaeso growled. "But if they make one move I don't like, I'll rip their little tentacles off their bodies one by one."

Ocella answered his comments with a scowl, then whirled around and went back into the octopod room. Claudia still held the golem octopod's fingered tentacles and stared at its black eyes. Varo raised a questioning eyebrow at Ocella.

"He disagrees," she said. "But we'll do it anyway. What have they been up to?"

"These two have been like long-lost siblings. They can't stop staring at each other and smiling. Or rather, she's smiling. I don't know what her friend is doing." He then nodded to the four octopods on the other side of the room. "They've just been standing there with their arms out. Haven't moved or made a sound."

Ocella walked up to Claudia and put a soft hand on her shoulder. She turned to Ocella with a look of contentment.

"They are so much like us," she said. "They have families they love." Claudia glanced at Kaeso as he entered the room once again. "And hate. They're scared, and all they want to do is go home. Are we going to help each other?"

"What have you told them so far?" Ocella asked.

"Only that we're trapped here, too, and that I'm a golem." Claudia's smile evaporated, as it always did when she remembered what she was. The octopod in front of her cooed softly, and used its other two tentacles to caress Claudia's hands. She turned back to the octopod and gave it a grateful smile.

"Ask them what this room is. The holo in the middle was showing their species. Is this where they've been kept?"

Claudia glanced past Ocella at Kaeso. "Is he going to glower at them the whole time?"

"Probably, but ignore him."

"This is a bad idea," Kaeso rumbled.

Ocella turned on him. "There's the hatch. Leave if you want to."

Kaeso's jaw clenched and unclenched. *Very convincing, my love.*

Ocella turned back to Claudia. "Ask them."

Claudia looked back at the octopod holding her hands. Whatever way they communicated only took a second or two, and the octopod cooed and whistled. One of its tentacles pointed at the four behind it and then at the now-empty holo display. The family continued to hold their tentacles splayed out, as if trying to make themselves appear bigger before a predator.

"They remember the vessel pulling their ship inside it, and then they woke up in a different room," Claudia said. "They left the room and wandered the vessel's corridors which were built to look like their ship. They ultimately found this room and saw the holo device. Apparently it's common on their world. They can control it with their minds and project images of their thoughts onto it. They were testing it and had only been here a few minutes before we arrived. They believe it is divine providence that we should meet like this."

Kaeso grumbled, "A lot of gaps in their story."

Ocella agreed, but didn't want to acknowledge Kaeso and give up her Vestal role just yet.

Claudia said, "Now they want to know how we got here. I can give them my story, but I don't know yours."

Ocella shrugged. "Ours is basically the same. Our ship was captured like theirs, and then we woke up in our cell. We left to go exploring for a while, but came back when we didn't find anything. Then you arrived, and we left again."

She omitted the details about how they entered the ship, what happened to Lucia, and how Kaeso arrived. Her omissions were an attempt to see if the octopods knew more then they were letting on. If they accused her of lying, that would prove they had ways to gain information that they had not revealed.

She didn't even glance at Varo and prayed to all the Pantheon he wouldn't dispute her or even flinch at her blatant lie. Varo was a good soldier, cool under pressure—for the most part—and a quick thinker. As the seconds ticked by, she knew he had caught on when he didn't say anything.

She knew Kaeso wouldn't react, because part of the numina tactic was letting the Vestal take the lead. He would follow whatever she decided to do. His only task at this point was to be as disagreeable as possible.

Claudia nodded, then turned back to the octopod to relay their story. The octopod gave no indication it thought she was lying, though Ocella wouldn't have known what such indications would be anyway.

Claudia looked at Ocella. "She wants to know if we saw any rooms besides this one and the one we were held in. She said they found what appeared to be an engine room, but they were chased out by another alien species before they could see much."

Ocella quickly debated whether or not to tell the octopods about the room they found which looked like a breeding chamber for octopod golems. Of course, if she told them that, she would be admitting she lied earlier.

She shook her head. "No, I'm sorry, we didn't see anything unusual. This is the first room we found outside our prison cell. Can they take us to this engine room they found?"

Claudia relayed the information back to the octopod, and it whistled and chirped a bit louder than before. The four octopods behind it suddenly chirped, whistled, and waved their top four tentacles frantically.

"The aliens in the engine room scared them," Claudia said. "They don't want to go back."

"Tell them it may be the only way we can get off this ship. If we can take control of the engine room—"

"What did the aliens look like?" Kaeso asked.

Claudia looked back at the octopod, then nodded. "She's going to put an image of what they saw on the holo."

The holo image above the floating disc flickered and then solidified. It was an image viewed from the perspective of the octopods. It showed what appeared to be an engine room with serpentine pipes of all sizes and colors weaving around each other. Large banks of tabulari sat at one side of the room.

But it was the aliens that made Ocella freeze. There were dozens inside the room. Several brought up hand weapons and fired at the octopods, which quickly closed the hatch and ran back down the dark corridor.

All the aliens had looked like Lucia.

Chapter Thirty

The Liberti gold mining colony was built below the surface of a moon called Lucubro, which orbited just above the icy rings of the Libertus system's lone gas giant, Cerberus. The only indications of its existence were the moon's beacon on Cordus's tabulari and the landing lights upon the moon's black, rocky surface.

That and the hundreds of refugee ships orbiting the moon. There were so many that Cordus could easily see their running lights with his own eyes. Ships of every size and configuration flew in a one-way orbit around Lucubro, awaiting their turn to land and receive either medical attention or supplies. There were other colonies across the Libertus system, but this was the closest to Libertus Primus.

The former Libertus Primus, Cordus thought. With the death of the first one, Lucubro was the now largest human settlement in the system, and therefore, Cordus supposed, deserving of the title "Primus".

"*Vacuna*, Lucubro control," announced a tired-sounding controller. "Proceed to the coordinates I'm forwarding to you now."

"Any word on when we can land?" Cordus asked. "We have an injured man who's dying—"

"You'll receive landing instructions when it's your turn," the controller said. He sounded like he had explained this hundreds of times before.

"Hours? Days? Please, my crewman could die if he doesn't get medical—"

"Days, *Vacuna*. I'm sorry. Lucubro control, out."

"*Cac*," Cordus swore, then terminated the connection.

From the pilot's couch next to him, Aquilina said, "You could tell them you've worked with Umbra. I'm sure that would get their attention."

She was still strapped into the couch, but Cordus had loosened the straps a bit to let her shift her body and avoid cramps. He doubted she'd have any trouble escaping the straps if she wanted to, but it would take some effort, and he'd have a pulse pistol aimed at her before she got too far.

"Assuming they even knew what Umbra is," Cordus said. "Umbra is still an organization that will literally kill you for saying its name out loud."

"Do you really think they can do that now?"

Cordus was silent. He had no idea what was left of Umbra Corps. Had some elements survived? Likely, since Umbra Ancilia were spread throughout the human universe.

But what kind of leadership existed? Did they influence the remnants of the Liberti government? Cordus had tapped into the system bands for news and had learned that "elements" of the Liberti government had fled to Lucubro, but he had no idea which "elements". Were they from the consular levels, senators, or bureaucrats from the sewer magisterium? How much control did they actually have?

The bands said surviving units of the Liberti Defense Force were searching for survivors. But every survivor they'd found was from a short-range shuttle that had escaped the planet before the alien toxin had taken full effect.

They detected no survivors on the planet. In fact, no life could be found anywhere, not even plant life.

Aquilina said, "A Roman medicus team could help Blaesus."

Cordus snorted. "Yes, just before they arrest him for violating his exile. And then arrest Dariya and Daryush as escaped slaves. Then arrest me. No thanks, we'll wait here."

But Cordus was desperate. He had visited Blaesus a half hour ago, and the old Senator did not look good. It seemed his efforts in reprogramming the delta systems had weakened him. His wound was festering, he was feverish, and he could barely talk. Cordus had awoken Ulpius from delta sleep—the Roman centurion had cursed at the turn of events—to look at Blaesus while Dariya kept a pulse pistol aimed at him. Cordus didn't need Ulpius to voice the situation's severity. His grim face had told Cordus everything.

"The infection is spreading," Ulpius had told Cordus outside Blaesus's room. "I pumped every antibiotic into him this bucket of a ship has, but they ain't making a dent. He will die in two days if he doesn't get something stronger."

Cordus had wanted to try Lucubro, hoping the gods would grant him a miracle despite every indication the moon would be flooded with wounded, desperate people. But denying his own intelligence had cost them more time Blaesus didn't have. They would have to fly to another Liberti colony, but it would take days with just their ion engines. They would need the quantum way line engines to get anywhere quickly, and

Aquilina still refused to give him the codes unless he agreed to return to Roma.

Aquilina's voice brought him back to the present. "You're the Consular Heir. If you declare yourself, you could pardon them."

Marcus Antonius appeared in his usual spot in the delta couch behind Cordus. "She speaks the truth, young Antonius. People will jump to follow your orders. It's one of the perks of being a god."

I'm not a god, and neither were you.

"True. But if people think you are, isn't that just as well?"

Cordus turned to Aquilina. "You're killing Blaesus by not giving me those codes."

"No," she growled, "*you* are killing him. Along with billions of Romans because you're too selfish to take on your responsibilities. If you unite the Republic, we can defeat these alien demons and save lives."

She paused, and then said in a calmer voice, "You're afraid. Gods, I wouldn't want to be consul either. I know how crushing the responsibility is just by watching my mother attempt it as dictator. But if you want to save your friends—*all* of your friends—not to mention several billion human beings, you must go to Roma and declare yourself. It is the only way."

It can't be the only way, Cordus screamed in his mind.

Marcus was suspiciously quiet behind him, and Cordus almost wanted to turn around to see if he was still there.

"We're still here, young Antonius," Marcus said softly.

I...I don't know what to do...

Marcus sighed. "You know what we want, so we won't pretend to be an impartial judge here. But the promises you make now can be broken later."

Save Blaesus, but sacrifice my honor?

"Or save your honor and sacrifice Blaesus. You may not like those choices, but there they are."

Oh, Kaeso, how did you make these command decisions look so easy?

Marcus chuckled. "If your Kaeso is like every other human commander in history, then the decisions were *never* easy. He made a decision because he *had* to make one, all the while praying to the gods he made the *right* one. And then forever after, he either felt the guilt of making the wrong decision or relief that Fortuna was with him. So many humans credit the gods for their successes, but are quick to whip themselves over their failures."

So what do I do when all decisions are the wrong ones?

Cordus couldn't see Marcus, but he could sense the Muse-image shrug. "Make one that's less wrong."

Less wrong?

"Marcus Antonius Primus was not the most eloquent man, but he was decisive."

It was one trait Cordus admired about his ancestor. And it was one trait he desperately needed now.

He sighed. *I suppose I can't wait for the gift of such a trait.*

He could sense Marcus's smile.

Cordus turned to Aquilina. "We will go to Roma, and you will get the Dictator's own medicus team to heal Blaesus. After he is recovering...I will declare myself."

A slow smile spread across Aquilina's face. "Very good, sire."

Cordus shuddered, then growled, "I'm not the consul now, so call me 'Centuriae' or 'Cordus.'"

Aquilina laughed. It seemed genuine and made Cordus's heart flutter. In a throaty voice, she said, "Very good, *Cordus.*"

Chapter Thirty-One

The corridor through which the octopods led them was octagonal in shape, six feet wide, and covered in a black, spongy material. Each flat surface had what looked like ladder rungs. Ocella wondered about the rungs until she saw the octopods use them. Each one leaped up to the rungs on the ceiling and then swung from rung to rung like monkeys in a jungle. It enabled them to almost fly down the corridor and forced the humans to jog to keep up.

Kaeso cursed many times as he struck his head on a rung. He was over six feet tall, so he had to run in a crouch to avoid the rungs. Varo was a foot shorter than Kaeso, but with a stocky build—a symptom of growing up on a planet with a relatively high gravity—so he had no trouble jogging in an upright position. However, he couldn't breathe well through his crooked and blood-clotted nose, as each breath came in gasps and nasal wheezes. Claudia, in front of Ocella and immediately behind the octopods, had no trouble keeping up. In fact, her golem body helped her run at a steady pace while she barely breathed heavy.

"Claudia would have been amazed at what I can do," the golem remarked without missing a stride. "She was not one for exercising. Did Umbra make you this strong?"

"Not like you," Ocella gasped. "Could you ask them to stop for a rest or at least slow down?"

Claudia gave her an apologetic glance. "Oh, of course. Sorry."

She stared at the octopods a moment. They hooted and whistled, and then all stopped. They dropped to the spongy floor and skittered back to the humans. The golem octopod went to Claudia, while the others stood on four tentacles, their upper four in the same splayed formation as when the humans found them. Ocella sat down and leaned her back against the soft wall, her chest heaving. Varo and Kaeso also leaned against the wall while sweat poured down their faces.

The octopods were still wary around the humans, which was understandable—Ocella felt wary around *them*. They were so strange. They were a pace tall when standing on all eight tentacles, but were as tall as

Varo while swinging from the rungs. The four 'fingers' at the end of each tentacle would look human if they weren't all gray and had an extra joint. Ocella had first thought they were naked, but quickly noticed that each wore a gray, form-fitting fabric around their bulbous heads that matched their skin. She wondered if the lack of color anywhere on them meant they were colorblind. Their glassy, black eyes blinked occasionally, and their beaked mouths looked strong enough to tear through flesh and bone. And when she got close to them, she caught the faint scent of that awful stench from the octopod breeding room.

But with all their strangeness, she tried to appreciate the fact that she was looking at a living, intelligent alien species, perhaps the first one any human had ever met face to face. Yes, the Muses were intelligent, but few humans knew they existed. And when most people imagined aliens, they thought of ones they didn't need a microscope to see.

Judging by the condition in which they had found this ancient vessel, Ocella wondered if these octopods were the last of their species. Had they been kidnapped like they said and then put into the vessel's blue ovals? Had their species been wiped out millennia ago? Was that what the vessel had planned for humanity?

Ocella felt as if she were flailing, that she was reacting to what happened to her rather than coming up with an actionable escape plan. Running through this corridor and the Vestal-numina act she put on with Kaeso were just attempts to do *something*, but without an end goal in mind. She had to have faith that sooner or later these vessel Muses *had* to make a mistake. And then they'd be ready.

Her thoughts turned to Cordus as they did every other minute. Had he survived Reantium? What was he doing now? She prayed he had done the sensible thing and returned to Caesar Nova, not Libertus like Kaeso had suggested.

But if he was the stubborn Cordus she knew, he was doing something stupid to try and rescue her and Kaeso, likely egged on by Blaesus and Dariya. She almost smiled at the thought of Blaesus reciting a speech to Cordus from some past senator extolling the virtues of Roman bravery and honor. Dariya would have rolled her eyes and spent three seconds telling Cordus something like, "They are our friends, so we go." Nestor would have—

Her stomach twisted. Nestor and Lucia. Both gone.

Ocella looked at Kaeso sitting on the floor with his eyes closed. He had kept his distance from the group during their jog through the octopod-sized corridor, but never too far. She couldn't imagine what he must be going through now. Lucia had been his pilot for almost ten years and Nestor the closest thing to an advisor he'd allow himself to have. They were part of the family he had adopted after he left Umbra. The family that replaced the one he had abandoned.

Now Nestor and Lucia were dead. She desperately wanted to go to him, talk to him. Not only did she want to comfort him, but she needed his comfort as well.

But their Vestal-numina act had to be maintained for now, and it was one of the things Ocella found most unbearable about this godsdamned vessel.

As if he could sense her thoughts, Kaeso opened his eyes and looked at her. They stared at each other without expression, their eye contact conveying emotions their act would not allow.

Claudia passed Ocella, breaking her gaze with Kaeso. Claudia stopped before Kaeso and seemed about to say something, but then turned around.

"What?" Kaeso said. He didn't look up at her, only stared down the corridor.

She stopped, still struggling, but finally said, "She forgave you."

Kaeso didn't react.

"Well, not at first, but eventually. When you...died, it took her a long time to forgive herself because she thought she caused it. I know how silly that sounds, but I was—er, she was a child. Then you showed up on Libertus six years ago..."

Kaeso's eyes narrowed, but he still wouldn't look at Claudia. Before he went to Libertus, he had assumed Umbra's facial augmentation would have masked his old self from Claudia. Claudia's suspicions came as a shock to Ocella as well, since her face no longer looked like the one she had before she joined Umbra.

"She never knew for sure, of course," Claudia continued, "but she suspected. Like I said before, you have her son's eyes." Her voice caught, and she paused as she tried to keep herself from crying.

This time, Kaeso blinked once, and his jaw clenched. Yet he still wouldn't look at her.

She calmed herself, and then said, "Anyway, I just wanted you to know that she forgave you."

Claudia waited for him to say something, but he just stared down the corridor.

She frowned, then turned to Ocella. "I think they want to get moving. This corridor makes them uneasy. They say it's too long."

Varo grunted. "Glad we're not the only ones who think so."

Ocella nodded, then stood. She looked back at Kaeso, who sat motionless. She crouched down and put her hand on his. He flinched and then looked at her with glistening eyes. Ocella could not tell if it was the corridor's strange light or if Claudia's words had affected him.

He stood without saying a word. He gave her hand a squeeze before pulling away.

"Golem," Kaeso called out.

Ocella tensed. Claudia glanced back from her position behind the octopods and watched Kaeso approach her. Though she seemed to pale the closer he got, she didn't back away from him.

"I would know more about my daughter," he said. "If you would tell me."

Relief spread across Claudia's face. "I would like that very much. I have so much to—"

"No," Kaeso said coldly. "*You* are not Claudia. You are a golem with her memories. As long as you remember that, we'll get along fine. Do you understand?"

Claudia's reaction couldn't have been more pained if Kaeso had punched her. "I understand," she whispered.

The octopod golem behind Claudia whistled and cooed. She turned around, wiping her eyes with her sleeve, and nodded. All five octopods leaped to the hand rungs on the ceiling and began their swinging sprint down the corridor.

As they jogged, Kaeso asked the golem about the real Claudia's childhood in a cold, clinical voice. The golem answered in the same tone without looking at him.

Oh, Kaeso, Ocella thought as she jogged behind them. *How can you listen to that voice and look on that face—the voice and face of your daughter—and still be such a cold bastard?*

Chapter Thirty-Two

Cordus had always thought it ironic that his last memory of Roma was its sewers.

He had been a scared child fleeing for his life with Kaeso and Ocella through the ancient Cloaca Maxima beneath the streets of Roma. The Praetorians chasing them had filled the dank, water-filled tunnels with a gas that had knocked him out. When he awoke, they were in a Praetorian facility on Terra's south pole, from which they eventually escaped to space.

Now, he was about to return to Roma. He had vowed it would never happen, but here he was.

Vacuna came out of the quantum jump near the alpha way line above Terra. Cordus expected startled queries from the Terra Way Station, but the com was silent. He gave Aquilina a questioning look. She sat in the command couch, unrestrained. He had released her, along with her Roman team, once he agreed to come back. He was giving them what they wanted, so he didn't see the point in keeping them prisoner.

Aquilina tapped the back of her head behind her right ear. "I told them we were coming. You should have a clear flight path to Roma."

"We're not docking at the way station?"

"You want Blaesus to have the best and quickest medical care possible, right?" Aquilina said.

Cordus wanted to take back his question as soon as he uttered it. It was the centuriae in him speaking. Docking at a way station, per standard procedure, meant disembarking with Blaesus on a stretcher and rushing him to the way station's nearest medicus. While the facilities on the Terra Way Station were good, they were no match for the Roman Dictator's own team.

The com chimed, and Cordus opened the channel.

"*Vacuna*, this is Roma Flight Control. Proceed to Terran flight path 001-001. You are cleared all the way to landing."

"Only the consul gets a path like that," Aquilina said.

Cordus ignored her and responded, "Acknowledged, Roma Flight Control. Proceeding to path 001-001. *Vacuna*, out."

The path would take them directly to the Palatine Hill and a landing pad within the Consular Palace grounds. Cordus remembered the flight path well. It was the one he and his family took when they returned from visiting Republic worlds.

Cordus programmed the path into the tabulari, and then let the ship fly itself.

"Your medical team will be waiting for us when we land, correct?"

"Yes."

"And Dariya and Daryush—"

"I told you, they will not be arrested."

Cordus nodded. "Because if none of those conditions are met, I will admit to being nothing more than a freighter centuriae through my dying breaths."

Aquilina gave him a severe look. "I know I haven't given you much reason to trust me, but you have to now."

"You didn't trust me with the way line codes. You entered them yourself, remember?"

She shifted in the command couch. "Trust comes in small steps and is built over time. You will come to trust me once you see me honor the bargain we made. And I will come to trust you when you honor your side. I know that even now you're trying to figure a way out of declaring yourself. But for my part, I swear upon all the gods of the Pantheon that I will honor my side of the bargain."

She sounded convincing to Cordus. Of course, she had said many things that turned out to be lies. But she was right about one thing—he had to trust her. If he didn't, he might as well turn the ship around now.

"So you've been communicating with Roma all along through your implant?"

"Yes, but it's one-way, like sending a letter through couriers."

"How? Umbra Ancilia had to use live Muses for their implants to work. I thought the Terran Muses were extinct."

The Muses in Cordus whispered in protest, saying they were *not* extinct, but he ignored them.

Aquilina shrugged. "We figured out how to communicate like them. Think of it as tapping into a com channel on the far end of the spectrum that only had static before. We found it wasn't all static, and that there were signals we never noticed. So we created implants that could tap into those signals."

"You're saying you have interstellar com that doesn't require Muses?"

She smiled. "You'll see when we get to Roma. Things have changed quite a bit since you left."

"Remarkable," Cordus muttered. "Umbra and the Saturnists couldn't figure that out."

She eyed him with annoyance. "You always discount Roman ingenuity. It was Roma that brought humanity out of technological darkness, after all."

"It wasn't just Roma."

"Yes, the Muses gave the consul direction in their 'Missives of the Gods'. But the thousands—millions—of engineers throughout the centuries who built those things were *not* infected. They provided their own innovations that took us in directions the Muses never described. The Missives were not detailed plans, just high-level theories. Human beings figured out how to build those things. *Roman* human beings. You should take pride in your heritage, Marcus Antonius Cordus. You'll be leading us soon."

Cordus remained silent. He wished he could believe in Roma like Aquilina did. He wished he could trust her to ensure the safety of Blaesus, Dariya, and Daryush.

He wished he could trust himself.

The bumps that the ship's inertia cancellers did not suppress brought Cordus back to the flight. White plasma formed around the command deck windows as *Vacuna* collided with Terra's atmosphere. After several minutes the plasma dissipated, and Cordus could see out the window. It was night over Roma, and high, bilious clouds were illuminated by the full moon. Some clouds were heavy with storms, lightning flashing throughout them.

He was a bit disappointed at the obscuring clouds. As a child, his favorite part of space travel had always been re-entry. On clear days he could see the European and African continents, and the deep blue of the Mediterranean, spread out before the ship like a vast *latrunculi* board. He would stare out the window of the shuttle and watch the 'boot' of Italia grow closer, and then the gleaming steel and glass buildings of Roman *suburbas*, which covered the middle third of Italia.

Thanks to his Muses, he had the memories of his ancient ancestors and would wonder what they would think of the sight before him. But all he had to do was look at his parents and siblings in the shuttle seats next to him to know—complete apathy. While Cordus would marvel at Terra's beauty, his family would either sit motionless in a Muse-addled trance or be giving orders to their secretaries. The Terran Muses never appreciated beauty, only power.

Now, flying back to Roma at night and through dense dark clouds, Cordus couldn't help but appreciate the symbolism of it—he was flying home, but into a dark storm he could not control.

Winds buffeted *Vacuna*, and Cordus noticed Aquilina shift in the command couch. "This ship can travel to any point in the universe, but you can't install a decent inertia canceling system?"

"Not enough room. Turbulence make you nervous?"

When Aquilina didn't say anything, Cordus grinned. "Finally, something that scares the great Praetorian Aquilina Servillia."

"I prefer not to be pushed around by something I cannot see."

"Didn't your Praetorian training include jumping out of aero-flyers?"

"That's different. I can control my parachute."

"So it's about control?"

She looked at him. "What does that mean?"

"It means you and I are alike. We want to control our own lives. We don't like to be buffeted by unseen forces. We prefer to work alone. Basically the exact opposite of being a consul."

She sighed. "I watched you lead my men on Reantium. They were not acting—they followed you because they wanted to, and they are not easy to impress. I see the way your crew looks to you, even though you became their centuriae through a field promotion. And they seem even harder to impress than my men. I know you don't want to be consul and that it terrifies you to your bones, but I believe it's something you can do."

Cordus stared out the command deck windows. "I have no choice in the matter anyway."

"For what it's worth, I'm sorry."

"Thanks, I suppose."

"Too many people want to be consul, and they're always the ones who shouldn't be consul. Perhaps its time for someone to take the job who *doesn't* want it."

"Makes me the ideal candidate," Cordus murmured.

When *Vacuna* emerged from a dense bank of low clouds, the lights of Roma spread out before them. They were two miles up, but the city's lights still reached from horizon to horizon. Raindrops tapped against the windows, then flew off in streaks from the ship's speed. Cordus's tabulari verified they were still on course toward the Palatine landing pad in the center of Roma.

"When we land," Cordus said, "will they—?" He looked at Aquilina, but her eyes were glassy and stared at a point much farther away than her tabulari. *Is that how I look when Marcus Antonius is talking to me?*

She blinked, and then a haunted expression fell over her.

"What is it?" Cordus asked.

"It was my mother. She wants to see us at once. She will meet us personally at the landing pad."

"The great Dictator herself will greet me? I'm honored."

Aquilina remained stone-faced before Cordus's attempted levity, and he suddenly felt foolish. "Has something happened?"

"She didn't say, and that's what worries me. She confides in me about everything, especially over implant com. She didn't this time."

"Do you think she no longer trusts you?"

Aquilina scowled. "Of course she trusts me, I'm her daughter. What worries me is that she may no longer trust the implant com. If someone can tap into that, we would lose our most secure com."

"Who could do that?"

Aquilina frowned. "One powerful warlord, a former senator named Quintus Arrius Wendatus, managed to buy off some Praetorian engineers who were close to our Muse-based research. Arrius is my mother's biggest rival, and they've had many battles over the last two years, but none decisive enough for either to gain an advantage. If he can tap into our Muse com, or gods forbid use implants..."

"We'll find out either way in a minute. We're at the Palatine."

Just as he remembered, the Palatine Hill was alit with multi-colored lights that illuminated the historic and massive Consular Palace. Beyond the Palace, on the Capitoline Hill to the northwest, sat the structures that were the heart of Roma—the ancient Senate House and the Temple of Jupiter Optimus Maximus, also gloriously alit. Each building had the iconic, towering marble columns and ornate bas-reliefs just below red-tiled roofs. A powerful nostalgia swept through Cordus at the sight. While his childhood was mostly a nightmare of feeling like a prisoner, the hours he spent exploring those structures were among the few bright spots.

Vacuna landed in the middle of a landing pad surrounded by a vast garden within the Consular Palace's walls. The pad was large enough to hold four ships of *Vacuna's* size, but this night it was clear.

Memories of the garden and the palace assaulted him with surreal intensity. The massive olive tree from which he had fallen when he was seven still towered over the lesser trees a dozen paces beyond the landing pad. The Fountain of Diana near the olive tree still spouted water fed from the ancient Aqua Marcia aqueduct that served the Consular Palace with water from the Valles Anio east of Roma. The palace columns and terraces surrounding the garden brought Cordus back to the days when as a child he would explore each one by himself, wondering why he was so different from his family. Wondering how he could escape.

He glanced at the path that led through the garden to the palace. As he suspected, a dozen or so toga-clad officials and red-uniformed soldiers stood nearby waiting for the ship to land. Off to one side, a group wearing light-green medical suits with matching head covers stood near a stretcher. Before them all stood a trim older woman dressed in a red Legion uniform, a purple sash draped over her right shoulder and chest signifying the Dictator's "temporary" post as the "first among equals". She had more gray in her close-cropped hair than black. Her back was straight and her chin level. Cordus got the impression that despite her current role, Vibia Servillia Gemmella was Legion to her core.

Vacuna touched down with a slight bump, and Cordus powered down the engines. The ship was suddenly quiet, something that always felt strange to Cordus after days and weeks on a starship. It would take him several more days on-world to get used to the lack of a background hum.

Aquilina arose from her couch. "Let me talk to them first. I already gave her the details of our bargain, but the senators will probably have questions."

Cordus frowned. "Did she tell them who I was?"

"I told her to keep it quiet until you declared yourself, just as you asked. But if implant com has been compromised, then anyone can know. Stay on the ship until I motion for you."

Cordus nodded, and they both left the command deck.

They met Dariya and Daryush in Cargo One, along with Piso, Gracchus, and Duran. Ulpius was with Blaesus, preparing him for transport to the Roman medical facilities. The three Romans seemed eager to leave the ship, while Dariya and Daryush understandably looked nervous.

Before Cordus could approach his two crewmen, Duran stopped him. "I think you're doing the right thing," he said. "A lot of people will follow you. Including us." Piso and Gracchus both nodded once in agreement.

Cordus wasn't sure how to respond, given they were willing to shoot him yesterday. So he simply returned their nods and then went to Dariya and Daryush.

Before he could say anything, Dariya growled under her breath. "That old man better live through this, or by Ahura Mazda I swear my spirit shall torment his after the Romans behead 'Ush and I for being escaped slaves."

"They won't kill you," Cordus said, trying to sound more confident than he felt. "I'll never cooperate if they do anything less than give you official amnesty. I'm too important for them *not* to cooperate." He paused. "Still...monitor the Praetorian bands Aquilina gave you. The com chatter may give you warning if things go badly. If that happens, you leave as fast as you can. Don't look back. Understand?"

Dariya muttered something in Persian and then nodded. She took Daryush's hand. Her large brother was pale and seemed ready to pass out at the slightest loud noise.

Cordus had discussed the situation with his crew before releasing Aquilina and the Romans from their delta couches. He had made it clear that if they refused to go along, he would call off his bargain with Aquilina. They both agreed to it without hesitation. Neither one liked it, but they knew Blaesus's life was at stake, and that allying with the Romans was the only way to rescue Kaeso, Ocella, and Lucia. Cordus couldn't imagine the courage it took for them to come back to the heart of the Republic, the place where they had once been enslaved, the place where Daryush had lost his tongue and Dariya her innocence. He prayed he could display the same courage in the days to come.

Aquilina approached her Roman men, and they all nodded to her. She looked at Cordus. "Ready?"

Cordus nodded. Aquilina went to the door controls and tapped them open. The door ramp hissed, then creaked and groaned as it descended. Fresh air—the familiar scents of the gardens dizzying Cordus with memories—rushed into Cargo One. Outside, the medical crew waited with their stretcher. As soon as the ramp was still, the medical crew bounded up. The lead medicus asked Aquilina, "Where is he?"

"Piso will direct you," she said. Piso told the crew to follow him, and he led them into the ship.

Aquilina said to Cordus, "I'll be right back."

Cordus swallowed, then nodded. He watched her stride down the ramp flanked by Gracchus and Duran. All three approached the group of Romans led by Dictator Gemmella. Cordus couldn't hear what they said, even with his Muse-enhanced senses, but he could tell by their rigid body language that not all was well.

Marcus Antonius walked past Cordus and stared out at the gardens. He took in a deep breath and sighed. "Ah," he murmured. "We missed this place very much. Here is civilization. Here is where one can live like a sentient being."

Cordus ignored Marcus and watched Aquilina. Several toga-clad senators behind Gemmella fired heated questions at Aquilina. She stood as straight as her mother, who didn't speak, and seemed to respond with quiet restraint. However, Cordus could see even from this distance that she was tense.

Dariya leaned close to Cordus. "I feel uneasy, Centuriae."

Cordus felt the same, but he didn't want to shake Dariya's confidence any more than it already was. What was the problem? Did they *all* know who Cordus was and about his bargain with Aquilina? Were they refusing to honor it?

The medical crew entered Cargo One with Blaesus strapped to their stretcher. The old Senator seemed a pale shell of the larger-than-life man he used to be. Cordus widened his eyes to dry the forming tears.

Ulpius strode behind them, giving the lead medicus the history of what he had done for Blaesus. "So the way I see it, he needs massive antibiotic treatments to kill that infection. I got the pulse pellet out, but he'll need surgery to—"

"We know what to do, Centurion," the lead medicus said dismissively. The grizzled Centurion frowned and clenched his teeth. He slowed to a stop near Cordus.

Cordus watched the medical crew take Blaesus down the ramp. "Thank you for all you did for him, Centurion. I won't forget it. No matter what happens."

Ulpius nodded slowly, watching after Blaesus. "He's a tough old dog, ain't he?"

"He is."

"He'll make it through. Just needs some Roman medicine. Yeah, he'll make it through."

Cordus didn't know if Ulpius was trying to convince himself or Cordus.

Ulpius finally looked at Cordus. "You'll make it, too, sire." He then turned and walked down the ramp.

Cordus sighed, then glanced at Dariya. She shook her head. "Do not expect me to start doing that. All that bowing, and 'sire' this, and 'my lord' that will give you a bigger head than you already have."

Cordus smiled. "Thank you, Dariya. I would hope for nothing less."

He turned to see six Praetorian soldiers stride up the ramp, all dressed in black body armor and with pulse rifles in their hands. Aquilina walked behind them, her face tight.

Anger simmered in Cordus. "Aquilina, the bargain was that my crew would have amnesty—"

"Your crew is free to go where they wish," she said. The Praetorians stopped in front of Cordus and aimed their weapons at him. "It's you they're arresting."

CHAPTER THIRTY-THREE

The octopods dropped to the floor. The golem octopod went to Claudia while the other four assumed their usual stances—four tentacles splayed above them, while they stood on their rear four. Ocella put her hands on her knees and tried to suck in as much air as she could. Kaeso and Varo also breathed hard. Even the four octopods behind the golems looked tired—the four tentacles splayed above them trembled, and their bulbous bodies squeezed in and out as they drew in quick breaths.

Claudia and the octopod golem seemed about as weary as if they'd been sitting still the whole time.

Claudia approached Ocella, Kaeso, and Varo. "The engine room is fifty paces up the corridor."

Through deep breaths, Varo asked, "How can they tell? This corridor is as unchanging as ours."

"They can still smell their own scent from the last time they were here."

"Pleasant," Varo muttered.

Ocella turned to Kaeso and Varo. "What's our play?"

Kaeso glanced at the octopods. "Depends on how they fight."

Claudia said, "They will fight if cornered, but prefer not to. They've already lost two of their family and don't wish to lose any more."

"Neither do we, golem," Kaeso said.

Claudia's cheek twitched at Kaeso's harsh tone, but she continued. "I said they'd *prefer* not to fight. Doesn't mean they're unwilling. We just need to make our plans clear to them. If they decide there is a chance at success, they will fight with us."

Ocella looked at Kaeso. "Solo gambit?"

"Risky," Kaeso muttered. "Especially without weapons."

"The *what* gambit?" Varo asked.

"It's an Umbra thing," Kaeso said.

"That clears it up..."

Ocella explained the tactic to Varo, who didn't seem any more thrilled with it than Kaeso.

"I know it's risky," Ocella said, "but it's all we have to work with. Maybe we could come up with something different if we had hours or days to plan, but we don't. I've been trying to think up something the whole time we were running. Haven't you?"

Kaeso and Varo both frowned.

"That's what I thought." She turned to Claudia. "Unless our alien allies have a better idea?"

Claudia shook her head. "They used to be cargo haulers. They can fight if they have to, but they're not tacticians."

Ocella looked back at Kaeso and Varo. Kaeso shrugged. "Solo gambit, it is."

Ocella stood before the hatch to the vessel's engine control room. The hatch's control pad was a gray glass square in the middle of the hatch. The golem octopod jumped up to one of the rungs above her, then swung its body forward so that two of its fingers tapped the pad. The octopod swung over to the side and then hung from rungs beyond sight of the door.

The door slid open with barely a hiss. Ocella froze. For a brief moment, she wondered if the octopods had led them into a trap. But her eyes adjusted to the room's darkness, and she saw it was exactly how it had looked on the octopod holo device. Large, irregularly-shaped tabulari dominated all the walls in the octagonal room. Sinuous pipes snaked around each other from the tabulari to the ceiling and walls.

Over a dozen naked 'Lucias' worked at the tabulari. None turned to Ocella as she stood in the doorway. She kept still for several seconds, waiting for the golems to notice her, but none did.

Cac. They're supposed to chase me, not ignore me.

Ocella glanced at Kaeso to her right. He and Varo leaned against the wall there. He gave her a questioning look, but she shrugged. She took a few tentative steps into the doorway.

None of the Lucia golems acknowledged her. It was as if the door had never opened.

Ocella was about to walk further into the room, but Kaeso hissed a warning. She knew he wanted her to abort the play since the golems didn't chase her like she thought they would. She knew he didn't want her trapped in the engine room if the door should suddenly close behind her.

She knew he didn't want to lose someone else he loved.

Ocella turned back to the Lucia golems, who went about their tasks like ants. "Excuse me," Ocella shouted. "Can someone show me to the latrine?"

She tensed, ready to jump out of the way if the golems should draw any hidden weapons. But none turned.

She looked at Kaeso, and he shook his head.

She stepped forward into the room.

"Ocella!" Kaeso cried.

When she entered the room, nothing happened. The door remained open, and the golems didn't so much as flinch from Kaeso's shout. Kaeso charged into the room and stopped beside her. He grabbed her arm, eyed the golems, and then said, "You weren't supposed to go in alone!"

"They don't even know we're here."

"Or they're pretending not to notice."

Varo entered the room, along with Claudia and the octopods. The octopods fanned out behind Varo and Claudia. The octopod golem—Ocella could tell it was the golem because it was the only one that would stand next to Claudia—splayed its tentacles the same way as the four behind it. As soon as they were all in, the door slid shut behind them.

The Lucia golems stopped what they were doing and turned as one to Ocella and the others.

"Follow," they said in the same tone. Then they all turned and filed off to the left, toward a large entry that irised open as soon as the first golem approached it. Beyond the entry was a dark, blue-veined tunnel with an opening fifty paces ahead. Bright green lights pulsated from the opening at the end, but Ocella could not see their source. The golems didn't turn to see if the humans and octopods were following.

Kaeso just stared after the Lucia golems with a mixture of disgust and trepidation.

Varo said, "We may as well see where they're going. Not like they couldn't do what they wanted to us anyway."

Ocella was about to ask Claudia what she thought, when she suddenly walked after the Lucia golems. Holding the golem octopod's tentacle, she said, "Follow," in the same emotionless tone as the other golems. At the same time, the octopod golem hooted to its family. The four octopods hooted and chirped rapidly amongst themselves, their tentacles still splayed. Within moments, however, they started following Claudia and the other octopod.

Ocella glanced at Kaeso. He stared down the corridor, his eyes fearful.

"Just like Menota," he muttered. He squinted at the brightness, but refused to look away. "In the vaults where the Cariosa Muses stored their archives."

There was a tremble in his voice, which made Ocella shudder. The Cariosa were infected by a Muse strain that was incompatible with human physiology. It drove their human hosts mad and eventually turned them into feral shadows of human beings. By the end, the average golem was more human than the Cariosa.

Ocella had never seen the Cariosa close-up. Based on Kaeso's previous descriptions, she prayed she never would.

"The Cariosa archives were in a strangely lit room like that," Kaeso continued, nodding toward the lights. "Maybe they hold this vessel's archives."

Varo sighed. "I really don't care anymore," he said in his nasally voice, then walked into the corridor.

Ocella scanned the control room. They were alone. The vessel did not seem to be forcing them into the corridor, so the choice appeared to be theirs.

She was suddenly very tired. Tired of making choices that never improved their situation, tired of worrying about Cordus, tired of grieving for Lucia, Nestor, and Claudia. What had felt like weeks of boredom mixed with terror mixed with despair had worn her down to the point where she didn't care what the vessel did with them anymore. Had it defeated her? At that moment, she felt it had, for she was suddenly content to let it guide her wherever it willed.

Kaeso took Ocella's hand, and she flinched. She looked at him, then squeezed his hand.

"Why not?" Kaeso said. He sounded as tired as she felt.

"Why not," she responded.

They both walked after the golems into the tunnel.

Ocella could barely make out the shadows of Claudia and the octopods ahead of Varo, for the green lights seemed to grow brighter and pulse faster the closer they got to the end. With less than halfway to go, the light became so bright that it even hurt her eyes when she closed them. Ocella had to shield them with her hand. A cold wind grew stronger the closer they got to the light. It got to the point where it howled in her ears and she had to lean into it.

"Gods," Varo grunted beside her, "maybe this wasn't such a good idea."

"Too late now," Ocella said. "Hope they dim the light, though."

Ocella didn't know what she was saying, and realized she was just talking to keep her mind off the fact they were walking toward a light that seemed as bright as Elysium. *Is the afterlife at the end of this corridor? Will I find Petra? Claudia? Cordus? What about all the people I killed throughout my life, including the Umbra Ancilia I gave up in Roma six years ago?*

And then she thought, *Why are we all so willing to walk into an unknown light and possibly die? Does this mean we've* all *given up?*

She had slowed down unconsciously, and it was only when Kaeso pulled on her hand that she realized she had stopped.

"I don't—I don't think I can go in there."

Kaeso put both hands on her cheeks. "Do you want to go back? Just say the word. No matter what we do, we'll do it together."

She wrapped her arms around him and kissed him in a way she hadn't in months. This was the Kaeso she had fallen in love with again, the man who stood at her side—and she at his—when the odds were against them. She didn't care who was watching. Let the octopods stare at them in confusion; let the vessel see they weren't in as much conflict as they let on; let Varo wonder at their sanity. She didn't care about any of them. Right now Kaeso was all there was. And by the way he returned the kiss, she was the only thing he cared about as well.

She broke away from him and held his face in her hands, staring into his gray-blue eyes. She had to blink away tears, but seeing the same tears in Kaeso's eyes only made more appear in hers. Ocella laughed.

"What?" he said with a grin.

"I just missed you."

"And I missed you. Now what do you want to do? Everyone's staring."

She didn't look beyond Kaeso to confirm this. She didn't want to break eye contact with him. "Let them. If this is our last time holding each other, then I want to make the most of it."

"If the vessel wanted us dead—"

"I know; we'd be dead. But whatever happens beyond that light..."

He held both of her hands. "We'll be together."

Varo stood several paces from them, waiting and shifting his feet. When they walked up to him, he said, "That was nice."

"Don't pretend you weren't uncomfortable," Ocella said.

Varo gave a relieved sigh. "Fine, that was awkward. You're making me damned nervous with this 'final good-bye' act. Let's keep some optimism here."

The octopods had already disappeared into the pulsating green lights, but Claudia stood just outside the entry. Ocella could barely make out her shadow before the lights.

"All will be well," Claudia shouted over the wind. She had the same flat golem voice she had earlier, as if the vessel had finally taken control of her like Kaeso suspected it would.

Ocella expected the same angry expression on Kaeso's face he always had around the Claudia golem, but he regarded her with sadness.

"We're coming," he said, then squeezed Ocella's hand. She squeezed back, and they began walking forward with Varo beside them.

Claudia turned and entered the green lights. As Ocella got closer, the lights seemed to dim, allowing her to look at them without shielding her eyes. The swirling lights looked like a thin film of oil on water, but she still couldn't see beyond them. Somehow a cold wind buffeted them from the film, though the film did not have any obvious pores from which the wind could blow.

Just before the film, she, Kaeso, and Varo all stopped as one, as if gathering their courage before stepping through.

Ocella looked behind her. The corridor was still empty, and she could make out the blinking tabulari in the quiet engine room at the other end. Did that mean they could turn around if they wanted?

Does that mean we can believe Claudia, that all will be well?

Varo stared at the light, then murmured, "Fine." He stepped through the film and out of sight.

Ocella looked at Kaeso, and he at her. She nodded to him and they both stepped forward together, keeping their eyes on each other.

The light blinded her, a fire consumed her, and she tried to scream through a ragged throat. But it took less than a second for darkness to end the pain.

Chapter Thirty-Four

Cordus paced the dark, narrow prison cell in the lower levels of the Consular Palace. It had been over twenty-four hours since he was captured, at least if his meal schedule was any indicator. When they had thrown him in here, they had given him dinner soon after, then breakfast, then lunch, and now he had just finished his second dinner. His normally voracious appetite was non-existent, and he had forced himself to eat the expertly prepared fried eel smothered with *garum* and vegetables.

His anger rose and fell with each hour, burning bright for a while before extinguishing in hopeless assurance that he had been a fool to accept Aquilina's bargain.

Even Marcus Antonius seemed frustrated as he 'sat' on the hard cot that took up one whole side of the cell. "This so-called Dictator's head will be the first one on a pike as soon as you get out of here. Once you declare yourself, the sycophants at her side will trample each other to gain your favor. That's how it happened when we took Roma from that whelp Octavian, and it will happen the same way here. Of course, you need to escape first..."

Cordus had barely spoken a word to Marcus. Or *thought* a word, rather. He knew the Romans were monitoring this cell, so he would not make them doubt his sanity by talking to thin air. Though he could communicate silently with Marcus, Cordus did not have the will to constantly refute his cries for brutal vengeance on their captors.

"...And why in all the hells do Romans today use golems instead of real humans as gladiators? Things were much simpler in Primus's day—you commit a crime, you get thrown into the arena. Not only did it keep crime to a minimum, but it also provided cheap entertainment for the plebeian mobs. A win-win scenario. Now prisons are overflowing with criminals because they know there's no..."

Though Cordus didn't speak to Marcus, the Muse-avatar's constant prattling was soothing. It made him feel less lonely.

He heard footsteps outside the door the same instant Marcus said, "Ah, our captors approach."

Several people paused by the door. Someone activated the panel on the other side, the door opened, and Aquilina stepped inside. Three Praetorians in black uniforms stood outside, each holding what looked like the fulgurators the golems on Reantium had used.

Aquilina half-turned to them. "Close it."

A Praetorian did as commanded. Once the door shut, Aquilina and Cordus simply stared at each other.

Aquilina broke the silence. "I'm sorry for this. This was not my call, nor even my mother's."

"Yet here I am."

"Things are complicated."

"Obviously. Where is my crew?"

"Blaesus is in the Consular Medical Center. He's recovering from surgery, but it will take some time before he's back on his feet. He may never be the same. The infection took much from him, physically and mentally."

Cordus nodded slowly. "Dariya and Daryush?"

The corner of her mouth twitched with a small grin. "They refuse to leave *Vacuna*. We've offered them fresh food, but Dariya says they're fine with the ship's packaged rations. I think they're afraid we might poison them."

Cordus couldn't blame them. After the treatment they endured as slaves to a sadistic Roman master, he considered it a miracle they even trusted *him*.

"Why am I here, Aquilina?"

She sighed. "There are some—well, most—in my mother's council that say they don't believe you're the real Marcus Antonius Cordus."

"You already took a blood sample from me. What more do they want?"

"They *say* they don't believe it's you. In other words, it's political not factual."

Cordus shook his head. "And you wonder why I don't want to be Consul."

"The only reason nobody has killed you outright is because too many people know you exist. They're rivals who are just as afraid of each other as they are of you. The only compromise they could come up with was hold you until your lineage could be confirmed."

Cordus threw up his hands. "Well if they can't read a godsdamned blood test, then I don't know what else to tell them. Keep me locked in here for the rest of my life, because I'd prefer this to dealing with these fools!"

Aquilina swallowed, then took a quick breath. "There is something you can do to make them believe—"

"No," Cordus said firmly. "They can all rot before I do that again."

"Cordus, it was the only way your ancestors kept Roma from tearing itself apart for such a long time."

Cordus locked gazes with her. "No. Find another way."

Aquilina shook her head, and then anger exploded from her in a torrent of words. "You are the most stubborn, ungrateful, selfish person I've ever known! All you care about is yourself, and everyone else be damned. Yes, you were born to this position, it's not fair, you had no choice in the matter. But if you won't do it, this Republic will fall further than it already has, and billions of people will die in the wreckage. But no, you go off in your little freighter ship and have a merry time with your crew skipping across the universe. Because who cares what happens to the rest of humanity, when you can have a pint of *bosca* with your mates in some backwater dive." She gave him a disgusted look. "You sicken me."

She turned and slammed her hand on the door twice. The door opened and she left without another word.

Marcus Antonius, still sitting on the cot with his back against the wall, cleared his throat. "Well. She's right about one thing. You are stubborn."

Don't you start.

Antonius was silent a moment, then said, "Do you know the story of the Battle of Alexandria?"

Cordus sighed. *Of course. I have your memories.*

"Good, then I won't have to go into the whole back story. My point is: What did Marcus Antonius Primus do?"

Cordus could see the memories as if they were his own.

Marcus Antonius Primus knew Octavian's forces were on their way, and he knew he was not ready for the battle. The musket and cannon manufactories were only just built, so Marcus's soldiers were still equipped with the standard swords, spears, and arrows of the day. The battle was coming whether Marcus wanted it or not.

Cordus had memories of staring at maps and locating a valley through which Octavian's forces had to travel to reach Alexandria. Marcus then set an ambush with the prototype muskets and cannons they had developed. They only had 1,000 soldiers, enough muskets for a squad, and four cannons to take on a force of 20,000 battle-hardened Roman Legionaries.

But Octavian's forces had never encountered muskets or cannon before. Marcus had waited for Octavian's Legions to enter the valley, then fired his muskets and cannons at strategic targets within the mass of troops. The fire was not meant to inflict mass casualties, for the force was too big—the fire was meant to take out generals and tribunes and induce panic.

And induce panic they did. With the explosive sounds and the virtually invisible death of musket balls, the Legionaries panicked and fled either up or down the valley, where Antonius's meager army was waiting for them. In such a bottleneck, Octavian's forces were slaughtered.

It was the beginning of the end for Octavian, for he never again mustered a force that even threatened Antonius.

"We'll tell you what he did," Marcus continued, answering his own question. "He used the power we gave him to surprise a foe that outnumbered him twenty to one."

I won't use the aura.

"Then you are a stubborn fool!" Cordus glared at Antonius, who quickly raised his hands. "The way we see it is you can either control your destiny or let it roll over you and take you where *it* wills."

You sound like a flamen of Fortuna. Since when did you become a philosopher?

"We've existed for 20 million years. We've learned a thing or two during that time."

Cordus sat down on the cot beside Marcus and leaned his back against the wall. *I spent so much of my childhood hating this place that, even now, knowing I'm in the Consular Palace turns my stomach into knots. Great Jupiter, my whole childhood felt like being stuck in this cell.*

Cordus brought his knees up and put his arms around them. *I just want to be like Kaeso and Ocella. Be some anonymous Saturnist soldier, doing my part to fight the Muses. I spent twelve years as Consular Heir, and it was twelve too many. Being consul means being in a cage.*

"There's no such thing as true freedom, young Antonius. Everyone has responsibilities. Some men must toil in the fields to feed their families; others have to rule an empire. Again, our point is don't run from your destiny—grab it with both hands and bend it to your will."

Fine words from a virus that enslaved billions of humans throughout history, not to mention all the other species you've infected.

"And that kind of success didn't come from us moping in a prison cell with our arms wrapped around our knees."

Cordus stood and began pacing again. *I will* not *use the aura. Aquilina should know that, especially after what I did to her. Why would she even suggest it?*

"She smells of desperation. What could make her so desperate that she would suggest you do the one thing she knows you would never do?"

Cordus paused. *Her mother is in danger.*

"Maybe. Could be a number of things. You may want to ask her next time."

Cordus realized he never did ask her what could make her so desperate. He'd been so angry that he hadn't thought of it.

He knew she was correct, along with Marcus Antonius, to some extent. Cruising the universe with his friends was something he *wanted* to do, but was it something he *could* do knowing he'd doom billions of people? The idea of one person—him—being so important was absurd. It was something he had scoffed at his whole life.

But what if it were true? What if he *could* save lives by accepting the destiny people were constantly telling him to accept?

He had wanted to be with Kaeso and Ocella and the rest of the *Vacuna* crew because they treated him like a normal human being. But he was not a normal human being. One look at Marcus Antonius beside him proved—

He felt as if a gear had clicked into place in his mind. His heart raced with hope at his new insight, even though an old fear clawed its way into his thoughts.

Marcus, tell me how the Muses communicate.

Chapter Thirty-Five

For the first time in months, Ocella felt the sun's heat on her skin. She was on a Terran-class planet. She wore no EVA suit. She lay on her back in a large field beneath a blue sky, a warm breeze bending the tall grass around her. Peace consumed her, and all she wanted to do was stare at the wisps of clouds floating across the—

She sat up quickly. The field in which she sat seemed endless. The grass stretched flat in all directions, from horizon to horizon. No cities or towns dotted the landscape, nor could she see any tracks indicating how she arrived here. And she was alone.

She stood, turned around and around, searching for something—anything—besides tall grass. Nothing.

"Kaeso," she breathed. Then she shouted, "Kaeso!"

Her voice seemed small and was swallowed by the infinite grassland, not even an echo to alleviate her sudden loneliness.

She tried to remember what had happened just before she opened her eyes. The memories slammed into her with the force of an anti-matter missile. The pain. Stepping through the film of light. The dark corridor. Holding Kaeso. Varo, Claudia, the octopods, and their imprisonment on the alien vessel. Memories before that came back to her in a torrent so vivid she had to stop thinking of them before the crush overwhelmed her.

She squeezed her eyes shut. "Kaeso!"

"Ocella," came Kaeso's voice from beside her.

She jumped, opened her eyes. Kaeso stood beside her looking as confused as she felt.

"Where are we?" he asked.

She ignored his question and wrapped her arms around him. He returned her embrace with equal strength. They held each other for a long time before Ocella pulled away and stared up at him.

"Do you remember anything after the light?" she asked.

He winced. "No. We walked in and then I was here. But when I try to remember things before the light…it's too much."

"Like you're reliving it again, with all your senses."

Kaeso looked uneasy as he scanned the grasslands. "This is like when I stayed awake during the way line jump. It all seems real, but it's not."

"You think we're in a way line? But the vessel has gone through the way lines before and we never..." A cold feeling gripped Ocella's chest. "Do you think all this time we've been in a way line dream?"

He shook his head. "I don't know about before, but I'd wager we are now. Popping into existence right next to you doesn't happen in the real world."

"Where's Varo? And Claudia and the octopods?"

Kaeso didn't answer.

Ocella scanned the horizons again. Nothing stood out from the endless grass. "I wish there was a landmark. A building, a hill, a godsdamned tree."

"What about that?" He pointed behind her, and she turned.

A huge columned building stood a quarter of a mile away. It looked like the Temple of Jupiter Optimus Maximus in Roma. Its red-tiled roof gleamed in the bright sun, and Ocella could even make out the bas-relief scenes just beneath the roof.

Kaeso stared at the building. "I was just thinking that I wanted answers, and then I saw that."

"Earlier, I was wishing for you and then you appeared. Wherever we are, it's not the physical world. Maybe we're..."

Ocella didn't want to think she was dead, but she thought that if this was Elysium, perhaps she would find Cordus—

No, the boy is still alive. I can't be dead.

Kaeso didn't respond, but there was eagerness in his eyes. If they were dead, then maybe the real Claudia was in that temple.

Or Petra.

A pang of jealousy swept through Ocella. *If this is the afterlife, then it feels no different than real life. So petty things like jealousy still exist here? Perhaps stories of the gods' human emotions were real after all.*

They walked side-by-side toward the temple, taking their time, for they both seemed to feel like they had all the time they wanted in this place. The closer they got to the Ttemple, the more it made the real Temple in Roma seem like a shadowy counterfeit. This Temple glowed with white light that emanated from the very structure itself. It hummed with a soothing power that put Ocella's fears and doubts at ease. The columns and architecture of the entire building were flawless, without scratch or blemish.

It was exactly how she had imagined the home of the gods.

Ocella and Kaeso ascended the white marble stairs to the temple's open doors, two wooden behemoths two stories high and a story wide, each as polished and perfect as the rest of the building. Through the entrance gleamed columns and polished gray floors. Sunlight streamed through openings above, and terraces ran along the upper stories. Marble statues of the minor gods and legendary heroes lined the walls to her left and right. She found she could recall the names and histories of each god or person the statues represented. It was like she still had an Umbra implant.

At the far end of the building stood three thrones, and each held a god of the Capitoline Triad.

Jupiter Optimus Maximus, king of all the gods, sat in the middle. His back was straight in his marble throne. He had a well-muscled chest and an angular face framed by dark-brown hair and a beard. He wore a white toga that shone as bright as the temple's marble columns.

To his right sat Juno, goddess of war, Jupiter's wife and chief councilor. Her braided auburn hair hung in loops over her shoulder, her complexion like alabaster.

To Jupiter's left sat Minerva, daughter of Jupiter and goddess of wisdom. She was just as beautiful as Juno, with similar features like the braided auburn hair and perfect complexion. But on Minerva's shoulder stood a large gray and white owl as tall as one of Ocella's arms. Its black eyes regarded Ocella with the same imperiousness as the three gods.

Kaeso suddenly laughed. Ocella glanced at him and then at the gods. All three stared at him with narrowed eyes.

"If you're gods," Kaeso said, "then I'm Romulus's bitch mother."

"Kaeso," Ocella murmured, putting a hand on his forearm. Perhaps they were in a way line dream, or perhaps not. She wasn't about to insult these beings until she knew which was true.

Jupiter's hand clenched the armrest of the throne on which he sat, and he leaned forward. "A mortal with no faith," he said with a rumbling voice. It did not boom throughout the temple, but Ocella could feel it vibrate every cell in her body. "Do you think you are the first to doubt us?"

"Hardly," Kaeso said. "But I've been awake through a way line before. I know how it plays with your mind. You're not real; this temple isn't real. You're just the Muses doing what you've always done—pretending to be more important than you are."

Ocella wanted to stop Kaeso. She feared that if this was Elysium, then the gods would capriciously throw her into the underworld for all eternity, and she'd never see Cordus again.

But a part of her wanted to see how they responded to Kaeso's accusations.

Jupiter stared at Kaeso for a long time, and then he turned to Juno. The beautiful queen of the gods shrugged. Jupiter then turned to Minerva, who gave him a knowing smile.

He turned back to Kaeso. "Very well, mortal. We are not your gods."

We're still alive, Ocella thought. She wasn't sure if she was relieved or horrified.

Jupiter turned his piercing gaze upon her. "No, mortal, you are very much dead."

Ocella stared at him. *You can read my thoughts?*

"Of course we can, child," Minerva said. Her owl fluttered its wings and shifted on her shoulder when she spoke. "We may not be gods in the sense you believe. But here, in this place, we *are* gods."

"What do you mean we're dead?" Ocella asked Jupiter.

He fixed her with a cruel gaze. "When you walked through that corridor, your bodies died. Now your mind is here, waiting."

When Jupiter said no more, Kaeso grunted. "Fine, I'll play along. What are we waiting for?"

Jupiter smiled. "Your new golem bodies. You will be centurions in our army when we invade Terra."

Chapter Thirty-Six

Aquilina entered Cordus's cell, shut the door, and then stood before him with her arms folded. Her gaze could have frozen a star. "You have something to say?"

Cordus drew in a breath. "You said you have devices that mimic Muse communication. Can I see them?"

"Why?"

"Because I have an idea of how to stop the alien vessel."

"Tell me."

Cordus held up a hand. "First, what kind of interface do your implant communicators use?"

"It's neural. One person on this end wears a wired head net that captures brain waves and then transmits them to someone with an implant. But we can't speak to each other like a normal com since there's a com lag—they send a message to me, I hear it, then I send a message back. Lag time can be up to a minute."

"So only one person on this end can communicate with one other person with an implant at a time?"

"Yes, but we're working on expanding the users who can participate."

"Good," Cordus muttered to himself. *Perhaps the gods are with us after all.*

Aquilina looked at him expectantly. "And your idea is...?"

Cordus explained what he wanted to do. She took it much better than he had expected—she simply stared at him with a blank face. "You're joking."

"I know it's a little desperate—"

"'Desperate'? Try insane. Nobody will agree to that."

"And if that vessel finds Terra, what then? You know what it did to Libertus."

Aquilina let down her Praetorian mask for just a second, and Cordus saw the terror in her eyes.

"It *has* found Terra, hasn't it?" he said quietly.

She nodded. "We think so. Since it left Libertus, it's taken the most direct way line route to Terra. It comes through the way line, kills the nearest planet, and then jumps through the next way line that leads here. Every ship that tries to attack it is destroyed. If it stays on its current course and speed, it will be here in four days."

Aquilina sat down on the cot, her shoulders slumped. "News has spread throughout human space about this thing. The Roman factions are gathering their ships for Terra's defense, at least the ones they're willing to give. Even the Zhonguo are sending ships, though it's a token few. They're keeping the bulk of their fleet for defense of their own worlds. Can't say we wouldn't do the same—"

"Aquilina," Cordus said, sitting down next to her. "We have no other choice."

She shook her head. "What you're suggesting is like killing the patient to stop the disease."

"Yes, there are risks. But if that vessel gets here, there won't be a Terra to salvage. You know *all* of humanity's warships wouldn't stop this thing. This is the only way."

He put his hand on top of hers, and she suddenly turned her hand over and squeezed his. She had the eyes of a drowning woman.

"Promise me this will work," she said in a shaky whisper. "Promise me you will *make* this work."

Cordus squeezed back. His heart raced at being so close to her, the scent of her hair, the warmth of her hands and body. He wanted desperately to tell her anything she wanted to hear, anything that would ease her fears and give her hope.

But he knew his plan was desperate, suicidal, and probably wouldn't work. Where was the hope in that?

He licked his lips. "I promise I will do all I can to protect my people."

Her eyes softened. She put a hesitant hand on his cheek, and Cordus flinched at the jolt that went through his body. He had the sudden urge to kiss her with all the passion that had built up in him since he met her, despite being in a prison cell and talking about the possible death of the Roman Republic. None of it mattered at that the moment.

"Very well," she whispered. Then she stood, suddenly all business. "First, we have to get you out of here."

Cordus wanted to weep at losing such a moment to his hesitation, but he gathered his wits and said, "Isn't this cell monitored?"

She shook her head once. "They didn't want a record of you being held, especially if you ended up being consul. The only way you'll be truly safe is if you publicly declare yourself now."

A shudder went through Cordus. He clenched his teeth and nodded slowly. "So how do I get out of this cell to do that?"

Aquilina grinned. "I have an idea. By the time I'm done, they'll be begging you to leave."

Chapter Thirty-Seven

The cell door opened, awaking Cordus from a rare moment of sleep. He sat up in his cot. Aquilina strode in, gave him a quick wink, and then stepped aside to let in Vibia Servillia Gemmella, Dictator of the Roman Republic. Up close, Cordus noticed she had the same piercing brown eyes as Aquilina.

"This is what's going to happen," she said in a tone that would not allow negotiation. "When we leave this cell, we will go to the steps of the Consular Palace. There, among the news criers, senators, and assembled citizens, you will confirm that you are indeed Marcus Antonius Cordus."

News criers, senators, and citizens? Just how many people are out there? Juno have mercy.... Cordus suddenly felt sick, and it took all his will to keep from vomiting on the Dictator's shoes.

Gemmella continued, "You will also announce that in the interests of a smooth transition in these times of crisis, you will work with my administration on the legal path toward your ascension to the consulship. In the meantime, I will continue my duties as dictator until such a transition can occur peacefully. I've prepared your complete statement."

She raised a hand, and one of her assistants behind her gave her a slate. Without looking at the assistant, she handed the slate to Cordus. "I suggest you memorize this, as it will appear more authentic than you simply reading it. I trust one with your...abilities should have no trouble remembering six sentences."

Cordus scrolled through the statement, which said essentially what the Dictator just paraphrased. He looked up at her, and she regarded him with the same cold calculation with which Aquilina had watched him at times. *I thought she believed in me; why does she not seem to trust me?*

Cordus stood. He was almost six inches taller than Gemmella, yet he still felt like she was looking down at him. "My crew—"

"Is no longer your concern—"

"They are my *only* concern. Right now I'm just a freighter centuriae held under mistaken identity. Does my crew have amnesty? I want your personal guarantee."

Gemmella's eyes narrowed.

"Because if they don't," he continued, "I'm staying in this cell."

After a few moments of silent staring, she said, "Tell me, Marcus Antonius Cordus, does your loyalty also apply to the Roman people you wish to rule?"

"I don't *wish* to rule anybody. I assume your daughter has already told you I take this path reluctantly. But history and religion say the consul serves the people rather than rules them. I would take my historic and religious duties seriously. *If* I were consul."

Gemmella did not smile, but her icy gaze softened. "You have my personal guarantee that your crew will receive amnesty."

"When can I see them?"

"After you declare yourself. Once you do that, you will have Praetorian protection."

"Is my life in that much danger right now?"

Gemmella barked a laugh. It was similar to Aquilina's, but did not have the playful quality. The Dictator's laugh was tempered by hard years and cynicism.

"We didn't put you in this cell for its amenities," Gemmella said. "There are factions who'd rather the Antonii stay dead. You're in much greater danger while you're undeclared than if you declare yourself. In the former situation, if those factions knew who you were, you'd be a *dead* freighter centuriae held under mistaken identity."

"Has Aquilina told you my plan to stop the alien vessel?"

Gemmella's eyes twitched and her jaw flexed. "Yes."

"And you will allow me to do it?"

Gemmella spoke slowly. "If the situation becomes so desperate that we have no other choice...then yes, I will allow it. But we have weapons the vessel hasn't seen yet. Your plan will not be needed."

Cordus acted as though he accepted this, but thought, *I'm sorry, Dictator, but it is* your *weapons that will not be needed.*

"Will you follow me?" Gemmella said.

Cordus nodded once. Gemmella turned and left the cell, followed by an assistant and two black-uniformed Praetorians. Cordus's legs suddenly felt as if they were cemented to the floor.

Aquilina gave his arm a gentle squeeze. "I'll be there with you the whole time," she whispered.

"What did you do to get me out of here?"

"Somehow, news leaked to the Republic bands that Marcus Antonius Cordus still lived and was in the Consular Palace. Even holos of your landing in the palace gardens were leaked. Over the last twenty-four hours, facial recognition experts from across the Sol system have confirmed it could be you. So everyone is demanding to know if it really *is* you."

"Your mother could not have been happy."

Aquilina smiled. "She's the one who 'leaked' it."

Cordus blinked, then shook his head and left the cell.

As he stepped out, he glanced at the four Praetorians surrounding the Dictator, then looked again. Gracchus looked much older in his ceremonial Praetorian armor; Piso's black, curly hair peeked from beneath his golden helm; Duran watched him with amused brown eyes. Ulpius wore the same dour look he always had, though he didn't look as grizzled now that he had shaved the gray stubble off his face and neck.

"Thought you were all Legion," Cordus said dryly.

"What gave you that impression?" Ulpius growled.

Duran grinned. "Lady Aquilina assumes she's our commander, but we've always been *her* Praetorian detail—"

"I'm warning you, Duran," Aquilina said in a deadly voice from behind Cordus, "call me 'lady' once more and you'll be guarding penguins at the South Pole Detention Center."

Duran snapped to attention. "Sorry, ma'am," he said, but his eyes still held amusement, as did those of Ulpius, Gracchus, and Piso.

Cordus smiled despite the circumstances.

Gracchus and Piso fell into formation around the Dictator and her three assistants, who spoke with her quietly. Ulpius and Duran marched behind Cordus and Aquilina. Cordus did his best to match Gemmella's purposeful stride. If he was about to become consul, he would need to act like her.

The walk through the holding cells beneath the Consular Palace was a blur. His mind could not focus on anything other than what he was about to do. He had feared and avoided this moment his entire life. Even when he was a boy, he had never wanted to be consul. Now he was about to claim leadership over 150 billion people spread across the universe. His hands trembled, and he constantly wiped his sweaty palms on his pant legs. Sweat beaded on his upper lip and forehead. His legs would not match the confident strides of the Dictator in front of him.

What if I just abdicated instead of declaring myself? What if I just named Gemmella the new consul and said it was the start of a new Roman dynasty?

"Because you gave them your word, young Antonius." Marcus Antonius strode next to Cordus, matching his pace. "And we know you'd rather die than break your word. An impractical code, but yours nonetheless."

I don't know if I can do this, Cordus thought desperately.

"Oh, you'll love it," Marcus replied, anticipation making him virtually bounce down the corridor. "There's nothing greater than the love of a mob. Makes you feel like a god."

Cordus grimaced, and Marcus added, "Or what we presume a god would feel. Of course, we're not gods, so we have no idea for sure."

Cordus realized they were in the columned hallway of the Consular Palace's entry, walking toward the open doors ahead. He could see gray sky outside, and the snapping red pennants lining the top of the Circus Maximus. He smelled rain on the humid breeze coming through the doors.

He passed the marble statues of old consuls, all Heroes of the Republic. Near the end of the hall, at the entrance, he saw a statue of his twelve-year-old self. Cordus had heard about it and knew it proclaimed him a martyr and Hero of the Republic for "standing tall before barbarism". His father, the last consul, had commissioned it after believing he succeeded in secretly murdering Cordus on Menota. As with all the statues in the hall, it accentuated his features, giving a twelve-year-old boy the muscles and bearing of a thirty-year-old. He certainly didn't remember feeling that tough and confident—he mostly remembered being terrified all the time.

"I suppose you'll have to take that down," Aquilina said at his side, her gaze on the statue. "That's for a dead child."

Cordus didn't say anything. He was too sick to speak.

"I was in the Forum when they unveiled it six years ago. I was only a child myself, but it inspired me." She looked at him. "It told me that even children could 'stand tall before barbarism.'"

"It's fantasy," Cordus whispered harshly. "I was never brave. That statue is nothing more than a cloak to cover my father's crimes."

Aquilina nodded. "True. But it *did* inspire me, and countless others, to serve the Republic. Is that a bad thing?"

Cordus didn't answer because he didn't know what to say. He didn't know anything anymore. He had sworn to the gods that he would never put himself in this position. Yet here he was, of his own choosing. In less than twenty paces, he would be standing on the palace steps—

White light blinded him, and then he felt the impact. He heard nothing as he flew backward, slammed into the two Praetorians behind him, and then landed on the polished marble floor. Sharp chunks of debris pelted him along with sickeningly warm pieces of what felt like raw meat.

He lay on his back, paralyzed by the blast and the lack of air in his lungs. He took in several gasping breaths and then coughed up plaster dust and mucus. He opened his eyes and slowly propped himself on one elbow. After starbursts faded from his eyes, he saw the people he'd been walking with a second before. They all lay on the floor among the debris, some moving, but most still. His hearing crept back accompanied by a terrible ringing, and then the sounds of screams and pulse rifle fire coming from outside the palace.

Find a gun, you fool.

He forced himself up; his body groaned with the effort. A Praetorian lay next to him. Duran. His neck was turned in an unnatural angle, his sightless brown eyes staring to the right. Cordus took his pulse rifle and swung it around toward the palace doors. He blinked the dust and wetness from his eyes. Pulse fire still raged outside, but nobody was charging in. The right door was off its top hinge and tilted against the doorframe. Only the jagged upper half of the left door remained. Seeing no immediate danger from the entrance, he scrambled to his feet, still aiming the rifle at the doors. His eyes flicked over the bodies and debris around the hall.

"Aquilina!"

His voice still sounded muffled to his recovering ears. The Muses were hard at work repairing any damage to his body. Likely everybody else was in much worse shape than he.

"Aquilina!"

Her dark braid lay beneath the upper torso of one of the dictator's assistants. Cordus rushed over and with one hand pulled the torso off Aquilina's head. He checked her pulse, found it, and almost sobbed with relief. She coughed and gasped, her entire body curling into a fetal position.

Thank Juno, she can move.

He turned her over and she continued to cough, but her eyes were open and staring at him. He helped her sit up so she could cough easier.

"What...?" she tried to say, but another coughing fit came.

"An explosion," Cordus rasped through his own ragged throat. "There's fighting outside."

She stared at him. "I can't hear," she shouted.

"Mine is only now coming back—"

Her eyes suddenly widened. "Mother?" she yelled, looking around.

She tried standing, but fell back to her knees. Cordus slung the rifle over his shoulder and helped her up.

"Mother!" she yelled again, searching the bodies.

Ulpius was on his feet. He looked dazed and spat gobs of debris, but he had his rifle up and aimed at the door. Everybody else still lay on the floor, either too wounded to rise or dead.

"Mother!" Aquilina screamed. She stumbled in the direction Gemmella had been before the blast. Cordus followed her with his rifle up, trying to avoid stepping on bodies. He tread around Piso, who lay on his back with his chest ripped open. Fortunately the Hiberian was dead.

Aquilina rushed forward and dropped to her knees next to a bloody form. Cordus stood over them both, glanced at Gemmella, and knew she was going to die. The left side of her face had been sheered off almost to the bone; her left arm was gone along with most of her torso. The whites of her ribs poked through her blackened and bloody skin.

Aquilina held her head. Amazingly, her right eye moved to Aquilina. The dictator whispered something, but blood leaked from her mouth.

"What?" Aquilina shouted, moving her ear next to Gemmella's mouth. "I can't hear you!"

It wouldn't have mattered if she had. Cordus's hearing was virtually healed already, but even he could not make out what the dictator was trying to say; only wet gurgles came. Then her chest stilled, and her right eye stared up at the ceiling.

More pulse fire came from outside, and this time shots tore up the remaining pieces of the jagged left door.

Ulpius, and now Gracchus, rushed over to Aquilina and Cordus, both with rifles pointed at the door. Ulpius yelled, "My lady, sire, we need to leave now!"

"Mother!" Aquilina shouted at the dead Gemmella. "What did you say? Mother, I can't hear you—"

Cordus yelled near Aquilina's head, "We have to go! They're right outside the door!" He reached for her arm, but she pushed him away.

"She's trying to tell me something! I can't hear what she's saying!"

Cordus slung his rifle and pulled her up by both arms. "Your mother's dead!"

Aquilina stared at him and then looked down at her mother. "But I...I didn't hear what she said..."

Cordus put both arms around Aquilina and gently, but firmly, pulled her along as he and the two surviving Praetorians raced back down the hall.

Chapter Thirty-Eight

"Centuriae or pilot, 'Ush?" Dariya said.

Daryush looked from the command couch to the pilot's couch on the command deck of *Vacuna*. He frowned with indecision.

Dariya gave an exasperated sigh. "'Ush, you had the pilot's couch last time, so take the command couch."

She knew the source of his indecision. The command couch was larger and more cushioned, which better accommodated his large frame. But the pilot's couch had a larger screen on its tabulari for a better view of the horse races on the Roman bands. The Romans may be bastards in most things, but they bred the finest horses in the human universe.

Dariya threw up her hands and sat in the pilot's couch. Daryush shrugged, then sat in the command couch and brought up the races on the smaller tabulari monitor. Dariya loved her brother beyond words, but his hesitant nature infuriated her at times.

She frowned as she scrolled through the local broadcast bands. She couldn't find any horse races, but she saw lots of news criers discussing the impending announcement that an Antonius had been found and was here in Roma. Criers stood in front of the open Consular Palace doors, awaiting the Dictator and presumably the last Antonius. They all speculated that it was Marcus Antonius Cordus himself, back from the dead.

Cordus, you fool, you should have let them all rot. You should never have come here.

She glanced at her brother, who had settled on an old broadcast of a horse race that seemed to be running through the sands of Arabia. He watched the race with a happy grin.

We *should never have come here...*

A rumble vibrated her couch. She knew small earthquakes were common in Italia, just as they were in Persia, but her instincts were on edge. She turned on the Praetorian bands that Aquilina had given her.

Men and women screamed over the sounds of pulse blasts. Some cried out they needed a medicus for wounded comrades, citizens, or themselves.

Dariya looked to the broadcast bands. The cameras jerked about as the holders tried to flee the scene, while at the same time record what was happening. The doors to the Consular Palace were blown apart and smoking. Black-armored guards stood near the doors, firing from behind white columns at someone in the crowd. Whoever fired back was disguised as a citizen.

Dariya sat up in the couch. "Cordus..."

Her eyes were drawn to the ship's external cameras. Not trusting the Romans one bit, she had kept them all on and had even turned on the motion sensors. Nothing could get within a hundred paces of the ship without setting off alarms.

And as soon as she saw movement, the motion alarms blared. Black-armored men with pulse rifles were charging from out of the garden toward the ship.

She lunged for the shield controls on the pilot's tabulari. A hum permeated the ship as the shield generators came on line, and then a translucent blue glow filled the external cameras. The shield encased *Vacuna* in a spherical energy, slicing through the ground on which the ship sat. The ship groaned and shifted as the landing pad beneath it became unstable from the shield scooping out a huge semi-spherical chunk of it. She engaged the anti-grav engines. The ship stopped moving as it rose a few feet above the crumbling ground and floated within the energy sphere.

Daryush grunted in alarm as he pointed at the external cameras. Through the blue glow, they saw black-armored men fire at the shield with pulse rifles. But the pellets disintegrated harmlessly upon impact.

They were protected. But with the shield in place, the public bands they'd been watching on their tabulari, along with the Praetorian bands, turned to static.

Dariya and Daryush shared a fearful look.

"*Caccing* Romans," Dariya snarled.

Chapter Thirty-Nine

A wareness came in waves.

First, she was warm and content. Then she realized she was alive. She soon discovered she had eyes that she could open, but they did her no good since all she could see was a dark blue haze. She did not care.

Then memories slammed into her, and Ocella woke up.

She floated in a warm gel that encased her naked body. She found she could breath the gel, but that did not ease her panic. She thrashed about, grasping for anything solid within the endless gel. She didn't even know where to 'swim' to, for she had no idea which way was up or down.

A shadow moved to her right, and she swung her head toward it. More shadows moved there, and they grew close enough for her to see their human forms. She moved toward them. Once she got closer, two sets of hands reached in and grabbed her arms. She tried to slip away, but she had no leverage.

The hands pulled her out of the gel and into a cold, brightly lit room. Ocella shut her eyes tight against the brightness. The light filtered through her lids, causing pain. She opened her mouth to scream, but gel spewed out. She turned on her side and coughed up streams of gel.

Gentle hands rested on her back and shoulders. "Get it all out," a male voice said. "Your new lungs will adjust. Just takes a minute or two."

When she could breathe without gagging, she slowly opened her eyes to find that they, too, had adjusted to the room's brightness. However, she realized the room was actually quite dim, though brighter than the cell in which they were held before—

Ocella stiffened, then looked up at the man standing beside her.

Gods. He has the face he had before Umbra. Older, perhaps, but the same.

Kaeso looked healthier and more relaxed than she could ever remember; perhaps back when they first courted twenty years ago, but certainly not after Umbra had surgically changed him.

He smiled. "Welcome back."

"Where...?"

"Hold on," he said, and then took a large blanket from Claudia, who stood near the head of the cot on which Ocella lay. Kaeso wrapped the blanket tightly around Ocella's naked, gel-covered body. "Let's get you warm first."

Claudia went and stood next to Kaeso, regarding Ocella with a sympathetic smile. "No fun being born, is it?"

"Born?"

Ocella feigned confusion, but she already knew what had happened. Memories came back to her in a torrent. She could access them the same way she could when she stood before Jupiter, Juno, and Minerva.

She was a golem.

"Kaeso" gently wiped her face with the towel. "I resisted at first, but it's not so bad. All the injuries I had before, the changes Umbra made to my body—all gone. This is the real me, and I've never felt better. You will, too, once you're a little warmer and we get some hot *kaffa* in you. It's actually quite good here."

No. If I'm a golem, I'm already dead. I'm not alive. This isn't me. Oh, gods, they've somehow trapped my soul! I'll never see Elysium. I'll never see Cordus again. My poor, dear boy...

Despair overwhelmed Ocella. Her body started to go numb, beginning in her fingers and toes, then spreading up her arms and legs. She couldn't move and she didn't care. Her breathing shallowed, and her heart skipped beats, then struggled to beat at all.

The sympathetic smiles Kaeso and Claudia wore were replaced with cold frowns, as if Ocella was a piece of machinery that didn't work the way they hoped.

"She's fading," Claudia said. "The invasion approaches—"

"It's all right," Kaeso said. "She'll come around." He sighed. "Let's get another body."

Then warmth and darkness embraced her.

And awareness came to her in waves....

Chapter Forty

Cordus thanked Fortuna that the Consular Palace had not changed since he left. He led Aquilina, Ulpius, and Gracchus through the labyrinthine halls, down into the basements, and through ancient corridors. For a while, Ulpius and Gracchus stayed back several dozen paces to ensure they weren't followed. Cordus assumed the Praetorians fighting near the palace doors had held back the attackers, for Ulpius and Gracchus reported no signs of pursuit when they later rejoined him and Aquilina.

Cordus took the survivors down a long, brick-lined tunnel with ancient wiring that lit the way with dim light fixtures. He stopped at a large metal door with rust around the edges. Cordus knew this place well. He pulled on the old latch, and the door opened with a loud scraping that echoed up and down the hall. They all held their breath and listened for footsteps. When Cordus heard none, he pulled the door wide enough to let them in. He stepped into the dark room, felt along the left side of the wall for the ancient light switch, and flipped it on. Light pads above them fluttered, then came on to illuminate the room. Cordus pulled the door close as soon as they were all in.

"*Dis Pater*," Gracchus breathed as he looked around.

They stood in a large storage room, a hundred paces long and wide, containing items that were centuries old—from the first tabulari to bins of clothing to old hand-made toys the consular children played with before the era of mass industry. All the items were labeled and stacked neatly on rows of wide shelves that stretched into the murkiness ahead. To their right sat an old ground car that used to run on steam, most of it covered in a moldering canvas tarp. The room displayed the Roman penchant for organization, but also showed how quickly Romans forgot their past—it obviously had not been visited in years.

Cordus led them down a row toward the back of the room.

"Been working in the palace for three years," Ulpius muttered from behind Cordus, "and I never knew this was here. More holes in this place than a senator's honor."

"How did you find this?" Aquilina asked.

Cordus glanced at her. It was the first thing she said since they fled the attack. Her eyes were still hollow, but her voice was calm.

"Couldn't stand my family, so I did a lot of exploring. Drove them crazy, too, because I'd disappear and they wouldn't know where I'd gone. This place was my favorite. Only came here three times, though."

"Only three?"

"After the third time, my father beheaded the slave who was supposed to watch me."

She was silent.

Cordus sighed deeply, trying to expel the memory. "Anyway, there's an old visum box here that I adapted to pick up the Palace bands."

"Those things are ancient. How old were you when you did that?"

Cordus shrugged. "Nine."

The light pads were dark above where his old visum should be, but there was enough ambient light for him to find the box. It sat in the corner of a storage room behind a small enclosure he had made years ago with boxes and tarps. If he hadn't known what he was looking for, he would have assumed it was just another stack of boxed junk. But Cordus flipped over a tarp as if he'd been here yesterday and entered the enclosure. His Muse-enhanced sight found the visum in the meager light, and he turned the on-dial. He smiled when the screen flickered to life and showed the same children's band he used to watch.

Nostalgia hit him like a blow to the stomach. His Muse-enhanced memory was always excellent with sensory details, but emotional memories usually weren't as vivid. This time was different. He remembered the loneliness that drove him down here in the first place, only for him to replace it with a different loneliness: a wish to play with children who weren't forced to play with him out of fear for their lives. He would watch the entertainment shows about children playing together in parks with toys or talking to fantasy animals. He marveled at advertisements depicting happy families doing happy things.

Normal lives that he knew he'd never have.

"Cordus?" Aquilina said from behind.

Cordus blinked, wondering how long he'd been staring at the children's band. He reached for the box's finder and searched for a news band.

"—the impostor was killed during his cowardly attack," said a grim-faced older man in a black uniform with Praetorian gold-rimmed scorpion sigils on his shoulders. He stood just outside the entrance to the Consular Palace. Behind him, portable lights showed the blown out doors, shredded by the explosion and subsequent pulse fire. The steps leading up to the doors, and walls around them, were pockmarked and blackened. "But we can confirm the impostor's men were all killed as well. Unfortunately...we were unable to save the Dictator's life. She died of knife wounds from the impostor's own hand just before he set off his bomb. The Praetorian Guard is now searching the area for the impostor's cohorts. They won't get far."

"Son of a whore," Ulpius snarled. "That's Prefect Tarquitius. He's head of the Praetorian Guard."

"Who got to him?" Aquilina asked in a hard but quiet voice. Cordus saw in her eyes the plans for her next assassination.

"To confirm," an off-camera news crier said, "you're saying this man"—a still picture appeared of Cordus when he stepped off *Vacuna* in the Consular Palace gardens—"is not the *real* Marcus Antonius Cordus, but an impostor?"

"Correct," Tarquitius said. "He only wanted to get close to the Dictator so he could murder her with a bomb surgically embedded in his body. The note he left us—the one I just read to you—confirms this."

"And what of Terra's defense?" the news crier asked. "Reports say Terra is the alien vessel's next target?"

"Senator Quintus Arrius Wendatus has graciously offered his forces up for the defense of the Terran system," Tarquitius explained. "Dictator Servillia and the Senator were conducting secret negotiations—"

Ulpius cursed under his breath. Aquilina whispered through clenched teeth, "Lies. Arrius was the only warlord who *refused* to contribute."

"—so the Senator will honor the deal both he and the Dictator were about to announce before this horrible crime."

"When will the Senator's forces arrive in the Terran system? The alien ship is only a day away at its current speed."

"As I said, the Senator and Dictator had already negotiated for the merging of their Legions, so the Senator's forces are already on their way. They should arrive before the vessel gets here."

"That's good to hear, Prefect. Now, are there any theories as to who was behind the Dictator's assassination? The impostor fooled many experts. Surely he had some powerful backing, yes?"

Tarquitius shook his head. "No evidence yet, but we do have suspects in custody who will provide the information we need soon enough. I cannot name our suspects at this time."

"They haven't had the time to torture their 'suspects' into confessing," Gracchus muttered.

Worry twisted Cordus's gut. *Blaesus, Dariya, and Daryush...*

"How could this have happened?" the news crier asked. "How did this impostor get so close to the Dictator and fool even the Consular

Medicus, who swore his blood matched the samples previously taken from Marcus Antonius Cordus?"

Tarquitius sighed deeply. "We've heard the rumors for six years. We all wanted to believe one of the Antonii lived, especially Cordus, who captured every Roman's heart after the Liberti assassinated him. With this alien threat, we all prayed for a savior who could unite Romans once again to fight a common threat. Well this impostor took advantage of that desire. We're not sure how he did it yet, but we will find out. Right now all Romans need to unite under a single banner. I'm not a political man; my only desire is to ensure the safety of the Republic. That is why I will support Senator Arrius's leadership during this present crisis. I urge all Romans who love the Republic to do the same."

"Thank you for taking the time to talk with us, Prefect Tarquitius."

Tarquitius nodded and then left the interview area.

The news crier turned to the camera and said, "Two hours ago, the *Vestales* removed the Sacred Flame from the Temple of Vesta for the first time in over a thousand years. They say it is just a precaution, but does it mean Roma is doomed? We'll find out after this message from Scipio's Meats and Confections. Whether weddings, dinner parties, or funerals, Scipio's can..."

Gracchus spit on the floor. "Tarquitius, you bastard."

Ulpius turned to Aquilina. "What are your orders?"

Aquilina continued staring at the visum. "We find Arrius."

Cordus stayed silent as they began discussing possible ways to kill the Senator. Cordus wasn't thinking of the Republic or vengeance or the alien vessel: he wondered if his crew were still safe. He wondered if *Vacuna* was still in the Consular gardens. He wondered if Ocella and Kaeso were still alive, somewhere, inside that alien vessel that everyone was trying to destroy.

Most of all he felt relief. He would not be consul today.

But his plan to stop the alien vessel still needed to go through if Terra had any hope of survival. Even with all Roman factions united, Cordus doubted their fleets could do anything. His idea was the only way.

"We need to get to your Muse com center," Cordus said, interrupting the assassination planning between the Praetorians. All three looked at him with stony faces. "Regardless of what's happened, my idea is still the only hope we have of stopping that vessel."

Aquilina's jaw moved back and forth. "That may be true," she said quietly, "but I would sooner see the Republic burn than unite under the banner of Arrius."

"Aquilina, I know what you must be feeling, but now is not the time—"

"You have no idea what I'm feeling," she snarled. "I just held my mother's bloody corpse in my arms. I know who did it, so I'm going to kill him."

Cordus glanced at Ulpius and Gracchus, and knew he'd get no support from them. They had just lost two friends and the dictator to whom they had sworn oaths. Their blood was boiling, and they wanted Arrius's head just as much as Aquilina did.

"Listen to me, all of you," Cordus said slowly. "You will have Arrius, I swear this to you. I will even help you. *But not now.* If we don't go with my plan now, we won't be ready when the alien vessel arrives."

Aquilina shook her head. "Arrius dies as soon as he arrives in the Terran system."

"Fine," Cordus said, "but he won't get here for another twenty-four hours. Plenty of time to prepare for the alien vessel. After that, you're free to go on whatever suicide mission you want."

Aquilina stared at him for a long time. In the flickering lights of the visum screen, she seemed the very likeness of Nemesis, with the pale skin and tormented eyes of the vengeance goddess.

"Or was that talk of self-sacrifice and saving billions of Romans just *cac*?" Cordus continued. "Now that *you* have to sacrifice for the greater good, are you willing to do it?"

Aquilina tilted her head to one side, then one corner of her mouth turned up in a smile that held no warmth. "We'll help you for twenty-four hours. But when Arrius arrives—"

"Right," Cordus said.

He knew she wouldn't listen to his arguments at this point. He just hoped she would come to her senses later when he really needed her.

Chapter Forty-One

As they approached the way line, Ocella watched on the vessel's wall-sized monitors. The way line was marked with a yellow cross-hair target; otherwise it would be invisible to the naked eye. This way line would take them to the Terran system.

The vessel was leaving behind the Pietas system—a system that had once been a thriving Roman province largely untouched by the civil war—as barren and lifeless as it had been before humans had terraformed it. The vessel had taken enough witnesses from among the population to obtain a diverse selection of experiences for the Observers and then eliminated all life in the system with its toxin drones. They would not leave behind anything that could one day rise to challenge the Observers. It had happened many times before the Observers had found the wisdom of eliminating all rivals.

Better to use the golems as hosts rather than naturally occurring species—there was no doubt regarding biological compatibility nor any chance of an anomalous being evolving to resist their strain.

Like Marcus Antonius Cordus.

Ocella now understood why they had not taken him on Reantium: They wanted him to chase the vessel in a vain attempt to rescue Kaeso and Ocella. They knew he was a unique individual and that his emotional experiences would be highly valuable to the new archives and as trade with other vessels of their strain.

But they had not counted on just how unique Cordus was until after they had absorbed the minds of Ocella and Kaeso. They now understood the quality of his character, that he could unite humanity against the Observers. Worse, they now understood his potential immunity to *all* strains, not just the Terran strain in him.

They had to find him on Terra and take him, then discover the biological mechanisms that produced such a being. His body contained the secrets to why he could resist the Observers. And so the attack on Terra would be an invasion, not an extermination.

As a golem, Ocella no longer held any affection for the boy, but her memories of doing so were still there. Her knowledge of Cordus was one of the reasons the vessel had chosen her and Kaeso to oversee its first invasion force in over six million years: They would have an easier time capturing Cordus if once recognized them.

Even Ocella's golem mind marveled how it had been so long since the Observers last undertook an invasion. The octopods were the last species they'd encountered, and they had been easily conquered. The Observers took their experiences, stored them in the internal archives, exterminated the octopods, and then slept until the humans—a new species with new experiences—discovered them. The Observers would return to their home after exterminating the humans and trade experiences with other vessels of the Observer strain. Though the Observers hid most of their thoughts from her, she could sense their growing excitement. They were eager for a fight after so long, to test themselves against another sentience.

She was happy the Observers shared this knowledge with her rather than blocking themselves like they had with the Claudia golem earlier. They had finally removed the block from Claudia, but Ocella could not imagine going for so long with the Observers' comforting presence in her mind.

Kaeso entered the control room and approached her. She still remembered her natural body's weakened physical response to his proximity. She did not look back on it with emotion, as she would have if she wasn't a golem. It was a memory now, with no regrets or opinions. Her purpose was to serve the Observers. Kaeso, along with Lucia, Claudia, and now Varo, were instruments that served different purposes.

She turned to Kaeso. "Are the legions ready?"

She could have asked him this with her mind, and he could have communicated with her from the legion decks spread throughout the ship. But she found it pleasing to use her voice, and he apparently did too. She supposed it was a remnant of their emotional attachments to each other, but the Observers did not object, so she continued to talk as a human would.

"All loaded into their drones and ready to fly," Kaeso reported. "I'm going to my drone once we enter Terran space. I wanted to stop here first and wish you the grace of the Observers."

Ocella glanced at him and allowed herself a smile. The remnants of their old bodies that the Observers allowed to survive surprised her at times. The Observers were wise beyond all measure, so there must be a reason for it. Her golem mind was not built to fathom the reasons, so she ignored those thoughts.

"And to you, Kaeso."

"See you on Terra."

Ocella watched him leave the control room. He seemed to retain more of his natural body's preferences than she did…except in one instance. Whenever her thoughts turned to Marcus Antonius Cordus, a hollow feeling spread through her body, making it hard for her to concentrate on her true duties. She wondered again at the Observers' hidden wisdom to allow such thoughts—

She was suddenly in the Temple of Jupiter Optimus Maximus, standing before Jupiter, Juno, and Minerva. They sat upon their thrones staring down at her. She knew they were not real gods—if such beings even existed—but they were the closest thing to gods in the universe. She prostrated herself before her Observers.

"What is your command?" she asked, her forehead touching the warm polished floor.

"Your thoughts are troubled," Jupiter rumbled.

"We feel your emotions, child," Juno soothed.

"You question our wisdom," Minerva said. The owl perched on Minerva's throne hooted softly.

"I am yours to command," Ocella said. She didn't know what they were asking or how to respond to their statements. She was their instrument. Why were they not giving her a task?

"Do you love us?" Juno asked.

Ocella lifted her head. "Love?" she asked, confused. "I am yours to command." *Why were they asking about love?*

"You are our child," Jupiter said with a deep, comforting voice. "We love you. Do you love us, your creators and your gods?"

Her natural body had once known love. She had memories of loving Cordus and Kaeso. She could access them anytime she wanted, but they were like reading a biographical history of someone she never knew. Sometimes a gnawing feeling came with the memories, as if something was about to burst from her skull if she didn't acknowledge it. That feeling was back.

She shook her head, trying to be rid of it. The feeling made her doubt the Observers. She would rather die than doubt them.

"I—I am yours to command," Ocella said.

The gods glanced at each other. They looked troubled, and it gave Ocella a feeling she only knew through her old body's memories. Fear. What could be so bad as to scare the Observers? Whatever it was had to be truly evil indeed.

"She still does not love," Juno said.

"The transition is not complete," Minerva said. "She is flawed, as are the others. We must create new versions."

"The invasion is at hand," Jupiter rumbled. "There is no time to create more. The anomaly must be captured and studied before it realizes its potential. This one"—nodding to Ocella—"serves us well enough, though is incapable of loving us. That will change in future versions."

Minerva and Juno both nodded their heads.

And then Ocella was back in the vessel control room, facing the wall-sized monitor. She blinked; the transition back to her golem body made her sway on her feet.

"Are you well?" Varo said from behind her. He put a hand on her shoulder to steady her.

"The Observers brought me before them, and I just returned."

Varo looked at her with awe. "What are their commands?"

Ocella stared at him. "They issued no commands. They asked me questions."

"What questions?"

The Observers had not forbidden her from discussing the visit with any other golem, so Ocella figured it was fine for her to tell Varo about it.

"They asked if I loved them."

"Love? I don't understand. Why would they bring you before them and not issue commands?"

"They didn't rescind their previous commands. We will continue to perform the tasks we were assigned."

Varo nodded. "We enter the way line to Terra in fifteen minutes. There is an armed way station nearby, but it will not impede our progress."

Ocella knew the way station, one of the better-armed stations in the Roman Republic since it led to Terra. It would do everything it could to impede the vessel, but could no more stop them than a gnat could stop a speeding aero.

What made her pause, though, was that Varo also seemed to prefer making his reports with his voice. Why did they not use the communication methods the Observers gave them? Why did she prefer to use her voice, too?

Were they really 'flawed' like the Observers suggested?

"Thank you for the report," Ocella said. "You may return to the piloting controls. When we emerge from the Terran way line, we will maneuver the vessel to the weakest point of their defenses. Agreed?"

"Agreed."

Varo strode across the room to his position at the tabulari panels that controlled the vessel's actions. The controls were nothing like those on human ships, which relied on a tabulari interface operated by hand motions. Ocella and Varo operated the vessel controls with their minds. It was much faster and more efficient than antiquated hand motions.

Ocella's mind saw the data regarding the vessel's progress toward the way line, its defenses, its preparations for its first invasion in six million years. All proceeded as planned by the Observers.

She should have felt satisfaction, but that gnawing feeling that she had when thinking of Cordus had not left her.

Chapter Forty-Two

Cordus knew how to get into the Temple of Jupiter Optimus Maximus undetected. Secret corridors between the Consular Palace and the temple had been built centuries ago—the Muse-infected Antonii and Collegia Pontificis had sometimes wanted to gather in secret without even the Praetorian Guard knowing.

He was more worried about getting to the implant com room. Aquilina said it was on the top floor of the Temple, near a com dish that broadcast the signal—based on mysterious Muse physics—to the universe. It was supposedly guarded by an entire cohort of Praetorians, all veterans loyal to the Republic.

Cordus led Aquilina, Ulpius, and Gracchus through ancient stone corridors beneath the palace that smelled of mold and the Tiber River. Most of the time they had to feel their way through pitch-blackness. Cordus remembered these corridors as if he had been a child yesterday, exploring them for exploration's sake. He had no trouble maneuvering around old torch sconces, pipes, and the occasional statue of a god or consul—obstacles that the Praetorians behind him cursed when they ran into them. Cordus often warned them when they approached something, but frequently to no avail. While Gracchus and Aquilina endured each collision with a stoic grunt, Ulpius cursed like an ancient drover pulling an obstinate ox.

"*Cac!*" Ulpius swore when his head struck a low-hanging pipe. "I'm more beaten up in this *caccing* corridor than I was on *caccing* Reantium!"

"Must you complain every time?" Gracchus grumbled in a rare show of irritation.

"I'm a centurion, boy, it's my job."

"How much further?" Aquilina asked calmly from behind Cordus.

Cordus ran both hands along the chipped plaster walls to his right. He knew they were adorned with frescoes over 500 years old, but the smooth paint he remembered as a child had given way to a film of dust. They hadn't been maintained as they were when the Antonii and Collegia still ran the Republic.

His hands found the alcove that he'd been searching for: It held a small bronze figurine of a naked Venus. He knew the doors were close.

"Another ten paces," Cordus announced, then took his hands off the walls and strode forward. "There shouldn't be any more obstacles. At least there were none six years ago…"

Ulpius grumbled under his breath, and Gracchus sighed. Aquilina said nothing.

Cordus found the smooth door at the end and then felt along the left side for the control pad. He placed his hand on the pad, and it glowed as it scanned him. The glow seemed as bright as a spotlight in the blackness they had endured for the last half hour.

"Won't that alert someone?" Aquilina asked.

"No, it's not linked to the Palace's tabulari bands. It's a standalone lock that scans for the Muses in me. If it finds them, it will unlock."

The door lock clicked open.

"We're entering the temple," Cordus said as he unslung his pulse rifle. "It's another secret corridor, but it's not limited to Muse-infected people, so there *could* be guards."

He dropped to one knee, his rifle aimed at the door, while Gracchus and Ulpius stood behind him with their rifles up. Aquilina put her hand on the door latch, counted down from three, and then pulled the door inward. Cordus tensed his finger on the trigger, scanning the corridor beyond for targets.

The empty corridor was decorated the same as the one they were leaving, but this one was well lit by light pads on the ceiling. It stretched off into the distance.

Cordus exhaled. Ulpius and Gracchus lowered their rifles. Aquilina looked around the door, then turned to Cordus. "Lead," she commanded, impatience dripping from her voice.

Cordus slung his rifle and then entered the corridor. "What makes you think you can even get to Arrius?" he asked Aquilina as they walked side-by-side.

"Anybody can be killed," she murmured, her hard eyes focused ahead. "All it takes is planning. Look what happened to your father. Look what happened to my mother."

"My father's killer traded his life and so likely did your mother's."

Aquilina didn't say anything.

"Well. You are a Praetorian to your core: willing to give your life for your leader. Are you willing trade the lives of Ulpius and Gracchus, too?"

The two Praetorians maintained a respectful distance from Cordus and Aquilina, as they had the entire journey. But Cordus had no doubt the two could still hear the conversation despite his low tones.

"They know their duty. We all swore oaths before the gods."

"Say you do kill Arrius. What then? More civil war as the other warlords fight to replace your mother and Arrius?"

Aquilina continued to stare ahead. "Arrius will die by our hands. Anything less would be an affront to the gods. What happens afterwards is up to Jupiter."

Cordus sighed and stopped walking. The two Praetorians stopped behind them, keeping their distance. Cordus took her hand in a firm grip; he was relieved she allowed him to do so. "Aquilina, if by some godsdamned miracle my plan works, I will need you to help me be consul."

She smirked. "You don't need me. You have all the wisdom you need in that head of yours."

"Things have changed over the last six years. That 'wisdom' is a bit outdated. It's like your idea to contact the news criers; I never would have known those people or come up with that idea. I need you if I'm going to be consul."

"So now you *want* to be consul?"

"There's nothing I want less. But I'd rather be consul than hand it to the likes of Arrius."

She looked away and pulled her hand from his.

"The more help I get from you, the better chance we have of making that happen. When I'm Consul, I'll make sure Arrius pays for his crimes."

Aquilina's jaw moved from side to side. "Once you're at the com room, there's not much we can do anyway."

"You can watch my back while I'm in there. No doubt the Praetorians there are loyal to Tarquitius. And no doubt some of Arrius's agents are prowling about. And who knows what the alien vessel will do once it realizes what I'm doing."

"Cordus, we're wasting time."

He turned and proceeded down the corridor. He hoped he could convince her to stay with him before they got to the com room. He understood her desire for justice; Cordus's own desire to get back at the alien vessel for stealing Kaeso and Ocella, and destroying Libertus, was his primary motivation right now. He wasn't sure he'd react any differently if he saw Ocella murdered before his eyes. But he needed Aquilina if his plan was to work.

Of course, there were his...other reasons. He still felt the electric jolts whenever they touched. He didn't know if she felt the same way. He thought she did, maybe, but his experience with women was limited to the memories of the Muses, and they were of dubious value. One thing he understood from them was that every woman was different, and that every generation was different. What were Roman women like today? What were Roman *Praetorian* women like?

A chuckle came from Marcus Antonius to Cordus's right.

I thought you were asleep, Cordus thought to him. *Haven't heard from you in hours.*

"Sleep is for mortals," Marcus sniffed. "Thinking of women, eh?"

What? You can't read my mind.

"No, but nothing quickens a man's heart like a beautiful woman, and yours seems to double-time whenever the lovely Aquilina is nearby."

I'm worried about her.

"Yes, it would be a pity if she dies. She'd make a fine wife."

Cordus stumbled, and Aquilina grabbed his arm to steady him. "You all right?" she asked.

"Yes. Just, er, lost in thought."

"Then come back and focus on your feet."

He nodded. Then to Marcus, he thought, *Who said anything about marriage?*

"Why not? She comes from a strong family, she's obviously intelligent, and she would be a perfect link to the old regime in your succession. Not to mention we bet she's an absolute tiger in—"

I'm not marrying her. Now shut up.

Marcus bowed his head once. "As you wish. We'll just, um, go back to sleep." And then he disappeared.

Cordus gave Aquilina a sideways glance. The light in the corridor was dim, but he could still see her sharp cheekbones and olive skin beneath black hair tied back in a long braid. Gone was the easygoing, flirty Aquilina she'd been on *Caduceus* and Reantium. Now her jaw was set and her lips pressed into a thin line.

But she was still as beautiful now as she was when Cordus first saw her in that jail on Reantium. He didn't want to lose her for reasons much more personal than the fate of the Republic.

When they reached the end of the corridor, Cordus found the locked door he knew would be there. He turned to the Praetorians. "There are two more doors on the other side. One leads to a small Temple Custudae post, and the other opens into a stairwell that accesses each floor of the Temple."

"How many *caccing* doors in this place?" Ulpius grumbled.

"Makes for better defense if the Temple is under attack," Cordus explained. "We'll stop at the Custudae post first."

All three Praetorians gave him a puzzled look, but then nodded when he explained what they would do there.

"Then we'll take the stairwell up to the top level." He looked at Aquilina. "Once up there, you'll need to lead us to the implant com."

She nodded. "Let's move."

They opened the door the same way they'd opened the last one. Seeing nobody beyond, they entered the small hallway, which was similar to the spartan corridor they just left. Just like Cordus remembered, the private stairwell was immediately to his right and the door to the Temple Custudae post was straight ahead. The door had a large window on it. The darkened office beyond looked empty.

Rather than use their previous door-opening tactics, Aquilina strode up and opened the door as if she belonged there. She left it open for the rest of them to enter. They all affected relaxed strides, but kept their pulse rifles unslung in case things went badly.

Fortuna was with them, however; there was nobody in the post. It was past midnight, so the only guards likely to be there were the night watch, and they would be out in the temple. Especially with the Dictator's assassination.

Cordus led them to a Custudae closet and they found what they needed—ceremonial Custudae uniforms. Each uniform had a gold breastplate, red-plumed gold helm, and black robes that fit beneath the armor. The helm was of particular interest to them because it would block most of their features.

They all found uniforms that fit, put them on, and quickly left the post for the private stairwell. Cordus led them up six flights of stairs until they reached the level of the implant com.

They stopped before the door and Cordus turned to Aquilina. "Your turn."

"This is where it gets challenging," she said quietly. "Praetorians should be guarding the place, not Custudae, so they will try to stop us. These uniforms should get us close enough to take them down."

Ulpius and Gracchus frowned at each other. "Damned nasty business, taking down fellow Praetorians," Ulpius said. "Them boys are just following orders."

Aquilina glared at Ulpius. "Like Prefect Tarquitius?"

"Never said we won't do it. Just saying I don't like it."

"Neither do I," Aquilina said finally.

She gave Cordus a hard look, as if waiting for him to say something. He knew what she wanted him to do. Bile rose in his throat. He knew it would save the lives of honorable men and women who were simply doing what they thought was best for the Republic.

All I have to do is enslave them, Cordus thought bitterly.

"If it comes to a potential fight...I will do what I can to stop it."

Aquilina nodded, then opened the door.

They entered a corridor that was not as opulent as the temple's public halls. Those halls were adorned with tapestries, murals, statues, and alcoves filled with more tapestries, murals, and statues. The flamens and Pontiffs did love their art. This hall, though not as dank and sparse as the corridors below, could have fit right in at any merchant's office in Roma's financial districts—gray carpeting, off-white walls, and wood doors with door-length windows at their sides. Each door had a control pad next to it, and all were marked with the name of an administrator or high-ranking flamen.

Cordus paused. Nobody was in the corridor.

This feels wrong....

"The Temple is on lockdown," Aquilina whispered, noticing Cordus's hesitation. "Tarquitius probably recalled all Praetorians to search for us. We either do this or we leave."

And go where? Cordus thought. This was his only chance to save Kaeso and Ocella. If he couldn't do that, he might as well be captured or dead.

Cordus nodded, and they entered the corridor.

They marched down the corridor as if they had important business. Aquilina arrived at the implant com door, which bore the mundane nameplate "Numinatus". Cordus smiled. *Office of the Numina* was an appropriate name to house a device that used Muse physics to communicate across the universe. It's what the Praetorians used to call Umbra Ancilia before they figured out the Ancilia were simply humans.

Aquilina turned to Cordus. "Once I put my palm on that lock pad, they will know we're here."

Cordus nodded. "If my plan succeeds, they will be too busy to care."

Ulpius growled, "Let's get this over with." Gracchus nodded his gold-helmed head in agreement.

Aquilina put her palm on the lock pad. It glowed blue as it scanned her hand, then the door clicked open. Aquilina reached for the door handle.

The door slammed into her, flinging her back into Ulpius and Gracchus. Two Praetorians charged through, all black armor and helms with raised pulse rifles. More of them poured out of the doors up and down the corridor, all screaming at Cordus's team to drop their weapons.

Cordus didn't have much of a choice with a dozen barrels in his face. He slowly put down his rifle. The others did the same, then put their hands on top of their heads.

Prefect Tarquitius walked out of the Numinatus room, his eyes angry.

CHAPTER FORTY-THREE

Prefect Tarquitius paced in front of the prisoners and then stopped before Cordus. He reached up and pulled the ceremonial Custudae helm off Cordus's head, then gave him an appraising stare.

"You look like him, I'll give you that," Tarquitius said. "Your surgeons did a remarkable job."

Ulpius spit on the floor next to Tarquitius's shiny black boots. "Because it *is* him, you whoreson traitor."

A Praetorian slammed his rifle butt into Ulpius's stomach. Ulpius grunted and doubled over, but then straightened slowly with a red face and a sneer.

Tarquitius's gaze never left Cordus.

Cordus searched his Muse memories. Tarquitius had been an apprentice of Scaurus, the former Praetorian Prefect, and Saturnist, who had helped Cordus flee Terra. From what the Muses told him, Tarquitius was loyal to the Republic, the Antonii, and his oaths. He had performed his duty, taking the lives of enemy soldiers or agents when necessary. There were no memories of cruelty by Tarquitius.

Is he still the man the Muse memories say he is?

"How much did Arrius pay you to betray the Dictator?" Cordus asked.

Tarquitius's eyes narrowed. "I'm no mercenary."

"That's right. You're loyal to the Republic and do what you think is best to secure it and make it strong. You served the Antonii and then whomever held the title of Dictator. But the constant rotation of dictators has worn on you. You see this civil war as a blasphemy that must be stopped. You want the Republic united again, but you don't care who does it, so long as this conflict ends. Better someone like Arrius become consul and stop the war than have it drag on in perpetual negotiations, deadlocks, and broken treaties. Is that about right?"

Tarquitius raised an eyebrow. "You think you've figured me out, eh?"

He drew the pulse pistol from his side holster and placed it against Cordus's forehead. It took all of Cordus's will to keep from releasing his bowels. He stared at Tarquitius, praying he masked his terror with determination.

Aquilina said in a strained voice, "Cordus."

He didn't look at her. He knew what she wanted him to do. *Not yet, not yet...*

"So tell me why I shouldn't kill you right now, impostor. You're the most wanted man in all the Republic. I'd be a Hero, given a Triumph even. Why shouldn't I take that?"

Cordus swallowed once. "Are you asking me or yourself?"

Tarquitius stared at him with cold, blue eyes. He had Nordic features with pale skin, blond-white hair. The wrinkles around his eyes shifted as he thought.

Don't make me do it, Tarquitius. Please Jupiter, don't force me do it.

The Prefect's head suddenly tilted, and Cordus saw a black com-ring in his left ear. He put his other hand on his throat to activate a voice sensor. "What?" he growled, his gaze and pistol never wavering from Cordus. He listened for a moment, and then his eyes widened. "When?"

He suddenly looked like a very old man. His cheeks sagged, and he gave a weary sigh. He removed his hand from his voice sensor then dropped his pulse pistol from Cordus's head. He stared at Cordus with a desperation that brought Cordus more fear than relief.

"Are you *him?* No more games."

Cordus lowered his hands from his head. "It's here, isn't it."

Tarquitius stared at him a moment longer, then nodded once. "Just came through the way line. Planetary defenses are engaging it now. My orders are to take you to a prison cell."

"Whose orders?"

Tarquitius's jaw moved back and forth. "Senator Arrius."

Cordus felt Aquilina tense at this confirmation of Tarquitius's culpability in her mother's death. He prayed she wouldn't do anything stupid right now.

"Prefect, let me in that room. I can stop that vessel. The Legions may only delay it at best, but they can't defeat it. Let me help."

Aquilina shifted next to Cordus. "You can prove it to him."

Tarquitius glanced from Aquilina to Cordus. "How can you prove it? Because if you can't convince me in the next five seconds, I'm taking you to a cell."

"Just for a moment," Aquilina said to Cordus.

Just for a moment. Surely I won't be damned for a moment's weakness? What's one more time...to save the Republic?

He swallowed, then said to Tarquitius, "You know the Antonii and the Collegia Pontificis were able to command the loyalty of any human being, yes?"

"They were touched by the gods," Tarquitius said. "I felt it when I was around them. But with you, I don't—"

Tarquitius inhaled sharply. The Praetorians standing around Cordus shifted in their places, their weapons wavering, some lowering them altogether. Even Aquilina, Ulpius, and Gracchus gave Cordus worshipful stares. The Muses rejoiced at him releasing their power; they reveled in the worship from others, which Cordus spent so much of his energy denying them. He wondered where Marcus Antonius was. *Probably too busy soaking in the worship like an addict in an opium den.*

Tarquitius cried out, "My Consul!"

He started to kneel, but Cordus shouted, "No!"

Tarquitius looked confused. Cordus immediately stopped releasing the Muse aura and ignored the disappointed cries from the Muses. It took a few seconds for the aura to dissipate. When it did, the Praetorians around him immediately brought their weapons back up as they shook their heads to clear them. Tarquitius blinked several times, but continued to stare at Cordus with the same awe as a moment before.

"I'm not consul," Cordus said, quieter. "And I will not allow you to kneel before me while I—" He tried to find words that would make sense to someone who was unaware of the Muses. "If you kneel, it must be by your own choice."

Tarquitius still looked confused, but he nodded. "I won't pretend to understand what you just did, but it's the same feeling I had when in the presence of your father. And that's proof enough for me. Lower your weapons."

Almost as one, the Praetorians lowered their weapons and backed away. Aquilina, Ulpius, and Gracchus brought their hands down from their heads. Ulpius and Gracchus seemed relieved, but Aquilina still stared daggers at Tarquitius.

"What do you need from me, my Con—" A sharp look from Cordus, and Tarquitius said, "What do you need from me?"

"Make sure I'm not disturbed after I enter that room. And put a detachment on the roof to guard the signal dish."

"Right. Centurion Drusus?"

A helmed centurion behind Tarquitius stepped forward. "Sir?"

"Station your men outside this door and in all the stairwells. Coordinate with the Custudii Prefect..."

As Tarquitius issued his orders, Cordus stepped in front of Aquilina's hate-filled stare at the Prefect. "I need you in there with me," Cordus said.

"You don't need me anymore," she said, still watching the Prefect over Cordus's shoulder. "You're here and all these fine men will protect you now."

"I don't need your protection," Cordus said. He took her hand, and she looked at him. "I need *you*."

A softness flickered in the cold mask she wore. For a moment, he thought he had broken through. But it was as if she realized this, and she strengthened the mask.

"Very well," she said.

Gracchus cleared his throat. "I'd like to volunteer to stay with you as well, sire."

"Gracchus, I'm not the consul—"

"Sire, with all due respect, you've been my Consul since you pulled my ass out of Reantium."

Ulpius nodded. "Agreed. But if it'll make you happy, I won't bend my knee until you walk out of there again."

Cordus didn't know what to say. He realized he had earned their loyalty not by command and not by using the Muses. He had earned it because they respected him. It was something his father and all the Antonii before him could never claim. He would die to protect these men, and they would do the same.

Ulpius broke the awkward silence. "Well enough of this sap. Go save the godsdamned Republic."

Cordus grinned and then walked into the implant com room.

Chapter Forty-Four

No ceiling light pads illuminated the com room; glowing tabulari and holo-monitors that lined the walls provided the room with flickering multi-colored illumination. The room was no more than ten paces square. A single, high-backed chair was fastened to the floor and faced the tabulari. A headset hung from the right corner of the chair's back. A rush of memories came back to him—his own memories, not from the Muses—of using a similar device to deactivate Ocella's Umbra implant six years ago, the night they had fled the Consular Palace.

"Well," he said, walking up to the chair, "they made the interface easy. What do these monitors do?"

"The ones on top are mundane com bands," Aquilina said. Two of the three monitors bore the Praetorian sigil: a gold scorpion on a red shield. The third displayed a publicly broadcast news band where a well-groomed female crier questioned a young centuriae in Terra's Naves Astrum. The sound was off, so Cordus could not hear the interview. A larger bottom monitor directly in front of the chair also showed the Praetorian sigil, but it was a three-dimensional display.

"The bottom monitor shows your message," Aquilina continued. "You focus your thoughts with images, sounds, and feelings which are transmitted to the other implant. The bottom monitor shows your transmission and then the response."

Cordus wondered if Marcus Antonius would show up on the monitors while Cordus was communicating with the vessel.

"Most definitely," Marcus said, leaning on the tabulari and peering at the monitors. "If you can see us, they will see us. They did a fine job figuring this out, considering they didn't have our guidance."

Maybe you'd better not show yourself, Cordus thought to him.

Marcus eyed him severely. "You're going to need us, young Antonius. That strain is more powerful than you can imagine. Even with the golem power, you will still need our council."

Cordus knew Marcus was right. But what would the others think when they saw Marcus Antonius Primus at his side on that monitor?

"We don't have time to debate this," Marcus said.

I know.

Cordus sat down. The chair was padded and comfortable, but it felt more like something into which a torturer would strap his victims. He took the head net, a mesh of clear elastic wires, and put it on. The net tightened so that it fit his head snuggly.

"Now wha—?"

The three mundane monitors above the large implant monitor flickered and then materialized into the same image. Three beings sat upon marble thrones, one man with two women on either side, all dressed in iconic white togas. Cordus knew who they were because their faces were on almost every public building in the Republic.

Jupiter leaned forward, his blue eyes shining with the fires of Elysium. He wore a fatherly smile that gave Cordus chills rather than comfort.

"My children," his voice boomed from the monitors' speakers, "your salvation is at hand."

Juno said in a motherly tone that was at once stern and sad, "Your leaders have failed you, so we have come to bring peace to the holy Republic. Your leaders will try to stop us, for they only desire power above your welfare."

Minerva, with an owl perched on her shoulder, said, "If you wish for peace, do not resist the angels we are sending to eliminate the current regime and its minions. Once Terra is secure, a golden age will begin that will surpass even that of the Antonii."

The images flickered again on the three mundane monitors, and then they returned to their previous state. The well-groomed crier stared open-mouthed at a monitor beside her before she realized she was back on camera.

"Blasphemy," Gracchus murmured.

"Yeah," Ulpius growled, "but enough will believe it's them. These Praetorian bands are supposed to be secure. If those aliens grabbed secure bands, they probably sent this out to every com device on Terra."

Aquilina said, "There are thousands of people outside and inside the Temple right now. The Temple monitors probably showed this, too."

The holo-monitors inside and outside the temple showed religious ceremonies to as many people as possible. If the gathering crowds panicked and believed the alien "gods" were real, some might take the alien side and try killing off Roma's leaders. When the "angels" showed up, things in the Temple could get violent.

"Aquilina, how do I get in?"

"If you were contacting another implant, we'd have the codes programmed into the tabulari; you could just look it up and send a transmission." She took a deep breath. "The vessel is not in the tabulari, so you'll need to search for it...somehow."

Cordus nodded. *Marcus, that's where you come in.*

"We are ready," Marcus said.

Cordus closed his eyes. The Muses whispered in his mind as they reached out to find the golem signals, just as they had done on Reantium. At first, they could find none on the com room's immediate level, but as their search expanded to other temple levels, signals began to appear to Cordus like tiny stars in his mind. More stars popped into existence as the Muses found golems outside the temple and in the surrounding buildings. The search expanded at an exponential speed, racing through Roma, then Italia, then the rest of Europa and the Mediterranean provinces. The stars in Cordus's mind exploded into a galaxy of signals, and kept growing. A part of his mind was shocked at how numerous the golems had become on Terra, but he had no time to think on it or pray for the safety of their citizen-owners once he took away their safety controls.

"We have all the golem signals on Terra, young Antonius," Marcus said from beside Cordus.

To the real gods of the Pantheon...forgive me.

Cordus mentally opened his hands wide to gather in all the power. It rushed into his hands as streaks of light too numerous to count. Thousands, millions, he had no idea. Their power filled him with a fire that did not burn, but made him feel...like a god.

He shook away that thought, and tried not to dwell on what the released golems were doing right now.

The vessel. Find the vessel.

Cordus searched the space around Terra and quickly found the alien vessel. He could not see it so much as feel the vibration of its immense presence. Its power overwhelmed any other source in the entire Sol system, like the sun outshone the planets. He drew in all the power from the golems and *leaped* for the vessel. He surged through the atmosphere faster than was possible for a mundane ship, only his thoughts limiting his speed. He flew through the atmosphere in seconds and entered the quiet cold of space. He knew he was not in space physically, that this was how his mind interpreted what was happening to him, but space felt every bit as cold as he imagined it would. It was agonizing; his body would have frozen solid. At least he could still breathe.

He found the vessel. Its amorphous shape seemed as big as the sun, though he knew that was not true. The power it emitted made it seem much larger to his mind's eye.

Black shapes, like hornets, streaked past Cordus from the vessel, all racing toward Terra. The drones. Terra's planetary defenses would engage them soon...if they weren't already distracted by the golems.

The vessel. Focus on the vessel!

Cordus willed himself to go faster, and he arrived at the vessel almost before the thought to accelerate left his mind. He approached the vessel at an alarming speed, and would crash into its obsidian skin in seconds. But he willed himself to go faster and then closed his eyes as he prepared for impact—

He fell into a patch of tall grass and rolled several paces before stopping. Dirt filled his mouth and eyes from the fall. He blinked away the grit and spit out strands of grass. After his eyes cleared, he looked around.

He was in a vast grassy plain beneath a blue, cloudless sky. A warm breeze swayed the tall green grass around him.

"I'm so happy to see you again, Cordus," a voice said from behind him.

Cordus whirled around. Ocella stood next to him, wearing the green dress uniform of a Liberti Defense Force centuriae. Her hair was longer, hanging down her back in a shoulder-length braid. She seemed younger than Cordus ever remembered. In fact, she looked only ten years older than Cordus.

Cordus stared at her. "Ocella, what—?"

"You have questions," Ocella said, holding out a white-gloved hand. Cordus slowly took it, and she pulled him up off the ground. "Come with me, and you'll have your answers."

Ocella turned around and marched toward a large temple off in the distance. Cordus stared at the temple; it looked like the Temple of Jupiter Optimus Maximus in Roma. Only *much* bigger.

Cordus glanced at Ocella again, her back straight and her stride purposeful. Why was she here in what should be the vessel's Muse mind? Why did she look so young? Disturbing thoughts struck him. Was it really Ocella or a Muse-generated copy? Where was her body?

Ocella turned around. She smiled, but it did not hold the warmth he remembered. "Do you want your questions answered or not?"

Cordus nodded once and then followed.

Chapter Forty-Five

Aquilina watched the lower monitor, seeing and hearing everything Cordus experienced. She marveled at how easily he had taken the Muse-based energy of the golems and then used that power to "fly" up to the alien vessel via the Muse com bands. Her own experiences with the implant com were much more mundane: just a recording of her mother standing in a drab room speaking her message. Cordus's experiences were dreamlike and real-time, limited only by his imagination. He sped past the incoming drones and then blasted through the alien vessel's shield. When he fell into the strange field, she began to hope. If he could penetrate the alien shields, he could defeat them.

"Good lad," Ulpius breathed.

Aquilina was about to agree, but her hope turned to dread when she saw Marcia Licinius Ocella.

"Who's that?" Gracchus asked, his blue eyes studying the monitor.

Aquilina sighed. "His mother."

"Mother? I thought she died."

"That is the Umbra Ancile who helped him escape Terra six years ago and who basically raised him ever since."

Ulpius grunted. "Well what the *cac* is she doing there?"

"Distracting him," Aquilina said.

The Muses were not stupid. If they had Kaeso Aemilius, they likely knew everything there was to know about Cordus. Especially his emotional buttons. They would use every weapon they had. Aquilina prayed Cordus could resist.

A tapping came from the door. Aquilina opened it to find Tarquitius standing there. She had to force herself not to put a pulse round in the man's brain right then and there. He had helped murder her mother. His life was hers.

But not now. Cordus needs me, and Cordus needs him. For now.

"What?" Aquilina asked.

If Tarquitius noticed the acid dripping from Aquilina's voice, he ignored it. "We have incoming drones. They're spreading across the planet. The Legion Aeris corps is engaging them, but there are too many. Some will be here in minutes. My men are protecting the implant com dish on the roof, but if something happens to the dish, only someone with an implant can access the systems to repair it."

"There are dozens of Praetorians with implants," Aquilina growled. "Use one of them."

Tarquitius frowned impatiently. "They're spread throughout the city looking for you. They won't get here in time."

Aquilina glanced at Cordus sitting in the com chair. His eyes were closed and he looked as if he was in a peaceful sleep. She had given him her word that she would protect him while he fought the vessel. It was a matter of honor. He was her Consul, but also more. She couldn't articulate what that "more" was. He was a good man and a good leader. Even after spending such a short time with Cordus, she could not imagine her life without him. And she knew very well he had feelings for her.

But if the implant com signal was lost...

"Gracchus, with me. Ulpius, guard Cordus."

Both Praetorians nodded. Gracchus unslung his pulse rifle and followed Aquilina out the door. Without a word, Tarquitius led them down the corridor through squads of black-armored Praetorians and Temple Custudii and to the stairwell that went up to the roof. They climbed two flights of stairs and then exited through a steel door onto the temple roof.

A cold wind blasted Aquilina. The lights of Roma twinkled in the pre-dawn, spanning the horizon in every direction. It reminded her of the view from her tower apartment in the Suburba, though not as spectacular since no building could rise higher than the temple. She loved that apartment, despite her mother insisting she move to the Consular Palace with—

A cold lump rose in Aquilina's throat, and she eyed Tarquitius's back as he strode toward the Muse com dish in the center of the temple's roof. Her right hand rested on her holstered pulse pistol.

I may not get a better chance...

She took a deep breath and dropped her hand to her side.

She spied squads of Praetorians and Custudii stationed across the roof. Mass driver cannons, their barrels pointed skyward, stood ready to rotate in any direction to combat the coming drones. The faint howl of sirens rose up from the city, warning citizens and slaves to take shelter. The crack of pulse fire occasionally echoed from all directions in the city, and Aquilina wondered if it came from looters or the rampaging golems Cordus feared he would unleash. Either way, they were not her concern.

The Muse com dish was small and nondescript compared to all the other com dishes spread across the roof. Four Praetorians guarded it, and Aquilina recognized Tarquitius's centurion as one of them.

"You can take cover with me in the bunker over there," Tarquitius said, pointing to a flat opening in the roof with stairs leading down to another door. "We'll only need you if something happens to the dish."

The last thing Aquilina wanted was to be in a confined space with Tarquitius. She wasn't sure she could stop her impulse to kill him. She was about to say she'd rather stay on the roof when the mass driver cannons erupted with fire. The sound wasn't as bad as the concussive force from each blast. The blasts increased the pressure on her ears and affected her balance.

"Incoming drones!" somebody shouted. All the Praetorians and Custudii took cover behind sandbagged fortifications while Tarquitius raced toward the bunker stairs.

In between the cannon blasts, Gracchus yelled, "My lady, we must take cover!"

Aquilina gritted her teeth and ran after Tarquitius, with Gracchus behind her. They charged down the stairs as explosions echoed around the temple and Consular Palace grounds. She glanced up at the sky to see blue streaks of light forking down around them. She had no more time to watch before Gracchus pushed her inside. He slammed the door shut just as a nearby explosion shook the entire temple. Dust and bits of stone fell on her head, and she had to blink the debris out of her eyes.

She had never been in the temple's roof-top command bunker, mostly because this was Custudii territory. It was a long room, but not very wide. One whole side was covered by tabulari and holo-monitors, each showing different areas of the temple complex. Six Custudii dressed in the same black armor as the Praetorians, but with Capitoline Triad sigils on their shoulders, sat at the tabulari communicating with cohorts stationed throughout the Temple complex. Aquilina noticed two Praetorian women sitting at tabulari near the far end of the room, also talking into their headsets.

"Status," Tarquitius called out.

A Custudae tribune quickly approached Tarquitius, just as another explosion shook the room. The young man flinched.

"No sign of the toxin they released on Libertus," the tribune said. "Drones are attacking Legion bases across the planet, but not in significant force. Probably diversionary strikes to keep them busy. The main focus of their attack appears to be Roma."

"They don't want to kill the whole planet," Tarquitius said. "That's something. What of Arrius?"

Aquilina flinched at the Senator's name, but she thought she hid it well.

"His Naves Astrum is engaging the vessel, but cannot breach its shield. The vessel seems to be ignoring them. Arrius is destroying the drones as they come out of the vessel, but there are just too many for him to get them all."

The mass driver cannons on the roof continued their thumping blasts, making the floor and holo-monitors shake. A massive explosion on the roof made Aquilina stumble. Everyone reached for the wall or a tabulari to steady themselves. They glanced at each other with fearful eyes.

"Direct hit on cannons five and nine!" shouted a Custudae at a tabulari. "All cannons now taking drone fire!"

Gracchus leaned toward Aquilina. "They won't last much longer out there."

"They need to protect the com dish," she muttered back. "Cordus can't get back without it."

"Could we just move the dish inside?" Gracchus asked.

Aquilina closed her eyes and accessed her implant for technical data on the dish. Information flew past her closed lids in streaks of letters, numbers, and diagrams. It took her implant seconds to search through the Muse com dish specifications. The com dish was on the roof so as to minimize any interference, but she could not find any spec saying the dish *had* to be on the roof. It was possible that bringing it inside would interfere with the signal, but leaving it outside at this point would surely destroy it.

She turned to Gracchus. "Fine idea, Praetorian. Want to help me get it?"

"Not really." But he unslung his pulse rifle and ensured it was set to fire.

Aquilina turned to Tarquitius. "We're going to move the com dish."

Tarquitius frowned. "It's raining drone fire out there, girl. You sure?"

"Yes, *old man*, I'm sure. If we don't protect that dish, Cordus can't defeat the vessel."

Without another word, Aquilina unslung her own rifle and followed Gracchus up the stairs to the horizontal door that protected the bunker. Gracchus heaved it open. They were greeted by a cacophony of mass driver blasts, sizzling drone fire, explosions, and the screams of men. They leaped out of the bunker, and then Gracchus slammed the door shut while Aquilina raced toward the com dish. The scents of ozone and smoke made her cough. Black shapes streaked above the Temple, then blue lightning blasted holes in the roof, cannons, and men around her. More black shapes slowed down and descended, though Aquilina could not tell if they were landing on the roof or the temple grounds. Roma's main power utilities appeared to be knocked out, for most of the city was now dark, with pockets of lights here and there. The temple compound was also dark on the outside to theoretically make it more difficult for the drones to attack. It did not seem to impede them at all, though.

They could turn Roma into glass if they wanted to, but they're not. They want Cordus alive. That will give us time.

The dish was still intact, but the Praetorians who'd been guarding it were behind their sandbag bunkers. Their black-helmed heads peeked up above the bags as they watched her and Gracchus run towards them. She stopped before the com dish and knelt down to study it.

"I need more light," she screamed to Gracchus. He nodded, then ran over to the Praetorians and shouted something.

As Gracchus retrieved a torch, she closed her eyes and tried concentrating on the specs for the dish. The terrible noise and shaking roof made it difficult. She had to spend several valuable seconds researching her implant's data to find the diagrams on the dish. She located the records she needed and held them in reserve until Gracchus returned.

He ran back to her, keeping his head low amidst the explosions. He fell to his knees beside her, activated the torch, and pointed it at the dish.

"Look for a thumb pad on the base," she yelled. Gracchus moved the torch around the base and located the pad.

The small thumb pad was well hidden—it matched the matte gray exterior of the dish's base—with only a black, oval outline to indicate its presence. Aquilina placed her thumb on it and then focused her implant to unlock it. A slot on the bottom of the base opened to reveal a flat tabulari with no interface, just a monitor the size of her hand. Tarquitius was right about the dish being inaccessible to anyone without an implant; the only way to interface with the dish was with implant communication. She needed to unlock the dish from its perch here without severing the com connection.

She was about to focus her implant toward the dish's interface when the sudden lack of noise startled her. The lightning had stopped, and the dark drones no longer swarmed above the temple.

She looked at Gracchus. His eyes widened as he stared over her shoulder. He whipped his pulse rifle around and fired several pellets over her head. Aquilina ducked away from the rifle, and then looked behind her.

A wave of spider-like creatures was racing toward them.

The Praetorian cohort outside *Vacuna's* shield began to withdraw from the landing pad and then ran up the garden path toward the palace's exit.

"Where are they going?" Dariya muttered, staring at the external displays.

Daryush grunted and motioned to one of his displays on the command tabulari. It showed a view from the west, toward the Temple of Jupiter Optimus Maximus. Dariya could see the roof through the shield's blue haze. Cannons fired at black shapes in the sky, which returned fire with blue forks of lightning. Orange explosions bloomed across the roof, and fires spread.

"They have bigger troubles than us now," she said. She strapped herself into the pilot's couch and then began the engine startup routines.

She could feel Daryush's accusing eyes. Without looking at him, Dariya said in Persian, "Cordus told us to leave if things went sour, and that's what we're going to do."

Daryush continued staring at her. She finally met his eyes and snapped, "I don't like it either, but we have to take care of ourselves. Just like we've always done, right?"

Daryush frowned, then turned away to stare at the command tabulari.

"Ush," she said with a softer voice, "the Romans killed our mother. They took your tongue. I will give my spirit to Angra Mainyu before I sacrifice anything more for them."

Daryush brought up a blank slate on the tabulari and then tapped out a message in Latin: *Cordus and Blaesus are not "the Romans". They're family.*

Dariya sighed, then turned off the shield and engaged the ion engines. The ship hurtled into the sky above the palace.

"I'm sorry," she said, her grip tight on the ship's controls. "We can't help Cordus and Blaesus."

As she set a heading for space, she prayed to Ahura Mazda that the alien drones would ignore them. And that she had the luxury of her brother's honor.

CHAPTER FORTY-SIX

The massive temple was farther than Cordus expected. He wanted to start jogging across the seemingly endless grasslands toward it, but Ocella strolled along at a leisurely pace and he didn't want to leave her behind.

"Can we hurry?" he asked.

She smiled at him. "Time does not flow here like it does in the mundane world. Your friends down in Roma do not experience things in the com room the same way you do here."

Fear bit at Cordus. How did she know about the com room? What else did she know?

"Are you Ocella?"

"Yes," she said. "But not the one you knew."

Cordus swallowed. "Is she...alive?"

"As you define it? No."

Cordus's legs weakened and he gasped for air. Nausea swept through his gut, and he put his hands on his knees. He stared at the grass and soil at his feet. *Oh gods, my mother is dead. They killed my mother. Kaeso, too?*

"Dear boy," the Ocella golem said, walking back to him, "do not grieve for her. All that she was is now in me. All her memories, emotions, and dreams for the future. I have them all. Including her love for you."

Cordus looked up at this thing pretending to be the woman he loved as a mother for six years. She seemed so young, her light brown skin smooth around her eyes and mouth, her black hair missing Ocella's silver strands. But she gave him the same patient look Ocella had given him the last time he saw her. Just before she and Lucia left to scout the Menota system.

It may have looked like her and had her memories, but it was not *his* Ocella.

"I want to see your masters now," Cordus growled. He stood tall again, stamping down the nausea. "Enough delay."

The young Ocella regarded him with kind eyes and then nodded, "As you wish."

They were suddenly inside the Temple of Jupiter Optimus Maximus. Cordus recognized the main altar chamber where hundreds of Romans gathered for mass rituals. But instead of an altar, there were three thrones. Upon those thrones sat the gods Jupiter, Juno, and Minerva. Each one was at least twelve feet tall. They looked just as impressive as they did in all the statuary and art throughout the Republic and every other world where the Pantheon was worshiped.

To Cordus's left, Ocella knelt prostrate on the floor before the three gods.

Jupiter put one fist on his knee and leaned forward, his blue eyes glittering with lightning. "You are the first being to meet us here without purification. That interests us."

"Is that what you mean by 'purification'?" Cordus said, nodding to Ocella.

Jupiter raised an eyebrow, as if Cordus had just asked if space was cold.

Marcus Antonius appeared to Cordus's right, a grin on his bearded face. Though Marcus looked confident, the Muses in Cordus's mind whispered fearfully.

"Impressive," Marcus said. He walked perpendicular to the thrones with his hands clasped behind his back, as if inspecting a cohort line on the battlefield. "Perhaps if we had appeared to the boy like this he would've shown us more respect."

Juno stared at Cordus, her contempt for Marcus dripping from her voice. "We do not hear the words of a strain that bows to mortals."

"'Mortals,'" Marcus said and then laughed. "It took us years to understand their culture so thoroughly as to manipulate them like this. You've done it in a matter of weeks. Congratulations!"

The three gods stared at Cordus, ignoring Marcus.

"What did you do to Ocella and Kaeso?" Cordus asked in a low growl.

The owl on Minerva's shoulder fluttered its wings. Minerva said in a serene voice, "They are part of us now. As you will be soon."

"What does that mean?"

"It means," Jupiter thundered, "that your mundane body will be brought to our vessel and examined."

Juno said, "Your coming here has helped us. We now know the source of the signal that projects your mind. We will retrieve your body presently."

Marcus continued to pace before the three gods, but spoke to Cordus. "You're a unique individual in our history, young Antonius. No species, in all the millions of years we've roamed the universe, has ever controlled us. Some were immune or incompatible, but none have *ruled* us like you. They want to dissect you like a flamen inspecting goat entrails."

"Like you would?"

"Of course," Marcus said, "but we can't. Plus...we're not sure we'd want to anymore. We've developed a certain, oh, respect for you over the years. Perhaps it's the same love and respect slaves develop for a benevolent master, or the acceptance your species gave us when we first infected your ancestor. Whatever it is, we stand with you now, young Antonius."

Juno sneered, looking at Marcus for the first time. "Your strain has become a slave to the mortals, just like the strain on Libertus. Blasphemy! When we retrieve the boy's body, we will burn you out of him."

Marcus bowed. "You are welcome to try, my lady."

When he straightened, he had a javelin in his right hand. Cordus had a microsecond to wonder where the javelin came from before Marcus flung it at Juno. The javelin flew straight and true into Juno's heart. Red blood spurted across her white robes. She gasped, staring first at the javelin and then at Marcus, before she slumped in her throne.

Jupiter roared. He stood, a fork of blue lightning in his right fist. He cast it at Marcus. Marcus raised his forearm, and a large, red shield emblazoned with the golden eagle of the Republic materialized. The shield deflected the lightning, but the blast sent Marcus flying backward twenty paces. He landed hard and then slid across the smooth marble floor.

Marcus leaped back to his feet, another javelin in his hand, and he threw it at Jupiter. The god tilted to one side. The javelin missed his chest by a breath, but continued on to slam into Minerva's stomach, who had stood up from her throne. Her eyes widened as she clutched at the javelin. She fell back against her throne, leaving bloody streaks down the white marble.

Minerva's owl shrieked and shot toward Marcus. He now had a gladius in his hand. He stabbed at the bird as it raked at him with its claws and beak. Jupiter flung more lightning at Marcus. This time the lightning struck Marcus's helm just as he sliced the owl in half. The two halves of the owl fell on the marble with sickening slaps; Marcus's golden helm clanged to the floor.

Jupiter threw another lightning fork just as Marcus flung his gladius at him. The gladius stabbed into Jupiter's thigh, causing the god to roar and fall onto the altar's steps. The lightning, however, hit Marcus in the chest, incinerating his armor and creating a massive hole. Marcus grunted and fell to his knees.

The entire battle had taken seconds. Ocella continued lying prostrate on the floor, never moving a muscle during it all. Cordus suddenly found the will and strength to move. He rushed over to Marcus to catch him as he started falling backward.

Cordus had no idea how Marcus could still live. The hole in his chest was two hands wide and Cordus could see the floor on the other side. The lightning had cauterized the surrounding tissue. Marcus's heart and most of his lungs was gone.

But they were not in the mundane world.

Marcus's face was pale, his body shaking. A weak smile appeared on his lips. "I think he got me," he said in halting gasps.

"What do I do?" Cordus asked. He could feel the Muse whispers weakening as they struggled to live. "How can I save you?"

"Can't be saved. No strength..."

"I can't do this without you."

Marcus laughed weakly. "We just remembered...today is your eighteenth birthday...you're a man in Liberti eyes now..." Marcus grabbed Cordus's shirt in a surprisingly steel grip and pulled him closer. "Be the man you were *meant* to be...young Antonius."

Marcus loosened his grip.

For the first time in Cordus's life, the Muses in his mind were silent.

Chapter Forty-Seven

Aquilina tried desperately to unlock the com dish as rapid pulse fire from the bunker behind her slammed into the oncoming alien horde. Gracchus fired from a laying position. The pulse fire ripped the creatures apart, but there were always more to take their place. The wave was slowly getting closer.

Aquilina pushed her thumb onto the dish's pad, trying to will her implant to unlock the dish from its magnetic moorings. Nothing happened. She couldn't focus with all these alien shrieks and that pulse fire.

This is why I joined the Praetorians and not the Legions! I hate battles!

Praetorians in the bunker screamed, "Targets behind us!"

Pulse fire was redirected behind the bunker, and an explosion announced the Praetorians were using grenades.

Aquilina pressed her thumb to the pad. *Open, godsdamn you!* "Cac!" she screamed, pressing harder.

A dark, multi-limbed form leaped at her. She ducked out of the way, but the creature clung to her with tentacles that had fingers on the ends. It quickly wrapped other tentacles around her throat. Her eyes bulged and her tongue flapped as the creature strangled her. She desperately reached for the knife at her belt, drew it, and stabbed at the alien's bulbous head. A gurgle escaped the alien's beaked mouth in the center of its body, along with the foul, ammonia-like odor of its breath. It released its tentacles from around her throat and fell to the ground. Aquilina dropped to her knees, gasping for as much air as her lungs could bring in.

Gracchus had tossed away his pulse rifle and was shooting aliens with his pulse pistol. But the aliens soon swarmed over him before Aquilina could help him. He fell to the ground, buried in tentacles and gray bodies.

More aliens leaped at Aquilina. She swung at them with her knife, stabbing some, but not enough. Their numbers shoved her onto her back, knocking the remaining air from her lungs. She couldn't breathe as aliens wrapped their tentacles around her throat once again, while others tied her limbs to keep her from flailing.

No weapons, she thought as she began to black out. *What a strange species...*

Pulse fire erupted in rapid bursts, accompanied by grenades that exploded so close that they deafened Aquilina. The aliens released their grip around her throat and limbs. Once again she gasped for air, but she couldn't move or hear anything. She simply looked up at the clear sky, marveling at how many stars she could see when the lights of Roma were turned off.

When was the last time a Roman saw a sky like this?

She knew her body and mind struggled with oxygen deprivation, yet she still could not muster the will to move or to think clearly.

Cordus needs me.

She thought of him strapped in that chair downstairs, wondered suddenly what he was doing in the alien vessel above. If he was still alive.

Tarquitius's face appeared above her, as did several other black-helmed Praetorians. He shouted something at her. She blinked, realized she didn't want this traitorous whoreson giving her any more help than he already had. She gathered her strength and tried to rise on her own. Her hearing slowly came back. Rapid pulse fire continued all around her. Alien bodies and pieces were strewn about the roof.

To her right, Gracchus lay on his back amidst alien bodies. His glazed eyes stared up at the sky, his tongue hanging from his mouth, his face purple. A groan escaped her throat that she felt more than heard. A sudden memory came to her of the pride on Gracchus's freckled face when she told him he had earned a place on her team. They were the same age, had been in the same graduating class at the Praetorian—

"They're overrunning us," Tarquitius shouted into Aquilina's ear, forcing her to stamp down her grief once again. "We need to get below, with or without that dish."

Aquilina looked down at the dish, still locked in place. Tarquitius tried to pull her back toward the door that led down to the temple, but she yanked her arm free and bent down. Her brush with death seemed to have cleared her mind, not to mention that most sounds around her were now muted. Her concentration focused sharply on the dish.

Unlock, she directed to her implant.

The locking mechanisms suddenly blinked a green color. A metallic *chunk* came from the dish, loud enough for her to hear. She picked up the dish and examined the small tabulari interface. It was still transmitting. She took two strides toward the door that led down to the com room, but stumbled and fell into a pile of wet alien parts. Disgusted, she tried to stand but was still too stunned. Tarquitius lifted her up by her arms before she could shrug away his hands. She didn't say anything to him and continued toward the door.

I need to get to Cordus. He's all that matters now. My men are dead. My mother is dead. He's all that matters now...

The door to the Temple was near the edge of the roof. As Aquilina and the Praetorians approached the door, a wave of aliens suddenly rose up over the edge and skittered toward the humans.

Without pausing, Praetorians near her opened fire on the horde. Alien bodies disintegrated under the pulse blasts slamming into them at twenty pellets per second. The Praetorians held them off, but more aliens always came from behind and took the place of the dead. Not even the piles of corpses the aliens had to climb over slowed them down.

Tarquitius screamed into his com. "All available units, to the roof now! I say again, all available units to the roof to protect the Consular Heir!"

Where are these monsters coming from? She glanced up at the dark sky, the east now indigo with the approach of dawn. *And where are the drones?*

She hugged the dish tighter. *They want this and they want Cordus. They don't want to risk destroying the dish or killing him. They want to overwhelm us with numbers rather than weapons.*

"I'm out!" screamed a Praetorian beside her. He flung down his pulse rifle, drew his pistol, and fired single shots at the aliens. More Praetorians ran out of pulse pellets and drew their pistols. The aliens grew closer as they climbed over their dead. All the Praetorians would soon be out of ammunition.

Tarquitius yelled once again into his com. "Repeat, all available units, report to the roof to protect the Consular Heir!"

Unless the units were just outside the roof door, they would not arrive in time.

The roof beneath her feet rumbled, then a loud whooshing sound arose that seemed to suck the breath from her lungs. White lights came from beyond the edge of the roof where the aliens were surging. The lights grew brighter until a spherical ship rose above the lip of the roof. Its landing lights illuminated the entire area and the seething aliens beneath it. Aquilina first thought it was a massive alien drone until she realized what it was a second later.

"*Vacuna*," she breathed.

"Who in all the hells is that?" Tarquitius screamed above the pulse fire.

"Our *Amesha Spentas*," Aquilina said. *The "beneficent immortals" of Persian heathenism come to rescue a band of Romans.* She barked a laugh that sounded half-sane to her recovering ears.

"What?" Tarquitius yelled.

She didn't bother to explain and didn't care if he heard her.

"They'll crush us if they get any closer!" he said.

The ship rose above the roof and hovered thirty feet over their heads. Such close proximity to the ship's engines made her teeth and skull vibrate. There was no noise from the engines, but their deep hum felt as if they would rattle her body to pieces.

Then she realized what *Vacuna* was going to do.

"Everyone gather beneath the ship!" she screamed. Tarquitius issued orders to the centurion next to him, who passed it along to the others. The surviving Praetorians and Custudii gathered in a tight circle directly beneath the ship.

Tarquitius screamed into Aquilina's ear, "Now wha—?"

A sphere of shimmering blue energy, like the waves off a black road on a hot day, appeared around the ship extending fifty feet from the hull. The sphere ripped through the roof and sliced into the floors below. Aquilina and all the Praetorians stumbled as the roof jolted beneath their feet. The aliens in the path of the shield were sliced in half or had limbs cut off. The aliens outside the shield ran into it, but recoiled when their bodies began burning and smoking. The aliens on the inside still charged at the humans, but they were far fewer in number now. The humans picked them off with their pistols and some used their knives to finish the job.

The humans and surviving aliens stumbled again as *Vacuna* slowly rose higher and away from the temple. The roof section beneath Aquilina groaned and shrieked, metal grinding against metal. Cracks appeared in the floor around the humans as the roof shifted from the movement. She struggled to keep her balance and hugged the com dish tight to her chest.

"Clear!" a Praetorian shouted behind her. More shouts of "Clear!" came from other directions as the human defenders announced that the last of the aliens inside the shield were dead. Now all they had to do was concentrate on not falling through any crevasses in the roof.

Vacuna flew them toward the temple's administrative building, a blocky rectangular structure that was connected to the temple via two glass bridges. She looked back at the Temple of Jupiter Optimus Maximus. *Vacuna* had taken a semi-spherical chunk out of the building, with parts of the roof, side, and top floor cauterized. Her heart froze a moment when she wondered if Cordus had been scooped up as well, but she remembered the com room was on the other side of the building.

Aliens still climbed the walls near where they had just escaped; however it seemed their numbers were not endless. Several dozen drones sat on the ground nearby, but she didn't see any more aliens coming out of them. As she watched, each drone rose into the sky and then shot up into the upper atmosphere toward where she assumed the alien vessel orbited.

Vacuna descended to the ground car parking lot in front of the administrative building. The lot was surrounded by a stone wall topped with electrically charged fencing that Aquilina prayed still had power. *Vacuna* gently lowered the roof section to the lot on top of cars already parked there.

"Hold on!" Aquilina screamed. A moment later *Vacuna* deactivated its shield. The roof section dropped about a pace with an earsplitting crash. Aquilina and everyone else fell down. The roof teetered, then tilted at a forty-five degree angle. Aquilina slid on her back, head first, down the roof structure toward the ground several dozen paces away, all the while concentrating on holding the com dish to her chest. She ultimately collided with a pile of hard debris and bloody alien bodies. Flailing humans slammed into her at the bottom. She scrambled backward, trying to avoid any more collisions. She leaped to her feet and ran away from the roof section, accompanied by other Praetorians and Custudii.

After a few dozen paces, she stopped and checked the com dish. Miraculously, its small tabulari monitor indicated it still transmitted normally.

She turned back to the wreckage. Black-armored humans stumbled away from the roof debris. Aquilina did not see any human bodies among the aliens. The deep, teeth-shaking hum of *Vacuna's* engines drew her attention behind her. The ship landed in a clear spot towards the end of the parking lot a hundred paces away. Aquilina jogged toward the ship and arrived just as one of its door ramps descended. Dariya and Daryush walked down the ramp. Daryush stared wide-eyed at the roof section, while Dariya scanned the black-armored humans near the roof debris.

Before Aquilina could say anything, Dariya asked, "Where is Cordus? The Praetorian bands said he was on the roof."

"He's still in the Temple and still in danger," Aquilina said. "You coming with us?"

She put a hand on the pulse pistol holstered at her hip. "Well we did not come back to save *you*."

"Understood. Thanks anyway."

As the three jogged toward the gathering Praetorians and Custudii, Dariya laughed. Aquilina glanced at the Persian woman. Dariya nodded toward the semi-spherical gouge in the temple roof. "I suppose it was not a complete waste of time. Ahura Mazda will be most pleased with me."

Despite all that had happened, Aquilina wanted to laugh, too. But the laughter died on her lips when she saw another wave of drones streak over the temple and land in the same place the empty drones had just left. Dariya saw it, too. They shared a determined look, and then all three sprinted for the temple entrance near the administrative building.

Chapter Forty-Eight

Aquilina, Dariya, and Daryush arrived at the back entrance to the temple next to where it was attached to the administrative building. Tarquitius and the rest of his men arrived at about the same time. He came to a stop near Aquilina and Dariya, his chest heaving from the run.

"I thank you for saving our lives," Tarquitius said to Dariya and Daryush. "But you will need to answer for destroying the Republic's greatest religious relic."

Dariya looked at Aquilina. "Is he serious?"

"Yes," she said.

She studied the ancient, ornately carved doors, and then spotted the discrete control pad on the left. She flipped open the bronze cover and placed her palm on the control pad. Nothing happened.

"The temple is locked down," Tarquitius said. "No one can get in or out."

"And those things are coming this way," Dariya said, staring behind them.

Aquilina turned to the parking lot wall. The breaking dawn illuminated it well enough for her to see aliens climbing over. Sparks and smoke erupted when the fence at the top electrocuted those who touched it. But the alien corpses simply draped over the fence, allowing other aliens to climb over them and leap down to the ground.

"We could go through the administrative building," a Praetorian centurion suggested.

"By the time we go through all the hallways and locked doors, the aliens will have Cordus. This is the most direct route. Tarquitius, you try the control pa—"

Dariya gave an exasperated grunt and fired her pulse pistol at the door handles. The handles exploded into cinders and smoke, and a gaping hole appeared where the locking mechanisms once existed. She pulled the doors open and glared at the Romans. "Are we going," she said, "or will you arrest me for destroying more relics?"

Aquilina nodded to Dariya, then charged through the doors. She still clutched the dish with both arms, checking it every now and then to make sure it still transmitted. As far as she could tell, it did.

The white-columned hallway emptied into the temple's main, circular altar chamber. Aquilina skidded to a stop in shock. The temple's backup generators still functioned; the lights in the high roof above illuminated hundreds of people standing, sitting, or laying prostrate on the floor around the altar. Black-robed flamens led them in prayers. Holo-monitors on the walls surrounding the main altar area displayed either the flamens or the text of the prayers they were chanting. The people seemed be a mixture of commonly dressed plebeians, senators in white togas, and well-groomed patricians; though it was hard to tell who was who since the clothes of all were torn, dirty, bloody, and burned. Mothers and fathers tried to comfort crying children. Most heartbreaking of all were the blank-faced children who sat alone without parents to console them, all the crying ripped out of them by the horrors they had witnessed.

Will they ever smile again? Will I?

Thankfully, the roof here seemed intact and had not suffered from the chunk Dariya had taken out of the temple.

Temple Custudii in dented ceremonial armor and uniforms stood near the doors, some with pulse rifles, others holding a ceremonial gladius that Aquilina doubted they'd ever been trained to use in battle.

Three Custudii jogged toward Aquilina and the others. One of them, a bald man with a bloody right ear and a centurion insignia on his chest, was red-faced with fury.

"You fools!" he shouted. "Why did you destroy that door? Now they can get in!"

"We didn't know all these people were in here," Aquilina said. "Gods, if the aliens come through that door…"

The Custudae gaped at Aquilina. "Aliens? I'm talking about the golems! They've gone crazy. Started destroying things and killing people. Most of the wounded you see here are from *caccing* golems."

Aquilina flinched, knowing Cordus's fears had come true. *Destroying the Republic to save it…*

"We didn't see any golems outside," she replied.

"Well they were pounding on the front doors ten minutes ago."

Tarquitius said to Aquilina. "You go to the Consul. My men and I will stay here and hold the door."

Aquilina stared at him. *Hold the door with what?* All of his Praetorians and Custudii were either out of ammunition or down to their last few pellets. But his tired eyes said he was well aware of the situation.

"Prefect Tarquitius," the Custudae centurion said, calming himself, "I did not realize it was you, sir. My apologies. We have a gladius cache if your men need them. They're ceremonial, but they'll cut anything you swing them at."

Tarquitius nodded to the centurion. "Get them."

The Custudae centurion turned to his men and ordered them to gather the rest of the gladius cache.

Tarquitius said to his soldiers, "Now we fight like the Legions of old at the birth of the Republic. A gladius worked well for them, so why not us, eh?"

The men gave him grim, determined nods. They turned and jogged back down the hall to the doors Dariya had ruined.

Aquilina said, "Fortuna be with you, Prefect."

"And you, Praetorian." Tarquitius then jogged after his men.

She looked at Dariya and Daryush. "Ready?"

Daryush grunted, gripping his pulse pistol in both hands. Dariya said, "Lead on, Roman."

Aquilina led the two Persians through the praying and wounded masses to a set of ornate doors on the other side of the altar area. Once through the doors, Aquilina was happy to see that the generators also continued to power the elevator. They filed in and she tapped the controls for the top floor.

As the elevator rose, Dariya asked in a quiet voice, "How is he?"

"He's trying to save us all," Aquilina said, glancing down at the com dish.

Dariya cleared her throat. "Our...sympathies on your mother."

Aquilina clenched her teeth and stared at the elevator's level monitor, watching the floor numbers rise. She nodded once. She didn't want to move her eyes or blink, for fear they would fill with tears.

"Our mother died before our eyes, too," Dariya continued. "Same day our old Roman master took 'Ush's tongue." Her voice grew hard. "Same day I killed that Roman, and me and 'Ush escaped."

Aquilina shifted her eyes to Dariya. "Did it help? Killing your mother's murderer?"

Dariya stared at her brother as he gazed at the elevator floor with a haunted expression. "It did not bring our mother back or 'Ush his tongue." She then gave Aquilina a level stare. "But yes, it helped."

The doors to the elevator opened, and all three brought up their pulse pistols. Aquilina shifted the com dish in her left arm as she aimed down the hall. It was empty, just as it had been when she, Cordus, Ulpius, and Gracchus arrived. The Praetorian guards were gone, likely to answer Tarquitius's earlier calls for all units to the roof. There seemed more dust in the air, though; unsurprising since a section of the temple roof had been removed nearby.

All three ran down the hall, Aquilina in the lead. When they got to the com room door, Aquilina shouted, "Ulpius, it's me."

After several long seconds, the door clicked open. Ulpius stood to one side, his pulse rifle in his right hand. He glanced at the com dish in Aquilina's arms.

"Too hot up there for it?"

"You could say that," she said as she pushed her way in past him.

"Why are you two here?" he asked Dariya and Daryush.

"Nice to see you too, Praetorian," Dariya grumbled.

"Gracchus?"

Aquilina shook her head once.

"*Cac*," he whispered. He shut the door behind Daryush and locked it.

Aquilina hurried over to Cordus, who was still strapped into the com chair. He still looked asleep, his features peaceful and calm.

But the drama unfolding on the holo-monitor seemed anything but calm. Cordus knelt next to the body of a dark-haired, bearded man wearing ancient Roman armor. A blackened hole the size of two fists ran all the way through his chest. The man appeared dead.

Cordus's eyes—and the view of the holo-monitor—swung around and focused on what looked like Jupiter pulling a gladius out of his leg. Juno and Minerva sat on their thrones behind him, javelins through their hearts.

"Ulpius, what in the name of Dis is happening?"

Ulpius stood next to Aquilina. "Best I can tell, that fellow on the ground was Marcus Antonius Primus. He appeared suddenly, then conjured up some javelins to throw at Juno and Minerva there. Jupiter didn't take that well, so he threw lightning at Primus and killed him."

When he saw Aquilina's incredulous look, he grunted. "Yeah, it's like some godsdamned religious drama up there."

Cordus faced the angry Jupiter. Juno and Minerva also began to move. Both regarded the javelins in their bodies, and then each pulled them out with one powerful motion. They tossed the javelins to the floor and then walked down from their thrones to stand next to Jupiter.

Cordus seemed to be fighting three gods.

An idea struck Aquilina. She set the dish down next to Cordus's chair, then hurried over to the holo-monitor's controls. She activated the interface and then scrolled through the options. She found the data feed she wanted, entered several passwords, and then verified the feed was active.

Ulpius said, "You sure you want to broadcast this to the world? What if he dies up there?"

"Then we all die," Aquilina said. "But if he lives, and he saves us...not even Arrius will dispute his claim. Who would defy the man who can defeat gods?"

Ulpius grunted. Aquilina stared at the holo-monitor, but became aware of Dariya and Daryush standing on the other side of Cordus.

All four watched the drama.

Chapter Forty-Nine

Cordus faced the three gods of the Capitoline Triad, the most powerful in the Pantheon.

That's what they want me to think. They're no more gods than I am.

"We do not want to kill you, young Antonius," Jupiter said. He yanked the gladius out of his leg and threw it away. The wound and blood on his leg evaporated until Jupiter's bare, muscled thigh was once again smooth and bronze.

The blood gushing from the chest wounds in Juno and Minerva had stopped. The blood on their white togas evaporated as well, leaving their gowns as immaculate as they were before Marcus attacked them.

"We want to help you," Juno said. Kindness softened her eyes as she tilted her head, looking at him like a mother would a son.

"We can give you your heart's greatest desire," Minerva said. Her owl, now whole again, sailed from the floor behind Cordus and landed on Minerva's alabaster shoulder.

"What is my heart's greatest desire?" Cordus asked.

Ocella and Kaeso appeared beside him, just as Marcus had, and they both said at the same time, "Freedom."

Cordus flinched, then looked at the two people he had loved most.

"I know, kid, I've been there," Kaeso said, putting a hand on Cordus's shoulder. "Everyone wanting *you* to solve their problems. When all you want to do is be free."

"No more taking care of someone else," Ocella said from the other side. "You can travel the stars, explore new worlds and old. Have new experiences that nobody has ever had. It's what you've always wanted."

Juno stepped forward, towering over Cordus by almost six feet. She knelt down on one knee, her eyes kind. She lightly touched his cheek with her fingers. "We desire peace. We always have."

"Then why destroy Libertus? Why attack Terra?"

Minerva approached, her steps light despite her size. "Because of them," she said, nodding toward the body of Marcus Antonius. "They, and all the other strains, are the infection that rots the soul of the universe. They upend the natural order by serving mundanes. It is the mundanes who should serve *them* and provide the experiences all the strains need to survive."

Ocella took his hand in hers. "We can be together again, like it used to be. Only now we can go wherever we want." She nodded to the three gods. "They encourage us to explore because it gives them new experiences."

"It took me a while to accept it," Kaeso said. "But once you do, you cannot imagine the freedom." He shook his head with a smile. "It's what I always wanted. And I know it's what you've wanted, too."

"The price?" Cordus asked Jupiter. The god stared at him from behind Juno and Minerva.

"Your faith," he rumbled.

"Give up your body..." Minerva said.

"...and become immortal," Juno soothed.

Cordus looked from Ocella to Kaeso. They both regarded him with all the love that proud parents would show their son. Cordus's real mother and father had never looked at him that way.

Only Ocella and Kaeso had.

They had taken the time to get to know him, to teach him how to be a real human being. They had raised the real Cordus, the person he was beneath the Muses and the Consular Heir. They knew his dreams for the future.

He swallowed once, then said, "What do I need to do?"

Juno leaned forward, her beautiful face only a foot from his. "Tell us where you are in the Temple below."

"What's he doing?" Ulpius asked Aquilina. They all watched the drama unfold on the holo-monitor through Cordus's eyes. "He's not going to tell them where we are, is he?"

"No," Aquilina said. "I believe in him. He will *not* abandon us."

She glanced at Dariya, who returned a wary one of her own.

I believe in him.

Aquilina unholstered her pulse pistol and held it at her side. Dariya bared her teeth, but turned her gaze back to the holo-monitor.

But I am not a fool.

"I have friends near my body," Cordus said.

"Your friends will not be harmed," Minerva said. "Unless they try to stop us."

"What will you do to me?"

"Enough questions," Jupiter thundered. "Do you accept the offer or not?"

"It is generous," Juno said with motherly patience.

The man-sized owl on Minerva's shoulder shifted its head, its black eyes staring at Cordus. Minerva added, "You will have the freedom you desire above all else."

Cordus glanced at Ocella, then at Kaeso. They both gave him encouraging smiles.

"Freedom," Cordus said. "Like them?"

"It's not what you think, kid," Kaeso said. "We're not chained to a single body anymore. If our golem body dies, we can leave it for another. Quickly, painlessly. *That* is freedom."

"All we have to do," Ocella said from the other side, "is give them our loyalty and our experiences."

"But you're golems," Cordus said.

"We're free," Ocella countered with a gentle smile. "Tell them where you are so we can be together forever."

"Come with us, kid," Kaeso added.

Cordus looked from Ocella to Kaeso. "I want that so much," he breathed.

Aquilina raised her pulse pistol and put the barrel against Cordus's head. Dariya and Daryush looked from Cordus to Aquilina. Emotions warred on their faces. They knew as well as Aquilina that if Cordus abandoned them, humanity was lost. They could not let him join the Muses and give them the secrets of his abilities.

Tears clouded Aquilina's vision as she watched Cordus's sleeping form. Her pistol hand trembled.

I believe in you. I believe in you...

"I've always wanted that," Cordus said. "I've told you both that since we first met. Do you remember what you always said?"

The comforting smiles of Ocella and Kaeso wavered.

"You said that was *not* the man I was meant to be."

Cordus knew this temple, this world, these "gods" were not physical. This was all a dream world within the alien vessel inhabited by the Muse strain. And in dreams, only imagination and will limited what one could do.

At least that's how Cordus prayed it worked here.

I need to be bigger, he thought. Ocella and Kaeso shrank away from him as his body grew to twelve feet tall. He stood eye-to-eye with both Juno and Minerva, their kind expressions turning to shock.

I need weapons. A pulse pistol appeared in his left hand and a gladius in his right. He thrust the gladius into Juno's throat, while at the same instant, he shot Minerva and the owl in their heads with the pistol. Minerva fell to the floor on her back, blood pooling around her head. Juno still hung on Cordus's gladius. Cordus knew they would soon heal themselves. He only had moments to defeat Jupiter.

But Jupiter was ready for him. The god had a fork of blue lightning in his hand and flung it at Cordus before he could remove his gladius from Juno's throat. He ducked behind Juno, the lightning slamming into her back. It blasted a hole through her chest and then continued on toward Cordus. He rolled out of the way, but lightning singed the top of his arms when it surged past him. He scrambled away from Juno's body and hid behind a nearby column that no longer seemed so wide now that he was twice as tall as when he arrived.

Jupiter issued a deep sigh, almost like a hum, that rumbled through the halls of the Temple. "So we finally battle," Jupiter said. "It has been a long time for us. We missed it."

More lightning slammed into the column Cordus hid behind, sending shards of marble everywhere. He reached around with his pulse pistol and fired several blind shots in Jupiter's direction. Cordus tried to peer around the corner, but lightning and marble shards kept him pinned down.

I did not think this out well. Juno and Minerva would heal soon, and then he'd be surrounded. He was on their vessel; they knew their terrain better than he did. They inhabited the vessel like the memories of Ocella and Kaeso inhabited in their golem bodies.

Cordus looked around. This place was the center, where the vessel was controlled. It had to be. So where were the controls?

He saw the vacated thrones to his left. All three glowed a faint blue, but Jupiter's throne seemed more vibrant.

Cordus needed to get to that throne and then...well, he wasn't sure after that. Was it the real gods urging him on? The residue of Marcus?

He didn't know, but he felt it to the core of his being that the key to defeating these Muses was on those thrones.

Another lightning blast hit the column, and this time the entire thing shook. Cracks appeared all around it, and he didn't think it could take another blast. He fired more blind pulse shots at Jupiter.

A humming sigh to his left. Cordus had no time to turn before a hand was around his throat. The hand lifted him off his feet and turned him around. He dropped his pulse pistol. Jupiter's face was no longer that of a benevolent father. His skin had turned a sickly green, his hair hung in greasy black strands, his teeth were sharp points, and his eyes were completely black. Cordus knew his Pantheon. This was Orcus, a god of the underworld and punisher of broken oaths.

Orcus's breath was foul when he snarled at Cordus. "I will feast on your soul, boy."

As soon as the battle started, Ocella had dropped to her knees and assumed a prostrate form before the Originators. Kaeso had done the same as they both awaited the inevitable conclusion of the battle.

Cordus will lose, she thought. *He will die. My poor, dear boy will die...*

Her body trembled as the shock of that realization roiled through it. This was not right. She should not feel these things. The Originators had assured her she would no longer be distracted by emotions. She was free, they said.

Why couldn't Cordus see this opportunity? Why couldn't he just accept the will of the Originators and do what he always wanted?

Lightning exploded against a column to her right. She risked a glance up from her prostration. Cordus hid behind the column, gripping the pulse pistol. Jupiter strode over to him, flinging lightning blasts upon the column. Cordus fired wildly at Jupiter, but the pulse pellets never got close. Jupiter's body melted into the sickly form of Orcus.

He's going to kill Cordus now. This couldn't happen. She was his protector. She had been since the moment she met him seven years ago, and especially since she helped him escape Roma. And all the years since then, keeping him safe from bounty hunters, Praetorian assassins, and Umbra Ancile eager to avenge their losses in Roma.

Ocella noticed Kaeso had turned his head toward the column as well. She could see his hands shake as he watched the terrible scene unfold. Was he feeling the same urge to protect Cordus as her?

His head suddenly turned toward Ocella and their eyes met. His desperate voice filled her mind. *What do we do?*

She was too paralyzed to respond. *My creators...my boy...*

Orcus lifted Cordus by the throat and told the boy he was going to die. Cordus's face turned purple, his tongue flapped from his mouth as he struggled to breathe. Orcus punched Cordus in the face several times, breaking his nose. Blood spurted. His struggles weakened.

A low moan originated deep in her chest and then emerged from her lips. It grew in volume and intensity into a scream and then a raging howl. Something in her mind snapped and figurative chains fell from her body. She leaped up from the floor, all her focus on Orcus. This monster held her dear boy—*her son!*—in his rotting hands. She charged toward the monster, protecting Cordus her only concern. Her body grew larger to match Orcus's height and mass, though she never consciously willed it. All she felt was rage toward this thing that was hurting one of the two people in the universe that she loved more than her own life.

Orcus turned at the last moment. He seemed much smaller now, almost a head shorter than Ocella. She felt a savage glee as she slammed into him with her shoulder and knocked him into a marble wall a dozen paces away. Cordus fell to the floor gasping and coughing.

But Ocella followed Orcus. She leaped on top of him and hammered her fists into his grotesque face. She rained blows on Orcus, now almost half her size, until his head was an unrecognizable pulp of green meat and white bone.

Cordus rasped, "Behind you!"

Ocella whirled around as two arrows hit her chest from Juno and Minerva, both of whom aimed longbows at her. The arrows knocked her back against the wall. She slid to the floor, her feet unable to support her. She felt herself shrinking in size to her normal height. Juno and Minerva both nocked another arrow and aimed at Ocella. Their faces were impassive, as if they were about to step on a roach.

Kaeso rose up behind them, a gladius in his hand. With one gigantic swing, he decapitated Juno and Minerva. Their heads flew into the air and their bodies slumped to the floor.

Kaeso stood over them, blood dripping from the gladius. "Heal that," he growled at their bodies.

Ocella wanted to smile, but she couldn't do much more than look at him. There was no pain from the arrows, but her mind was slipping away. She knew that if she closed her eyes, she'd never open them again. Not even in a new body.

Cordus was by her side. Blood streamed from his broken nose. She found the strength to smile at him. He was alive. It was all that mattered.

Cordus stared at the arrows in Ocella's chest, willing them to go away in the same way he had willed himself to grow into a giant. He drew from the power of the golems on Terra. He took more than he knew he should, releasing them to potentially kill and hurt other people. He didn't care. His mother was dying.

When the arrows would not disappear, he tried pulling them out with his hands. They would not budge, no matter how hard he pulled or how much strength he willed into his arms. Ocella was unconscious, but moaned with each pull.

He cursed in frustration. "Why can't I remove them?" he cried.

Kaeso knelt beside Ocella and took her hand in his. Cordus had never seen such pain on his typically stoic face.

"Why can't I remove them?" Cordus repeated to Kaeso.

Without taking his gaze off Ocella, Kaeso said, "This isn't your world. It's theirs."

A wet chuckle came from behind Cordus. He whipped around to see Orcus beginning to move. His head was still a mash of green tissue and bone, but it restructured itself before Cordus's eyes.

"We are gods here, boy," Orcus gurgled through his ruined mouth.

The headless bodies of Juno and Minerva twitched as white bone slowly grew out of their neck stumps. The bone took the form of skulls, and then tendons crawled up the skulls.

Cordus jumped up and ran to Jupiter's glowing blue throne. Juno's hand grabbed for his legs. He leaped over her grasping hands. He charged up the steps and then sat down in Jupiter's throne.

Nothing happened. There was no change in the throne's glow. He didn't know what he expected. He scanned the throne for an interface, but it was all smooth white marble.

What am I supposed to do? He instinctively reached for the Muses, but recoiled in despair when all he got was silence. Their underlying whispers had always been in his mind, even when they did not answer his queries. The silence was maddening and sad.

Orcus laughed again. His head was looking more like the hideousness of Orcus than some one who had been beaten. "*We* are the gods here, boy," he repeated.

Juno and Minerva had also sat up. Veins, muscles, and fascia crept up their skulls. Eyes expanded into their empty sockets, and their fleshless mouths pulled back into ghastly smiles.

Cordus searched the throne again for anything that might let him gain control of the vessel.

Orcus stood, took two strides toward Ocella and Kaeso. Kaeso swung at Orcus with his gladius. Orcus knocked the weapon out of Kaeso's hand and grabbed him by the throat. He reached down and grabbed Ocella with his other hand. He held them both out to Cordus. Kaeso's eyes bulged as he struggled in Orcus grasp. Ocella hung limp, the two arrows still in her chest, her eyes closed.

"Submit to us, or we will erase them from our archives."

"You can be with them forever if you submit," Juno said. Pink flesh now covered her hairless head.

"Give us the location of your body," Minerva said. Dark hair sprouted from the top of her head and looped down around her shoulders.

Cordus stared at Kaeso and Ocella. Tears formed in his eyes.

I don't know what to do...

Cordus heard Marcus Antonius's voice from his memories. *Everyone has responsibilities. Some men must toil in the fields to feed their families; others have to rule an empire.*

Cordus clenched his teeth. *It's not what I want to do. But it's what I must do.*

He rose from the throne and willed his height to match that of the three gods below him.

"I am Marcus Antonius Cordus, descendent of Marcus Antonius Primus and Consular Heir of the Roman Republic. *You* will submit to *me.*"

The entire temple shuddered beneath Aquilina's feet. Ulpius, Dariya, and Daryush glanced around nervously. Another explosion, this time closer, made cracks appear in the ceiling. Dust rained down on them.

"*Cac,*" Ulpius muttered. "Sounds like they don't want him alive anymore."

Aquilina could imagine the drone ships hovering above the temple raining down blue lightning in an attempt to destroy it—and Cordus—before he could take control of the vessel.

A buzzing from the high-security Praetorian com nearby made them all jump. Aquilina tore her gaze from the holo-monitor to activate the signal.

"—coming from the alien ship," a hurried female voice said. "They match the description of the toxin drones that attacked Libertus. Repeat, this is the command ship of the Arrius Astrum Naves reporting to all Legions defending Terra—the alien vessel is releasing drones matching the description of the toxin drones that destroyed Libertus."

The signal crossed all bands; it would be playing on all com devices in every home, business, car, and citizen's pocket.

Aquilina turned back to the holo-monitor as another explosion made a part of the ceiling fall to the floor behind her.

Whatever you're going to do, Cordus, hurry.

⤜⟫⟫⟩ ⟨⟨⟨⟨⤛

Orcus, Juno, and Minerva flinched back from Cordus. The light in the temple went from bright sunshine filtering down from the skylights above to a darkened milieu of roiling black clouds. Even the marble within the temple seemed to blacken and crack.

Orcus growled, "Get down from there or your friends and your planet die."

"I am Marcus Antonius Cordus, descendent of Marcus Antonius Primus and Consular Heir of the Roman Republic—"

As he said this, the marble thrones next to him flickered and then melted into a single black sphere. The sphere undulated. Blue veins formed on its surface looking like the skin of the vessel. It slowly contorted itself until it finally settled on a shape that Cordus recognized.

The command couch on *Caduceus*.

"THIS VESSEL IS OURS!" Orcus screamed. His voice thundered through the temple, its rage causing more cracks to emerge in the columns and floor.

But this time he sounded scared.

Cordus descended the steps from the command couch, the weight of his feet cracking each step. He towered over the gods. Juno and Minerva stepped away from him. Gone where the serene and motherly gazes from before. Now there was only fear.

The Muses cannot control me, but I can control them. Even this strain. It's what I've always *been able to do.*

"I am Marcus Antonius Cordus, descendent of—"

Debris fell from the temple ceiling, huge chunks of marble, brick, and timber. The ground rumbled.

Orcus tossed Kaeso and Ocella to the side, a spear suddenly in his hand. He flung the spear at Cordus.

Cordus saw the spear and brought up his forearm. A large shield was there to deflect the spear. It bounced off the floor. Juno and Minerva both loosed arrows at Cordus. Though they were only ten paces away, Cordus had no difficulty bringing his shield around to deflect their arrows. The goddesses fired volley after volley at him as Orcus continued to throw spears, but he blocked them all with hardly any effort.

This was how it felt when I controlled the Terran Muses. They've lost, but they don't know it yet.

He threw his shield at Minerva and Juno. The impact knocked them dozens of paces across the Temple toward the wide open entrance. Orcus, now just as large as Cordus, leaped at him and wrapped his fingers around Cordus's throat.

"We are your gods," Orcus snarled, his breath stinking of death. "You will submit to *us!*"

Cordus reached up and grabbed Orcus's wrists. He slowly pulled Orcus hands away from his throat. Orcus's eyes bulged.

"You are not gods," Cordus growled. "You're a little germ with a big ship."

He smashed his forehead into Orcus's nose twice. Orcus stumbled backwards, stunned by the blows. Before Orcus could recover, Cordus thrust his hand into Orcus's chest. But instead of the hot organs Cordus expected, blue light erupted from the wound he had created. He felt the rest of his body being pulled into Orcus.

Orcus screamed. Juno and Minerva screamed from the other side of the temple.

And then Cordus took control of the vessel.

Aquilina's ear com beeped as another explosion almost collapsed the entire ceiling in the com room. Tarquitius's voice yelled over the sounds of pulse pistol fire, clashing steel, and human and non-human grunts and cries. "The aliens are spreading throughout the temple. They seem to be searching the entire complex, so I don't think they know where you are yet. But I just saw one group head up the back stairs towards you."

"How many?"

"A lot!"

Aquilina turned to Ulpius. "They're coming up here."

He nodded grimly and went to the door. He opened it a crack to peek through. Then he opened it all the way and stepped into the hall. He stood outside, looking from left to right.

Dariya and Daryush joined Ulpius in the hall, their pulse pistols drawn and ready to fire. Ulpius nodded to them. They stood back-to-back, Dariya and Daryush facing left, Ulpius facing right.

"How are your men faring, Tarquitius?" Aquilina asked.

"Not good. We have the aliens coming through the back door, and most of them got past us already. Now the golems are trying to ram down the front doors. We're giving a gladius to every citizen who can stand, but..."

Tarquitius didn't have to finish for Aquilina to understand how hopeless he viewed the situation.

"Any way the Consul can speed things up?" he asked.

"I can't reach him now," Aquilina said, looking at Cordus. "We have to be patient."

Tarquitius grunted. "Right," he said, then broke the connection.

Pulse fire from the door startled Aquilina. Ulpius fired again down the hallway.

"They're coming out of the stairwell," he shouted. Dariya and Daryush turned and fired down the hall, too.

Aquilina rushed over and peaked around the corner. The gray, octopus-like aliens filled the hallway and skittered toward them. Pulse fire tore them apart, but more just flooded over the dead. There was no way pulse fire would stop the onslaught.

"Back inside," Aquilina shouted.

Dariya and Daryush jumped through the door. Ulpius let off a final blast of rifle fire, then dove through the door just as Aquilina slammed it shut and locked it. She heard the aliens gathering outside, their fingered tentacles tapping around the edges.

Ulpius stood back, his pulse rifle pointed at the door. "Hope they don't have a ram—"

A loud bang came from the other side of the door, and then another. The edges around the door handle and lock bulged inward with each bang. The doorframe soon began to crack and then splinter around the lock.

"*Cac*," Ulipius said.

"Behind the chairs!" Aquilina shouted.

As soon as everyone ducked behind a tabulari chair, the door lock blew apart, sending shards of wood and steel exploding across the room. Ulpius fired at the aliens streaming through the door. Dariya and Daryush screamed and fired into the alien mass. All three killed many, but not enough.

Aquilina fired her pistol, but was down to one pellet before she knew it. The aliens rushed forward. She focused on Cordus's sleeping body.

I'm sorry, Cordus. I wasn't good enough to protect you. I won't let them dissect and torture you. At least I can give you peace.

She raised her pistol with its last pellet to Cordus's head. Before she could pull the trigger...the room turned quiet.

She turned her eyes to the aliens. They stood before her on four tentacles, with the front four raised like a fan above their bulbous gray heads.

"What are they waiting for?" Ulpius growled. "Finish us!"

But they didn't move.

Aquilina looked up at Cordus and then checked the holo-monitor.

The first genuine smile in days crossed her lips.

CHAPTER FIFTY

Cordus floated above Terra. He did not feel cold or warm, just numb. The planet spread out before him; he could focus on any country, city, street, or individual. He found he could see their atoms, if he chose.

He noticed Roman Eagles flying around him firing missiles, plasma cannons, and mass drivers. None of their weapons touched him. A faint blue glow surrounded him whenever a projectile was turned away or destroyed.

He also saw drones swarming toward Terra. The toxin drones.

Stop, he said.

They stopped.

Come back.

They turned around and came back toward him.

He looked down on the planet, focusing on the octopod ground forces and drone attackers all over Terra.

Stop. Come back.

The octopods stopped their ground assaults. The drones flew back.

"It's a wonderful vessel, is it not?"

A male child's voice came from beside Cordus. He now stood in a room shaped like the inside of a sphere, with space and Terra surrounding him. Three children stood next to him, one boy and two girls. The boy had dark curly hair. One girl had long dark hair and a small, snowy-white owl perched on her shoulder. The other had auburn hair tied in two braids that ran down her back. All three wore white togas of ancient design.

"We built it 15,900,127 of your years ago," the dark-haired girl said. Her owl cooed at her voice.

"We like it far better than a mundane body," the auburn-haired girl said.

"You can tell it to restructure itself if you don't like the design," the boy offered. "It's very easy."

Cordus stared at them. "Where are Ocella and Kaeso?"

The boy shrugged. "Bring them here if you wish to see them."

Ocella. Kaeso.

They both appeared before him. Ocella—arrows no longer protruding from her chest—rushed over to Cordus and hugged him tightly. He returned the embrace with equal strength. Kaeso stood behind her with a proud grin.

"Well done, kid," Kaeso said.

Cordus pulled back, looking at them both with tears in his eyes. "You're both dead aren't you?" It was more a statement than a question.

Their smiles faltered.

"You're just the personalities the Muses built around your memories," Cordus continued. "My Ocella and Kaeso are...gone."

Ocella and Kaeso nodded.

Cordus turned to the three children. "What will you do when I leave this ship? When I return to my body on Terra?"

The boy tilted his head. "We will take back control and destroy your planet."

"We will try to kill you as well," the auburn-haired girl said.

"You have angered us deeply," the dark-haired girl said. Her owl flapped its wings in agreement. "Only your will is keeping us from destroying you now."

Cordus eyed them sardonically. "Thanks for your honesty."

"We are under your command," the boy said. "We cannot deceive you."

"I could root you out of this ship."

All three shook their heads. The boy said, "We are too deeply integrated. You could no more destroy us than you could the strain that lived in you. You cannot kill us, only control us."

The auburn-haired girl said, "And you would have to stay here to maintain control."

"How? My body is still down there."

The dark-haired girl said, "You can sever the connection."

A tendril of white light, no bigger than a spider web strand, connected him to his body on Terra. The tendril undulated as if swaying in the wind. He then found a gladius in his hand.

The auburn-haired girl said, "Your mind will stay here, but your body will die. You will become part of the vessel. Like us."

Cordus took in the stars around him, the planet below, and all the ships flitting about nearby. The power and freedom he had with this ship was everything he ever wanted. The things he could do, the places he could explore...

Ocella put a hand on his face and gently turned him toward her. "You can't stay."

Cordus stared at her. "But we could be together."

Kaeso stepped forward. "There's a world down there full of scared people who need a leader to give them hope."

"I'm not strong enough to—"

"You are," Kaeso said firmly.

"I just...don't trust myself to be consul," Cordus protested.

Ocella said softly, "I know. That is why it must be you."

Cordus turned away, his eyes and senses taking in the universe. *Gods, why tempt me with everything I ever wanted if I was meant to do something else?*

He remembered Aquilina in Roma. She was standing guard over his body right now. He hoped it had been an easy task, considering he was still alive and could see the com signal. She believed he could inspire others to make the Republic a better place.

He remembered Dariya and Daryush. He hoped they had somehow escaped in *Vacuna* and were on the other side of the universe by now. They deserved their own ship and the freedom it gave them after the hard life they had known at Roman hands. Despite all that, they had given Cordus, a Roman, their loyalty.

He remembered Blaesus. He prayed the old man still lived after the alien attacks in Roma. He embodied the best parts of the Roman principles of law. The Republic would need people like him now more than ever.

He remembered Nestor, killed by golems on Reantium, which seemed like years ago. He had had more faith in the Pantheon than anyone Cordus had ever met, including many flamens. He had lived a charitable life according to his faith. Cordus prayed Nestor's soul was welcomed in Elysium with a triumph that overshadowed Heracles.

He remembered the Praetorians Piso and Duran, who died before his eyes. He hoped Ulpius and Gracchus still lived. All four followed him because he honored them with respect, a leadership quality he learned from Kaeso. Their allegiance to him had strengthened Cordus and given him courage.

He thought of the countless Romans throughout the Republic with the same values of honor, faith, and charity, who were being used by petty warlords. It was a horrific injustice.

Cordus knew he could not fix the Republic overnight. Probably not even in his lifetime. But there was no one else who could begin the process right now. Perhaps Vibia Servillia Gemmella had had the strength and honor, but she had died because she believed in Cordus. So many people had died because they believed in him.

Perhaps it's time I put my faith in them...*and believe in myself.*

Cordus turned to the three children. "I cannot stay, but I cannot leave you in control of this ship."

They stared at him like mindless golems awaiting his command.

Cordus looked at Ocella and Kaeso. They both knew what he had in mind. But if he destroyed this vessel, their personalities in the vessel's archives would cease to exist. "I...I can't let..."

Though they were not Ocella and Kaeso, he still could not bring himself to say the words.

"We know," Ocella said. She put both hands on his face. "It's all right, my dear boy. It's all right."

"Do what you have to do," Kaeso said. He pulled Cordus into a tight embrace, and Cordus could feel his hard body shaking. "He was proud of you before. He'd be even prouder now."

After several moments, Cordus slowly released Kaeso and then turned to the three children. "I'm going to send this vessel into the sun with a course I will lock in. This vessel is too dangerous to exist, especially with you still around. How do I keep you from taking control when I leave?"

The boy looked at Cordus's hands. He now held three sets of shackles. "Put those on us. They will prevent us from taking over the vessel, at least for as long as it takes to fly into the sun."

Cordus stared at the children and searched their thoughts for deception. As with the Terran Muses, he sensed an underlying anger at his control. But they could not lie to him.

He ordered them to hold out their hands, and they did so dutifully. After he had shackled the children, he turned back to Ocella and Kaeso. He opened his mouth, but didn't know what to say that he hadn't already said.

Kaeso broke the silence. "Claudia was also taken. Can you bring her here before...?"

"They took Claudia from Libertus?" Cordus asked. Kaeso nodded.

Ocella said, "And Lucia, and Varo. And some octopod aliens who helped us."

Cordus nodded sadly. He focused on the faces of Lucia and Varo, and they suddenly appeared before him looking confused. He didn't know the faces of the aliens, but he sent out a query for the aliens who helped Ocella and Kaeso. Five octopods appeared next to Lucia and Varo.

"You are released," Cordus said to all of them.

Claudia gasped and ran to her father. They hugged each other tight.

Lucia and Varo blinked, then gaped at the stars, the planet, and the three shackled children. Lucia growled and made a move toward the children, but Cordus stood in front of her.

"They can't harm you now," he said. "Besides, there's nothing you can do to them anyway. Do you understand what happened to you?"

Lucia shifted her gaze to Cordus. Her anger faded to sadness and resignation. She nodded. Kaeso put a hand on her shoulder.

"He declared himself, Trierarch," Kaeso said.

Lucia turned back to Cordus with a raised eyebrow. "Well, it's about time," she said, and then bowed her head. "Sire."

Cordus explained his plan to destroy the vessel. She nodded crisply throughout and took her orders like the legionary she once was.

"We'll take care of it," she said, glaring at the three children. "They won't escape." She turned back to Cordus, and, with embarrassment, said, "I'd appreciate it, though, if you could maybe…" She paused and took in a breath. "Maybe posthumously reinstate me—or *her*—to the Legions. With honor."

Cordus nodded. "You have my promise. Everyone will know the honor with which you've conducted yourself these last years."

She stood at attention and gave him a crisp Legion salute—a fist over her heart and then a straight arm forward.

One of the octopods approached Cordus. It hooted and clicked, but Cordus had no trouble understanding it.

You honor us by bringing us before you, Sail Master. This vessel destroyed our civilization. Remember us.

Cordus accessed the vessel's archives and learned what happened to the octopods' culture. It was indeed exterminated by the vessel. In an instant, he learned everything the vessel knew about the octopods. He hoped those memories would stay with him when he returned to Terra.

Cordus nodded to the octopod. "I will remember, Sail First Arm," he said, referring to the octopod's rank among his people. Satisfied, the octopod returned to his companions.

Cordus took them all in. Kaeso and Ocella, Lucia and Varo, Claudia, the aliens, the three children. They all watched him. Kaeso and Ocella with pride, Lucia and Varo with respect, Claudia and the aliens with curiosity, and the three children with the blank looks of pre-programmed golems.

Cordus willed the ship to break Terran orbit and fly with all conventional speed toward the sun. It did. There was no tabulari readout, but he knew it would take less than fifteen minutes for it to dive into the sun. He locked the course.

He raised his hand in goodbye to Ocella and Kaeso. They raised their hands to him.

Cordus willed himself back to his body. He released his grip on the golem energy and let it fall back into the golems throughout Terra. The journey back was the opposite of his journey to the ship. He flew past Arrius's Naves Astrum, then down through the clouds of Terra, then to Europa and Italia and Roma. He plunged through the roof of the Temple of Jupiter Optimus Maximus...

...and gasped for breath in the com chair. Aquilina stood by him, trying to calm him. It took several moments for him to take in enough air to feel like he could breathe normally again. Ulpius stood behind Aquilina with a grin. Then, to his surprise, he saw Dariya and Daryush smiling at him from the other side of the chair.

"You did it, Cordus," Aquilina whispered to him. "You saved us all."

Cordus nodded and then began to weep.

Aquilina stroked Cordus's hair as he sobbed bitter tears. She understood. If she did not keep control, she would be crying over her mother every moment.

After some time, Cordus stopped crying and closed his eyes. At first she was alarmed that his life was slipping away, but his breathing had the rhythm of deep sleep.

"So what in the all the hells are we to do with them?" Ulpius said.

The octopod aliens stood frozen with their top four tentacles splayed out around their heads. She walked toward them. The ones she approached skittered out of her way, but did not make any other moves.

"You sure that's wise?" Ulpius said. He held his empty pulse rifle like a club.

"Only one way to find out."

She continued walking through them and then out into the hall. The hall was filled with octopods in the same frozen stance.

Indeed. What in the hells are we to do with you?

The stairwell door at the end of the hall burst open and Tarquitius strode out, a gladius in his hand. He shook his head at the frozen octopods and then made his way through them toward Aquilina. He lowered his sword once he reached her, but continued regarding the aliens nervously.

"Damnedest thing," he breathed. "They had us beat. Just a few of us left. Then all of sudden they just stopped. The golems, too. They're just standing outside the temple."

"Did the people see what happened on the monitors?" Aquilina asked.

"Oh yes. Quite the drama, that was. If they weren't fighting off aliens and golems, they were watching. I imagine most people across the planet saw it. How's he doing in there?"

"He's tired, but fine." Aquilina glanced behind Tarquitius. "Where are your men?"

"What few I have left are downstairs making sure those golems and aliens don't wake up—"

Aquilina brought up her pulse pistol and shot Tarquitius in the head. The Prefect didn't have time to put a surprised look on his traitorous face. He simply fell backward onto the path he had created through the aliens.

Aquilina turned to see Ulpius standing behind her with an unreadable expression.

"Cordus is a good man," she said, holstering her pistol. "In the coming days, there will be things that need to be done. But they are things he *won't* do. Things he *shouldn't* do. *We* will do those things."

Ulpius gave her a hard stare and then nodded slowly.

Aquilina opened an unlocked office door. She grabbed Tarquitius under his arms and began dragging him into the office. Without a word, Ulpius grabbed the traitor's legs, and they unceremoniously dumped the body into the empty room.

The Originators raged against their shackles.

As soon as Cordus disappeared, Ocella watched the Originators grow from innocent-seeming children into the twelve-foot giants they had been in their temple. She knew that her feelings of loyalty toward them had been the Originators controlling her thoughts. There was a part of her that even now wanted to free them and bask in their approval.

But she couldn't do it even if she wanted to. Cordus had locked the shackles tight. The Originators could no longer control the ship or change the course Cordus had set. They were all going to dive into the sun and oblivion.

"We will rip your *caccing* heads from your *caccing* bodies!" Jupiter shrieked at them.

Spittle flew from Minerva's lips as she screamed, "We will devour your livers while you watch!"

Juno struggled against her chains, her wrists bloody. "We will cast you to the gorgons and let them rape you for eternity!"

The others glanced nervously between the Originators and the growing sun in the spherical room. Like Ocella, they tried to ignore the screams.

Varo said, "Will we go to Elysium?" He had to raise his voice over the vile curses coming from the shackled Originators.

"We're already in Elysium," Lucia muttered, watching the sun get closer.

Claudia leaned close to Kaeso. "Do you think we'll feel pain?"

Kaeso looked at her with unbridled love. "No, daughter," he said. "It will be quick."

She smiled. He wrapped an arm around her.

Kaeso held out his other hand to Ocella. She took it, meeting his eyes. Their thoughts flew back and forth, expressing emotions and love they never could have conveyed with words. For this one moment, Ocella was suddenly grateful for their golem bodies; they never could have given their love to each other like this as humans.

The sun filled the entire room now. Ocella turned to Lucia and held out her hand. Lucia looked at it, and then Ocella. With a wry grin, she said, "I hated you when you first arrived."

"I know," Ocella said. "I hated you, too."

"You grew on me, though." She took Ocella's hand in a firm grasp. "I'd say it will be an honor to die with you, but we're already dead, eh?"

Lucia turned to Varo and held her hand out to him. "Want to join this orgy of sappiness?"

Varo took Lucia's hand and then said to them all, "I hope to see you all again soon."

The octopods skittered over to Varo, and Sail First Arm held out a fingered tentacle to him. Varo smiled and took it into his hand. Sail First Arm then entwined his tentacles with the other four octopods in his family.

"We're afraid," said a boy's voice.

Ocella looked at the Originators, who had returned to their child forms.

The dark-haired girl said, "We don't want to die."

The auburn-haired girl asked, "Will your gods accept us, too?"

The innocence and fear emanating from them brought tears to Ocella's eyes. She no longer felt their rage.

Claudia held out her hand to them.

The three children, with shackles clinking around their wrists, hurried over to Claudia. They held each other's hands. The boy clung to Claudia like a scared child to his mother.

They all stood in the spherical room, hands connected. Ocella did not care that the vessel had reached the sun's corona, or that its shields had failed, or that the outer hull had started to burn.

She did not mind that she and Kaeso were heading toward oblivion. Their bodies were there, anyway, and she had faith their souls had already met in Elysium.

All she cared about was that Cordus had become a good man. He would face many challenges in the coming days and years. But with Jupiter's grace, he would face them all with strength, courage, wisdom, and humility. He had become the man he was meant to be. She could let him go now.

The sun's light enveloped her, and she smiled.

CHAPTER FIFTY-ONE

Cordus awoke with a start in the com chair. He'd been dreaming of Ocella and Kaeso, but the details quickly faded from his mind. All he could remember was their unconditional love for him. After several moments failing to remember the dream, he decided the emotions were really what mattered anyway.

But everything else came back to him in a rush. He shut his eyes again and prayed for the oblivion of sleep.

"Welcome back, Roman," Dariya's voice came from his left.

Cordus opened his eyes. Dariya stood next to him, while Daryush stood behind her giving Cordus a toothy grin. "Sleeping the day away is not proper behavior for a centuriae."

"How long was I out?" he rasped. Cordus tried to swallow, but his throat felt drier than Apulia in the summer.

Dariya shrugged. "Ten minutes or so."

"So not quite a whole day."

"Feels like it, considering the company," Dariya said, nodding behind Cordus.

He gathered his strength and then leaned over the side of the chair to look behind him. There were at least ten octopod bodies lying in the com room with more in the hallway. They all had wrapped their tentacles around themselves, as if bedding down for the night. They were not moving. They must have died when the vessel finally entered the sun and its communications with them ceased.

"How long have they been there?"

"They were about to tear us limb from limb until you stopped them," Dariya said. "I do not know what you did up there, but they listened to you. Then just a few minutes ago, they all lay down as if going to sleep, but I do not think they are sleeping anymore. They look dead to me." She paused, and then in a quiet voice, said, "Is it true? Lucia, Ocella,...Kaeso...?"

Cordus looked at her. "I'm sorry."

She gave a shaky sigh. "What will we do now?" she asked under her breath. Daryush's lost expression said much the same thing.

"What do you want to do?" Cordus asked.

"We do *not* want to stay on this planet any longer than we have to. Even the Persians here are too Roman."

"Then *Vacuna* is yours," Cordus said.

Dariya stared at him. "What about Blaesus?"

"His days of exile are over. I'm going to need him if I'm to survive Republic politics."

Dariya's mouth twitched. "Thank you."

Daryush clapped his hands and rubbed them together, eager to get back to the ship and do all the tinkering he'd always wanted to do.

Dariya smiled at her brother, then said to Cordus, "Come with us. Leave this craziness to all the crazies here."

"I wish I could. But these are my people, crazy or not. I need to help them as best I can."

Dariya nodded. "Well, then they are already better off than they have ever been."

Cordus appreciated the compliment, but the Republic was still technically in a civil war and Roma was in ruins. How were they better off? Would they ever be 'better off' with him leading them? Cordus didn't know, but he knew he owed it to all the people who fought and died for him to make it happen.

He leaned forward, steadied himself on the chair's armrests, and stood on shaky legs. Vertigo overwhelmed him, and both Dariya and Daryush steadied him.

"You need to see a medicus," Aquilina said from the door. She and Ulpius stepped around the octopod bodies crowding the door and entered the room. Aquilina took his right arm and draped it over her neck. She guided him out the door and through the octopods in the hall. Somehow, after all she had been through, Cordus could still smell the faint scent of jasmine in her braided, wispy hair.

"Thank you," he said. "I can't wait to hear about *your* adventures."

She tensed. "It was...interesting." She said no more, and he didn't feel like pressing her for details. *Jupiter, Juno, and Minerva—don't let her run off after Arrius. Please keep her by my side.*

Ulpius, Dariya, and Daryush followed them into the hallway. The corridor was filled with octopod bodies, all lying in the same position as the ones in the com room, with their tentacles wrapped around themselves. Cordus half expected them to jump out of their slumber and attack, but he could not see any movement from them, not even breathing motions from the sides of their bulbous heads.

They made their way through the octopods and down the elevator to the main temple level. When they opened the doors to the altar area, Cordus was shocked to see the butchery before him. Octopod bodies and pieces lay strewn about the floor of the vast temple hall. Praetorian and Custudae bodies lay among them, alongside the bodies of plain-clothed citizens. Most of the human corpses held a gladius in their hands. The fighting here had been vicious and close.

There was no movement among the carnage.

"Gods, did *anybody* survive?" Cordus asked aloud.

The others seemed just as stunned, for they didn't say anything.

The doors at the temple's main entrance were opened wide, and sunlight streamed through them. Cordus heard the murmurs of a large crowd combined with the low chanting of prayers. He stepped through the slaughter toward the fresh air, the sights and stenches enough to give Cordus a lifetime of disturbing dreams.

Movement caught his eye to his right. A lone golem female, with the standard dark hair and white complexion, sat on the floor with her back against a marble statue of Apollo. Her yellowish innards spilled from a large gash in her abdomen. Her head and eyes followed Cordus and his group.

"How may I serve?" she asked in a gurgled voice. Yellow golem blood dribbled from her mouth when she spoke.

Aquilina exhaled, staring at the golem. "At least their controls are back in place."

Cordus nodded wearily.

They marched past the female golem, passing more golems that still functioned despite their wounds. All followed Cordus with their eyes or heads. The golem bodies grew more numerous as they approached the temple doors. The floor was slick with their yellow blood and biological circuitry. He prayed that his use of their power had saved more human lives than were sacrificed. *Gods, if you exist in Elysium, let it be so.*

They stepped past the last of the golem and human bodies, past the giant marble statues of Jupiter, Juno, and Minerva, and then emerged into the sunlight just outside the temple doors.

They all stopped and stared.

Thousands of people had gathered in the great square in front of the temple. Several black-robed flamens led them in prayers of thanks to all the gods of the Pantheon. Human and golem bodies littered the square and the steps leading up to the temple. On the horizon, smoke billowed into the bright morning sky from numerous fires throughout the city. The sirens of fire brigades warbled and echoed. Above the city, Roman attack flyers left crisscrossing contrails as they screamed across the sky.

The chanting tapered off as the black-robed flamens noticed Cordus. The Pontifex Maximus, a gold braid around the shoulders of his black robes, approached Cordus. Cordus didn't remember ever meeting the Pontifex so he didn't know the man's name. His white hair was wispy, and his robes were ripped and stained. The old man looked exhausted, but tears brimmed in his red eyes as he regarded Cordus. He slowly bent down to one knee, then both knees, and then lowered his head to Cordus.

The flamens near the Pontifex did the same. Kneeling spread to the citizens at the foot of the Temple steps and then, like a slow wave, to the citizens in the square beyond. Cordus could see kneeling people all the way to the Senate House two hundred paces away.

Aquilina squeezed his hand. She watched him with soft brown eyes and a reassuring smile. The morning sunlight made her face glow, and he had never seen anyone so beautiful. If she were not standing beside him right now, he would have run in the other direction.

Instead, he took in ragged breath as he surveyed the kneeling throngs before him.

"*Cac*," he exhaled.

EPILOGUE

Uller Mus climbed the numerous steps to the Zhonguo Imperial Palace. The Zhonguo Sphere's capital world, Pan Ch'ao, had a gravity slightly greater than Reantium's—1.05T to be exact—but it felt good to his legs. Uller was born into slavery on Abundantia, a world with 1.12T, and had lived most of his life there, until he was sold to Aulus Tarpeius when he was thirty-six Terran years old. Tarpeius hated worlds with higher gravity than Terra-standard; he said it prematurely aged a man. And so they had settled on Reantium in part because of its lower gravity.

Uller grinned inwardly. *That worked out well for me, though not for him.*

He was flanked by an entire cohort of Divine Riders, the Zhonguo Emperor's palace guard. Like their Praetorian counterparts, each wore ceremonial armor while in the presence of their sovereign: gilded bronze helms with red plumes, bronze scale armor beneath gilded shoulder guards. Each carried a shiny, stylized pulse rifle made to look like a short spear. They reminded Uller of the rifles the Roman Legions had carried when they conquered the Zhonguo's ancestors on Terra over nine hundred years ago.

The Zhonguo Chancellor, a eunuch named Zheng Yang, led the procession up the steps. He was a fat man with a bald head who wore elaborate, flowing robes that made him look fatter. Despite his bulk, however, he climbed the Palace steps with ease and little shortness of breath. The air was warm and humid, which made the large eunuch's fitness even more impressive. Uller had just left his shuttle five minutes ago and sweat already dripped from his forehead.

The Imperial Palace was every bit as massive as the Consular Palace in Roma, but with classical Zhonguo architecture: sweeping gabled roofs with yellow tiles, red walls with gold trim, and carvings and paintings of dragons along almost every wall and column. While the Consular

Palace was made of marble, the Zhonguo preferred wood for their religious and imperial centers, though their cities were made of steel and concrete like all modern human cities.

When they reached the top of the steps, they entered the palace through massive wooden doors. The Chancellor and the Riders led Uller into the main audience chamber just inside the entrance. At the far end of the chamber was a gold-painted, wooden throne carved to look like the clawed hand of a dragon. Upon it sat Emperor Pan Ku, dressed in multi-colored robes even more billowy than the Chancellor's. Uller was about the same age as Pan Ku, but the Emperor's hair was dyed black and his cosmetic surgeons had done a remarkable job keeping any hint of age at bay. He looked about twenty Terran-years old, with smooth, glossy skin and no facial stubble or wrinkles. He sat straight-backed and statuesque on the Zhonguo throne, his eyes focused on the city outside the door. The chamber was packed on all sides by Divine Riders, bureaucrats, and dozens of Imperial courtiers dressed just as colorfully as him. Holo-monitors were built into the walls, depicting glorious vistas from worlds in the Sphere's twenty-two star systems. The court grew silent as Uller and the Riders entered.

Chancellor Zheng Yang approached the foot of the Emperor's dais and bowed deeply. The Emperor did not move or shift his eyes. The Chancellor then turned to Uller.

"Uller Mus," the Chancellor said in ancient Han, "you come before us not as an emissary of our friends the Daqin, but as an individual. A slave to be exact. Your master on Reantium was tragically killed in the golem uprising there, which you say was related to the troubles the Daqin experienced with the alien vessel that attacked them and Libertus. You have told us that you bring a great gift to benefit the Zhonguo people. The only reason you stand here is because your master, Aulus Tarpeius, was a wealthy and powerful man among the Daqin. Why should Emperor Pan Ku, the True Son of Heaven and Lord of Ten Thousand Years, listen to a former slave? Why should he not send you back to your Daqin masters as a gesture of good will between our nations?"

Uller swallowed, and a quick stab of fear shot through him. *I can't go back. I can't be a slave again, nothing more than a golem with a soul.*

"Courage, Uller Mus," said a voice from his right. "We promised you greatness, and we always keep our promises."

Uller cast a quick glance at Marcus Antonius Primus. He wore ancient Roman armor, his fists planted on his hips. Uller knew only he could see Antonius, so he tried not to let his eyes linger on the apparition.

A surge of confidence suddenly flowed through him. It was the same confidence that helped him betray Tarpeius after Uller injected himself with Cordus's Muse-infected blood on Reantium. Marcus Antonius Primus had appeared to him immediately after and showed him how to set the Reantium golems free. How to set Uller Mus free.

Uller sighed quietly, then gave the Chancellor a steely gaze. "If you return me to the Daqin," Uller said in perfect Han, "you will never learn the secrets of Daqin power. The secret that enabled them to go from riding horses to starships within two hundred years."

The Emperor seemed unimpressed; he kept his focus locked on the cityscape behind Uller.

The Chancellor smiled. "Lofty words from a slave. How do we know you can deliver these...secrets of which you boast?"

Uller reached up to the pendant around his neck. Almost as one, the Divine Riders surrounding him stepped closer and leveled their rifles at him. Uller ignored them, brought the pendant over his head, and held it out to the Chancellor.

The Emperor never flinched.

Chancellor Yang sniffed. "The True Son of Heaven has no need for Daqin baubles—"

"In this pendant you will find a blood sample. It is the blood of Marcus Antonius Cordus, the last Antonius."

"An interesting religious relic," the Chancellor scoffed, "but the Emperor fails to see how—"

"The Daqin have humiliated the Zhonguo for centuries," Uller continued. "From taking your lands in Terran Asia to Daqin pogroms that attempted to destroy your culture. You fled Terra and reestablished your nation among the stars of Heaven. Don't you wish to repay the Daqin for their crimes?"

The Chancellor sighed, seemingly bored. "As you say, the Daqin are a nation in ruins. But we already have the strength to assert our rights, and the Daqin can do nothing about it."

Marcus Antonius leaned close to Uller. "Now set the hook."

"True," Uller said, "the Daqin cannot hurt you *now*, but neither can you hope to conquer them. Even as fractured as they are, their Legions are still strong and will likely unite with an Antonius as consul again. It is only a matter of time before they are strong again, and a threat to you." Uller dropped his voice low. "But what if I told you how to destroy the Daqin without your forces even firing a single shot?"

The Chancellor raised an amused eyebrow. "And what is that way?"

"Inject this blood into your body, and you will learn the secrets of a hundred dead *alien* civilizations. Civilizations from the distant past that were more powerful than the one that just attacked the Daqin. *This*, dear Chancellor, is the source of Daqin power."

A murmur arose from the people in the court.
Emperor Pan Ku finally turned his eyes to Uller.
Marcus Antonius barked a laugh. "We have a new home."

Read MUSES OF THE REPUBLIC, book three in the Codex Antonius series.

AFTERWORD

Thanks for giving *Muses of Terra* a read. If you enjoyed it and have the time, please leave a review, I'd appreciate it.

If you're ready for more adventures in the Codex Antonius universe, continue with the next novel, *Muses of the Republic*.

Check my website (https://robsteinerauthor.com) for a full list of my novels.

If you'd like a quick note when I release something new, please sign up for my newsletter on my website. For social media fans, you can find me on Twitter, Facebook, Goodreads, and BookBub.

Acknowledgments

Thanks to my alpha readers: Heather Kliesner, Gidget Kirk, Marcia Sacks, Mike Lippo, and Chris Hooker.

Thanks to my editor David Drazul (dedzone.net) for the clean shine and lemony scent he always puts on my manuscripts.

Thanks to my design team at 100covers.com for the fantastic cover, and thank you Stone Perales for the alien starship illustration.

And as always, thank you Sarah and Amelia. Sarah, for your love, support, and professional insight on sentient viruses; Amelia, for letting me practice my storytelling skills through our action figure adventures.